THE GENESIS MACHINE

INCEPTION, DECRYPTION, REVELATION

K. J. GILLENWATER

KJB WRITING SERVICES, LLC

THE GENESIS MACHINE

INCEPTION

BOOK ONE

K. J. GILLENWATER

CHAPTER 1

July 2022
Fort Madison, Iowa

PETTY OFFICER RYAN LEDBETTER stepped through the rising waters outside the secure perimeter of the NAVSECGRU detachment headquarters on Fort Madison. Rain pummeled him and ran off his raincoat in sheets. His watch cap was soaked through.

"This is bullshit. We should be following evac procedures." He shone his flashlight through the murky dark, and it bounced off the chain link fence which surrounded the compound. "There's nothing out here. Rounds are done." He snapped off his flashlight and headed for the gates. He'd be damned if he'd wade through rounds the rest of his twelve hour shift. The commander should've let them leave hours ago.

"Wait." Seaman Bradley Conlon, his watch partner, stood still. "Do you hear that?"

Newbies always took this watch shit too seriously. "There's nothing there, Conlon. Come on, let's go back inside." His flashlight flickered out. He shook it. The light wavered. "Dammit."

A tremendous roar filled his ears. Like a tornado. A shrieking blast of sound. Instinctually, he covered them to protect himself from the noise. His whole body shook with the force of it.

Conlon was yelling something at him. He pointed at the sky.

Ledbetter looked up. Overhead, less than twenty feet above them, a huge ball of fire streaked by.

The object lost altitude rapidly and headed toward the swollen Mississippi, which edged the base. It slammed into the shallows sending flames and chunks of debris everywhere. Within minutes, the fire was doused by the flood waters and rain.

Ledbetter pressed the button on his walkie talkie. "This is Petty Officer Ledbetter. I think a plane crashed. We need emergency vehicles on site ASAP." He ran toward the rubble even before he was done speaking. "Come on Conlon. There might be survivors."

Conlon held back. "That was no plane."

Ledbetter turned and slowed his run through the mushy, flooded grass. "What do you mean?"

"It was just a big ball. There weren't any wings, no tail." Conlon splashed down the slope to him. "Let's go check it out."

Through the sheet-like rain they slipped and slid their way down the riverbank. Visibility was practically nil. Ledbetter shook his flashlight once more. It popped on. He played the white light across the grassy shoreline, now under a foot of water and rising. The beam caught a jagged edge of something sticking up from the ground.

"Over here." Ledbetter headed for the strange thing only a few yards away. The water came up over his chukka boots, wetting his wool socks. He paid it no mind. The object in the shallow water grabbed his attention.

A blob, about eight feet across and cracked open like a nut, sat in front of him. Smoke rose from the center, and the whole thing hissed in the rain and damp. He reached out to touch one jagged edge. His fingers hit something spongy and slimy. Like snot. "What the hell?" He yanked back his hand and wiped it on his dungarees. A chill ran through him.

Conlon stood right behind him. "What is it?" He reached out to touch it, too, but Ledbetter stopped him.

"Don't. I don't know what the hell that thing is, but it ain't no plane, and it ain't no meteor." Ledbetter picked up his radio once more and pushed the talk button. "This is Ledbetter again. I think you need to get someone down here."

CHAPTER 2

Defense Language Institute, Monterey, CA
August 2023

CHARLIE CUTTER SLICED into the water, her arms in perfect rhythm. The silence under water soothed her as she focused on her freestyle stroke—her routine four times a week. Her mind clear, her breathing timed.

One, two, three. Breathe. One, two, three. Breathe.

Swimming was one of two things she'd been naturally gifted at from an early age.

Two more laps, and she'd be done with her two thousand meters.

She hit the end of the pool, prepared to flip, but a hand touched her arm.

She came up out of the water with a gasp. Concentration broken. The quiet calm of her routine interrupted.

"Petty Officer Cutter?" A pimply-faced seaman in his summer whites crouched down at the edge of the pool.

Charlie looked past him at the clock on the wall. She'd been on her best time. Dammit. "Could you hand me that?" She nodded at her plain white towel sitting on a bench near the women's locker room door.

The seaman's face reddened, but he did what she asked.

Newbies, like this one, who waited for a new cycle of language classes to start, pulled odd assignments to fill in the empty days. A linguist-in-training at the Defense Language Institute might wait months for his spot in class, which meant he spent every day 'on duty.' Only the lucky ones got plum assignments. Looked like this poor seaman, bewildered and nervous, must've gotten a crap job of some kind.

Charlie climbed out of the pool, adjusted her racing suit, and wrapped the thin towel around her. "What can I do for you, Hansen?" She read the nametag pinned crookedly to his pressed white cotton shirt. He'd been lucky there'd been no surprise uniform inspection this morning at muster. The Petty Officer-in-Charge would've noticed that.

"Commander Niels wanted me to find you. Your roommate told me you'd be here at the gym." He cleared his throat. "I didn't know you'd be in the pool."

Was it her fault the kid had probably never been this close to a woman in a swimsuit before? She was surprised he'd made it through the rigors of Boot Camp with his spindly arms and nervous jack rabbit twitches. "Lieutenant Commander Niels?" She'd met him once, the day after she'd arrived in Monterey. He'd been a classmate of her father's. Even from three thousand miles away, Captain Harrison Cutter kept tabs on her.

"Something about your orders?" Hansen stood at parade rest, a horrible habit leftover from training. It took a few months for most to lose such an obvious newbie trademark. "I have a van parked out front. I'll wait for you there."

She dried her hair with the towel. "Give me five."

Charlie, her hair braided but dripping under her cover, shivered in the passenger van. Although it was mid-August, air conditioning was unneeded in the mild Central Coast climate. She gave Hansen the evil eye from the bench seat behind him, but he kept his gaze focused on the winding road.

"So tell me, how hard is it?" Hansen stopped at the bottom of the hill and sneaked a glance at her in the mirror. "Class, I mean."

"What are you taking?" DLI offered every language under the sun. She'd even run into a few civvies from the FBI here to take a Tagalog course once.

"Persian-Farsi."

"My roommate's taking that. Not bad, she says. Do you know French?"

"No."

"Well, I've heard it's similar to French. I'm sure you'll be fine. Forty-seven weeks, just like Russian, and I survived."

"Yeah, but you're—" He broke eye contact with her and made the turn toward the administration buildings. "—different."

Her heart seized up. She'd heard that before. Languages came naturally to her, maybe a little too naturally. Her teachers, little old ladies from the Ukraine and Russia, had suspected she'd studied Russian before. She hadn't. "Don't worry, Hansen. You'll be fine. It takes a lot to rock out."

"Guess I'll find out in September."

Charlie nodded. Most students did well at DLI. But most of them studied their hearts out. Flashcards with vocab, doing assignments for hours in their heavy workbooks, listening to the foreign news stations. For her, that was all a waste of time. Her brain latched onto language like a wolverine did its prey. Russian had been a bit more of a challenge with its four declensions, however. After a few weeks she'd gobbled down the grammar rules so quickly, her instructors kept her busy with new vocabulary while teaching the rest of her class. Most expected her to pass her Defense Language Proficiency Test, or DLPT, with an across the board four-rating on a five point scale. Almost impossible for someone new to the language.

"Here we are." Hansen parked outside the two-story cement block building that served as the Navy administration headquarters for the language students.

"Thanks. Good luck in class." She stepped out of the van and made sure her cover sat level on her head and her white cotton uniform skirt was wrinkle free. The commander of the naval detachment would notice those details. The last thing she wanted was Lieutenant Commander Niels reporting to her father about her less-than-perfect appearance.

When she walked inside, a young admin sat behind a desk. By the hashes on the sleeve of her uniform, Charlie could see she was an E-5, Petty Officer Second Class.

"I'm here to see Lieutenant Commander Niels." Charlie took off her cover. The inside brim was damp from her hair. A slight chill ran through her. She'd been a good student, never been in trouble, and did well on her physical fitness tests. Had her father decided to meddle again?

The E-5 pressed a few buttons on her phone and talked quietly into the receiver. "The Lieutenant Commander wants me to send you up."

Charlie headed for the stairwell. She was so close to finishing her class—of course her father would intervene and make a mess of things. Calling in a favor, probably. He couldn't sign her up for Officer Candidate School without her permission, could he?

She headed right for the commander's door, a wooden placard with his name painted in gold lettering next to a ship's wheel. She knocked.

"Come."

She took a deep breath and opened the door.

Lieutenant Commander Niels had ruddy cheeks and a halo of gray hair around a shiny bald crown. "Petty Officer Cutter, have a seat, please."

Charlie stood stiffly in front of his desk. She had to know. She couldn't wait for him to explain the point of her visit. "Sir, I want to be a linguist. I wouldn't have joined if I didn't. If my father thinks that I'd give that up to please him, well—"

Niels cracked a smile. "Please, have a seat, Cutter. Your father didn't have anything to do with this meeting."

When she heard those words, she lost her train of thought.

Why else would he ask her here? She sat in the hard metal seat with a blue fabric cushion—standard Navy issue.

Niels settled back in his chair. "It's come to my attention your skills would be better suited to a different assignment than your original orders. I've never seen this type of request come across my desk. Instead of heading to Goodfellow in Texas after graduation, you've been reassigned to the Naval Criminal Investigative Services."

"What?"

He raised an eyebrow.

"I'm sorry, sir, but I don't understand. I have orders to Japan—Misawa. I want to be airborne. That's why I joined." Did her father have something to do with this unprecedented shift in plans despite what the commander said? He'd never liked the idea of his daughter being enlisted much less riding in a spy plane gathering enemy comms. "If Captain Cutter gave you some idea that I'm unhappy here—"

"I told you, Cutter, I haven't spoken with your father. In fact, I'm rather insulted you'd believe that as commander of the naval detachment here at DLI I wouldn't have any say over the students in my purview. Or that I'd listen to a suggestion from an old Academy friend. That's not how things work in the Navy." Lieutenant Commander Niels's eyes snapped with fire, and his once smiling mouth turned down in a frown.

"No, sir."

"Good. Now, let me continue. You have new orders. After you've finished class, you will be headed directly to the Washington Navy Yard and will check in there to find out more about your assignment."

"Yes, sir."

"Do you have any questions?"

A million questions ran through her head, but most of them not ones she'd ask the Lieutenant Commander. "They want a CTI straight from school with no equipment training? Why me?"

"The request came directly from the head of BUPERS. As I said, I've never had a request like this before, but you're an exceptional student, Cutter. This is a great opportunity for you." He handed her a manila envelope with her name scribbled across the front in black marker. "I wish you luck, sailor."

"Thank you, sir." She took the envelope.

"Take that with you and hand it to the Officer-in-Charge. Your PCS orders will be ready with the rest of your classmates' after graduation."

He stood up. Her cue to leave. "Yes, sir."

Once she'd left his office, her mind raced. Her father had to be wrapped up in this somehow because it didn't make any sense. She was nobody. A brand new E-4 fresh from language training. What could she possibly have that NCIS would want? Besides wasn't their mission internal? They investigated crimes within the Navy and the Marines. It didn't make sense.

The envelope grew heavy in her hands. No matter who'd been behind this switch, she was upset. Everything had been perfect. She was supposed to take her final language exam, transfer to Goodfellow Air Force Base in San Angelo for equipment training, and then flight school, followed by her final orders to Japan flying recon out of Misawa.

She wasn't a desk jockey.

She strode past the admin's desk and headed out the door, popping her cover back on her head. Hansen waited for her in the van, its engine running while parked next to the curb. She strolled right past him.

From her skirt pocket she plucked her cell phone. She chose a number out of her contact list and, while she waited for an answer on the other end, headed straight for the barracks up the hill.

"Cutter here," a gruff voice rumbled in her ear.

"What did you do?" She could hear the strained anger in her own words. The accusations she wanted to let fly. But she was determined to keep a cool head this time. Show him she could act the grown up and not like the typical teenager he still liked to compare her to. "Why did you have them change my orders?"

"Charlene, what are you talking about? Where are you?"

Why did he call her that? He knew she hated it. "You know

very well where I am. You're screwing with my life again. Why don't you just admit it?"

He sighed. "I'd love to say I have been. Trust me, I've been chomping at the bit to get you out of there—but I swear to you, I've kept my word."

He sounded sincere. Charlie, her pace so quick she was out of breath, stopped in mid-stride. "You swear?"

"Yes."

Silence settled. Charlie's mind raced. "Then I don't understand." If her father wasn't involved in all of this, what was going on?

"You say you received new orders?"

"Yes. To some place called—" She opened up the manila envelope. "—NCIS-A Division. Do you know what that is?" Her father had been in the Navy her whole life. Captain Harrison Cutter was a well-respected intelligence analyst at the National Security Agency. She might butt heads with him frequently, but occasionally he was good for a few things.

"No. But why would they want you? That's police work. You're only a linguistics major."

The usual dig at her choice in college majors. She reined in her temper as best she could and let the slight roll off her back. "Look, I was hoping you might have been responsible for this, that's all. But since you clearly don't believe I'm qualified for the job in the first place, I guess I can throw that idea out the window. Say hi to Chad for me when you see him."

"Charlene, I didn't mean—"

Charlie hung up. He had a way of cutting her down every time she talked to him. Nothing was ever good enough for him. The last thing she needed to hear was his typical lecture about how she'd failed his expectations and why she made a huge mistake enlisting in the Navy rather than going to OCS.

She needed to burn off some of her anxious energy. A few more laps in the pool would do it. Her roommate thought she worked out too much, too hard, but it was one way for her to clear her head and forget about her dad's disappointments in her life choices.

There had to be a way out of this. If her father hadn't been the one behind it, she'd figure out who was. Damned if some idiot from NCIS would be telling her what to do. They'd already changed her orders once. There must be a way to change them again.

CHAPTER 3

CHARLIE SAT in the security lobby of Building forty-two—a nondescript, blocky structure. She needed a good swim to shake off her nerves. After working for months to perfect her language skills and be the best damned Russian linguist the Navy had, she found herself at the Washington Navy Yard surrounded by a bunch of civilians and contractors.

As she waited for her security badge and an escort to lead her to her new office and a job she knew nothing about, she stifled a yawn.

Last night she'd arrived at Reagan National with her duffle bag and a phone number scribbled on the back of her manila envelope—her sponsor. She'd dialed the number. No one answered. After waiting a half hour for someone to call her back, she'd given up, flagged down a taxi, and wandered around base with her overloaded bag and a wheeled carry-on looking for the Navy barracks.

"Petty Officer Cutter?"

Charlie looked up from the outdated magazine she'd been reading to see a tall, thin woman with chin-length curly hair standing in front of her. "Yes?"

At the same time, the security officer behind the desk called out her name, "Cutter. Your badge is ready." He held a laminated badge with her picture and a metal clip.

The woman in front of her smiled. "I'm Petty Officer Storm. Call me Lisa, please."

Charlie eyed her sleek tan trousers and bright blue short-sleeved sweater. "Where's your uniform?"

"Why don't you go grab your badge, and I'll explain everything on the way to the office."

A Navy assignment, a petty officer, and no uniform? This was growing more interesting.

Charlie rose from the couch and collected her badge from the man behind the counter, signing her name into the log.

"If you ever forget your badge," the man told her, "you need to stop in here to pick up a temporary badge for the day. If you lose your badge, make sure to contact base security immediately. Your badge is your responsibility. If it does end up lost or stolen, don't expect a slap on the wrist."

Charlie nodded and clipped it to the pocket of her uniform shirt.

"Let's go." Lisa stood at the door, holding it open for her. "Commander Orr is waiting for you. We've got a lot to cover in a short period of time to make sure you're up to speed."

Charlie stepped out of the security office. Wow, the foot traffic had picked up considerably since she'd arrived at 0730. Beyond the lobby and the security office, stood a row of turnstiles. Each was equipped with a separate slot and a red/green light. A soldier in camo stepped up to an empty turnstile, pulled his security badge down from its retractable line around his neck, and slid it into the slot. When he pulled it free, the light turned from red to green, and he pushed through the turnstile. Behind him another worker lined up for the same process.

Lisa stepped in line behind a few others and signaled Charlie to follow her. As they waited their turn, Lisa gave her some instructions. "Don't pull your card out too quickly, or you might cause an error. Too many errors in a row, and you'll be locked out."

"Locked out?"

"Just means you'll have to make a stop at the security office and have them straighten you out. But I'm sure you can tell they don't like mistakes in there."

The man's speech about losing her badge and what that might

mean still rung in her ears. Before she could ask any more questions, Lisa was sliding her card into the slot. The turnstile clicked, and she pushed through to the other side.

Charlie stepped up for her turn. Since she only had her badge clipped to her pocket, unlike everyone else who had it attached to a retractable line, she had to unclip it to put it into the reader. She slid it in and out, taking her time. The light stayed red. Her palms began to sweat. It wouldn't do on her first day of work to make mistakes. She didn't want to go back into that security office and explain that the reader wouldn't accept her card.

Lisa held up her own security pass and turned it around. "You put it in backwards. It has to go in like this." She showed her how the card had to be put in the slot with the magnetic strip facing away from her.

Relief shot through her. The line was building behind her, so the pressure was on. Quickly, she re-entered her card the correct way, and the green light came on.

Charlie caught up to her new co-worker.

Thank goodness she'd made it through.

To the right several people entered codes into keypads that lined the walls. A big metal drawer popped open for one person.

"What's that?" she asked.

"That's where we collect our office key every morning. Well, that's where Commander Orr gets it from. He has to pick it up and drop it off every day. Lieutenant Kellerman also knows the combination in case it's needed."

"But we're inside a secure facility. Why would they need a key?" Charlie thought her clearance would give her all the access she needed.

Lisa smiled and led her down the hall toward a bank of elevators. "There are multiple levels of security here. We work with compartmented information. Each office has its own secrets. You'll see. I can't tell you much more about it here." Lisa nodded at the stream of workers headed toward their respective offices.

Thousands of people worked in this building. She'd watched them pass by while she waited in the security office. The layers of cars parked outside revealed a lot more went on inside the building than she'd realized. With only a few floors visible from the street, she wondered where they all disappeared to.

Charlie and Lisa hopped into an elevator. A half-dozen military and civilian personnel got inside with them. There was a row of buttons. Only a third of them were marked. One through seven were clear as day. Then, beneath were the unmarked buttons. The arrow above the door indicated they were going down.

After a few people pressed some of the unmarked buttons, Lisa reached forward and pressed the button on the bottom of the left column. "That's our floor. Don't forget it."

Charlie nodded. She wished someone would tell her more about who she was working for, why they'd chosen her, but Lisa had made it clear they couldn't talk about much here in the open. Even amidst all of these other military and government workers with security clearances as high as hers. She kept her mouth shut.

The elevator slowly emptied out. People trickled out in bits and pieces as they descended down further and further. Eventually, it was only the two of them and one lone Marine. The elevator slowed. The last floor. Theirs.

"Follow me." Lisa led her to the left. A series of doors on either side of the hallway greeted her. Each one had a keypad and a slot on the wall next to the doorknob. There were several shorter hallways leading off the main one with signs indicating room numbers in each wing. Lisa made another left down another hallway. The door at the very end of the hall was marked 1271. Lisa slid her security badge into the slot and pressed some numbers. The door clicked.

"I'll give you the code once we're inside the office. Memorize it. Never share it with anyone. It changes every six months. Hope you have a good head for numbers." Lisa turned the knob and opened the door.

———

The office behind the door looked like any other office. Cubicles. Computers. A stained coffeemaker next to the printer.

"Welcome to NCIS-A Division." Lisa led her down a short

row of cubicles. "Chief, Petty Officer Cutter is here. This is Chief Ricard."

In the last cubicle at the end of the row a face popped out. He leaned back in his chair to take a good look at who was headed his way. Chief Ricard, red-faced and round-cheeked with a receding hairline, gave her a wink. "Cutter." He smiled. "Good to have you join us. Stormy, I can take it from here. Why don't you grab our new team member a cup of java." He stabbed a chubby finger in her direction. "Cream? Sugar? How do you like it?"

"Black is fine." The coffee had smelled burned to her when she entered the office, but no one could be in the military without a heavy coffee addiction. Burned or no.

"My kinda gal. You're all right, Cutter." He spun his chair around to face her head on. Unlike Lisa or 'Stormy,' he wore his tan chief's uniform. She needed to find out what kind of dress was required here. "Have a seat. We'll show you to your cube in a sec." He rested his hands on his ample stomach, which was barely within regulation weight, she guessed.

Charlie grabbed an empty chair and rolled it out into the aisle. She set her cover and her purse on the desk behind her.

Chief Ricard snatched a folder off his desk and opened it. "Petty Officer Charlene Cutter. Language school. Top of her class, it says. Pretty impressive PT scores as well."

"I prefer to be called Charlie."

He shifted his gaze to her face. "Cutter. We go by last names around here."

"Right." Although the chief appeared about as harmless as a teddy bear, he clearly had a tough interior.

He focused back on her folder. "I'll bet you're wondering how you pulled this assignment."

Her heart thumped. "Yes. The Commandant back at DLI didn't give me much to work with. I thought I was all set for Misawa." The disappointment still burned inside her. Now instead of flying with recon planes over the Kamchatka Peninsula, she was sitting in a room with no windows, one door, and a dozen cubicles. Not exactly the exciting military career she'd envisioned when she signed up.

"The Commander wants to brief you in detail once he arrives. He had an early meeting this morning upstairs. But I'm supposed to settle you in, introduce you to the rest of the group, make sure you're set up. That kind of thing." He thumbed through her papers.

"I understand, Chief." She hadn't seen where the 'rest of the group' was. This part of the office was strangely quiet. Not even the tapping of keyboard keys. Where was everybody?

The door banged open. An explosion of conversation filled the quiet office.

"Let's go, people. Hop to it. We have to have our asses on a plane out of here in less than ninety minutes. Got it?" A tall Hispanic man in a white shirt and striped tie strode into the office. He swept right past the aisle where Charlie sat with the chief and headed for an office door in the rear. "Where's the Commander? Chief!" He spun around. His dark eyes alight with an energetic fire.

His gaze settled on Charlie. "Who's this?"

Chief Ricard set down her file and stood. "Petty Officer Cutter. She's that linguist they brought on board." He directed his next words at her. "This is Special Agent Demarco."

Demarco scanned her for a moment, as if he were sizing her up. "You have your passport?"

"A passport? Where are we going?"

"This time we're headed to North Dakota. But tomorrow it might be Mongolia. You need to be prepared for any contingency."

"I applied for one back at DLI. Haven't gotten it yet."

"You're fresh from school?" Demarco's face curdled into annoyance. "This is who they give us? Some wet-behind-the-ears newbie?"

Chief Ricard offered up her file. "You should see her test scores. They're off the charts."

"Just what I needed. Someone to babysit. We've got shit going down today, and this is the best they can do?"

Charlie's stomach churned. She wished she could be anywhere but in this office. Who in the hell sent her here if she clearly wasn't wanted?

"The commander put in the request. Maybe you should ask him," the chief said.

Demarco ran a hand through his short black hair. His handsome features marred by the obvious stress her presence was putting him under. He grunted. "Where is everyone? We need to get out of here, ASAP."

"Why do we need to go to North Dakota?" She'd just arrived here and now she was headed out somewhere else? She hadn't even had a chance to be briefed.

"You, sit." Demarco pointed at her. "Chief, you better as hell track down everyone now and make sure they're ready for transport." He headed toward Lisa. "Stormy, I need you to contact the doc and let her know we'll likely be bringing back samples. This is a big one."

Chief Ricard picked up the phone by his desk and started dialing. Lisa ran for a red phone on the wall marked 'secure.'

Bringing back samples of what? What was going on? Everyone had something to do except her. She was in the way. Lost. Clueless. She didn't like feeling out of the loop.

Chief hung up the phone, "The meeting's been over about ten minutes. Commander Orr and Lieutenant Kellerman should be here any second. Should I finish briefing Cutter?"

Demarco let out a breath. "Stormy can catch her up on things once we're in the air. Right now I need your help making sure the equipment is ready before take-off."

Chief nodded, strode over to Lisa's desk, and dropped Charlie's file on it.

Lisa finished up on the phone. "Doc's ready for whatever we might bring back. She told me to remind you to take enough vials this time." She smirked. It was obvious to Charlie that Lisa found Demarco to be as much of a jerk as she did.

Demarco headed toward a door at the back of the office marked 'Supplies' and pulled out a set of keys. "Just finish getting ready, would you? Orr and Kellerman should be back any second, and we need to be prepped and packed."

Charlie bristled. What did this jackass know about her aptitude for the job? Someone clearly thought she was qualified, but she knew her place. She was new to the job and a third class Petty Officer with only an education to thank for her rank. For now, she had to suck it up. Later on she could prove her worth. If they needed a linguist, she sure as hell could show this special agent she had the chops to keep up with the team.

CHAPTER 4

LISA PICKED up the manila folder. "Want to take a seat?" She gestured at an empty office chair beside her. "I'll have to give you the short version."

Charlie made her way to the front of the office and took the offered chair.

Lisa opened the folder and peered at the same statistics and background Chief had perused moments earlier. She whistled. "Impressive."

"Right. I get it." Charlie's patience was wearing thin. Her first day, and she had no idea why she was here and was about to take a plane to North Dakota. Someone better start talking. "Are you going to brief me or do I need to find this Commander Orr?"

Lisa shot her a surprised look. "You're a go-getter." She set down the folder that contained Charlie's military records. "We don't have much time. I'll give you the quick down and dirty because we need to be on that plane. I'm thinking you aren't game for that until you know what we're up to. Am I close?"

Charlie relaxed and nodded. Finally, someone would shine a light on why she'd been diverted from her original orders.

"You've been assigned to NCIS-A or A Group, as we like to call it in here. Most of the people outside this office—the ones we shared the elevator with, the turnstiles, the parking lots—have no idea what we do."

Charlie took in the beige cubicles and fluorescent lighting. Looked a lot like any other boring office. "So what do you do?"

"We're a secret division that investigates extraterrestrial activity."

"Extraterrestrial activity?" What a crock. The rest of the office would jump out at any moment, yell surprise, and then spray her with Silly String. A first day joke on the newbie. She was no stranger to that. "You have to be joking."

Lisa spun her chair around to face her computer. She entered a password, and her computer desktop came alive. Splashed across the extra-wide screen was Lisa's email client. "This is where we're going today." She opened an email and clicked on a photo attachment. "A local farmer witnessed this crashing into a lake two nights ago in the middle of a pretty bad rain. Lots of flooding. It's going to be tricky to handle, but we've managed worse."

Charlie couldn't speak. On screen was a picture of a strange object, the size of a two-door compact car. Nothing about this object looked manufactured. It was green and gooey with a hatch-like opening. Strange markings covered part of it. A skinny man in a rain slicker stood to the side, knee-deep in muddy water. He was as white as a sheet.

"We're flying out there today to take samples, transport that thing to our lab, and give those guys a plausible story about what landed near this man's property." Lisa closed the file and shut down her computer.

"You're telling me this is something from outer space?"

"Stormy, let's go." A tall man in his late twenties with a military haircut, black-framed glasses, and dressed in civvies peeked around the cubicle. He gave Charlie a quick once over and then turned his focus back on Lisa. "Plane's ready."

Her new co-worker tucked Charlie's folder into a cardboard box on her desk. "We don't have a lot of time. Commander Orr needs to give you the full briefing." She grabbed the box.

Charlie stared at the odd object on the computer screen. Her mind was a blank. She didn't know what to think. Aliens? On earth? For real? If everyone around her weren't so serious, she'd probably burst out laughing.

Someone shut off the lights. "Let's go, people. We need to get the hell out of here."

Demarco. Jerk of the highest order.

She knew she wouldn't receive any answers from him. Lisa seemed kind enough and eager to give her the heads up on her new job. But Charlie agreed with Demarco—why in the heck did this office want a linguist? What possible input could she provide?

Charlie followed Lisa out the door. She had nothing on her, but her uniform, and now she was headed to North Dakota. For how long? She didn't even have a toothbrush with her for God's sake.

———

Seated inside the C-17 aircraft twenty minutes later, Charlie surveyed her new co-workers. They all bustled about the cabin, ignoring her as she sat on one of the jump seats along the wall.

Demarco stood near the front, clipboard in hand, checking off things as they were put away.

Did he ever stop scowling?

Lisa stuffed her cardboard box into a cargo net attached to the wall, but grabbed Charlie's personnel file before finding her own seat near the front. Lisa immediately opened up the file and began to read.

Chief Ricard unloaded two large metallic cases and set them inside a cargo box the size of a garage freezer. His face appeared one shade darker and redder than when she'd first met him in the office. He plopped into a seat next to Lisa.

The youngish man with the glasses carried a military-style duffel bag and held an iPad in one hand. He took a seat across from Charlie, tucked his bag under his seat, and tapped away on the tablet.

A fifth person entered the aircraft. Like Chief Ricard, he wore a uniform—officer khakis with gold oak leaves on his collar. Charlie had not met him before, nor had he ridden with the rest of them over to the airstrip. This must be Commander Orr.

He carried a small bag, which he handed over to Demarco.

Demarco checked something on his clipboard and then set the bag lightly into the cargo netting next to Lisa's cardboard box and some other soft-sided bags.

Orr headed her way. He had a slight smile on his face and extended his hand. "Welcome to the team, Petty Officer Cutter."

Charlie stood and accepted his hearty grip. "Thank you, sir." She didn't know what else to say. She had no idea why this man selected her as part of the strange office. She had so many questions no one seemed interested in answering.

He stood only about four inches taller than she, but his presence filled the cabin. "I'm sorry you had such an abrupt introduction to the shop. We haven't added a new teammate since Kellerman joined the team about nine months ago."

Kellerman must be the one with the glasses. The only name she didn't recognize. "Is it always like this?" Everyone on the plane was filled with nervous energy. She could sense it. A much different atmosphere emanated from the group than when she'd met most of them an hour earlier.

Orr laughed. "You mean, dropping everything and flying off to the middle of nowhere?" He looked over his shoulder at Demarco who was still checking cargo and furrowing his brow as deeply as he could. "What say you, Demarco?"

The annoyingly handsome Demarco looked up from his clipboard, confusion clear in his eyes.

"Are we crazy sons of bitches?" the commander asked.

"Hell, yes." Demarco smiled, white teeth bright even in the yellowish fluorescent lighting that filled the cabin.

Charlie huffed inwardly—a gut, feminine reaction to that mega-watt smile.

He's a jerk, Charlie.

Orr took a seat next to Charlie and indicated she should sit back down. "I would rather have given you the full spiel in my office back in 1271, but right now we don't have that luxury. I know you're probably wondering why you were assigned to NCIS-A."

"I thought maybe you needed a really good Russian linguist." She thought proudly of her language proficiency scores and how she'd been looking forward to putting her language skills to use at something more practical than the academic career she'd been headed toward before she joined the Navy.

Orr smiled. "I haven't even looked at your scores, to tell you the truth."

Charlie's heart sank.

"I was more interested in your work before you joined the military. Your research into the Voynich Manuscript."

Charlie blinked. That wasn't what she'd been expecting to hear. Her pre-military life seemed as if it had happened decades ago. "You're interested in my linguistics work?" Her mind blipped back to her graduate school days. Living off of a small stipend, sitting through lectures on syntax, phonology and dialects, learning bits of Finnish, Chinese, and Swahili for fun. Seemed idyllic now.

"Kellerman, let me have your iPad."

The bookish Kellerman looked up from the tablet, and his face tinged pink. Charlie glanced at the surface of the tablet and caught a glimpse of a half-completed Sudoku matrix. She bit her lip to keep from laughing.

Kellerman cleared the screen with a finger tap and handed it across the cabin to Commander Orr.

Her new boss dug into a folder on the main screen of the iPad until he opened up a very familiar document—her master's thesis on the Voynich Manuscript.

The manuscript was a mysterious document that had mystified cryptographers for centuries. It consisted of more than two-hundred and forty pages of handwritten gobbledygook and illustrations and had been discovered in an Italian monastery by a Lithuanian bookseller named Voynich in 1912. Every expert, every master of code had failed to decipher the mysteries locked within the elaborate document. Many theorized it had been written by Leonardo da Vinci; others believed it was a bunch of junk. Charlie had been fascinated with the document since she'd first heard about the text in her freshman linguistics course at Baylor University.

"How did you find my thesis? I never finished it." The more

she found out about this assignment, the more she wondered who had been pulling the strings. That thesis had been left on her laptop back at her parents' house. Once she'd quit grad school and abruptly joined the Navy, she thought it would be the end of that bit of writing.

"Your academic advisor told us he was disappointed you didn't finish."

"I was going nowhere with my analysis. The money was running out. I didn't feel like taking out a bigger student loan to end up with a half-baked idea."

"It's not half-baked. You have some great guesses in here that might lead to a—"

"A great guess is not what I'm interested in achieving, Commander Orr. When I first started that paper, I really thought I was onto something. Thought I saw a solution other people didn't see."

"But what if you did?" Orr flipped to the last page of her incomplete thesis.

Her failures in academia were not something she thought she'd be facing in her new assignment. "Why am I here, Commander Orr?"

He closed the file with a tap of his finger. "Your theories aren't bunk." He opened up a jpeg file. "The Voynich manuscript is a language. A real language. Not a code."

Orr handed her the iPad.

Charlie's gaze fixated on the picture he'd opened up. It was a blown up version of the photo Lisa had shown her earlier in the office. At this larger size, she could identify a familiar script scrawled across the unidentifiable greenish blob. The script was blurred, but the whorls and loops were definitely Voynich. "Where did this come from?" Only one document existed in the world with this writing. No other.

Orr took back the iPad. "We're about to show you."

CHAPTER 5

THE PILOT'S voice came across the loudspeaker. "We're cleared to go. Is everything secure?"

Orr headed to the front of the cabin to use the intercom and left Charlie in her seat with the iPad clutched in her sweaty hands. She couldn't take her eyes off the picture.

How could this possibly be? How could there be a strange green blob out in North Dakota that had the Voynich script on it?

She expanded the picture with her fingers to take a better look at the writings. Maybe Orr was mistaken. Maybe it only looked like Voynich script. When they arrived at the farm or wherever this blob was supposed to be, her boss would find out he'd recruited her for no reason. She was worthless to the team. All of this mystery about aliens and outer space...what would they do with her? Send her back to DLI? Give her new orders to SERE training in Maine? She'd wanted to be airborne and Survival, Evasion, Resistance and Escape training would be the first step in the right direction.

As she studied the blurry markings on the enlarged photo, she sensed a presence next to her and got a whiff of his Axe cologne. She didn't realize men over twenty wore that stuff.

"Sorry the quality is crap." Kellerman took a seat next to her. "Someone needs to let Farmer Joe know that they have better cell phone cameras these days."

"Be straight with me. Have you guys really found evidence of aliens?" The blurry quality of the photo made it impossible for her to determine without a doubt if the writing was the same as Voynich or not. No point in going crazy looking at a pixelated green blob for the next several hours. May as well wait to see the real thing. Then she could make her determination as to whether or not Orr and the rest of NCIS-A made a mistake bringing her on board.

"We think so." He rubbed his hands down his pants legs. "I've seen some pretty crazy stuff since I got this assignment." He darted a glance toward the front of the cabin. "But I really should let Commander Orr read you in. He should have time after we take off."

The Top Secret security clearance she'd been given did not include access to all the details of every government project with a Top Secret designation. She still needed the additional Sensitive Compartmented Information access—or SCI—to actually understand the purpose and scope of her job.

"How long have you worked here?"

"Since about January."

"Are you Intelligence?"

Kellerman cracked a smile. "No, I started out in Cyber Warfare Engineering. I studied Computer Science at Northwestern. Not sure what you call me now. The paychecks keep coming, so it doesn't matter to me."

Charlie focused her gaze on Demarco who was now paging through her file. "Guess you already know everything about me." Demarco was probably looking for any weakness to peg her on: a sick day, a less-than-perfect score on her last advancement exam, an inspection failure. He seemed like the type who would relish that kind of discovery.

Kellerman's neck turned red. Bright red.

"Crew, listen up." Orr's voice echoed through the metal cylinder of the cabin.

Charlie wished she had more time to explore Kellerman's reaction to her comment.

The commander took a seat next to Demarco. "Time to strap

in. We're cleared for takeoff. Just a reminder, this baby doesn't come with flight attendants and cocktail service. Snacks are in the cooler. Head's up front. We should be at Minot Air Force Base in about five hours. Then we have about a two-and-a-half hour drive to Camp Grafton. Any questions?"

Charlie raised her hand.

"Cutter."

"Are we staying overnight?"

"Yes, Petty Officer."

Demarco smirked.

Jackass.

She felt foolish for even asking. Of course they'd be staying there overnight. After more than seven hours of travel it'd be quite late in the evening even with the time change. She didn't want to bring up the fact she was the only one with no overnight bag in the cargo net. She swallowed the lump in her throat. "Thanks." She'd figure it out somehow. With Demarco around, she'd never admit to any failings.

"Anyone else?" Orr pulled the straps over his shoulders and connected them into the buckle across his lap. "We'll have our brief at 1330. Dismissed."

Kellerman crossed back to his original seat and dug around in his pack for something. Guess any conversation was over with him. For a moment she wished she were back at DLI sitting in the chow hall with her flashcards learning more Russian vocabulary. For most of her adult life she'd been a researcher and a student. Her mind longed for the stimulation of new information. Five hours on a military plane with not even a seatmate to talk to sounded hellish. At least Kellerman had left her with the iPad.

She touched the close button on the photo of the blurry blob. If the plane was taking them where this blob was, she'd learn more if she saw the thing in person. Sure, the writing looked like Voynich, but it could be random markings for all she knew. Until Orr or someone else on this plane gave her the background about the object, she was only along for the ride. She needed to know origins, how this was related to aliens, and what their expectation was of her in this new role as resident linguistics 'expert.'

Her advisor at Baylor would've been a better choice for this assignment. Professor Klingman had introduced her to the strange manuscript and encouraged her to continue exploring its mysteries in her graduate research. Whenever she'd been discouraged, he'd helped her through it. Maybe she could suggest the professor as a replacement candidate if this didn't work out.

The memory of the day she'd told Klingman she wasn't going to finish her master's degree made her cringe. She'd never been one to fail at anything. When she showed up at home in San Antonio with her laptop and all her belongings, her father had reminded her of that. *Cutters don't quit, Charlie.*

She tucked away the memory of that day in the back of her mind. It brought up too many negative feelings.

Charlie focused her attention on the iPad, found the Sudoku app Kellerman had been using, and started up a game. Everything else seemed to be password protected. Without knowing its possibly confidential contents, she wasn't sure if she should be handling the device. Could the photo of the blob really be unclassified?

———

Charlie awoke to a hand on her shoulder.

"Hey, the Commander wants to brief you now."

Charlie opened her eyes and saw Lisa bent over her. When did she fall asleep? She sat up quickly, embarrassed she'd drifted off with a bunch of strangers around her. The iPad had disappeared from her lap. She touched her hair.

"You look fine. Come on." Lisa urged her toward the back of the plane where Commander Orr and Special Agent Demarco waited.

Great.

Her mouth was dry. She wished she had a minute to look at herself in a mirror. Curiosity, however, drove her forward. She used the line of jump seats along the wall of the aircraft to guide her. Unlike commercial aircraft, this plane had no windows. Beneath her feet, recessed handles lined the floor indicating more storage compartments. To make sure she didn't stumble, she kept her eyes on the floor.

"Have a seat, Cutter." Orr gestured to a more traditional-looking airline seat in a row of six.

She picked one, leaving some distance.

Demarco handed her a piece of paper on a clipboard. "I need you to read this and sign it."

She read through the document. Along with all the warnings about prosecution if she revealed any classified material, it gave her access to SCI documents marked with both the KLONDIKE and YARDARM control systems. She signed her name at the bottom and dated it.

Demarco took it from her, signed his name next to hers, slid it into a leather briefcase, and snapped it shut. "What you are about to read cannot be talked about outside of this plane or the office. Do you understand?"

"I've been through the clearance process. I signed the read in document. Yes, I understand." So far only Demarco rubbed her the wrong way. She bit her lip to avoid saying anymore. It wouldn't be good to give him a reason to dislike her more than he already did.

"This will explain things to you." Orr handed her a red manila folder full of papers. "If you have any questions, let me know."

She took the folder from him. "I will. Thanks."

Orr smiled; Demarco scowled. They both left her sitting in the back of the plane and made their way forward to their seats.

She sat for a moment looking at the red folder in her lap. So NCIS-A tracked aliens. Even if she didn't one-hundred percent believe it was true, the contents of the folder should tell her what she needed to know. Then she could judge for herself if she'd ended up in some wacky secret branch of the Navy or if this was real.

Charlie opened the red folder. Her hands sweated. Her brain told her aliens did not exist. She wanted to read the contents with an open mind, but it was hard to do when the word 'alien' only invoked a mental picture of Spielberg's E.T.

The first things inside the folder were a series of pictures.

Different photos than the one on the iPad. The light quality was terrible, but the object in the foreground was unmistakable—another pod. She flipped the photo over to see if it was marked on the back.

When was this taken?

Nothing. No markings.

She scrutinized the picture again. One close-up photo of the pod had the glare of a flash splattered across its dark green surface. The Voynich-like markings were clearly visible. Her finger traced across the familiar letter pattern.

There had been another pod before this one.

She set the picture aside. Eager to read the documents that filled the folder. The first was a report. The date in the upper right hand corner stated it was written in July 2022—one year earlier.

TOP SECRET KLONDIKE

To: Director, Naval Criminal Investigative Service, Mr. S. Trainor
From: LCDR Jacob McDowell
Subject: Unidentified Object—NAVSECGRU Fort Madison, Iowa

Site report from NAVSECGRU Fort Madison indicates crash landing of Unidentified Object (UO) at 2230 hours on 15 JUL 2022. Witnesses attested to loud noises, fire before UO landed in the Mississippi River.

Petty Officer Ledbetter and Seaman Conlon were first on scene. Ledbetter and Conlon both described a large round object about eight feet in diameter. Organic in nature, green or black in color. Hull had been breached by the crash. UO disintegrated in rain and flood waters before team arrival. Unable to attain specimen due to degradation in the field.

Photographs attached to report show size, shape, color and possible writing-like markings on external shell.

Ledbetter testified to seeing fleeing figure, which emerged from UO after crash. No clear description given beyond estimated height (6 feet) and anthropomorphic shape. Search of the surrounding areas revealed no tracks or trace of anything coming from the crash site.

Conlon did not corroborate Ledbetter's testimony.

Further investigation unwarranted due to lack of evidence. Filed under UO until further identification is possible.

Suggested actions: None at this time.

The report was thin. Charlie had been hoping for more details. Many questions had popped into her mind. The photos were the only evidence of this first pod. She wished she could interrogate the two sailors who claimed to have seen the crash.

The rest of the folder was filled with a dozen local accounts of the same mysterious crash in 2022. People who lived near the site were interviewed, their details written down by hand on sheets of lined paper. Names, addresses, and phone numbers of people who probably had forgotten all about the strange fiery crash during the storm.

Charlie wanted more. This file told her nothing. Why all the secrecy and special handling when this read like another Roswell incident? It was a junk report written by an overworked Naval officer who most likely wanted to escape the rain and go home to his wife and kids.

Where was the explanation for the current situation? Where were the details of the 'pod' and its origins? Certainly an expert in extraterrestrial life would've weighed in on this craziness by now?

This was her briefing into NCIS-A?

Charlie flipped through a dozen of the handwritten reports. The very last page caught her attention. Another classified document from a year ago.

TOP SECRET KLONDIKE

To: Director, National Security Agency
From: LCDR D. Orr
Subject: New Investigative Division

Requesting creation of new investigative division under the purview of NCIS in order to respond to recent events. Request made for the following reasons:

Second UO sighting identical to report from 15 JUL 2022

Additional evidence obtained that points to OTE (Other-than-Earth) origins

Samples obtained that need further study outside regular channels

Implications could be substantial; therefore, additional classification and study is necessary.

New division would require two additional cleared personnel for support. Reference Report #3A15972C for further details of related events.

Charlie leaned back in her seat. Stamped at the top and bottom of the document all in caps was the word YARDARM—the SCI designator for classified material associated with NCIS-A.

The NCIS-A division was brand new. No wonder the file was thin. Or maybe this was only the part of the documentation that pertained to her job on this team.

Where was the additional information about this secondary event? This meant the pod in North Dakota was pod number three. There were no more documents in the file. Did they have pictures from the second pod? Was this pod also covered in Voynich-like markings? Did they retrieve any other evidence? Did anyone else see a possible human-like figure emerge?

Adrenaline coursed through her at the possibilities.

Charlie picked up the blurry photographs again. She needed to start taking notes on this stuff. If she was brought on the team to figure out the meaning of the strange symbols on the pods, then she would need to work on crafting a database. One of the reasons deciphering the Voynich text had been so daunting was the lack of multiple documents using the same symbol system. The more examples of writing she had, the possibility of cracking the code grew more likely.

Despite her doubts about the existence of aliens, she needed to take her job seriously. This is why she'd left her graduate studies, didn't she? To find something meaningful in life, more exciting. Plus, she'd never been able to truly uncover all the mysteries the Voynich document held. Here was her opportunity. The keys to solving the mystery. Right at her fingertips. No deadlines. No professor breathing down her neck about proving her thesis. No one telling her she was wrong.

As part of this team, she was the linguistics expert. That is what Commander Orr told her. No one would question her theories. She'd have full authority to follow any rabbit trail she liked.

Maybe this whole extraterrestrial thing was crazy. Maybe it was nothing more than a handful of kooks running around meeting with nutjobs and conspiracy theorists. She was only a cog in a much larger wheel, which meant she could focus on her one little piece of it and leave the big stuff to someone else.

There was comfort in that.

She closed the file, pictures and all, and headed back to her seat for a pen and a notebook.

"Whoa, hold on there, Cutter." Demarco snatched the folder from her hands.

"Hey, I need that." His eye line was slightly higher than hers. Did it bother him they were almost the same height? "I need to take some notes."

Commander Orr was deep in conversation with Chief Ricard at the front of the plane. Charlie wished she could shove Demarco out of the way and sit down with the commander for a franker discussion about her job and these old reports.

"This is classified material." Demarco's eyes snapped. "You've read it; now it needs to be checked back in before we land."

The patronizing son of a bitch. "Commander Orr brought me on because you don't have anyone on the team with my kind of skills. Why don't you let me do my job?"

"I'm the head of security on this team, Petty Officer." Demarco emphasized her rank with a curl of his lip. "It's *my* job to make sure our documents are secured properly."

Petty Officer Storm appeared out of nowhere and put a hand

on Demarco's forearm. "Give her a few minutes to take notes, Angel. You'll have time to lock it up."

Lisa's quiet words calmed the Special Agent. "Fine." Demarco's voice came down a notch or two. "You've got exactly ten minutes."

Charlie took back the folder. "Thank you." Her shoulders had tensed up. She forced herself to relax. Thank God for Lisa. Clearly, she knew how to calm the savage beast. So much for not having to prove herself anymore. Demarco might be harder to win over than the Linguistics Department at Baylor.

Demarco turned and headed back to his seat.

"His bark is worse than his bite," Lisa whispered. "You just have to know how to handle him."

"Thanks for the help. Guess I've got a long way to go before I fit into the team." Charlie sat in her seat, and Lisa joined her. "I feel as if I've got a lot of catching up to do."

Lisa smiled, which exposed a gap between her front teeth. "You'll pick it up. Look, if it makes you feel any better, Demarco told me I was a glorified secretary on my first day and that my most important job was picking up his coffee order."

"You're kidding."

"I wish I were. Demarco's one of those guys who wants everything to go back the way it used to be: men in charge; women in the back seat."

"Guess I shouldn't be hoping for much, then."

"Exactly. That's who the guy is. You can't change him. He might look young, but he's got the mind of my grandfather when it comes to the role of women in the work place. Don't let it get to you."

"I'll try not to."

Lisa squeezed her hand. "You'll be just fine." She caught sight of Commander Orr waving her toward him and took her leave.

Focusing back on her notes, Charlie wrote TOP SECRET YARDARM at the top and bottom of a page of blank paper she'd managed to find. Scrutinizing the faded photographs, she began creating a sketch of each symbol she could discern. At some point, she'd need to craft a more permanent document, but for now this would do.

"Would this help?" Quiet Kellerman leaned across the aisle and handed her a spiral notebook. "Demarco passed these out to us. I never use mine."

"Thanks." Charlie accepted the plain black notebook.

"Don't forget to give it to him when you're done. He can store it in the locker before we land."

"I have to go through him every time I want to access my notes?" Charlie imagined the glowering face of Demarco. That wasn't something she looked forward to.

"When we're traveling. When we're working in the office, you can leave your notes in your desk."

"Right. Secured office."

"Right." Kellerman cracked the tiniest of smiles.

Determined to prove herself a worthy asset to the team, Charlie sketched out her notes as quickly as possible. Then, she confidently headed straight to Demarco, handed him the folder and her notebook, and looked him straight in the eye. "Done. You can store these now."

Special Agent Demarco quietly took the materials and gave a curt nod.

Charlie sighed inwardly. One chink from his armor had been removed. Only a thousand more chinks to go.

CHAPTER 6

THE C-17 LANDED LIKE AN ELEPHANT, heavily and with no elegance. The savage jolt woke Charlie from a fitful sleep. Her stomach lurched. Nausea grew. The spare lunch Lisa had handed out to everyone—peanut butter sandwiches and a bottle of water— didn't quite fill the empty, nervous pit inside her.

A wisp of hair slid into her eyes. Charlie adjusted a bobby pin and re-secured the loose strand into her French braid. Her white navy skirt held a days' worth of wrinkles in it. With nothing to change into, she considered the possibilities. Would they be checking into a motel where she could hang her uniform in the bathroom and mist out the wrinkles with hot water from the shower? Or were they going to rush straight to the scene to investigate the mysterious pod? Although she was eager to examine this 'alien' pod for herself, she worried about the lack of proper gear.

"Minot reports a temperature of eighty-five degrees. Steady rain." The pilot's scratchy voice came across the intercom. "Please stay belted in until we give you the go-ahead."

"Heads up, folks. We have half a day before nightfall and a lot of ground to cover." Commander Orr appeared invigorated and alert—his regulation haircut perfectly combed and looking crisp, uniform clean and free of wrinkles. "Stormy, you show Cutter the ropes when we arrive on scene."

What a relief to hear she'd be teamed up with Lisa. They'd

gotten on well together in the short span of time they'd known each other. Maybe because Charlie was the only other woman on the team, but for now that was enough to carry her through the day.

The plane came to an abrupt halt.

After a few moments of silence, the pilot's voice crackled on the intercom again. "All clear. All clear."

Everyone unbelted. Charlie followed suit.

Lieutenant Kellerman packed up his gear. Demarco, up in front of the plane with the commander, fiddled with the crate of secured items. Chief Ricard removed boxes and bags from the netting and handed a few things off to Lisa.

Charlie had nothing to collect and no clue what her job should be at this stage. She ran her tongue across her teeth and wished for a piece of mint gum. "Do you need any help?" Kellerman was closest to her.

He hoisted his bag over his shoulder. "That's okay. I got it." He headed for the back of the plane behind the rest of her co-workers.

Charlie followed Kellerman with her meager belongings in hand. Rain pounded on the roof of the big plane, and the drops sounded like gunshots. She wished she'd brought a jacket with her that morning to the office. The weather had been warm and dry in D.C., and the extra layer had seemed unnecessary. Her shoulders slumped.

The back of the C-17 opened up like a trap door. Rain poured down in sheets. A gust of wind blew into the cabin.

They'd landed on the tarmac about a half mile from any building or shelter. Charlie set her cover on her head, glad for the bit of protection it gave her. As she took the ramp one step at a time, she anticipated the drenching she was about to receive with dread.

Everyone else wore rain gear and didn't seem to mind the weather.

Charlie stepped into the storm, and the rain pummeled her black cardigan sweater which covered her white cotton shirt. At least the humidity from the storm might release some of the wrinkles in her uniform. The wind whipped at the edge of her skirt.

She put her head down and caught sight of a bus waiting about fifty yards from the plane.

Dry warmth embraced her. Charlie, startled, looked to her right. Special Agent Demarco wrapped his trench coat around her shoulders. "Where's your coat?"

"I don't have one."

"You need to learn to be prepared, Cutter." He slowed his stride to match hers as they approached the waiting bus. "Our team has to be ready to move when the call comes in. There's no time to screw around packing a bag. Next time, you come to the office with your gear."

Charlie pulled the edges of the coat closer around her body. "I will." Even though Demarco had rubbed her the wrong way from the start, the gesture had been a kind one. Maybe he wasn't so bad after all.

Demarco waited until she stepped up into the bus first and then followed. "I'm sure Stormy can loan you a few things once we're done for the day. Keep the coat until we're back in D.C. I've got a poncho in my bag I can use."

"Thanks." Charlie took the first empty seat at the front of the bus. She scooted to the window, assuming Demarco would join her.

He slipped past her, however, and sat down across from the commander further back. The two of them immediately were deep in conversation.

She slid her arms into the coat Demarco had given her. He'd noticed her dilemma and had offered a helping hand. That went a long way to bridging the gap between them. In such a small office, it wouldn't be good to start off on the wrong foot. Maybe she'd misjudged the man.

Charlie stared out the window at the storm. A mystery waited for them a few hours away. Until she saw the pod with her own eyes, she wouldn't believe there was anything alien about it. It didn't matter what the classified materials revealed to her. She'd spent months with the Voynich manuscript. Everything about it said 'earth' to her.

She took her phone out of her purse and searched online for

the manuscript. It had been a couple of years since she'd laid eyes on it. The document used to be as familiar to her as her own brother.

She found the page she was looking for: an intricate image of a dragon with a long, curling tail, standing on a globe with three flaming orbs inside it. The dragon had a wound that rained droplets of blood on the orbs, which looked as if they sat in a lake of blue water. Four columns of writing appeared underneath the colorful artwork.

"What's that?" Lisa leaned over the back of the seat.

Charlie held the phone out for Lisa to see the screen better. "It's a page from an old manuscript."

"Can you read that stuff?" Lisa pointed at the writing on the ancient page.

"No, but I was working on it a few years ago." Charlie tapped on the screen to black it out. Her intention had not been to dredge up old regrets; she'd only wanted to familiarize herself with the writings to be prepared for whatever they encountered at Camp Grafton.

"I'm sorry." Lisa scrambled around the seat and sat next to her. "I didn't mean to pry."

"That's okay." Charlie knew Lisa's questions were well meaning. The last thing she needed to do was push away a possible friend. "Commander Orr thinks I can help decipher some of this stuff for you. I want to make sure I'm prepared. It's been awhile since I've worked with these documents."

"You've been at the language school, right?"

"Yeah. In Monterey."

"Not a bad gig."

Charlie nodded. "It's a beautiful place—expensive, but beautiful." She thought of the views of Monterey Bay from the 'hill' on which the military language school was built. On sunny days it was like paradise. She could walk to the beach or the pier, stroll the small downtown of Monterey or walk a little further into Pacific Grove. Giving up six hours of her day for language class and a few hours a night to study was a good deal compared to other Navy training schools. "What about you? Where did you go for training?"

"Florida." She smiled and flashed her gapped teeth.

"That's not so bad either."

Lisa shrugged. "Pensacola's okay. We were about fifteen minutes from the beach, though."

"Nice." Charlie imagined the warmth and humidity of sunny Florida. Monterey might've been beautiful, but it also could be cold and foggy for most of the summer.

"Nice if you have a car. I was pretty much stuck on base for two months."

Charlie reconsidered the idea. "That would suck."

"Exactly."

Conversation lulled. They both stared out the window at the passing landscape. As they moved further away from the base in Minot, the storm slowed to a drizzle.

"I was hoping it would clear up before we got to Grafton," Lisa said. "Last time, we had to do all of our work in the rain. By the time we were done collecting all of our samples, taking pictures, and interviewing witnesses, I was soaked to the bone."

"Will Commander Orr give me an assignment when we arrive? I'm not sure what I'm supposed to do."

"Demarco's pretty much the point man. He's been with the group longer than I have." Lisa was fully engaged now. "The commander is kind of our management guy. He interacts with the higher ups, keeps them off our backs."

"What about the Chief?"

"He's in charge of all our equipment. If we need anything, a camera, an iPad, whatever, we check it out from him. He logs it in the book. He's also the one who does the on-site repairs. Like our personal MacGuyver."

Charlie smiled inwardly at the comparison. Richard Dean Anderson's attractive head superimposed onto Chief Ricard's portly body. "And Kellerman's the computer nerd."

"I heard he came from an assignment at Area 51 before he ended up in our office."

"He didn't mention that detail." Charlie tucked that away for future reflection.

"In case you didn't notice already, he's a bit introverted. He's not the biggest conversationalist. I leave him alone and let him do his thing. That seems to be what he prefers."

Demarco appeared in the aisle next to Lisa. He turned and faced the back of the bus and interrupted their conversation with an announcement. "Everyone, we'll be at Grafton in about five minutes. Our goal is to collect as many samples as we can. We're hoping for better luck than last time. With the rain slowing down, there's a good chance we'll be able to bring something back this time. Keep your eyes peeled. Anything out of the ordinary, report it to me immediately. Commander Orr will be in charge of interviewing witnesses. Stormy, you help him out. Kellerman, I want you and Chief in charge of photos and retrieving any samples at the scene. Be careful not to contaminate anything." He pointed a finger at Charlie. "Cutter, you're with me."

Although Charlie was grateful to Demarco for loaning her his coat, she wasn't so sure about having to work with him. He'd shown nothing but scorn for her and her background since she'd walked in the door.

"Let's not disappoint Dr. Stern this time." Demarco finished his speech and headed to the back of the bus.

"Dr. Stern, is she the doctor mentioned back in the office?" Charlie asked Lisa.

Lisa filled in the knowledge gap. "She's our forensics expert. She likes to stay in D.C. as she's pretty attached to her work."

The bus took an exit off the highway marked 'Devils Lake.' After a few miles they drove across a spit of land that had water surrounding them on either side. The land was flat for miles around. Not a hill or mountain in sight. The choppy, dark lake reflected the stormy sky above. The rain had slowed to a mist, and a bit of blue sky attempted to break through in the distance.

Nerves took over. After today, she might believe there were extraterrestrials on earth. The possibility was frightening, but exciting at the same time.

The bus turned through the gates at the entrance to Camp Grafton, a National Guard station. They drove past the guard shack and parked near a low lying brown building. An officer in BDUs waited for them in the rain.

"Are you ready?" Lisa whispered.

The bus door opened.

"Yes," Charlie heard herself say as she stood up and headed out into the wet and damp to face whatever waited there for her. "I'm ready."

CHARLIE SHIVERED and followed Demarco through the woods that lined the edge of Camp Grafton. One section of the National Guard installation sat along the edge of Devils Lake where the pod had been found by a local farmer whose land abutted the camp. A vigilant National Guardsman, who'd been stationed there the night before in case of flooding from the storm, arrived on scene not much later to capture additional photos of the find.

"Pick up the pace, Cutter." Demarco pushed through the heavy brush and trees that blocked their route. He shifted a heavy backpack as he moved. "We don't have much time."

"I'm trying," Charlie puffed.

They had left Orr and Lisa back at the bus. When they arrived, the officer in charge of Camp Grafton had been waiting for them and led the commander and Charlie's new friend into a brown brick building where witnesses waited to be interviewed.

Charlie kept up as best she could with Demarco's blistering pace. She thought she was in good shape, but he somehow managed to stay several yards ahead of her no matter how hard she pushed herself. The heavy bag she'd been encumbered with back at the bus wasn't helping things any.

Although Chief and Kellerman were supposed to be taking photos at the scene of the crash, Ricard didn't even try to keep up with Demarco and Kellerman had hung back with his team mate. So Charlie and Demarco had pressed ahead without them.

"What are we looking for?" She wanted to have some idea of his expectations for her.

Demarco didn't answer.

The rain had slowed to a fuzz. Wet drops slipped from Charlie's cover and rolled down her collar. They had to be almost there. The sound of gentle waves lapping against the shore made that clear. She shifted the heavy bag to her opposite hand.

Demarco disappeared into the trees.

Charlie followed his footsteps, which had made obvious impressions in the sandy dirt.

"Hey! Cutter, hurry up." Demarco's booming bass voice split the quiet of the woods. "We have something here."

Charlie's heart sputtered unevenly. Her mind flashed to the Voynich Manuscript. Was this going to be the moment she made a discovery? Her dream in graduate school had been to crack the code, translate the text, and wow the world with her linguistic capabilities. She'd be able to write herself a ticket to any university she wanted. The scholars who'd studied the text for decades would be bowled over by the young graduate student and her work.

The trees thinned. Charlie burst through the tangle of branches and bushes to find herself on a rocky strip of land with grasses drowning in flood waters. The lake in front of her was muddy with choppy waves. Demarco stood about fifty yards away. She headed in his direction.

As she edged closer, her gut tightened. A gigantic, lopsided pile of green goop in the shape of a sliced open watermelon sat in about two feet of water.

The pod.

"Damn." Charlie couldn't help herself. Looking at the pictures and reading the reports hadn't really resonated with her. But seeing a pod in person—that rendered her mute. Goose bumps rose on her arms and scalp. Aliens were real.

"Stop gawking and start taking notes." Demarco crouched down in the knee deep water to take a closer look. "Dr. Stern is going to flip out." He touched the edge of the pod with his fingers and rubbed them together. "Slimy. Organic for sure."

Charlie dug into her bag and yanked out one of the notebooks that had been kept in the security box on the plane. She carefully wrote "TOP SECRET YARDARM" at the top and bottom of the first page. Her hand trembled. She took a deep breath. Freaking out would not help at this point. She'd only piss off Demarco and screw up her first day on the job. She needed to be as calm as the Special Agent seemed to be.

"Pod is approximately eight feet across and made up of dark green organic material. The roof is missing. No signs of life." Demarco circled around it, stepping deeper into the lake. He ran his hand along the pod as he walked and filled a test tube with the goo.

"Do you see any markings?" Charlie moved closer to the object, peering inside. To her unschooled gaze, the green lump of gunk inside looked like a seat of some kind. Rising from the floor were structures that could be mechanical pieces. Levers and knobs set in green goo. "Whoa, did you look inside?"

"Stay back." Demarco noticed how close she was to it. "We don't know if this could be harmful stuff or what. Where the hell is the Chief? This thing is disintegrating fast."

As if the pod heard him, a chunk of it slid into the lake and disappeared.

"Fuck." Demarco was now up to his hips in the murky lake. "Do you have a phone on you?" He wiped his hands on his poncho and placed the test tube in his pants pocket.

"Yes." Charlie pulled her smart phone from the pocket of his trench coat. Strange that Demarco didn't want her to approach it, but yet he had pod slime all over his hands. "Want me to take pictures?"

"Yes. Be warned, though, you'll have to hand your phone over to the Chief. Once those pictures are taken, you've got classified material on it. You won't get it back."

She hesitated.

"We'll give you a new one. Don't worry."

She snapped pictures of the exterior from the shore and the

strange interior. She used the zoom feature to take up close photos of the seat-like structure inside. When she used the same zoom on the mechanical-looking parts, her breath caught in her throat. "The markings. Do you see them?" She stared at the screen of her smart phone and snapped several photos. "It's the same."

They were Voynich-like markings for sure. She'd recognize the loops and whorls anywhere. How could it be that a book written hundreds of years ago could have the same writing as this pod? Could the manuscript really have been written by an alien, stranded centuries ago on earth? And if there was writing on the inside of the pod, then couldn't it be possible it contained life from outer space? Thinking, breathing, intelligent life?

The whole idea of the discovery and its implications for the world overwhelmed her. So unbelievable. So remarkable.

My God.

One whole side of the pod caved in, falling on top of the interior structures and burying the writing she'd only just photographed.

"Dammit." She took as many pictures as she could and stepped deeper into the lake, her shoes filling with water. The pod disintegrated rapidly. Once the side collapsed, the lake poured in and weakened the object further.

"Charlie, where's Demarco?" Kellerman called from the shore. He and the Chief had finally arrived.

"What?" When had Demarco taken off? They'd both been examining the pod. Far down the beach she could see a figure about to disappear behind a curve of land that followed the edge of the lake. "Demarco!" She didn't know why she bothered calling his name. He was already too far away to hear her. "Here, take my phone and snap more photos before this thing is gone."

Charlie waded back to shore and tossed her phone to Kellerman. What had Demarco observed that caused him to leave the scene?

Kellerman caught the phone before it hit the gravel. "Sorry it took us so long. Chief left his tripod in the bus, and we had to go back."

"Whatever." Charlie's gaze focused on Demarco. He'd almost disappeared from view. "I took some good ones before it started to fall apart. You finish up. I'll be back in a minute. Take more samples."

Kellerman said something to her, but she wasn't listening. She trotted in her soggy dress shoes toward the shrinking figure of Demarco. Not wanting to be slowed down, she'd left her heavy bag on the shore with Kellerman and Chief. "Demarco, wait!"

The figure didn't stop.

What the hell? Why didn't he say anything to her? What had he seen?

She focused on the point of land a half-mile in front of her. He'd managed to travel quite far in a short period of time. She pushed herself to run harder. Her breath came out in ragged gasps, and her lungs burned. Swimming was more her style, but she'd had to run in Boot Camp, and that wasn't too long ago.

She leapt over drift wood and rocks that were scattered along the beach. In some places, the rising waters of the lake practically buried any possible path along the shore. She'd had to slow down a few times to skirt the flooding by entering into the wood line and find a new place to continue.

The figure she'd been watching at the edge of the lake disappeared around the bend, but now she was only about a fifty yards from the spot. It had definitely been Demarco she'd seen. As she'd closed in on him, she recognized his poncho flapping in the breeze.

She reached the bend and made a turn, hoping she'd see him not too far ahead.

He'd vanished.

Uncertain where to go next, she made an abrupt stop. Her feet throbbed in her shoes. Not exactly made for running with their flat soles and zero arch support. She'd probably regret the run in the morning.

Where did you go, Demarco?

She scanned the rocky strip of beach. Only about a foot of land remained uncovered by the rising lake.

Footsteps in the sand.

Yes!

She'd found his trail.

As she approached the tracks, she stopped dead. Her heart fluttered.

Next to Demarco's boot prints was a distinct second set of prints. Not another set of shoe prints, but prints of someone who'd passed through here barefoot.

Her mind couldn't comprehend what she was seeing. The feet that had made the second set of prints didn't look human. Didn't look like anything she'd ever seen. There were two 'toes' with a split down the middle that reminded her of a pig's hoof. Yet the print had a distinct heel and arch.

What in the hell was Demarco following?

Charlie set aside the fear that set in when she saw those strange prints in the sand. She had to find Demarco. Had he seen the creature that made them?

She followed them to the edge of the brush and woods that lined the lake. Demarco had headed this way. Would she find him nearby?

Instinct told her to remain quiet. She drew on her limited experience with hunting. Her father had wanted her to become as expert a marksman as her brother, but she couldn't stand the idea of killing something. He'd taken her on three deer hunting trips, and all three she'd ended up in tears. Her brother would kneel on the ground next to his kill, and she'd be hiding in the tent waiting for it all to be over.

The crack of a breaking branch startled her. The noise had come from the woods. Was it Demarco? Or the creature?

Fear kept her immobilized. She didn't know if she could move forward. Everything inside her was telling her to stay put and wait for help to arrive. This was her first day, dammit. Her first day. She didn't know protocols. No one had warned her of this possibility. She had no weapon, no training, and now she was in an incredibly vulnerable position.

She took a step back.

Another crack.

Her breathing sounded loud to her own ears. She made each

breath as shallow as she could. Her gaze focused on the trees and shrubs in front of her.

"Cutter. What are you doing here?" Demarco stepped from the woods.

Relief flooded her. "You left me on the beach. I saw you way down here and thought you could use some help." Charlie felt the fool. She had no way to provide any help had he needed it. Had he found the creature that made the prints? His calm demeanor told her 'no.'

"Why did you abandon your assignment? Did you take enough pictures? Has the pod disintegrated?" The special agent wiped his sweaty forehead with the back of his hand. His hard gaze unnerved her.

"Kellerman and Chief showed up. I left the camera with them." She squinted at her superior. The sun had broken through the heavy cloud cover and shone in her eyes. She couldn't hold in her question any longer. "Did you find it?"

"Find what?" He stood still with his face in shadow. Charlie had a hard time reading his expression.

His answer knocked her back. Her confidence in what she'd seen, shaken. "Whatever made those weird footprints on the beach. It looked as if you were following them." She shifted her weight onto her other foot. "Is that why you came down here?"

"I thought I saw something...a movement. A shape. I wasn't sure. So I thought I'd better check it out." He brushed past her. "Then when I saw these, I thought I was on to something." He crouched down in the tall grass that rimmed the beach and parted it to reveal another of the strange prints.

Charlie hunkered down next to him. "Yes, I saw them, too. The alien. He left them here." Her thoughts skipped ahead. "The pod landed last night during the storm. The creature escaped from the pod and ran from the scene. But how did his footprints survive the rain and the flooding? Shouldn't they be washed away by now?"

"Whoa, slow down, Cutter. You're getting ahead of yourself. These are just shoe prints."

"Shoe prints?" Charlie couldn't believe it. She'd been fooled by a pair of shoes?

"When I saw these prints, I was in the same place you were. I headed into the woods, and then realized I'd let my imagination run away with me."

Demarco did not seem like the type to have any imagination whatsoever. Pressed pants, shined shoes, fresh haircut.

"Once I entered the woods, the sand turned into mud. Deeper prints. More definition. Definitely shoe prints. Some kind of brand that looks Japanese with the split toe." He cocked a half-smile at her. "I appreciate your enthusiasm. We need someone like that on our team. Commander Orr is always wrapped up in the red tape whenever we arrive on scene and Chief can't keep up with the pace. This time, though, it was a wild goose chase. It happens."

Charlie touched the print. "Guess I have to learn to slow down. Be more observant." She wiped the sand from her hands and stood. "All this alien stuff is new to me. I only want to do a good job." She could've kicked herself for revealing her worries to a man who'd already doubted her usefulness to the team.

"Why don't you head back to the crash site. Kellerman and the Chief are going to need your help." He pulled a small electronic device from his jacket pocket. "I need to take temperature measurements—air, water. You go on ahead of me, and I'll catch up."

She needed to grow accustomed to the ups and downs that came with this job. How silly of her to think they'd figure out the meaning of these pods on her very first day. "Will do. Sorry for dropping the ball." Did Kellerman manage to take more pictures before the pod deteriorated completely?

"It's all right, Cutter. This job has a steep learning curve. You're only beginning to scratch the surface." Demarco walked down to the water's edge and stuck the tip of his device into the lake. "We have to make sure we collect plenty of samples to bring back with us. This is the most intact pod we've ever encountered."

Cutter took that as her cue to leave Demarco to his tests. "I'll let Chief know where you are. See you back at the bus later?"

"Yes. I shouldn't be too much longer."

Demarco took sample after sample of lake water. How many samples could he possibly need? Charlie turned and headed back toward the crash site. She could see tall, skinny Kellerman and short, pudgy Chief Ricard circling the pod remains. Time for her to pull her weight.

CHAPTER 8

"HEY, where did you run off to?" Kellerman caught sight of Charlie as she returned to the beach where the mission had begun. He held an open case full of test tubes stuffed with green goo from the pod.

"I thought Demarco needed help." She tilted her head toward the distant point of the lakeshore where she'd seen the special agent thirty minutes earlier. "Turns out, he was fine without me. Did you take any more photos?" She hoped Kellerman would drop the subject of Demarco and focus on their assignment. Disappointment lingered after finding out the prints were nothing more than a shoe tread.

"A few. I have your phone around here somewhere." Kellerman held the heavy case against his side with one hand while he searched his pockets.

She expected him to drop the case any moment.

"It's okay." She reached for it, intending to rescue it, if he lost grip. "Demarco told me I wouldn't get it back anyway."

Confusion clouded Kellerman's expression. The case slipped. She flinched.

"Classified material."

"Sure." He shifted the case back into a more solid two-handed grip. "Guess you're going to need a new phone."

As if on cue, her phone played the distinctive Russian

National Anthem she'd chosen as her ring tone when she'd gotten into the DLI Russian program. It was definitely in one of Kellerman's pockets. "Sorry." Her face heated. "You can let it go to voicemail."

Kellerman jumped at the simultaneous vibration. "Back pocket. Grab it." He turned slightly to make it easier for her.

"That's okay. I don't mind if it goes to voicemail." She wasn't about to dig into her male co-worker's back pocket to reclaim her phone.

"I got it." Chief came up from behind and snatched the phone from Kellerman's pants. "Heads up." He tossed it in Charlie's direction.

She fumbled it, and it fell into the sand. "Whoops." When she bent over to retrieve it, she saw her father's name on the screen.

Dammit.

"Answer it already." Chief trundled past them with another case in his arms. "We're pretty much done here, and your ring tone is driving me fucking batty."

Charlie pressed the answer button. "Hey, Dad, you always have such great timing." She glanced at Kellerman as he passed by her with his case, following Chief Ricard into the woods and heading toward the bus.

"Are you busy?" Captain Cutter had a knack for calling at all the wrong moments. When her boyfriend of three years had broken it of in college. When she'd received her first speeding ticket. When she decided to quit her master's degree program. Yes, his timing was impeccable.

Charlie scanned the empty beach. "Looks as if I'm free for a few minutes. What's up?" She took a seat on a flat rock about twenty yards from what little remained of the pod. She couldn't believe how quickly it had melted.

"Your mom wanted me to call. She's worried about you. The new job and all. How was your first day?"

It was as if their disagreement from the other day had never even happened. He'd always been this way. Brushing aside arguments as if nothing had gone wrong. Pretending as if everything was hunky-dory when it had really gone to shit. "Fine. My first day was fine. In fact, I'm still working."

"I'm sorry, Charlene."

Charlene. Again.

She tamped down her annoyance. Most people her age would be happy to have a parent call and ask about their first day of work. She, on the other hand, found it intrusive and overbearing. "Even if I were done for the day, I wouldn't have much to say. You know, security and all."

Her father worked at the NSA, which was a short drive from Washington Navy Yard. He had a clearance and knew the rules.

"Right. I understand that. Your mom had me call because I think she believes we can talk about work since we're both in the Navy. I didn't have the heart to explain it to her. You know how she is."

Charlie pictured her mother at home, prepping dinner for her father. Angela Cutter's main ambition in life had been to be a wife and mother. Now that Charlie and her brother were grown up and gone, her mother had turned her attentions to pampering her husband with elaborate home cooked meals and meddling in her children's lives. "Tell mom I'm doing fine. I'll give her a call tomorrow when things are calmer."

"Will do."

"Have you received your new orders yet?" He was due for a new assignment soon. He and her mother had been stationed at Fort Meade, Maryland for three years. Not a bad gig, really.

"Should hear from BUPERS any day."

"What are you hoping for?"

"Your mom would love to go overseas. Japan, I think. But I'd like to teach again. We'll see."

Demarco made his way toward her. He must've finished with his tests. Probably wouldn't look too good if she were chatting on her cell phone, which was now likely the property of NCIS-A, to have a chat with her dad. "I should go. I have more work to do."

"Sure, honey. I understand. I'm sorry for interrupting your day."

At the last moment, she realized she needed his help. "Dad,

before you hang up, do you think when you get home tonight you could email me my research?"

"I thought you were done with that. In fact, I distinctly remember you telling me to drop your laptop off a cliff."

When she'd quit the graduate program at Baylor her research had hit a wall. She was not moving ahead as she'd anticipated at the beginning. Failure lurked around every corner and undermined her ability to decode the Voynich Manuscript. She'd not been used to failure. "I just need it, Dad. Could you email it, please?"

"If you were going to finish the research, why didn't you stick with it? Why did you give it up to enlist in the Navy?"

Same old issues. Time and again. "I'm not having this conversation now, Dad." Demarco was only twenty yards away. The last thing she needed was for him to hear her in a shouting match with her father. "Can't you do what I asked without any opinions or judgment thrown at me?"

"I could've gotten you an appointment to the Naval Academy, like Chad. I don't know why you always have to choose the hard way, Charlene."

"Charlie. I like to be called Charlie." Her voice rose higher than she intended. "How many times do I have to tell you that? Never mind about the files. I'll call Mom. She'll do it for me." She hung up and tossed the phone on the sand in front of her. Why did every conservation with him end up this way?

"Hope you don't mind if I keep calling you Cutter."

Demarco arrived at the most embarrassing point in her conversation. Great. "Cutter's fine." She huddled in her borrowed coat as the wind picked up.

"I'm going to have to take your phone now." Demarco picked it up and wiped off the sand. "Classified materials. I'll buy you a new one when we're somewhere less redneck."

Charlie smiled. Demarco could've made a bad situation worse, but he chose to spare her. "Is there anywhere less redneck in North Dakota?"

He held out a hand to help her up. "You've got a point. Maybe we'll wait 'til we return to D.C."

She accepted his assistance. "Unless you think Devils Lake has an Apple Store?" His hand was pleasantly warm, his grip sure.

He chuckled.

Yes, Charlie had actually made Mr. Tightass laugh. She considered her day a success.

They headed toward the woods to rejoin their group at the bus. Charlie looked forward to taking a hot shower and getting some sleep. It had been a very long day.

"Hey, help!" A cry came from the woods. "Cutter!"

Demarco took off before she could even react and plunged into the thicket.

The voice had sounded like Kellerman's. "We're coming!" Charlie raced toward her team member who needed her help.

————

Kellerman sat on the ground with his hand pressed to a bloody gash on his forehead. Ricard lay crumpled in a heap not much further away.

Demarco crouched over Ricard and tested the pulse in his neck. "What happened?" He directed his question at the young lieutenant.

Charlie pushed Kellerman's hand away from his wound. "Who hit you?" He had a good sized slice to his forehead. Possibly from a rock or a tree branch. There were plenty in the woods.

Kellerman shook off her ministrations and held his head in his hands. "Fuck, fuck, fuck!" He stood and scrounged for the remains of the case he'd been carrying. "He hit me over the head and took the samples."

Alarm rose up in Charlie. "What?"

Demarco focused back on the attack. "Who hit you? Where did he go?"

"Is Ricard okay?" Charlie couldn't think about the attacker. She had to deal with the situation in front of her first.

"Which way, Cole?" Demarco pulled a taser from his pocket. *Where the heck did that come from?*

"Hey, where do you think you are going?" Charlie couldn't

believe Demarco would dash off into the woods and leave two wounded co-workers behind. "You can't go running off by yourself. Let me help these guys make it back to Commander Orr, and I'll go with you."

"There's no time for that. Those samples are all we have. Someone must've been watching us the whole time."

Charlie took in the scene. Kellerman's case had been cracked open. All the test tubes she'd seen on the beach were gone. Ricard's case was missing entirely.

"I can take care of Ricard." Kellerman wiped the blood out of his eyes and made his way over to the unconscious chief. "You two go find the guy. Hurry."

Ricard moaned.

At least the chief was alive.

"Which way did he go?" Demarco asked.

"That way, I think." Kellerman pointed west into the woods along the lake.

"Fuck, Kellerman." Demarco stripped off his poncho. "We'd better find this guy or we're in a load of shit. Let's go, Cutter."

She nodded and paired up with Demarco. "Call the commander," she directed at Kellerman. "Let him know you guys need help out here."

She stuffed down her worries about Ricard's condition. She needed to be alert in order to help Demarco locate the person who'd attacked their people. Her mind flashed back to the strange footprints she'd seen earlier. Could it be that Demarco had been wrong about them? Maybe someone had been biding his time until he saw an opportunity to attack.

"Come on." Demarco plunged into the woods, his taser aimed straight ahead.

Charlie chased behind over limbs and downed trees, through scrubby bushes and underbrush. Minutes went by. Demarco pressed on.

The sun sat low in the sky. It would be dark soon. She hoped they could find some trace of the perpetrator before it was too late.

"Here. Look." Demarco pointed.

Ricard's case lay on its side. Test tubes had spilled out everywhere. All of them were smashed. As if someone had done it purposefully.

"See if you can salvage anything." Demarco indicated several indentations in the mossy ground and a broken tree branch. "See that? He went this way. I'll be right back."

"Wait. Give me my phone." Charlie held out her hand. "If you aren't back in ten minutes, I'm calling the Commander."

He pulled it out and handed it to her. "All right. Ten minutes."

When he hesitated, she shooed him away. "Go, go, go. I've got this. I'll pick up everything. You just get the bastard that did this."

Demarco nodded and disappeared into the darkening woods.

———

Charlie scooped up the remains of the test tubes. A little bit of green goo remained in several of them. With pincher fingers, she picked up each shard and placed it in the case. In the growing dark, it was hard to make out all the debris, but she worked methodically from the case outward. She had no other choice.

Maybe if they went back to the lake, they could still salvage more samples?

At the rate the pod had been deteriorating when she'd seen it last, that seemed unlikely. But maybe it was worth a shot. These samples were too important.

Her focus narrowed to the small patch of ground in front of her. The green substance could answer a lot of questions about what the pod was made of and where it might be from. Shouldn't Dr. Stern be able to tell the difference between a substance from earth and a substance from outer space?

She wished she had some gloves. She'd watched enough forensic specials on tv to know the way she was handling these small shards made DNA transfer unavoidable.

She glanced at her watch to keep track of the time. Only five minutes had passed since Demarco had continued on without her.

As she picked up every bit of glass she could find, she paused in her work and stood back for a better look at the scene to make sure she didn't miss anything. One larger piece of a test tube had fallen outside the range of her vision. It looked as if it might have some blood on it.

Blood.

From the person who'd attacked Kellerman and Ricard? This could be crucial evidence to save. She thought over the possibilities and took in her surroundings. Picking up a large maple leaf, damp and half decayed from last fall, she used it to carefully collect the shard. Wrapping it up in the leaf as best she could, she set it on top of the glass pieces already inside the case.

A crunch behind her made her freeze. The attacker had circled back for her. Her gut clenched.

"I lost him." Demarco emerged from the trees.

Thank God. Demarco.

The tense atmosphere lifted. No longer alone, she felt safer with the special agent there.

"I fucking lost him." He kicked at the base of a tree.

"What happened?"

"He vanished. I reached the edge of the woods on the other side of the base, and the trail ended there. I don't understand. We were right behind him. We had to be."

Demarco gripped the taser.

"You can put that away now," Charlie said quietly.

"Oh," He finally noticed he'd been pointing it toward her. "Sorry." He tucked it in the back of his pants like a pistol. "This whole day has been bizarre. I'm not thinking straight."

"That's okay." Charlie locked up the case. "I don't know what's considered normal for this group. Glad to know you think it's bizarre, too."

"We need to be on guard. I don't know where this guy's gone." He scanned the forest around them. "He's willing to attack two of our people, so he might try it again. Last thing I need is for the newbie to end up hurt."

Charlie was rankled at the comment, but it wouldn't do her any good to put up a fuss. Demarco had an issue with her, and she had to learn how to work through it. Show him that she was as useful and smart as anyone else on the team. Maybe then he'd respect her.

"I collected as much as I could." She showed him the locked case full of shards and bits of goo. "We should really join up with the group. Find out more about what happened."

"Unlock your phone for me." Demarco handed it to her.

She held the phone in front of her face until it recognized her image.

He dialed a number. "Commander Orr, it's Angel. Are Kellerman and Ricard with you?"

Charlie shifted her attention to the sounds emerging from the woods. The night creatures had awakened and strange noises came at them from all directions. She longed to be back in the safety of the bus, headed toward a motel room.

Demarco explained to the commander about the attack, the missing test tubes, and the unsuccessful chase.

Charlie wished they could keep walking. They'd done what they could. The perpetrator was gone. They weren't the cops. They didn't have CSI gear with them to track this person. Was this even related to the pod discovery? Or a random crime?

"We'll be there in ten." Demarco hung up and pocketed the phone.

"Kellerman and Ricard are okay. Someone from the National Guard depot has called for an ambulance. Ricard needs to be checked out, and Kellerman probably is going to need some stitches."

"Glad help is on the way."

"The commander said he was able to collect more samples from the pod. Stormy had an extra case. They might be more cont-aminated with lake water than the ones we had originally, but at least it's something."

"Maybe they can use what I was able to save." Charlie wished he'd pay a little more attention to her. It was as if he hadn't even been listening when she'd showed him the case she'd recovered. "I even found a shard with blood on it."

"You did?" Demarco had her full attention now. "Why didn't you tell me?"

"I did."

Demarco's jaw set in a line. "You never told me you had recov-ered any blood."

"You didn't ask." Charlie couldn't help but bite back. He was unpleasant, holier-than-thou, and condescending. The kindness of lending her his coat completely wore off. "I managed to recover some of the pod material plus a piece of glass with blood on it. It's all in the case."

Demarco snatched it from her. "Let me carry it. The last thing we need is another mistake." He headed back in the direction of where they'd left Kellerman and Ricard.

Charlie fumed. How dare he judge her as a screw up. She'd done nothing to deserve that. Although she wanted to grab the case away from him and knock him over the head with it, she knew it would bite her in the ass and probably only prove him right in some way. She had to take the high road at this point and pick her battles with him. As this was only her first day, the last thing she needed to do was piss off her team.

While she tramped after him in the dark woods, she hoped tomorrow would be a better day. She looked forward to meeting back up with the rest of the team and reviewing the day's events and where they'd go from here. She also wanted a good look at the photos they'd taken. Once she received her Voynich research, she could start working on comparing the two. Maybe she could help figure out where this pod came from, if someone had been on it, and who had attacked them.

CHAPTER 9

CHARLIE AND DEMARCO emerged from the woods in time to witness an ambulance pulling away from the parking lot near the base commander's office. Orr, Lisa, and Kellerman stood in a huddle by their bus.

"Is Ricard going to be okay?" Demarco joined the small circle.

Charlie hung back. After one day with this group, she didn't know where she fit in yet. She was anxious to return to a secure office where she could review the photos, hopefully access her graduate school notes, and compare the writings on the pod to the Voynich writings. For now, though, she could only follow Demarco and the rest of the NCIS-A team around like a puppy dog and wait for orders.

"The EMTs seemed to think he'd be okay, but he needs to have an MRI to find out the extent of his injuries," Commander Orr said. "We don't fly out of here until tomorrow anyway, so it's probably a good idea for the chief to spend the night in the hospital. They'll transfer him to the Minot clinic in the morning."

Although Kellerman held a blood-soaked rag to his forehead, he seemed eager to talk to both Demarco and Charlie. "Did you find him? The guy who hit me and Chief?"

In the short time she'd gotten to know Kellerman, Charlie didn't think of him as an excitable kind of person. This attack, however, brought out the badger in him. "Demarco lost him on the other side of the base," she answered.

Demarco flashed her a hard stare.

Whoops. Guess the straight-laced special agent didn't like being called out when he failed to follow through.

"We tracked him through the woods, but he got away." Demarco opened up the circle for Charlie to join. "Maybe someone was waiting for him in a vehicle. That's the only explanation I can think of. We found your case."

He held up the case with the broken contents locked away inside.

Charlie could've punched him for claiming 'they' had found it together. "Do you have any tape? We need to seal it up. We have DNA inside."

"DNA?" Orr took the case. "What kind of DNA?"

"Blood. On one of the broken vials. There's also some tiny samples left from the pod."

"I managed to collect a few more samples." Lisa held another case similar to the one Charlie had recovered. "Not sure how pure they are, but I'm hoping Dr. Stern can do something with them."

"I might have enough for her to work with. We'll see." Charlie had many questions about this mysterious attacker that she wanted answered. "Who could've known what we were doing out here? I thought this was all top secret activity."

"There are plenty of people who could've found out about the pod from the farmer," Lisa said. "I read the report in there." She motioned toward the commandant's office where she and Commander Orr had had their meeting while the rest of them were gathering their samples. "The guys on watch duty thought it was a meteor. Big, loud, flaming like a rocket engine. Enough to scare anyone that the end of the world had arrived. They met up with the farmer only a few minutes after he'd found it at the edge of the lake."

"The only reason the woods didn't set on fire was the rainstorm. Flooded most of the county," Commander Orr said. "We received the call only after it had been routed through Minot Air Force Base, which routed the call to NSA, which routed the call to our office. Plenty of people in the middle of all that could've sneaked out here to see what we were up to."

"You think they took any pictures or samples before we got here?" Charlie wondered if the mysterious attacker had arrived before they did and had taken better pictures of the writings.

"They sealed off the crash site immediately after impact." Demarco took out his taser and placed it back in its case, which sat on top of the other supplies they'd brought with them. "I doubt he would've made the move on Kellerman and the Chief, if he'd been able to collect his own samples. He stole the case, remember?"

"He destroyed it and the samples. If he wanted to keep them, he wouldn't have left them behind in the woods," Charlie pointed out. "Even according to you, the guy was long gone before we ever started tracking him. If he'd been interested in the samples, he could've gotten away with it easily. Instead he broke all the vials, cutting himself in the process."

"Good point, Petty Officer Cutter." Commander Orr clapped her on the shoulder. "Very astute observation. In other words, this person came here to sabotage our investigation."

Demarco's face darkened.

"Thanks, Commander." The more she thought about the events of the day, the more it made sense to her. The footprints in the sand, the chase down the beach...someone had done that to draw them away from the pod and away from the samples and pictures they'd been collecting. Four against one would've made the odds very bad for someone looking to destroy any evidence of the pod. But with her and Demarco at the other end of the beach, it would've been much easier for a lone attacker to take down Kellerman and Chief.

"Who would have reason to do something like this?" Lisa asked. She'd already packed up both cases, carefully sealing the recovered case with yellow tape to ensure the blood evidence remained intact and untouched until they returned to D.C.

"Conspiracy theorists, militia groups, you name it," Demarco said. "There's always someone who believes the government is inherently bad and wants to keep secrets from the American public."

"But aren't we keeping secrets from the American public?" Charlie asked.

"Yes, but part of the job of the government is to protect its citizens." Orr locked a stack of file folders in a box. He lowered his voice. "Until we know what these pods are, where they come from, and if they are extraterrestrial, it's our job to keep this a secret."

"It's been a long day," Lisa interjected. "We collected a lot of data, and it's going to take time for us to dig through it all. Why don't we save the theories for another day, shall we? The guy ran away, but he didn't take anything. We're not going to figure this out right now." She grabbed the two sample cases and loaded them in the secure storage area under the bus. "I'd like to find our motel and take a shower, if that's okay with everyone else."

Demarco aided Lisa with the task of loading their equipment. Kellerman boarded the bus, with his head wound unbandaged.

Commander Orr drew Charlie aside. "I know this hasn't been easy for you. There's a lot you still need to learn about our office, our job, and what's expected of you."

Charlie wanted to unload how she felt about her first day on the job, but sensed the timing was wrong. "I'm trying to play catch up as best I can."

"You need to trust me. When we're out on site like this, we can't be as open as we would like." Orr scanned the parking lot around them. "We have to do our best to follow security protocols. There will be a time and a place for us to discuss our work more freely. Have patience."

Charlie nodded. She'd only recently received her clearance and should've known better than to broadcast their activities in such a public setting.

"Why don't you board the bus with Kellerman? We'll finish loading everything."

"I'm sorry, Commander."

"Don't be sorry, Petty Officer. We need you on our team. Don't you ever doubt that."

———

Charlie swiped the key card through the door lock at Devils Lake Motel and entered her room—two queen beds covered with depressing brown comforters, a small fridge, and a flat screen tv. Not bad for middle-of-nowhere North Dakota.

She shivered. The maid must've left the air conditioning on all day even though it had been less than warm at the lake. She kicked herself for handing Demarco back his trench coat when they'd exited the bus.

Charlie adjusted the thermostat and picked up the motel directory. Even though night had fallen by the time they'd arrived at the motel, she hoped a store was within walking distance that carried toiletries.

As she flipped through the meager business offerings of Devils Lake, she glanced out the window. Across the street a gas station with a mini mart still had its lights on. Worth a shot.

She put her key card in her skirt pocket and hoped her room would warm up before she returned from her errands.

The Devils Lake Motel was located a few blocks from Highway 2. The town appeared deserted. No cars were visible on the road. The only sound was the loud scratchy rhythm of cicadas.

When she entered the mini mart, the female clerk glanced up from the romance novel she was reading. "We close in ten minutes." Her greasy brown hair had been pulled back from her shiny, pimply face with a pink rubber band. The clerk scanned Charlie from head to toe. Probably wasn't typical for someone in a Navy uniform to stroll in the door.

Charlie glanced at her watch. Almost nine o'clock. "I should be quick." She searched the short aisles for anything useful picking up toothpaste, a toothbrush, a comb, a small round brush, a bottle of hairspray, and deodorant. At the back of the store she spied T-shirts and sweatshirts with 'Devils Lake' on them. She grabbed one of each and a pair of sweatpants.

"Do you have any of those disposable cell phones?" Behind the counter, Charlie saw minute cards for sale for a variety of pay-as-you-go cell phone plans.

The girl got up from her stool and grabbed a flip phone package from the case near the lottery tickets. "This is all we got."

"I'll take it." Charlie dumped the rest of her items on the counter.

The girl took her time scanning each item. The sweatshirt, T-shirt, and pants had to be punched in separately. As Charlie waited to pay, she glanced out the plate glass window. A figure lurked near their bus. It was too dark and too far away for her to determine if it was someone from their team.

"Cash or credit?"

Charlie fished her wallet out of her purse and handed the clerk her credit card. She returned her gaze to the bus. At that very moment, an eighteen-wheeler blew by, obscuring her view. By the time the truck passed, the figure had vanished.

"You put it in the machine yourself." The clerk pointed at the reader on the counter.

"Sorry." She put her card in the chip reader slot. "Thanks."

The clerk handed her a bag and a receipt. Then she picked up her romance novel.

The bell on the door jangled.

"We're closing, sir." The clerk set her book down for a second time.

Charlie looked over her shoulder at the new customer.

Kellerman had entered. He seemed surprised to see Charlie. "Hey."

"Hey." Charlie smiled. He must've been the figure out by the bus.

"Thought you'd be dead asleep by now."

"That's a nasty gash there." The last time she'd seen Kellerman he'd been holding a rag to his forehead. The jagged cut oozed fresh blood.

Kellerman reached up to touch the wound. "Thought I'd see if they had any bandages. Didn't want to mess up the motel towels."

"First Aid. Aisle Two." The clerk, her nose deep in her book, pointed to the correct aisle. "I gotta close up soon."

Kellerman and Charlie searched the aisle for the right sized bandages.

"Do you like Spiderman?" Charlie held up the two boxes available. "Or Hello Kitty?"

"How about some gauze and tape instead?" Kellerman grabbed a box of gauze off the shelf.

Charlie imagined computer nerd Kellerman with Hello Kitty bandages stuck across his forehead and smiled. "You have something against Hello Kitty?"

Kellerman laughed. "My brother would kick my ass if he thought I was even considering it. He caught me playing Barbies with my little sister once and told all of my friends. I was a pariah at school for a month. He still brings it up at Thanksgiving."

Charlie returned the boxes to the shelf. "I would've kept your secret."

"But Demarco wouldn't."

Charlie saw an opportunity to suss out more details about her co-worker. "What is his problem, by the way?"

"Demarco?" Kellerman carried his gauze and tape to the counter.

"Yeah. Does he have a problem with me or is it all women?"

The clerk rang up the purchases.

Kellerman handed the woman a ten dollar bill. "Demarco's hard core, that's all."

"Hard core jack-ass?"

Kellerman didn't bite. "Deep down he's a good guy."

"Could've fooled me."

"He doesn't trust you yet."

They both exited the mini mart and headed back to the motel. The clerk snapped off the outside lights as soon as they left. Guess she wanted to make sure no more last minute customers ruined her evening.

Charlie thought about Kellerman's explanation as they crossed the street. She was new to the team, true. She understood that. Guess she'd have to prove to Demarco that not only was she trustworthy, but that she brought some skills.

They'd reached the bus in the parking lot. The locked storage section under the bus was wide open.

"Shit!" Kellerman exclaimed.

Charlie instantly thought of the figure she'd seen outside the bus moments before Kellerman had appeared in the mini mart. If it hadn't been Kellerman, who had she seen? And what had they taken?

Kellerman pawed through the boxes and bins that were stored inside the locked bus compartment.

Charlie held back. There wasn't room for two of them under there. "Is anything missing?"

"I'm not sure." He checked the locks on all the secure boxes. "I didn't help load it."

Charlie spied one of the sample boxes still inside the storage compartment. But where was the box with the yellow tape? The one with the blood sample inside? "The other sample box is missing. I don't see it."

Kellerman moved more quickly after that revelation. "Are you sure it wasn't put in one of the equipment boxes?"

Most of the items had been stowed inside large metal boxes with keyed locks. "I'm certain. Besides, the other box is right there." Charlie pushed past Kellerman and scooped up the remaining sample box.

Who had left the samples unprotected and sitting inside the compartment?

"Dammit." Kellerman sat back on his heels. "What the hell is going on? The commander needs to see this."

Charlie pulled out her brand new cell phone, still in the package and inactive. "You can use this."

He glanced at the uncharged, most likely unusable phone. "Go find the commander. I think he's in room 216."

Charlie hesitated. "Will you be okay alone out here?" She wanted to tell Kellerman she'd seen someone out in the parking lot earlier, but something made her pause. It had been interesting that Kellerman had appeared in the mini mart only minutes after Charlie had seen a shadowy figure hanging out near the bus.

"Just go." Kellerman closed the compartment door. "Someone broke the lock. Shit."

"I'll be back in a minute. Don't worry." Charlie trotted toward the motel lobby entrance. "Commander Orr will fix this." She said that last sentence mostly to herself. Even though she'd only met him that morning, she trusted Orr. He exuded some of the same characteristics as her father—serious, unflappable, tough. She would tell him what she saw in the parking lot moments before the break-in discovery.

The hotel desk clerk, an older woman with gray-streaked hair and orange lipstick, greeted her. "How are you this evening?"

Before heading up to Orr's room, Charlie had a thought. "Do you have a security camera in your parking lot?"

The woman nodded. "Put one in three years ago after the Elks Club convention."

Charlie sensed the clerk wanted her to ask about the convention, but she was in no mood to chat. "Please make sure you keep tonight's video. We had a break in."

"I'm so sorry." The clerk tapped her fingernails in a nervous rhythm on the counter. "I should probably call the night manager. He should be here by nine-thirty. Do you want me to call him?"

"My boss will probably want to talk to him. Maybe give him a heads up." Charlie grabbed a pad of motel note paper and a pen that sat on the counter. "What's his name?"

"Merle. He's been the night manager here for fifteen years."

Charlie scribbled his name on the paper. "Thanks." She ripped the top paper off the pad and shoved it in her pocket.

"No problem, honey. Sorry about the break-in. I didn't see anything, and I've been here since seven." The clerk pointed at the clock above the entrance.

Charlie headed for the stairs at the end of the first floor wing of rooms. She took the stairs two at a time, stopped in front of room 216, and knocked. God, she hoped Commander Orr wasn't too upset. What if the blood evidence she'd collected was now in the hands of an enemy?

The door swung open to reveal Special Agent Angel Demarco in a towel.

Charlie's face grew hot at the sight of his well-sculpted bare chest, muscular arms, and the thin material wrapped around his waist that left very little to the imagination. Damn Kellerman for giving her the wrong room number. She should've asked the desk clerk to double check for her before she bolted upstairs.

"Cutter, what in the hell are you doing here?" Demarco didn't seem pleased but did nothing to cover up.

"Kellerman told me this was Commander Orr's room." She sputtered and averted her eyes. Better to focus on Demarco's face. "Someone broke into the bus storage compartment. Do you know what room he's in?"

"What? Come in here." Demarco grabbed her and pulled her into his room. The door shut with a slam.

Charlie yanked her arm free. "I need to talk to the commander."

"Slow down, Cutter. Slow down." Demarco rubbed his wet hair with an extra towel. "Sit."

Although she wanted to bolt out of the room and find the Commander, she found herself following the special agent's commands. The tone of his voice made her obey rather than leave. She hoped Kellerman was okay alone in the parking lot. "We need help. The desk clerk has video. Maybe we can find out who did this." She took a seat on one of the two queen-sized beds in the room and put her bag of clothing and toiletries in her lap.

"What were you doing in the parking lot?" Demarco grabbed a pair of pajama pants out of his duffel bag and headed for the bathroom.

Of course the jerk would find something wrong with her story. "I went across the street to the mini mart...look, why I was out there has nothing to do with what happened."

Demarco disappeared into the bathroom, but left the door partially open so they could continue their conversation. "Did you see anything? You said Kellerman was there with you."

Charlie knew Kellerman was waiting for her. This delay was ridiculous. By the time she was done answering Demarco's questions, the perpetrator would be long gone. "When I was across the street I thought I saw someone by the bus. I couldn't make him out. Then, later when we crossed the street—"

"Kellerman went to the mini mart with you?"

She wanted to kick the man in the shins. "He showed up after I got there. Do you want to hear the rest of this or not? I really need to talk to the commander. Do you not understand how important that is?"

Demarco came out of the bathroom more suitably dressed in a pair of plaid pajamas, but no shirt. It was as if he enjoyed making her uncomfortable. "You saw someone by the bus. Kellerman shows up. You both cross the street and—?"

"That's when we noticed the storage compartment had been broken into."

"Anything missing?"

"The sample box we taped closed. I didn't see it in there."

Demarco raised an eyebrow. Finally, some kind of normal reaction out of the man.

"What room is the commander in?" Charlie demanded. "We need to start an investigation. Retrieve the video footage. Call the police. Shut down the town. Whatever we have to do to get that evidence back."

"We can track it." Demarco sat on the other bed and cracked open his laptop.

"What?"

"I put air tags on both sample boxes—is that what you call them? Give me one minute, and I can tell you the exact longitude and latitude of their location."

Thank God for technology. Maybe Demarco could find it. "What about Kellerman?" Charlie wondered what the computer geek thought of her prolonged absence. She needed to get back to him.

"Hold on." Demarco opened up an application. "I have to find the item in the list, hit 'search,' and let the computer do the rest." He worked the touchpad with his forefinger and scrolled to the correct item.

If they found the box, they would likely find the person who stole it. Would it would turn out to be the same person they'd chased through the woods earlier that day? Maybe the mysterious attacker didn't want them to have a sample of his blood or the pod or both.

"Got it." A crooked smile appeared on his face. "Stormy gave me an inservice on these little things. Really handy. She uses them all the time on her kids' backpacks. Here you go." He turned around his laptop so she could see the map on his screen. A little green dot flashed.

Charlie took in the information. The dot was located in their motel. "The box is here?"

"Looks like it." Demarco turned the computer back in his direction. "I should be able to narrow down the range, if I can remember how to do it."

"Can you figure out what room?"

"Give me a second." He tapped on his keyboard. "It's across the hall." Demarco looked up and his gaze burned into her. "Kellerman's room."

CHAPTER 10

DEMARCO OPENED up the nightstand drawer and pulled out his taser.

"What are you doing?" Charlie couldn't imagine Kellerman as the thief. Yes, it seemed suspicious that he'd appeared in the mini mart only a few minutes after she'd spied someone lurking around the bus, but he'd been attacked only hours earlier in the woods. Was Demarco suggesting by his actions that Kellerman had injured himself to cover his tracks?

"You can stay here." Demarco set the taser on the bed and put on a T-shirt. "I'll take care of this." His brown gaze hardened.

Charlie grabbed the taser and backed up. "This is crazy. You can't believe it's Kellerman."

Demarco took a few measured steps toward her. "Give me back the taser, Charlie."

It was the first time he hadn't called her 'Cutter.' She reached for the doorknob. "No. This is ridiculous. You're jumping to conclusions."

"He hasn't been in the office very long. Not much longer than you, actually." He leveled his gaze at her. "The work we do is too important to screw up. We aren't about to get this close to finding some real evidence, some tangible proof of alien life, only to have a weasel like Kellerman run back to Nevada with it. Give me the taser."

"No. I won't. I'm not going anywhere until you get Commander Orr in here." She thought about her options. Dash into the bathroom and lock herself in? Head out into the hallway and bang on Kellerman's door?

The bathroom would be a dead end. Demarco could easily bash in the door. If she ran into the hallway, Demarco would be seconds behind her if she tried to grab Kellerman's attention. She only had one option if Demarco refused her command. Charlie pointed the taser directly at his chest. "Don't come any closer."

Demarco raised his hands. "Whoa, hey, slow down. You don't want to hurt someone with that thing."

"I won't, if you do as I ask." Charlie willed herself to remain calm. She had no clue how to operate a taser, but if she had to, she'd figure it out. It looked enough like her father's .45. "Get Commander Orr in here."

He took a step backward toward the bed. "We're going to lose that case. Is that what you want?" His gaze darted over at the open laptop. "The box is on the move." His whole body tensed. "We have to go."

Charlie kept the taser steadily aimed at Demarco's torso. "Shut up. Call Orr. I want to talk to him." She didn't know why she trusted Orr more than she trusted Demarco, but since the special agent acted so irrationally when confronted with the missing box, she had to rely on someone. Orr had the authority to put Demarco in his place until they sorted this whole thing out.

Demarco's face turned red. "Fuck, fuck, fuck." He picked up the phone and dialed. He stared at her. "You don't know what you're doing, Cutter."

"Just get Orr." Charlie willed her hand to be still. She'd never done this before. Threatening someone with a weapon was outside her realm of experience. She was riding on instinct alone. "If Kellerman really does have the box, the tracker will show us exactly where he is." Maybe that would calm him down. No need to panic if the box could be found at a moment's notice.

"Commander, sorry I'm bothering you so late. I have a situation in my room." Demarco gave her a hard look. "Cutter's lost her mind. Could you please come here?"

He hung up before Charlie could complain about his choice of words. She regripped the taser in her sweaty hand. "Don't try anything stupid."

"What do you think I'd try to do to you? Kellerman's probably gone already. I don't have any beef with you. Put it down. You look ridiculous."

Each second that ticked by Charlie doubted herself a little bit more. Did she make the wrong choice? Did she just find herself out of a job?

Someone knocked on the door. "Angel, what's going on?"

Charlie backed up with the taser still pointed at Demarco. Now that she'd set on that course of action, she felt she had to stick to it. Even if she was losing trust in her own judgment. She felt for the doorknob and opened the door. "Come in, Commander."

Orr stepped into the room. "What in the hell is going on here?"

"She's crazy." Demarco didn't waste any time. "Thanks for adding such a valued new member to the team."

Charlie didn't appreciate the sarcasm. "Commander, there is something weird going on, and I don't know what to make of it."

"And that requires you pointing a taser at Demarco? I don't recall you being qualified in that particular weapon." The commander easily plucked the taser from her sweaty fingers. "There'd better be a good explanation for this, Petty Officer."

Orr made her feel like a little kid with that move. If they'd only listen to her for a minute, they might actually get somewhere.

Demarco relaxed, leaning back against the headboard. "Yes, explain it to him, Cutter. I'm sure he'd love to hear your theories."

"It isn't a theory." Charlie knew Demarco would never take her side on this. Orr was the key. "Kellerman didn't take that box."

"What box?" Commander Orr directed his question at Demarco.

Charlie answered it before the special agent had a chance to take over. "The box we'd sealed at the crash site with the blood evidence of the attacker. Demarco seems to think Kellerman stole it."

"A box was stolen from our secure compartment?" Orr tensed. "Why didn't anyone tell me?"

Charlie didn't have time to explain more. Someone had the case. They needed to find out who. "There's a tracker device on the box. See?" She turned Demarco's laptop to show her boss the blip on the screen. The screen was blank. "What the hell? Where's the tracker?"

Demarco gave a tight smile. "I told you we needed to move. Kellerman's probably miles down the road. There'll be a refresh in a minute." He tapped on the touch pad to update the information.

"Kellerman stole the evidence?" Orr handed the taser back to Demarco. "He was thoroughly vetted before we offered him a spot on the team. He has a top secret clearance. There were no connections in his background to any organizations or foreign governments. I can't believe he would betray us like this. What motive could he possibly have?"

Charlie watched as the tracker data updated. "It's still in his room. Let's go ask him."

She headed for the door before either of the two men could respond. In a moment she stood outside Kellerman's door.

At her knock, the door opened.

"Where have you been?" Kellerman stood in the doorway, the sealed box in his hands. "I found it."

Charlie grabbed the box from him and checked the tape seals. "Where was it?"

Demarco and Orr caught up to her moments later.

"Hey, Commander." Kellerman greeted his superior and opened the door to let everyone inside. "Am I glad to see you."

No mention was made of their earlier suspicions. Charlie knew Demarco didn't want to admit he'd rushed to judgment in front of her.

"Lieutenant," Orr greeted the junior officer. "Cutter told us about the break in."

"Don't worry, I managed to relock the compartment. Stormy's standing guard for now."

Demarco took the box out of Charlie's hands. "Where did you find this? Cutter told us it was missing."

"I thought it was, too. But we were wrong. It was buried under the other boxes. We overreacted."

Charlie could feel the heat of a blush flood her cheeks. She had been positive the box wasn't in the compartment. They'd looked through the whole space. That yellow tape would've stuck out like a full moon on a starless night.

Kellerman continued his story, "After Petty Officer Cutter went looking for you, Commander, I called Stormy, and we did a thorough inventory. All items on the list were accounted for. Once I pulled everything out, I found the sealed box."

"Why would someone break in and not steal anything?" Charlie needed more of an explanation. Although she trusted Kellerman, something wasn't right with the scenario. "It doesn't make sense."

"Agreed." Commander Orr nodded. "Has anyone bothered to find out if the motel has video of the parking lot?"

"Yes." Charlie glanced at Demarco, waiting for an objection. "The front desk clerk told me they have a camera out front and that the night manager should be able to give us the footage."

Orr took control. "Demarco, go talk to the night manager about the footage."

Charlie deflated. The video had been her idea.

"Lieutenant, you are in charge of the box." Orr opened up the closet by the bathroom to reveal a safe embedded in the wall. "It should fit in there."

"Yes, sir." Kellerman took possession.

"And what about me, sir?" Charlie asked. In a room full of testosterone, she felt oddly unnecessary.

"You and I will take turns standing watch at the bus. I'll take the next shift. You relieve me at 0200."

The clock on the nightstand read ten o'clock. Her turn was four hours away. Even though the commander probably expected her to sleep, she had other ideas.

Everyone left Kellerman's room for their assigned duties. Charlie headed in the direction of her room, but once the hallway was empty, she took the stairs back to the lobby. If she didn't insert herself into the investigation, she'd always be an outsider in the office. She'd pulled a taser on a superior, which could end her career if she didn't get ahead of things. The security camera had been her idea. She should be involved in what clues they could glean from its footage.

———

At the bottom of the stairs, Charlie quietly opened the door. From her vantage point she could see the special agent leaning over the counter, smiling and talking to a middle aged man in a golf shirt and a pair of khaki pants. Looked like the clerk she'd spoken with earlier had ended her shift. This must be the night manager, Merle.

She was too far away to hear their conversation, but if she stepped any closer she might be seen.

Screw it.

Why did she care if Demarco saw her anyway? He already thought she was an idiot. How much lower could his opinion of her go?

She boldly stepped into the lobby. "Are you Merle?"

The man behind the counter looked up and gave her a smile. "That's me." He was missing a front tooth and, on closer inspection, Merle looked to be in his late thirties. A decade or two of hard drinking and cigarettes probably prematurely aged the man and gave him the smidgen of a potbelly that puffed out his shirt.

"You were supposed to be resting," Demarco ground out.

Charlie ignored him. "I asked your clerk to save tonight's footage from the parking lot. Can we take a look at it?"

Demarco had his NCIS badge laid out on the counter. Its shiny gold shield glinted in the overhead lights. "The camera's down. There's no footage to view."

Her heart sank. This was going to be her moment. The moment she graduated from being the newbie in the office with zero experience to possibly being the helpful newbie in the office with some sleuthing skills. "Are you serious?" Her adolescent whine sounded ridiculous to her own ears.

Merle frowned. "I don't know why Donna told you it was

working. When the storm hit, we lost power for a few hours. When the electricity came back on, the power surged and blew the computer in the back. We gotta buy a replacement before we're up and running again."

"Give it up, Cutter. We don't have anything." Demarco stuffed his badge into his pajama pants pocket. His damp, black hair curled slightly around his ears. "If you're going to stand watch later tonight, you need to rest."

"Sorry guys." Merle shrugged. "Wish I could help."

Once again she'd failed.

Demarco must've noticed her dejected appearance. "It's okay. Like Kellerman said, whoever broke in didn't take anything important." His gentleness surprised her.

"Yes, that's the good news."

"We should probably double check Stormy's inventory in the morning, though," said Demarco. "I had trackers on the secured things."

They headed back to the elevators. The adrenaline that had been keeping her going had worn off. Exhaustion settled in. She'd been in D.C. that morning, and now she was in Timbuktu, North Dakota. Demarco was right. She'd better sleep, or she'd be nonfunctional soon. "I'm glad to hear that."

Demarco reached to press the elevator call button at the same time she did. Their hands touched. Charlie yanked hers back as if burned. Demarco grinned, but said nothing and pressed the 'up' button.

Charlie cringed at her childish reaction. Time to change the subject. "Have you heard anything about Chief?"

They stepped inside the empty elevator.

"I'm sure the commander will update us when he knows anything. We have Camp Grafton on high alert." Demarco pressed the second floor button. "They're doing twenty-four hour guards at all entrances and keeping records of all vehicles coming and going until we figure out who attacked him."

"Don't you think he's long gone by now?"

"Maybe." The elevator opened, and he ushered her out first. "But our blood evidence may give us some more data to work with, so we'll want to keep track of everything. It's all about the details."

They shared the quiet corridor for a few moments. Charlie paused in front of her room before unlocking it. Without clearing the air between them, she'd have trouble sleeping. "I wanted to apologize for earlier...the taser." Admitting weakness was not something she liked to do, but in this case, if she wanted to be accepted at her new job, she needed to learn humility.

The special agent leaned against the wall and crossed his arms. "You haven't used one of those things before, have you?"

"Was it that obvious?" She slid her key card through the door lock.

"Maybe." He waited as she opened her door.

"Guess I'll see you in the morning." She flipped the light on in her room.

Angel Demarco lingered.

What was he waiting for?

"Be careful on watch tonight." The commanding tone his voice usually held was gone. "You remember how to shoot a .45?"

All Navy shipmates were trained on how to operate and shoot a .45 pistol in Boot Camp. He knew that. "Of course."

"Good." The special agent's tone shifted. "Might come in handy. Good night." Demarco pushed off of the wall and headed down the hall toward his room.

As the door closed behind her, Charlie checked her watch. Eleven o'clock. She should be able to catch a couple hours' sleep before her two o'clock shift. She set her watch to go off at one a.m., with a second alarm set for one-thirty, if she slept through the first one. She glanced at the desk and zoned in on the coffee maker. A few cups of coffee shouldn't take much time to prepare. She'd done plenty of night watches at DLI. This would be no different.

Her energy level crashed after so much adrenaline. She kicked off her shoes, flopped onto the bed fully clothed, wrapped up in the comforter, and fell into a deep sleep.

———

Charlie's alarm blared. Six-thirty a.m. Her eyelids drooped. Out of coffee, since she'd drunk it all last night to prep for her four hours of uneventful watch duty, she stumbled into the bathroom and tossed cold water on her face. A short cat nap after her watch had only made her more tired. Their bus would be leaving in thirty minutes. She shrugged out of her wrinkled clothes and hopped into a tepid shower.

Their plane would be leaving Minot at ten. She hoped Chief would be able to make the flight. She hadn't heard an update on his condition since he'd been wheeled into the ambulance.

Someone knocked on her door.

Dammit.

She turned off the shower, grabbed a towel, and wrapped it around her. "Who is it?" Soapy water dripped down her legs. She shivered on the bath mat.

"You all packed up?" Lisa asked on the other side of her door. "I'm here to make sure your stuff is loaded on the bus."

"I don't have any luggage. I'm good." She barely had a toothbrush with her. She'd be walking out of the motel with only her purse and a caffeine headache.

"Oh, I forgot. Breakfast is down in the lobby whenever you're ready. Bus is out of here at oh-seven-hundred."

"Gotcha." Charlie rubbed her hair dry with an extra towel she pulled off the rack above the toilet. She had no make-up, no styling tools. Back to Boot Camp basics. Thank God the motel provided a blow dryer.

She reluctantly pulled on the sweatshirt and sweatpants she'd purchased the night before—baggy but comfortable. They'd be back in D.C. later today, and she could return to her temporary quarters at the base motel. She'd arrived at her new assignment location with two full suitcases and nothing else. The Navy would be delivering her shipped items in a couple of weeks. But at least she had fresh clothes and toiletries waiting for her once she returned.

She dried her hair and grimaced at the straight ends that flipped up every which way around her head. She should've asked Lisa if she had a straightening iron she could borrow. Her shoulder-length hair was barely long enough to put up in a braid. Without more styling tools at her fingertips, it didn't want to obey her desires.

Ugh.

She leaned toward the mirror. Without any mascara or lipstick, she looked like a twelve-year-old. Her nickname in Boot Camp had been 'Kiddie Cutter.' She'd hated that nickname. Her Recruit Division Commander or RDC had coined that term her first day at Great Lakes. Who knows why. She wasn't the only girl who'd appeared younger than her age when all the make-up and hair styling was stripped away. But for some reason, her RDC had flagged her for teasing almost immediately.

After nine weeks in Boot Camp, she'd been glad to leave behind the name. Not many graduates were headed to DLI. Only a handful were on the plane with her. None of them had been in her unit. 'Kiddie Cutter' disappeared into her past. But this morning, she faced it once again.

Demarco would likely be one who would notice and find a way to use it against her. She braced for the reaction he'd have to her innocent appearance.

She checked her watch. Ten minutes to seven. She'd need to rush if she wanted anything to eat.

She grabbed her purse, stuffed her wrinkled uniform items into a bag, left her key on the bureau with a three dollar tip for the maid, and headed out the door.

Commander Orr joined her in the hall. "Get much sleep, Cutter?"

Thank goodness he didn't comment on her appearance or her clothes. "A bit. What about you?" The commander appeared identical to yesterday: pressed clothes, shiny shoes, hair combed perfectly. He probably never felt out of sorts. He didn't seem like the type who would leave unprepared for the unexpected.

He shrugged. "I can sleep on the plane."

"True. I was just glad that my shift was uneventful."

They stepped into the elevator together.

"I hear that. I'll feel better when we have everything packed up and back in the office. We have a lot of evidence to sort through, pictures to upload to the database, notes to transcribe."

He left off the particulars of the evidence. She knew why. Speaking openly about classified topics was verboten. Only within the walls of a SCIF—Sensitive Compartmented Information Facility—would it be safe to discuss all the details of their trip and what transpired.

"Dr. Stern will be happy to finally have some solid samples to work from." The elevator door opened to the lobby and Commander Orr waited, letting Charlie exit first.

"I've heard a few people mention Dr. Stern." She'd filed the name away for later. Now seemed like the perfect time to find out more about the absent member of the NCIS-A team. "Why didn't she come with us?"

Her boss led her to the buffet line where her co-workers milled around the tables selecting breakfast items. "Dr. Stern doesn't work for us exclusively. We only use her time when our investigations pan out. I'm sure you'll meet her when we return. She was hoping for great samples this trip. I'm sure with you on the team, you and Dr. Stern can work together on the photos."

Charlie nodded. They'd have time later to discuss further the details of those photos. She was eager to dig into the mysterious symbols and compare them to her graduate research. Maybe she'd even have an opportunity on the plane. She hadn't looked at her graduate work in long time. It might be good to refresh herself on where she'd left things before she'd abandoned her studies and joined the Navy.

"I have a seat for you over here, Charlene." Lisa waved at her from across the lobby.

Charlie wanted to correct her new friend on her preferred nick-name, but decided now was not the time to fuss. She grabbed a mug, filled it with coffee, and piled a plate with fresh fruit, a bagel, and cream cheese. She smiled at Lisa and made her way over to the table.

"You look different." Demarco said as she passed his table. He sat with Kellerman near a window facing the parking lot. "When they said they were sending us a newbie, I had no idea how new."

Instead of taking on his slight, she ignored him and continued on her way.

"Leave her alone," Kellerman said.

Charlie warmed at the defense. Kellerman might be a nerd, but at least he was a gentleman.

CHAPTER 11

CHARLIE SMILED at Kellerman and joined Stormy at a table.

"Interesting outfit," her co-worker pointed out, a grin on her face.

"They didn't have much available in my size at the gas station across the street."

"Sorry your first day had to be so crazy. Next time you'll be ready with a go-bag at work. We're used to last minute assignments."

"This is normal? I thought A Group had only been around for a year or so?"

Her features dimmed. "Not here." Stormy nodded in the direction of Merle who was wrapping up his night shift by serving breakfast to guests.

Charlie had a lot she wanted to ask, but work with a security clearance had its problems. They'd have to wait until they were in a secure environment before openly talking about anything related to A Group. "Oh, sorry." She focused on her bagel and fruit.

"No harm. No foul." The two women ate in silence and watched as the men from their team went for seconds at the buffet.

"We're out of here in five, folks." Commander Orr dumped his empty paper plate in the garbage and set his mug in the self-busing area.

Only a few other motel guests were eating breakfast that early in the day, so they had the room mostly to themselves.

Kellerman smiled and nodded as he passed them both with an empty tray and headed out to the parking lot. Orr and Demarco stood near the floor-to-ceiling window that looked out over an overgrown lawn. The front end of their bus was visible to the far left.

Although the two men were engaged in deep conversation, the arrival of more guests created loud chatter, which drowned out anything she might've been able to overhear.

Last night had been strange, and she didn't yet trust Kellerman or Demarco. Something about what she'd witnessed didn't make any sense. She glanced at Stormy. Would the older petty officer be someone she could share her thoughts with? For now she felt removed from her team, as if she were a stranger in her new assignment.

"Come on," said Stormy, picking up her tray. "Let's get out of here."

Gladly, Charlie glommed onto the woman. Lisa Storm had been the kindest of them all, so she wanted to make every effort to be kind in return.

"Do you have any family?" Stormy asked as she dumped her breakfast garbage into the bin.

"Yes." The question caught her off guard. "I've got a brother, Chad. And my parents. What about you?"

"So you're not married?" She scanned Charlie from head to toe.

The sweatsuit probably made her think Charlie wasn't exactly a catch. Her face grew hot. "No."

Stormy nodded. "Well, no rush, you're young."

"Maybe someday down the road," she said. To her, a husband and children were more than 'down the road,' they were miles and miles away, and she had plenty of road to travel alone until she reached them.

They made their way amicably out the front door. The bus's engine rumbled as it idled in the lot.

Charlie spied Orr and Demarco still inside talking near the window. If it wasn't a public place, she would've suspected they were conferring about their trip to Devils Lake and last night's break in. But as Stormy had pointed out, talking about classified topics outside of a SCIF wouldn't be allowed.

Demarco looked out, and his eyes locked with hers. A wave of goose bumps ran over her flesh. Charlie quickly averted her gaze. How mortifying he'd caught her staring.

"Stay away from that one," Stormy warned.

She swallowed. Her new work friend had seen the exchange between her and Demarco. "Oh?"

As her co-worker boarded the bus, she explained, "He's got a sordid history with a lot of women on base."

Instead of asking Stormy to clarify what 'a lot' meant, Charlie followed her on board. But she had a hard time forgetting the way her body flushed and her heart raced when his gaze had caught hers.

———

Charlie strapped herself into one of the jump seats and geared up for the flight home. Everyone was aboard with the exception of Chief Ricard who had to stay overnight at the hospital due to his head injury.

Now that they'd completed the information gathering portion of their investigation, she was eager to do her part—compare the Voynich Manuscript to the photos she snapped on her now secured cell phone.

As the pilot taxied down the runway at Minot, the Russian national anthem echoed through the fuselage.

Orr stood and maneuvered to the origin of the noise using the seat backs and hanging straps to steady his movements. He reached the cases with their evidentiary materials.

"It's my phone, sir," said Charlie.

"I gathered as much," he said and unlocked the case with a key he had on a lanyard around his neck. "Someone forgot to turn it off when it was placed in the case."

Orr gave a hard stare at the whole team.

Kellerman had his headphones on with his eyes closed. Probably lost in some music.

Demarco tapped on the iPad and didn't even seem to notice a phone rang at all.

Stormy and Charlie were the only two paying any attention.

"I should've thought of that." Charlie grimaced.

"Unusual situation, Cutter. Next time, Ricard will make sure you're better equipped for your assignment." He pulled out the still ringing phone and walked it to her. "Answer it, and then shut it off, would you? I know you probably have family and friends who are wondering what happened to you."

Charlie took the phone. It was her mother. The only person worrying, she was certain. "Hello, Mom."

The plane sped up and rumbled down the runway, the whine of the jet engines deafening.

Charlie stuck a finger in her free ear. "I can barely hear you."

"Where are you?" The worry in her mother's voice was unmistakable. "Your dad said you needed your research and then left for some meeting yesterday. I don't know where you kept your documents, honey."

"I'm at work." The plane lurched forward, and Charlie almost lost the hold on her phone. The take-off tilted her sideways. "Everything should be on my old laptop. The one in the closet downstairs." She calculated if her mother could handle the many updates the operating system would want to accomplish after having been turned off for almost two years.

"What, Charlie?"

"At work." She had to shout into the phone as the plane engines drowned out her voice.

Demarco looked up from the iPad and gave her a frown. Her loud words had interrupted his concentration. Well, too bad for him. Her research was important. She needed it to support the team.

"My thesis materials are in the folder labeled 'Voynich' on my desktop."

"Boy-nitch?" Her mother's voice filled with confusion. "I don't know if I can figure this out, I'd better wait for your father—"

"No, Mom. I need these files as soon as possible. You can do it. It's Voynich. Do you have a piece of paper?"

"Hold on."

The entire team had their eyes on her. Charlie's cheeks heated. She turned her head away, so she could at least block out the staring eyes. Who cared if she looked foolish? She needed her research to do her job on the team and decipher those strange markings.

"Mom? Are you there?" The silence on the other end of the line made Charlie wonder if they'd lost connection during the takeoff.

"All right. I'm back, honey."

"Okay, it's V-O-Y-N-I-C-H. In a folder with that name on the desktop of my computer. If you could zip it and send me everything in there."

"Voynich, I see, how silly of me." Her mother giggled. "What an odd name."

"Yes, Mother, very odd." Her humiliation was now complete. "So please send me those files as soon as you can. Today would be great."

"Today? Well, I've got my cleaning to do, and then your father has some going away luncheon that I have to attend. You know how they like the officers' wives to be at everything."

Charlie could picture the eye roll on the other end of the line. Her mother hated formal events. "I'll be back in my office soon, and I'd love to have those files waiting. I need them for my new assignment."

"Why didn't you say so? I'll make sure you have them in an hour. How's that?"

"Perfect. Thanks, Mom."

"No problem, honey. Hope you can come see us for dinner one of these nights. We're only a couple of hours away from you. Well, not during rush hour, but you know what I mean. We'd love to have you. It's been a long time since you've been home."

"I'm sure I'll find a time to come visit. Maybe after I settle in on base."

"Yes, that would do. You just let me know."

"You got it." Charlie hung up the phone and walked it over to her boss. "Here you go, Commander."

"Do you need to transfer any of your phone numbers while I have it out?"

Without even a moment's hesitation, Charlie said, "No, I'm fine. I've got them memorized."

Kellerman had his headphones around his neck and stared at her. "Memorized? All of your contacts?"

She gulped. "Yeah, don't you?"

"Um, nobody does," said Kellerman.

"They don't?"

Stormy chimed in, "No, we don't."

Charlie decided it was best to reel in her big mouth. "Well, I mean my parents' number, my brother. You know, those numbers."

Stormy squished her eyebrows together, and Kellerman narrowed his eyes.

Charlie forgot sometimes about her unique ability to remember bits and pieces of data. It's what made her so good at languages. At least, that's what she told herself. Her brother Chad also had the same memory skills as she, so she never questioned it much. Sure, a few friends in college thought of her as 'weird,' but she'd heard of others with photographic memories. She'd shrugged it off back then, sure that there were a lot of other people like her and her brother in the world.

Apparently, that was not the case.

For the rest of the flight, Charlie spent time programming contact information and email addresses into her throwaway phone.

Unlike the flight out, nobody interacted much on the return trip. Maybe Ricard's absence had more of an impact on the team than she had been expecting. Or possibly everyone was tired. Had it been only yesterday when she'd shown up at headquarters?

When they landed back at Andrews Air Force Base Orr stood up and addressed the team.

"Tomorrow we'll need to rip through this data ASAP. I want preliminary reports by 1500." The commander pointed at Kellerman. "I want material analysis. The pod. Is it similar to other samples from last summer? Where did it come from? Why does it dissolve so quickly in water?"

Kellerman had taken back the iPad from Demarco and tapped on it rapidly. "Yes, sir."

"Demarco."

"Sir."

"The preserved blood and other evidence from the woods. I want you to escort those items directly to Dr. Stern. I've already contacted her, and she's ready to receive everything we collected this afternoon. I want you to leave directly from here and meet up with her at the lab."

"Yes, sir."

"Stormy."

The thirty-something redhead took a breath. "Yes, Commander."

"Catalog each item in the database as per usual. And give Cutter's cell phone an ID in the system for tracking, strip it of the photos, and then dispose of it. Zip all the photos and upload them to the photos folder on the share drive."

"Dispose of it?" Charlie couldn't help herself. "But I thought I'd get it back...eventually."

Demarco gave her a steel gaze from across the fuselage. She'd spoken out of turn, and he didn't like it.

"Sorry, Petty Officer," Orr said. He crossed his arms and leaned against the doorframe that led to the cockpit. "Those photos are highly classified, and there's no way to completely erase them from your phone. It will have to be destroyed. It's protocol."

"Oh." Charlie thought about the loss of data, passwords, links. Her whole life existed on that phone. No wonder Demarco wanted her to take pictures with her cell phone. Why hadn't he come prepared? Shouldn't he have been ready with a camera, if he knew what they might encounter?

She shot a glance at Demarco. He locked eyes with her for a moment. The strange look in his gaze unnerved her, as if he could read her mind. She looked away and shuddered at the cold wave of uneasiness that ran through her.

"You will be reimbursed for the loss, of course. Stormy can help you with the paper work when we are back to the office." Orr looked once again to Stormy. "Chief usually handles the equipment, but—"

"Absolutely, sir. No problem, sir." Stormy wrote a note in a small notebook in her lap, then looked at Charlie and grinned.

"Now, for your assignment, Petty Officer Cutter," said the commander with a slow drawl.

"Yes, sir?" Although Charlie already thought she knew what her assignment would be, perhaps Orr had something else for her to help with. She very much wanted to fit in with the team and feel as if she were contributing. Maybe all the odd feelings she had about Demarco and even Kellerman would disappear once they realized her usefulness.

"Will you be ready for a preliminary report tomorrow afternoon with your findings?"

Charlie prayed her mother figured out how to send her files. "Yes, I can be ready with a preliminary by then." It had been awhile since she'd been buried in Voynich files, but the idea of possibly making a connection between that ancient text and the symbols found inside the pod heightened her senses.

"Stormy will show you how to access the photos once she's uploaded them to the share drive."

Charlie nodded and sneaked a glance at Lisa Storm. Her heart warmed at the idea she wouldn't have to interact with Demarco in order to do her job. In fact, maybe she'd hardly have to work with him at all. Even on such a small team, the division of work was definite. All of her time should be spent on language analysis, an area in which he had no expertise.

Her mind lit up at the notion of returning to her beloved research. It didn't matter to her that a connection to an alien pod and an ancient document made zero sense. Could she piece together the two examples and possibly decipher a meaning? An electric thrill zinged through her.

———

Wearing a crisp, fresh white uniform with her hair styled, Charlie made quick work of the security line the next morning. She slid her badge into the reader with confidence and sailed through to the hallway beyond. In her arms she carried a stack of papers—her research. She'd printed it out using the base motel's office printer, her temporary housing until she could find a permanent residence.

Excitement bubbled to the surface as she entered the elevator and rode down to the correct floor. She itched to reexamine the photos she'd taken in North Dakota.

The elevator door opened. People exited.

Demarco stood glowering in front of her.

"Petty Officer Cutter. Just the person I was looking for."

"Oh?" Instead of making a right turn and heading down the hall to her new office, Demarco grasped her elbow and maneuvered her back inside the empty elevator. "Excuse me?"

His warm hand on her bare, cool arm sent a shiver up her spine.

"I'm taking you to Dr. Stern's office with me."

The elevator door shut, and they were alone.

"Agent, I have work to do this morning." Charlie used his formal title to remind herself what a jerk Angel Demarco could be. "Commander Orr gave me an assignment and—"

Demarco released her arm and leaned against the brass rail that ran around three sides of the elevator. "You have plenty of time to put together a report before this afternoon's meeting. I want you to meet Dr. Stern. She's an important part of our team."

Charlie's hackles relaxed. It was a kind gesture. "I appreciate that. I suppose I could spare a few minutes."

"Plus," Demarco said with a wry grin, "she doesn't like me very much. Maybe you can break the ice with her."

"Someone doesn't like you?" Charlie asked. "Shocking." She raised an eyebrow.

"Don't tell anyone I said that." His typically controlled features relaxed into a genuine smile with a dimple.

When did he have a dimple?

As Charlie reexamined her feelings toward the special agent, he continued, "I've been insisting Dr. Stern and I are on good terms because I have the experience dealing with evidence. I have the training. I need to do the job. But if Orr found out there was friction between us, well, I can imagine Kellerman jumping right in to 'help.'"

"Your secret's safe with me."

"'Thanks."

The elevator slowed as it reached their destination.

Charlie followed Demarco into a well-lit hallway on the fifth floor. Even though none of the floors had real windows—any truly secure building couldn't have them—the designers of the facility had gone to a lot of trouble to ensure the lighting gave the appearance of natural light. The basement wasn't afforded such amenities.

"She's right down here."

At the end of the very long hallway they approached an unmarked door with a keypad on the outside and a card reader similar to their office down below. Access control in a top secret environment didn't stop at the front entrance.

Demarco slid his badge into the reader and entered a long string of numbers. He didn't share the code with her, which surprised her. But maybe this would be her one and only time visiting with Dr. Stern.

The door buzzed, and Demarco opened it.

———

They entered a most bizarre place.

Dr. Stern's office was smaller than anticipated. No larger than a two-car garage. It was jammed full of equipment and small fridges and chemicals and test tubes. But what caught her by surprise was the decor.

At first, Charlie could only marvel at the random canvases on the wall. Amateur art. Mountain landscapes, beach scenes, a chicken, a wine glass, poorly proportioned fruit. All painted in garishly bright colors.

"Who's this?" a honey-coated voice asked. "And where are my samples you promised last night?"

Charlie drew her gaze away from the paintings. A stout, middle-aged woman with sepia-toned skin, warm brown eyes, and hair cut close to the scalp peered at her over reading glasses as she sat at a utilitarian metal desk in one corner of the room.

Demarco cleared his throat, and his face reddened.

Charlie held back a laugh. Big, tough Angel Demarco scared of something. Delightful.

"This is Petty Officer Charlene Cutter. She joined our team two days ago."

"Well, aren't you a pretty little thing?" Dr. Stern said.

Charlie's cheeks heated at the blunt compliment. "Thank you."

"And polite, too." She cracked a broad white smile. "So glad to see more women in A Group. It was starting to smell like a locker room down there."

Demarco redistributed his weight from one foot to the other.

"And the samples?" Dr. Stern's tone turned decidedly colder. "You didn't screw it up again, did you?"

Charlie bit her tongue. This was too good.

"There was a delay in transport from Andrews. We expect everything to arrive here within the hour."

"I see. You think I don't see through this little thing going on here?" Dr. Stern waved a finger. "Trying to deflect from your incompetence by bringing this nice young lady with you?"

"No. Not at all."

Dr. Stern leaned back in her chair and crossed her arms. "Uh-huh."

"Cutter—" Demarco began.

Dr. Stern corrected him, "Petty Officer Cutter."

"Yes, Petty Office Cutter." Demarco stumbled over his words, "She, ah, well now, she's new—"

"You said that."

"And she's an important part of our team."

News to Charlie's ears. He'd made her feel as if she were more of a nuisance and only good for handing off boring tasks he didn't want to do.

"Really? Well, then." Dr. Stern turned her gaze back on Charlie. "What is it they want you to do on the team?"

"I'm a linguistics expert. My specialty lies in deciphering ancient texts. Specifically the Voynich Manuscript. In fact—" Charlie opened up the manila folder filled with her graduate work and flipped through the stack of papers. "I managed to access my graduate work and was about to start in on some comparisons when Agent Demarco asked me to come with him."

Dr. Stern rose from her chair, a spark of interest in her eyes. "How fascinating." She plucked the top paper from the stack. "Although I have a knack for science, I always wished I had the gift to learn another language."

"Scholars haven't been able to decipher this one. It's been centuries." As she explained the mystery of the text on the page, Charlie's heart skipped a beat. That old excitement she'd had in graduate school, that she'd thought she'd lost, roared back to life with the merest hint of interest from Dr. Stern. "The script has no relation to any other written language on earth. At least no relationship that bore out a translation."

The scientist dropped the sheet on top of the stack of papers in the folder. "When you're done with your work, I'd love to learn more about it." She gave a quick smile and turned her gaze back on Demarco. "She'll be presenting her work to the team, I assume, at some point."

Charlie's confidence grew in that moment. From newest member of the team with zero clue, to expert on a topic that interested a scientific mind with years of experience. Maybe her work had meaning and usefulness after all.

Demarco swallowed. "Yes, I'm sure she will. We highly respect her expertise in the field."

Charlie almost fainted at the gushing praise. It must've taken all of the special agent's energy to make such wild claims. He didn't believe a word of it, she was certain. "I'm hopeful the photographs we took yesterday will help me build working knowledge of the writing. It did have a remarkable similarity." For a split second she thought about what that could mean for human history. Could an alien species have been present on earth centuries ago and gone undetected?

"I'll be on the lookout for the invitation then." Dr. Stern touched Charlie on the shoulder.

The door buzzed. Someone in the hall announced their presence.

"THE SAMPLES." Demarco rushed to the door.

Dr. Stern snapped on the red siren light, which indicated possible uncleared personnel entering the room. Without the appropriate clearance, the only way someone outside could gain entrance would be for all cleared materials to be hidden from view or placed in a secure drawer or cabinet.

"Give me a moment." Dr. Stern quickly swept a stack of papers into a desk drawer. "Okay, we're good."

Angel Demarco opened the door. Two army privates in camouflage, one male and one female, rolled in a cart with a couple of the hard cases that had traveled with A Group on the plane.

"Your signature, ma'am." One of the privates handed Dr. Stern the transfer paperwork required.

"Thank you very much." Dr. Stern inked her signature with a grand flourish.

The two exited the room, and Dr. Stern snapped off the red siren light.

"The samples you wanted." Demarco unlocked the cases. "Chief was attacked in the woods as he was carrying it to our bus, so there's substantial damage to some of the vials."

The case opened, and the smashed vials were revealed enclosed in plastic baggies to preserve as much as possible.

"There might be dirt in there, too, I had to pick everything up off the forest floor," said Charlie.

"You touched the materials with your bare hands?" Dr. Stern's brows shot up.

Demarco did nothing to rescue her from the question.

"Someone attacked the chief. I was in a bit of a hurry." Her explanation sounded weak to her own ears.

Dr. Stern looked over the contents of the first case. "This looks like mostly pod materials, similar to what was recovered last summer. But I'll do some tests to make sure it's the same unusual make-up."

Demarco unlocked the second case to reveal the extra pod samples Stormy had collected. "It disintegrated pretty rapidly after we arrived. But we managed to capture biological material." He pointed to a single shard of glass enclosed in a test tube on which a smear of red appeared. "Maybe Chief's attacker."

"Suspected alien DNA?" the doctor asked with a hint of awe in her voice.

The special agent hesitated and took a quick sideways glance at Charlie. He was holding back with her in the room. Charlie could sense it. He'd told her on the beach that he hadn't seen anyone in the woods when she'd found those odd footprints.

"I saw strange footprints in the sand near the crash site," Charlie plowed ahead. She didn't care if Demarco was pissed. "They didn't look human."

"Oh?" Dr. Stern carefully plucked the sample with the biological material from the case. She held it up to the fluorescent lights above her and examined it. "We were so close last year to obtaining a sample from another crash site, but then the vial disappeared along with a few others. That's when I instituted a policy about sample transport for the team, isn't that right, Agent Demarco?"

Charlie understood now why Dr. Stern had no love for Demarco. He'd screwed up somehow in the past.

"We have to go, doctor." He headed for the door. "We both have to work on our reports for this afternoon. Isn't that right Petty Officer?" He gave her a hard stare almost daring her to defy him.

"Yes." Charlie wanted to spend more time with the interesting doctor. She'd learned more about her team in ten minutes with Dr. Stern than in the last twenty-four hours.

"Please stop by again," said Dr. Stern who focused intently on the open cases in her laboratory rather than on the exiting visitors. "I'll have results for you in a day or two, if you could let Commander Orr know."

"Will do." Demarco slipped outside into the hall with Charlie not far behind.

The door shut with a kerthunk.

He headed down the hall toward the elevator without a word.

Charlie thought over the news about disappearing vials and wondered about the bus break-in at the motel in North Dakota. She'd need to keep her eyes and ears open. Perhaps her co-workers weren't as trustworthy as they let on.

Charlie sat at her newly assigned desk in the A Group office and pored over her Voynich research. Stormy had showed her how to navigate to their secure shared drive where the photos she'd taken yesterday were stored. As she scrolled through them, her fingers tingled. The symbols looked incredibly similar to the Voynich Manuscript.

The whorls and swirls of letters that edged the ancient text were repeated on pieces of the partially disintegrated pod. She had to set aside her disbelief at how this was possible and focus on the deciphering.

In her research, she had attempted to find repeated symbols that were the most common in order to break the code. Although the manuscript had been named after the Polish book dealer who purchased the manuscript in 1912, the assumption was the original author of the manuscript was Italian because of the vellum on which it had been written. So she had used Italian writing from the fifteenth century as a first comparison. Then she'd used basic decoding to attempt to figure out an alphabet of sorts. It was at that stage she'd hit a wall. Frustration and lack of confidence had resulted in her quitting the pursuit of her masters' degree and joining the Navy to do something else she loved: learning languages.

But with the new Voynich-like markings found within the pod, she had a possible association for each 'word' in the photo.

"Hungry?" Kellerman peered over her cubical wall.

Charlie's stomach rumbled. She'd been so focused on her work she didn't even realize how much time had passed. "When's our meeting this afternoon?"

Kellerman came around the cubical wall and took control of her mouse. He leaned in and navigated to her calendar. "Here."

He smelled of shaving cream—a not unpleasant smell—but Charlie rolled her chair back to put some distance between them.

"I'm sorry." He backed up aware he'd invaded her personal space. "It was easier to do it myself. Sometimes I can act without thinking." He pointed at the calendar that appeared on her screen.

Charlie, not wanting to dismiss an attempt at friendliness, replied, "That's okay. I appreciate it. I couldn't even figure out my email this morning." She scooted closer to the screen to read the calendar appointment. "That's right. Fifteen hundred."

"So lunch then?" the young lieutenant asked. "I know the best choices in the chow line. Trust me."

"Sure." Why not? She needed to get to know her team mates and what better way than over a free military lunch. "Should we ask the others?" She stood up and scanned the office.

"I don't think anyone else is still here."

"What time is it?"

"Thirteen hundred."

"What?" She checked her watch. "Wow, did I lose track of time."

"I can be a lot like that sometimes." He pushed up his glasses and smiled.

"Well, show me the way, please. My stomach would be most grateful." She grabbed her purse and cover.

"Absolutely."

As they were about to head toward the door, her desk phone

rang. She hadn't given the number to anyone yet, so she stared at it for several seconds.

"Are you going to answer that?" Kellerman asked.

Confused, Charlie picked up the phone, "Petty Officer Cutter speaking."

"Good afternoon. It's Dr. Stern."

"Oh, Dr. Stern. I was wondering who might be calling." She glanced at Kellerman.

He sighed.

"Do you think you could stop by my office today?"

"Sure, is there something you need?"

"Your DNA."

The request made her forget about her hunger. "Excuse me?"

"You mentioned this morning you'd touched the samples, and I completely forgot to ask you for a DNA swab."

Charlie hesitated for a few seconds.

"It won't take more than a few minutes. You remember how to get to my lab, right?"

"Yes, I remember."

"Great. Right now would be perfect, if you don't mind. When I start on my testing plan, I don't like to be disturbed."

Kellerman gave her a questioning look.

"Sure, I could stop by in a few minutes. No problem." She shrugged, knowing her lunch date had no idea what she'd agreed to.

"Fabulous. Thank you, Petty Officer."

Charlie hung up.

"What did Dr. Stern want?" Kellerman asked. "I didn't even know you'd met her."

"We met this morning. Demarco took me to her lab."

The lieutenant pulled a grimace.

"I have to stop by to give her a DNA sample."

"Well, then let's go." He escorted Charlie to the door. "I'm starving, and I'd rather not eat alone."

They exited into the hall and headed to the elevator. "How long have you been with A Group again?"

"About nine months," Kellerman replied

"It's a relatively new organization. Do you still feel as if you are getting to know everyone?"

He pushed the 'up' button and then stepped back to wait for the elevator. "I suppose."

"How did you end up here?"

"Requested it." Kellerman kept his gaze on the closed elevator door.

Charlie mulled that over for a second. "How did you even know about it?"

"I have friends in high places maybe." He pushed the button again. "What about you?"

"Honestly, I don't know exactly. I was finishing up language school when I got orders to A Group."

"Must've been the commander. He seemed to know a lot about your background and your work."

The elevator dinged, and they climbed aboard.

"I guess." Charlie shrugged.

"What do you think about the assignment to our office?"

"I left my graduate program because I felt my research was going nowhere. But now I feel reinvigorated." Aware they couldn't discuss the details of their work outside their cleared spaces, Charlie kept the topic vague.

"Nice. That's sort of how I feel. I wanted to apply myself where I'd do the most good. My previous work—well, I was only a cog in the wheel. Not my thing."

"I get that." Although Charlie wanted to ask more about the work he'd done previous to the A Group assignment, she knew due to security reasons he wouldn't be able to share. She could only speculate what kind of work someone did at Area 51.

They reached Dr. Stern's lab and, since Charlie didn't know the code to enter, she pressed the call button on the wall to announce her arrival.

"Hopefully, it won't take too much time to give my sample," she said.

The door opened, and the red siren light flashed in her eyes.

"Lieutenant Kellerman, how nice to see you," said Dr. Stern. "You didn't take long acquainting yourself with Petty Officer Cutter." The doctor gave a knowing smile.

Kellerman's neck turned bright red.

"He was nice enough to ask me to lunch."

Dr. Stern eyed the tall man. "Is that so?"

"Yes, ma'am," answered Kellerman. He rubbed the back of his neck.

"Well, that's very kind. Come, let's take that sample so you can go to lunch then." Dr. Stern headed to a counter along the far wall. Several colorful paintings of farm animals stared down at them.

The doctor opened a drawer full of packaged swabs.

"I see you like to paint," Charlie said unable to keep her eyes off a painting of a black-and-white cow standing in a field of daisies.

The doctor unwrapped a swab and stood in front of Charlie. "Open wide please."

She opened her mouth. Dr. Stern swept the swab along her inner cheek on both sides.

"My cousin has one of those paint-and-sip places in Fairfax." She took the swab and popped it into its plastic container. "All done."

Charlie glanced around the lab. "You painted all of these?" There must have been two dozen paintings in all. Each one more colorful and ridiculous than the last.

"I find it an enjoyable way to pass the time." Dr. Stern walked them to the door. "If you by some chance have nothing to do one of these Saturday nights, I'm always looking for someone to come with me."

Charlie considered the idea. She and Dr. Stern with paint palettes and glasses of chardonnay making small talk while they painted together. She held back a laugh. Absurd. "I'll think about it. Thanks."

As they exited into the hall, Kellerman teased her, "Guess you made an impression on Dr. Stern."

Charlie lightly shoved him in the arm. "Oh, shut up."

His smile faded, and he grew quiet as they stepped inside the elevator.

———

Charlie and Kellerman arrived back at the office an hour before the All Hands meeting. Lunch had been awkward, but at least she'd filled her empty stomach with some halfway decent grub. Her lunch partner had helped her navigate the less trustworthy dishes and hone in on the better tasting ones. Free food had its shortcomings.

When they walked in the door, the deep voice of Chief Ricard greeted them, "I told 'em I wouldn't believe it unless I saw it with my own eyes—the LT on a date with the new girl." He grinned widely from his position by the coffee maker.

"Chief," Kellerman said, ignoring his teasing comment, "you look good."

Ricard touched a bandage above his ear. "A little knock on the head, nothing big. A few stitches, a couple of Motrin, and I'm back in tip top condition."

"That's good to hear." Charlie breezed past the implications of accepting a lunch invite from the young lieutenant. She'd have to make sure she didn't make lunch with Kellerman into a regular event. "I have a few things to wrap up before our meeting, if you don't mind."

Chief toasted her with his full mug of coffee. "By all means, Petty Officer. I don't want to keep a lady from her work."

She slipped past the two men who continued to chat about the chief's injuries. During lunch as she'd navigated the awkward conversation with the lieutenant, she'd found her mind half focused on the manuscript and the similarities in the writing in her photos. Kellerman sensed her disinterest at one point, as they'd eaten their cake slices in silence near the end of their lunch hour. She'd felt bad, but to rediscover an excitement about her research lifted her spirits more than she thought possible.

A couple of years ago, the whole project had hit a brick wall, and it had crushed her interest in continuing in the program. But with this new information, her mind came alive with all synapses firing. Furiously, she typed away at her preliminary report, taking snapshots of enlarged spots on her photos and inserting them next to similar images in the Voynich document. She added arrows and explanations, possible definitions, and a final conclusion that the two writings were definitely related.

Incredible.

With twenty minutes left before their meeting, she cobbled together a slide presentation for the office. The details were less complex and focused on a few examples she thought her team could understand without her background and education. Unmistakable similarities that could be explained no other way. She hoped Commander Orr would be impressed.

Her calendar appointment for the meeting popped up on her screen, breaking her concentration. She hit print, entered her code for tracking copies, and selected enough for everyone. She scooped up the collated and stapled piles from the machine near the meeting room and handed them out to everyone seated at the big oval table and took an empty seat across from Stormy.

Commander Orr stood at the head of the table, a presentation laptop next to him, and a white screen on the wall. As he reviewed the print out she'd provided, Charlie's stomach flip flopped.

"Petty Officer Cutter," her boss said making eye contact. "Why don't you present first? Your report looks quite fascinating."

Charlie gulped.

She'd spent the whole day on her analysis. These people had no idea what she could add to the team. Even Charlie didn't realize, until she'd seen the writing in the pod, how perfectly suited she was for this assignment. The frustration she'd experienced when her orders had been unexpectedly swapped melted away as she approached the front of the room. Her discovery bubbled up inside like a mountain spring after a torrential downpour.

On the laptop, she navigated to the shared drive where she'd saved her slide presentation.

"Everyone, we might have made the discovery of a lifetime," Orr announced.

Stormy dimmed the lights.

The room was as quiet as a language exam during finals.

Charlie began to speak.

CHAPTER 13

"THE VOYNICH MANUSCRIPT is a document dating back to the fifteenth century." Charlie stood at the head of the table and scanned the meeting room. "The first owner known to history was Georgius Barschius from Prague in the seventeenth century. The document contained an unknown script and was intricately decorated with pictures of plants, stars, and chemistry annotations."

Charlie changed the slide, which displayed two snapshots of the manuscript side by side. The writing on the pages was strange and beautiful, full of odd loops and lines of text sprinkled throughout the colorful drawings, mostly of plants and flowers.

"Barschius sent a letter to Rome asking for help with the translation of the text. No one was able to translate the unusual writing."

She clicked to another slide that focused solely on the symbols that made up the mysterious language.

"Looks like elvish," Kellerman said. "You know, 'Lord of the Rings'?"

"Nerd." Demarco snickered.

Charlie ignored the two men and continued. "The next time the book appears it's 1912. An antiquarian book dealer named Wilfrid Voynich came into its possession, thus the name 'Voynich Manuscript' stuck. The sale was conducted in secrecy, but

Voynich claimed he came across the manuscript in a chest in an ancient castle in southern Europe."

She clicked to the next slide—more pages of the manuscript, which depicted either the chronological year or other celestial events on circular drawings with intricate notes and pictures.

"Voynich became convinced that the cipher text must mean it was an important document. No other document from that time period had been written in code. Attempts were made to decipher it, but decades and centuries passed with no luck. Until now."

She clicked to the next slide. One of several photos she'd taken of the pod's interior before it had disintegrated in Devils Lake.

Stormy gasped.

"When I did a preliminary comparison of the writing inside the pod to the Voynich text, I found striking similarities between the two." She took her laser pointer and drew a circle of light around a symbol from the pod. "This one stood out to me immediately. It's repeated throughout the original text."

She clicked to a new slide showing a page from the Voynich Manuscript next to the pod photo.

"I'm sure you've all heard of the Rosetta Stone. It was the stone, which allowed for the translation of ancient Egyptian hieroglyphics into Greek. An incredibly important artifact that resulted in a whole new understanding of Egyptian history once the code was cracked. The writing from the pod that we were able to capture—this is our Rosetta Stone to decipher the Voynich Manscript."

She clicked to her last slide, which showed every distinct symbol she was able to capture from the photographs with possible translations.

"Because the pod clearly was used as a transport object of some kind, I attempted to understand the meaning of a symbol based on its relation to the interior of the pod." She used her laser pointer again to draw attention to a symbol next to what looked like a seat belt or restraining device made of the same gelatinous material as the pod. "This symbol probably has something to do with safety, latching, belting, locking." She pointed at another symbol next to a handle in front of the seat. "This symbol probably is related to movement: forward, backward, faster, slower."

The room was silent. She knew they were likely as excited by this discovery as she.

"I know it's a lot to take in. I'm only just beginning to examine these symbols and compare them to the ancient text. It took decades for the Rosetta Stone to yield results, so we can't expect instant translation. The next step will be to compare these early results to the text itself to see if I can find any like 'words.' That should help me untangle the meaning behind the manuscript."

She clicked to a final slide that said: "Questions?"

Commander Orr spoke first. "We don't have decades to translate this, Petty Officer. You are aware this a time sensitive project?"

His words of criticism hit like a physical blow. She'd thought they were silent due to amazement, but maybe she'd read the room incorrectly.

"I understand that, sir, but I am only one person."

"The one person specially brought on this team because we thought you had the expertise to translate this."

"I do have the expertise," she said.

"I am sensing that you are more interested in translating the manuscript rather than getting to the bottom of the writing inside the pod. This job isn't about pursuing your pet project on the government's dime."

"That's not what I thought, sir. Not at all."

"What I heard is that this will take decades of time. That it is impossible to produce a translation faster than that. What good does it do us to know that a symbol could maybe mean 'backward'? I need to know where these pods came from. Who was in them? What is their purpose? Why are they here? Your presentation, to be honest, was not up to the standard I was expecting at this meeting."

Charlie's face heated at the dressing down in front of everyone. "I'm sorry, sir."

"I have a question." Demarco tilted back his chair, drawing all eyes his way.

Commander Orr dropped his pen on his notepad and crossed his arms.

The special agent plowed forward, cutting through the tension in the air. "What do you think the connection is between this manuscript and the writing in the pod? What is your theory for the similarities?"

"Excellent question," she said. Who would've guessed Demarco would give her a lifeline? "If this team was assembled to study alien life on earth, then we must consider the possibility that a being traveled here in the ancient past using the same methods."

Stormy and Kellerman nodded their heads. The commander focused his gaze on his notes in front of him.

"Wouldn't that beg the question about the appearance of these supposed aliens?" Kellerman asked. "In order to blend in during the fourteen hundreds and create this manuscript, wouldn't the alien have to have the appearance of a human?"

"We don't know if an alien created this document," Demarco said.

"True," Charlie replied. "But the fact that no other document has ever been found with text similar to the Voynich manuscript would lead me to believe only a single being was capable of creating it. And perhaps something stopped this being from creating more than a single work."

"And for some reason these beings, as far as we know, didn't visit earth again until the last few decades," Kellerman added. "We need to figure out why."

"Agreed," said the commander. "I think Petty Officer Cutter has a lot of work ahead of her. It would be premature for us to speculate until she translates more of the text. I expect a more robust presentation next week." He gave her a pointed look.

Charlie exited out of her slides and returned to her seat.

"Special Agent Demarco, you're up next with your report about ambient conditions and their effect on the pod."

Demarco rose and took position at the head of the table.

Charlie wished she could sink into her chair and disappear. Although her fellow teammates had rescued her from further embarrassment with their questions, her stomach roiled at disappointing her new boss.

Demarco cleared his throat.

Charlie focused her attention on the front of the room.

The special agent winked at her.

She ducked her head and scribbled on her notebook, contemplating the nervous energy that filled her.

———

The office had grown eerily silent in the last hour. Charlie checked the time on her desktop computer: quarter past seven. The emptiness in her stomach reminded her she hadn't eaten in hours.

After the dressing down by Commander Orr in the meeting earlier, she'd buried herself in her translation work by comparing minute differences between symbols in the pictures and those in the ancient text. She would not disappoint her boss again. She could do the translation. She knew it. It would just take super human effort on her part to push past the first few 'like' symbols and wring out a definition that jibed with the pages of sample text she had.

The commander didn't understand translating the Voynich Manuscript using the symbols found in the pod was the key to understanding everything.

Her eyes burned from so much screen time in the darkened room. Charlie kept a small bottle of drops in her purse. She squeezed two in each eye, blinked a few times, and headed for the coffee at the back of the room.

She was startled to see Angel Demarco pouring the last of the coffee into a plain white mug. Hadn't he left with the rest of the gang a while ago? Ah, the door key. Only he and Orr had access to lock up the office for the night.

"Don't cry, Petty Officer." Demarco grinned and stirred powdered creamer in his mug. "We have some instant here somewhere." He opened up a lower cabinet to search.

She wiped her eyes. "It's eye drops."

"Gotcha." He winked for a second time that day and set the instant coffee jar on the counter.

Even though she wanted to say something biting, make fun of him for winking at her or just irritate the hell out of him, she found she could not. He'd been too damned kind to her today. "Thanks for your question in our meeting."

"It was a good presentation." He stepped back to let her access the counter and craft herself a cup of instant. "Orr was out of line."

"I'm surprised you'd say that."

"He's the one that wrote up your orders and then he doesn't even give you the time to do your work? That's bullshit."

"Orr wrote my orders?" Although the commander had mentioned her graduate work on the plane to North Dakota, she hadn't really thought about how hands on he'd been with selecting her for the job.

"How else do you think you ended up here?" He gestured to the quiet, empty space surrounding them.

"I don't know—" Charlie couldn't think through the options. "He was familiar with the manuscript and my research, but I guess I thought orders came from BUPERS and went through a process."

"He'd gotten a scrap of writing last fall from another pod, ran it through a database, and that's when he found out about the manuscript. Who knew you'd also be a military linguist? He didn't have to convince you to come work for him, he could order you to do it."

"Another pod?" Although she'd been given the basic information about YARDARM, the last report in the folder had referred to a document that hadn't been provided to her.

"It wasn't in the packet?" He sighed. "After the arrival of the first one, when those two kids on watch duty at Fort Madison witnessed a pod landing in a storm, Orr started up A Group. He needed someone with a security background, and I volunteered." He stirred his coffee with a plastic stick. "There have been a few other incidents since then."

Her breath caught in her throat. More?

"Orr is obsessed with figuring this thing out. He's convinced the symbols are the key to understanding everything, and I think he's right. But he needs to give you time to do the work. Like you said, they didn't translate the Rosetta Stone overnight."

"I'm surprised you paid attention."

"Why would you say that?" He leaned a hip against the counter.

She pressed the special spigot on the sink and let hot water fill her mug. "You made it pretty clear yesterday that I'm a nuisance."

He studied her face. The intensity of his gaze unnerved her. "I don't think you're a nuisance. I think you could actually help me. I see that now."

Her stomach fluttered. She liked that he praised her work, but Stormy's words at the motel in Devils Lake floated in her mind: he had a sordid history with women.

"You hungry?"

"Starving," she answered without thinking.

"Let me take you out." Demarco downed his coffee in one swallow. "Don't want you to burn out. Since I'm your superior, I order you to stop working." He flashed a smile.

Sorry, Stormy, but she wanted to know what else Demarco knew. "All right. But it had better be good food." They'd be gone an hour or so, and then she could return to her work.

"I promise. It'll be the best Italian you've ever had."

As she followed him out of the office, the Voynich symbols floated around in her mind and organized themselves, much like her innate ability to learn new languages. A surge of dopamine washed over her. Although she'd explained to the team it would take time to translate, she'd held back the fact she knew far more than she was telling them.

"Italian sounds perfect."

———

Carmello's, Demarco's Italian restaurant of choice, was located a half-mile walk from their office at the Washington Navy Yard. The sticky August evening made Charlie aware that her antiperspirant wasn't up to the challenge. Although she wore her

Navy-issue black cardigan indoors to combat the air conditioned chill of the basement location, now the item stifled her.

"Can you hold this for me?" She handed her purse to the agent who wore a button-down shirt with tie and khaki slacks.

He held her purse like a football. "You don't have to wear your uniform to work."

She wrestled out of the sweater until she had stripped down to her summer whites—a short-sleeved cotton shirt and white cotton skirt paired with her sturdy black leather oxfords. "I'm still waiting on the movers."

"You didn't pack any casual clothes?"

She huffed, "They stuck me on a plane so fast I barely had time to grab my toothbrush."

He nodded, handed back her purse, and they continued on their way.

"So you're good at this translation stuff?" he asked.

She knew a free meal would come with an interrogation. Why else would he be interested in spending an awkward hour across the table from her? "I've always been good at words, languages, grammar." She shrugged. "One of my special gifts."

"Grammar, ugh."

She smiled. "What do they say? Learn a skill nobody else likes."

"That's true."

"I'm sure you have a few skills that come in handy from time to time." She thought back to that moment in the woods when an attacker had taken down two of their team.

"We all have our talents." He pretended to karate chop her shoulder. "Hi-yah."

Charlie let out a laugh at the goofball move. Not the same hardcore Demarco she'd met the first day. A warmth filled her chest, and she viewed the special agent in a bit of a new light for a fleeting moment.

A well-dressed couple strolling in the opposite direction gave them a wide berth. The female half of the duo scanned Charlie up and down before returning to her conversation with her companion.

Demarco sobered. "I know we can't talk details out here, but I'd like to understand as much as you can tell me."

"I gave you everything I had this afternoon. You think I'd hold out on the commander?"

"You've been at your desk for the last two hours. Seems as though Orr lit a fire under your ass."

He had, but Charlie didn't yet trust the special agent to share more.

As they reached the corner, someone bumped Charlie from behind and snatched her purse.

"Hey!"

The thief elbowed her in the side so hard, she stumbled and fell into the gutter.

"Are you okay?" Demarco reached out a hand.

"I'm fine." Dirty water from the gutter had splashed onto her pristine white uniform, making a mess. "He took my purse...and my security badge." A lump formed in her throat.

Demarco took off after the figure who wore sagging jeans and a white T-shirt. As her co-worker ran down the street chasing her assailant, he let out a string of obscenities.

The sting of scraped palms brought her back to her position in the gutter. Gross. Gracelessly, she stood and swiped her stinging hands on the back of her skirt, as if that would clean off the dirty water and trash she'd landed in.

Demarco disappeared around the corner.

Within seconds, the sound of shouting and tires squealing echoed down the block.

Charlie trotted toward the noise.

Her dinner date rounded the corner with her security badge in hand, a bloodied lip, and a wide smile on his stupidly handsome face.

CHAPTER 14

"THANKS," Charlie said putting on the badge, which she had affixed to a lanyard, and tucking it into her blouse for safe keeping. "That's the second cell phone I've lost in two days."

"Sorry I couldn't recover the whole purse for you, but that guy had an accomplice waiting." He brushed his hands on the legs of his khaki pants.

"I heard." She sighed. Her best summer whites were ruined. "Looks like I'll be buying new uniform items at the Px tomorrow. This was my best skirt."

"My place is a few blocks from here." He stood with hands in his pockets. "You can borrow some of my clothes. We can order a pizza."

From casual dinner in a public place to private pizza party for two at his apartment? She bit her lip.

"I feel as if I need to make it up to you. I'm the one that wanted to go to Carmello's." Already he was tucking in his button-up shirt that had pulled loose from his khakis and straightening his basic, boring red tie.

One-hundred percent anal.

And what would such a person's apartment look like? She had to admit a gnawing curiosity made her say, "All right. Pizza it is."

He wiped his brow with his arm. A sheen of sweat glistened

for a moment and then disappeared. Angel transitioned from thief-chasing hero to unsmiling agent in seconds. "Follow me."

They headed across the street from the corner and passed by rows of federal-style townhouses adorned with black wrought iron railings and matching black shutters, which set off the attractive brick-red exteriors. Mature red maple and sweet gum trees lined the edges of the sidewalks and, since it was the bloom of summer, provided a pleasant canopy. Between the matching townhomes stood less elaborate, boxy two story homes painted cream or blue, which gave a patriotic flair to the neighborhood.

"Have you lived here long?" Charlie imagined finding her own place to live. She'd requested off-base housing. "Seems like a perfect spot. You could walk to work."

"Eh, not long."

"Where were you before A Group?"

"I've spent my whole career in the DC area."

He didn't elaborate. Closed door. Do not ask again. The end.

"Here we are." He stopped in front of one of the many town-homes and headed for the stairs that led down into a basement section of the building. "I'm in the lower-level."

When she passed through the front door, she was transported to the jungles of the Amazon. Where a living room and kitchen should be, potted plants of all sizes were the guests of honor. Trees, flowering plants, even vines, which crisscrossed overhead and spanned archways, filled the space to overflowing.

"Wow."

Demarco sat in a brown armchair that blended in with two seven-foot tall ficus trees and removed his shoes. "I like houseplants."

"I guessed as much." She stood in the entryway. "Should I—?" She lifted her foot and rested it on her thigh so she could remove one of her dress shoes.

"You don't have to."

Too late. She held the shoe in her hand and laughed.

His lips curled up as if he were bemused.

"After wearing these all day, it feels good to walk around bare-foot." She removed her other shoe and pushed them to one side.

To take it all in, she strolled around the apartment space. "You said you haven't lived here very long, but how did you manage to grow all of this so quickly?" She touched the thin, delicate stem of a bright yellow orchid flower and marveled at its beauty.

"I guess I have a green thumb." He punched a number on his flip-style phone and put it to his ear. "Pepperoni okay?"

She nodded. The lush surroundings made her forget about the theft on the street, the strangeness of her job, and the on-again off-again cold shoulder Demarco displayed. Ferns, cacti, vines, trees, houseplants of every size and variety dazzled the eye.

She reached the kitchen. Fewer plants in this space, which made sense. How else would he be able to prepare food or eat when choked by greenery?

In the fridge she found a collection of locally-brewed beer. Why not? "Is it okay—?" She held up a bottle.

"Yeah, sure, bring me one. The pizza will be here in about thirty minutes."

"Sounds good." Charlie had intended to use their dinner out as a time to mine more information about their work. What she knew only scratched the surface, and today in the meeting, the urgency Commander Orr had displayed made her think there was more going on at a higher level. The more intimate setting had relaxed her and threw off her focus.

She handed him the beer.

"Oh, the clothes I promised." Demarco set his beer on a glass side table dotted with African violets and trotted through the kitchen into a short hallway beyond.

Left alone, she grew more curious about how the special agent lived. She hunted for books, DVDs, magazines, anything that might give her a window into the man inside. Oddly, she couldn't find a thing. Shelves hidden by hanging vines only revealed potting soils and fertilizers. In fact, she couldn't even find a television. Where one should be, across from the sofa on a wide expanse of wall, he'd hung shelves on which to set more plants.

Maybe he'd given over this space to his plants and those normal living room items were kept in the bedroom?

"Will this work?"

She had her head inside one of his kitchen cupboards and jumped at his voice. "I'm starving. Hope the pizza is delivered soon." She grabbed a couple of plates to cover her snooping.

Demarco held a gray T-shirt and a pair of running shorts with an adjustable waist. "You're tall." He tossed them at her.

"Thanks. Where can I change?"

"There's a guest bath right there." He pointed out a door hidden by more plants. "Then maybe you want to use my phone to cancel your bank card or something?"

"Dammit." Not only that, but her military ID. What a pain in the ass that was going to be.

"Give me a minute to change." Charlie locked the door and quickly slipped out of her ruined uniform. She caught sight of herself in the oval mirror above the sink. Dirt smudged her cheek and strands of hair had slipped loose from her French braid. She turned on the water and scrubbed her face clean in her underwear before donning Demarco's clothes.

The T-shirt smelled like him. Clean, yes, but a subtle masculine fragrance she couldn't place. Then she attempted to tuck the loose strands of hair back into formation. When the improvement to her appearance was minimal, she sighed, folded up her uniform and joined her dinner companion.

"It fits okay." She stood in the dining space with her arms out to her sides and spun around. "Do you have a bag I could put my stuff in?"

Demarco leaned against the kitchen counter, arms crossed, and regarded her for a moment. He opened a drawer next to him and grabbed a plastic grocery bag. "Here you go."

As she slipped her uniform into it, a question popped out of her mouth, "You never did tell anyone what happened in the woods."

"We're not in the office, Cutter."

"It's a simple question, not attached to any particular incident or location. What did you see in the woods?"

His gaze burned into hers. "I didn't see anything."

"Bullshit."

The doorbell rang, which was followed by a loud knock.

"Pizza's here." He handed Charlie his flip phone. "Why don't you make that phone call?

She gripped the phone tightly. "What did you see, Angel?"

He visibly stiffened.

Demarco carried the pizza box to the small table in the dining area, dodging the extended branches and leaves of his plant collection.

Charlie stood with phone in hand.

"Make the call." Whipping open the pizza box, he grabbed a large slice, folded it in half and took a bite.

"I don't have the number."

He set his half-eaten slice on the open lid of the pizza box and retrieved his bottle of beer from the other room. "You seem to have every other phone number memorized."

"Family, friends, yes. Random bank emergency numbers, no." She grabbed a plate and chose a slice of pizza. "Why won't you talk about the person you chased in the woods? Doesn't that have to be part of your report?"

He sat at the table and finished off his first slice. "Have I done my job as the security expert on the team? Yes. Do you need to know everything? No."

As she ate, she mulled over his answer.

"Would you sit down, please?" He kicked out the empty chair. "You're making me nervous hovering there."

She took him up on the offer. "By your answer, I will make my own assumptions, then."

"Fine." He picked up a second slice and drank a swig of beer.

"The only way I can fully support the team is by completely understanding what we are up against. I feel as if I only have a little peek inside rather than an invite to the party. Why? Doesn't everyone want me to connect the dots?"

"You've been here for two days. Maybe slow it down. Focus on your work."

Charlie had hit a wall. "Do you have any family? Brothers? Sisters?"

"Why do you want to know?" Resting both fists on the table, he paused his eating.

"I was making casual conversation. Is that not allowed?"

He rubbed his chin. "I had family once." A slack expression appeared.

When he didn't elaborate, Charlie abandoned the desire to press for more. Maybe Stormy knew more about Demarco's past.

"Tell me about your family." His gaze softened, and he leaned back. "I know you have a mother and a father."

Her face heated. He'd overheard more than one private conversation when she wasn't on her best behavior. "And a brother, Chad."

"Chad and Charlie." He smirked. "Cute."

She sighed. After joining the military, answering personal questions became rote. Every assignment, every new roommate, it was the same old thing.

"And where are Chad and Charlie from?"

If she opened up, maybe so would he. "We're Navy brats, which means we're from everywhere and nowhere." Maybe that would be enough of an answer for him.

"So you've traveled a lot."

"I guess you could call it that."

"I always wished I could travel more."

"Why don't you then?" she asked.

He hesitated and nodded his head. "You'd think it would be that easy, but sometimes things stand in the way of what you want."

His words resonated with her in a way he probably didn't expect. She kept her thoughts to herself. "Look, it was nice of you to offer dinner and all of that, but we don't need to be friends, you know."

"I know." He scanned her face.

The scrutiny unnerved her.

"What do you want from me?" Her stomach turned sour, and her appetite fled.

"Why do you think I want something from you?"

Dressed in his clothes and sitting in his kitchen, she felt vulnerable. The desire grew to leave his strangely decorated apartment. This was too intimate a setting for two co-workers who'd only just met. Stormy's words rang in her head about Demarco's reputation. "I should really go back to base and call my bank." She pushed her plate away.

"Let me give you a ride. I'm parked right out front."

"That's not necessary." She carried her plate to the sink and grabbed her clothes. "I know my way back."

"I insist."

She worked hard to keep her expression neutral.

"Ah," he said, casually closing the pizza box and gathering their empty beer bottles, "you don't trust me. What do you think I'm going to do?"

Her body froze, and her heart thudded. "I don't want you to go out of your way for me."

"It's really not a problem." As he set his plate in the sink, his arm brushed hers. "You just had your purse stolen. I don't think Commander Orr would be too appreciative if his linguistics expert didn't make it in to work tomorrow."

"I'm going to walk." She backed away from him. "Follow me, if that's what you want." The scent of the borrowed shirt hit her nose, and the once beautiful indoor jungle pressed in on her.

———

Charlie walked at a brisk pace, Demarco a few steps behind. Why didn't he turn around and go home? The best way to purge her growing discomfort was to change into her own clothes, maybe swim a few laps. Yes, a good swim would straighten her out in no time. It always did.

But having the special agent hot on her heels didn't help. He was half the reason she wanted to be alone...the other half? Well, the other half continued to process the Voynich comparison. Although Orr had reprimanded her for giving the appearance of being more interested in translating the manuscript than figuring out the origin and purpose of the pods, he didn't know what she'd found buried in the manuscript. A possibility so bizarre and so mind boggling, she wanted to examine the manuscript further to be sure she was on the right track.

"You missed the turn," Demarco corrected gently. "Tingey Street."

Without saying a word, she made a left turn onto the next block.

"That will loop you back to Tingey."

"Excellent," she snapped.

By the time she reached the base motel, her temporary home, most of her anxious energy had worn off. Her walking companion had kept his distance, and she grew used to his calm directions if she veered off course.

When she reached the doors of the motel lobby, she paused and faced him, "Thank you, but as you can see I made it back safely."

Demarco stood ten feet distant and absently played with the wristband of his watch. "I hope you have a good evening, Charlie."

She nodded and entered the lobby. Instead of continuing to her room on the second floor, she found a window that looked out toward the parking lot. Demarco stood at the edge of the curb, waited for a car to pass, and then headed back in the same direction they had come. She lingered there, unable to leave until his figure became a distant blur.

———

Ten minutes later she exited her motel room in a fresh white uniform—white blouse, with name tag and medals transferred from the stained one in the plastic bag, and white pants pressed perfectly with creases down the middle. Although she longed for a swim to soothe her nerves, her mind focused on her obsession: the manuscript. It waited for her back in her office. A desire to dig deeper, work harder, and confirm what she believed gnawed at her.

The base had grown quieter. The summer sun had set, and twilight lit up the deep blue sky with an eerie glow.

She crossed the base and entered the main building. A few offices ran 24/7 operations, so it was not unusual for someone to run their badge this late in the evening. A single guard sat on a stool near the card readers. As she ran her card through the access control slot, he barely looked up from the magazine he read

The green light appeared. She pushed through the turnstile. Once she reached the elevator, she realized her mistake: the key. She couldn't enter the office now that someone had returned the key, and that someone had been Demarco when they'd left together to eat dinner.

Dammit.

Yes, she knew the code to enter the office, but she'd forgotten about the key system Stormy had pointed out on her first day.

She abruptly turned and exited through the turnstiles.

This time, the guard watched her carefully as she left. Her unusual entrance and exit caught his attention. She was sure someone would ask about that at some point. Would it travel back to the office? To Commander Orr? To Demarco?

Her stomach soured at the thought Demarco would know. He'd left her at the motel, and she'd given the impression she was headed to her room.

She let out a breath and pushed through the front door and into the summer evening.

———

The gym stood open twenty-four hours a day. The advantage of being on a military schedule and having to maintain fitness was that access to workout spaces was unlimited. She slipped inside the quiet building, nodded to the solitary individual tasked with working the desk overnight, and entered the women's locker room.

Empty.

She disrobed and donned her one-piece suit, a plain navy blue one she'd received at Boot Camp. Not the most flattering, but it had been free. The constant chlorine exposure had started to wear down the elasticity, and she knew before too long, she'd have to purchase another. Maybe tomorrow after work when she visited the Px to pick up new uniform items, she could find a replacement suit.

She stowed her dry clothing, gym bag, and shoes in a locker, and then stood in front of a full-length mirror to brush out her braids and pull her hair into a ponytail. Sculpted biceps and shoulders stood out to her, a different body than she'd had before going to Boot Camp. She'd always been moderately interested in exercise, but in Boot Camp she'd found a natural gift for sport. She'd never pushed herself. But her RDC made sure she was motivated to strive beyond her normal physical limits.

A love of swimming kept her coming back to the pool. Although all Navy personnel were required to take a physical fitness test twice yearly, she had the choice of a one-and-a-half mile run or a five-hundred-meter swim.

But the physical changes to her upper body surprised her. She flexed her arm to see the result and hoped that regular swimming would maintain that new shape.

Although the sign next to the door to the pool read 'closed,' she'd bypassed signs before in Monterey. The lack of a lifeguard didn't bother her, and nobody was going to be checking this late in the evening to make sure the pool was clear. Most sailors preferred using the treadmills and ellipticals than the pool.

The lights were turned off, but enough residual light flooded through the windows on the double door entrance from the hall that she'd be able to make out the numbers on the lap clock. She wanted to improve her times before her fitness test in October.

She chose the lane closest to the locker room door in case she ran into a problem. But seeing as how the person sitting at the entrance barely acknowledged her, well, she wasn't worried. She slipped on her goggles.

Making a sleek dive, she knifed into the eighty-five degree water. The first few laps she warmed up with a relaxed breast stroke.

One. Two. Three. Four.

Perfect rhythm. She hung onto the edge for a few seconds, pushed off, and switched to freestyle. Each breath, each stroke was as natural as walking.

Her work on the manuscript occupied her thoughts. The odd shapes and swirls looped in her mind, soaring in and out, placing themselves in patterns on a black canvas. Creating words and meaning out of gibberish. She closed her eyes. Barely aware of her body.

Instructions. But for what?

A recipe for an organic compound. Weight and measurements. Types of plants.

A page floated ahead in the dark. A wheel of symbols and letters. It rotated faster and faster and faster. A blur. An impossible blur. Time passing. Hours? Days? Years?

Her fingertips slammed into the concrete.

She gasped and grabbed the solid edge.

An electric zip ran through her.

A machine.

The writer of the manuscript had been building an organic machine.

"Cutter, you swim?" Commander Orr stood in the shadows of the closed pool room, a white towel looped across his neck. He whistled. "Did you compete? That was an amazing lap time."

Charlie whipped off her goggles. "Sir?" An answer escaped her. An organic machine rotated in her mind, made of plant material. Layer upon layer, built by hand. Crafted by a long-dead mystery creature. Orr's questions rankled her. She pushed herself out of the pool. Water ran off her body.

"Didn't mean to interrupt your workout. Thought I was the only one who swam off hours."

She padded to her towel. "That's okay." She wrapped it tightly around her. "I need to go."

"Petty Officer, you don't need to."

"See you tomorrow, sir. Oh-seven-hundred." She squeezed water out of her ponytail. "I've got a lot of work to do. So much work." Her heart sped up.

The creature in the ancient past had been building a pod.

CHAPTER 15

"HERE YOU GO." Chief Ricard handed Charlie a brand new iPhone in the office the next morning. "To replace the one we had to take."

"Did Demarco—?" She scanned the small office for the agent's dark head. Across the room, she spied him through the window of Orr's office deep in conversation.

Ricard powered it up. "I programmed it with all your numbers and contacts." To prove it to her, he scrolled through her contacts list. "Can you sign this?" He handed her a receipt form and a standard black government ballpoint pen that looked to date back to the 1980s.

"Uh, sure." She scribbled her name and handed it back. Later on today, she needed to find a free moment to call her bank and report her stolen card amongst other things.

"Great." As he was about to walk away, he changed course and snapped his fingers. "Almost forgot. Orr wants to see you in his office." He pointed at the now open office door.

Demarco had disappeared.

"Thanks." She set her new phone on her desk and took a few sips of hot coffee to steel herself for the meeting. Although Orr had been kind last night at the pool., she didn't want a repeat of the All Hands meeting yesterday.

She grabbed a pen and a yellow legal pad and knocked on the open door. "You wanted to see me, sir?"

He waved her in. "Come on in, Petty Officer. Have a seat." He gestured at two empty chairs in front of his desk. "And close the door."

She clasped the legal pad closely to her chest and pressed her knees together. Her jaw clenched down. Stress filled every pore.

Orr tented his fingers and leveled his gaze. "I wanted to apologize to you."

Lightness filled her.

"My reaction yesterday in our meeting was unprofessional. I should've expressed my thoughts in private with you and not in front of the whole group."

She stared back. A million responses formed: *Thanks. No problem. It's okay. I'm over it.*

A drink of water would really help.

The phone on his desk rang.

"Give me a second here." He answered, Orr speaking."

Charlie's armpits were damp. Although she'd gotten past the fear of further reprimand, why hadn't her body received the notice?

"You're sure?" Orr broke out in a smile. "Hot damn, that's fantastic." He focused his gaze on Charlie and widened his eyes. He nodded. "Excellent. Thanks for your work on this."

He hung up.

"Looks like we got a radar signature."

"A what?"

His demeanor had made a one-eighty shift from serious apology to exuberant joy.

"A signature. A goddamn signature." He opened the door and stepped into the office. "We can track the pods, everyone. Holy hell, we can track the pods." He let out a whoop and smacked his hands together.

Charlie clutched her precious yellow pad. Was their meeting over? Should she leave?

Ricard and Stormy hugged.

Kellerman did a fist pump.

Demarco stood aloof and off to one side, as if a dark cloud had settled directly over him. No expression. No reaction of any kind. The usual Demarco moodiness.

"I've told them to keep us all apprised. If that radar signature shows up again, anywhere in the world, you'll all know about it immediately. This means everyone is on call. You receive a text about it, we all meet back here ASAP no matter the day or time. Prepped and ready to go. Got it?"

"Yes, sir," Ricard saluted.

"Got it, commander," Charlie said. Even more pressure to have a go-bag ready. Screw the moving truck, she'd have to give in and buy some civvies that very afternoon.

"And that means for the next ninety days, at least, no leave is approved."

Stormy frowned.

"We seem to be in some kind of pattern here. Three pods in a years' time. We can't risk missing the next one. We need an intact pod to move our research further along."

Charlie hovered behind Orr. "Sir, if you don't mind?"

"Sorry." He stepped to one side to unblock the door. "Second apology of the day. That's a rare thing, Petty Officer." He laughed a booming laugh. "Enjoy it while you can."

"Yes, sir."

Kellerman stood near her cubicle. "That's some very awesome news."

"Yeah."

"You sure lucked out being assigned here when you did. The last six months have been boring as hell."

"What did he mean by three pods?" She didn't intimate that Demarco had shared with her the additional pod arrival.

He ticked off with long, lean fingers. "Last July at Fort Madison, December in Idaho near the Acoustic Research Center in Bayview, and then the latest one in North Dakota. The first two were before my time."

She fought to keep her expression neutral. "Any idea what they found at the sites of the other two? More Voynich remnants?"

The images that entered her mind last night at the pool returned. More samples meant more confirmation that her translation was correct.

"The December pod was a bust. Landed on the shore rather than in the lake during a heavy snow and exploded into a million pieces from what Stormy told me. Any chance at recovery was blown. Any contact with water, and the pods and all their contents disintegrate. Pieces that small?" He blew air out his nose. "Not a chance."

The visual of a pod and all its 'contents' exploding made her nauseous. "Why so much time between landings?"

"How do we know we've gotten wind of all the pods?"

Charlie turned the information over in her mind. Her discovery couldn't be held back for long. She wanted to share with Kellerman what she'd found in the manuscript, but gut instinct held her back. "That's true. There could've been more. Earth is a large place."

"Well, the fact we now have a radar signature to track will help with that. If pods are landing elsewhere, we will be the first to know about it."

"Do you really think aliens are in these pods, Lieutenant?" She leaned against the wall of her cubicle.

"What else could be the reason for them? The shape. The space inside. Even your preliminary translations point to a transportation device, levers and other functional items inside for a traveler."

"I know. But I still can't wrap my mind around it."

He rested an arm on the top of the cubicle and leaned in. "You'd be surprised at what we know." The young lieutenant's gaze darted down the aisle. "I can't really say much, but just accept it."

A tightening in her chest reduced her breaths to shallow ones. "You mean your work at Area 51?" she whispered.

Kellerman peered over the edge of the cubical walls and then focused his gaze on her. "Yes." He lifted an index finger to his lips and then shifted his weight. "I've been wanting to ask you something."

"Oh?"

He rubbed the back of his suddenly red neck. "I thought maybe you might want to go to a movie sometime or dinner?"

Her face heated. "Um." Not a single word entered her mind. Not one. If only a bolt of lightning would zap the building and knock out the power. That would be a welcome relief from the awkward pause. "Well, I—" *Do it. Give him a chance. Why not, Charlie?* What was she so afraid of? He was a nice guy.

Where did that coffee cup go? Her mouth dried up like the Sahara Desert.

The main door to the office swung open, and a recognizable voice filled the air.

"How are my team today?" Dr. Stern bellowed. "Where is everyone?"

The cubicle set-up hid a lot of the activity behind bland beige walls, but also kept the wrong eyes from accidentally glimpsing top secret work.

"Dr. Stern," greeted Commander Orr, his lips still locked in a joyful grin. "Please do come in. We'd love to have more good news today, wouldn't we, team?" He lifted his hands and nodded with eyebrows raised.

Kellerman sniffed and gave Charlie a glassy stare.

"Let's talk later," she whispered.

His shoulders slumped, and he faced Orr and Dr. Stern as they shook hands outside his office.

"Commander, nice to see you again. I know I don't normally show up in your office unannounced, but—"

"Not a problem. Not a problem. You're welcome anytime. You're one of the most important members on our team." He invited the doctor into his office. "We can talk privately, If you'd like."

With all of the morning's interruptions, how would Charlie ever finish the translation work? The commander expected pod translations, which she could probably figure out now, if she only had a quiet moment to spare.

"This concerns the whole team," said Dr. Stern. She had shed her lab coat and arrived wearing a very stylish mid-length dress in a lovely coral color and a pair of strappy heels. Out of her lab, the doctor came across as much younger than Charlie had originally surmised. "Can I use your meeting room?"

"Of course." Orr's face clouded. "Let's go team. We've got work to do, so let's make this quick."

Upset he didn't get first crack at Stern's news?

The team filled the chairs around the table and waited expectantly for the doctor to share her findings. Charlie hoped for more about the possible occupant of the pod. The blood she'd managed to salvage could be connected to alien life.

Stern stood front and center, hands on wide hips. "I wish I had better news for you, but I wanted to deliver this in person to answer any questions you might have."

Demarco cracked his knuckles as he stood near the door. He'd chosen not to sit.

"The pod material collected was too contaminated for a complete analysis. I know this is disappointing. These were fresher samples, and we were all hopeful. The smashed vials had direct contamination from the forest, and the complete samples from Stormy had fully disintegrated in the water inside the tubes and bonded with the pod material similar to our last samples." She paced in front of the retracted projection screen. "The blood sample recovered by Petty Officer Cutter was a very small sample. The lack of material present required a different process for DNA analysis. Unfortunately, I cannot do that type of analysis at my lab here. I arranged for a lab at the National Security Agency to do the testing. It could take up to fourteen days for the results."

Orr pulled his chin. "This lab, do they have the appropriate clearance levels?"

"I made sure to discuss the sensitivity of A Group's work with the head of the lab, and he understood our concerns. They do highly sensitive work at that facility, and that is the reason I chose them. Your sample should be as safe there as it is in my lab." Dr. Stern scanned all the faces in the room. "Any other questions?"

Kellerman raised a hand.

Dr. Stern pointed.

"Will the results be available on the intranet here in the office, or will it be a printed report delivered?"

Strange question. What did it matter?

"A Group has a limited intranet here at Washington Navy Yard, but I'll attempt to have them deliver the report via secure networks. The printed report should be delivered with other top secret materials somewhere around that two-week timeframe. When it arrives, I will contact the team and give a presentation of the findings."

Kellerman rested his elbows on the table. "Sounds good."

"Anyone else?" Dr. Stern asked.

Stormy raised a hand. "Will I be able to make a copy of the report to keep in our files here in the office?"

"Yes. If the secure network avenue fails for delivery, I will make it available to you. I understand how important it is to keep track of each piece of evidence."

A classified copier sat in the main office space. They each had a personal code they had to enter to monitor what they printed on the machine. All copies were counted and tracked to ensure no one made inappropriate copies or walked out of the secure facility with documents they shouldn't have.

"Any other questions?" Dr. Stern waited a heartbeat or two. "I know this was not the news you wanted to hear today. Time is passing quickly to decipher the origin and meaning of the pods, but I want you to know I'm in this with you for the long haul. I won't let you down. We will hopefully find something meaningful in the blood evidence that may further our understanding of what's happening. I'm still excited I was chosen to be part of this amazing team, so don't lose focus on the bigger picture. We can piece this puzzle together and find out why these pods are here. I'm sure of it."

"Thank you, Dr. Stern," said Commander Orr. "We very much appreciate the time you took out of your busy day to deliver this news personally."

"My pleasure." Dr. Stern smiled. "This is the assignment of a lifetime."

"Well, everyone, looks like it's back to work. Demarco, I want that write-up on Devils Lake by the end of the day. Kellerman and

Ricard—meeting at 1100 to go over the details of the attack." All three men nodded. "Doctor, before you go, I'd like to meet with you in my office for a moment, if you could."

"Of course, Commander. But could you give me a minute?" She made eye contact with Charlie and smiled. "I have a question to ask your newest member."

Orr raised an eyebrow, but didn't ask any questions. "Petty Officer Cutter?"

"I'm happy to answer whatever questions you might have, doctor." Charlie smiled.

The commander ushered everyone out of the conference room and left Dr. Stern and Charlie alone.

"You wanted to ask me something?" Charlie remained seated and viewed the older woman who had a spark to her brown eyes.

"I do." Dr. Stern gave a quick smile and then sat in the chair right next to her. "I like you, Petty Officer Cutter."

"Well, that's kind of you to say." Her bewilderment at the statement was tempered by a warm feeling from the compliment. "Is there something I can help you with? Perhaps you wanted me to give you that overview of my findings so far?" Could she trust Dr. Stern with her discovery in the Voynich manuscript? She'd appeared very interested in her linguistics work upon their first meeting.

"I am definitely interested in your translation work, but my question is more of a social one."

"Oh?"

"I mentioned that my cousin runs a paint-and-sip business in Fairfax."

"Yes, I remember." How could she forget? The woman's whole lab was covered in proof of that statement.

"I'd like to invite you to a paint-and-sip class this Saturday at her studio." The serious scientist turned into a fun-loving artist within seconds. "She has a few spots left in her Starry Night Owl class, and I told her I could help her fill them. I'll pay for the whole thing, even buy you a glass of wine. She's been working so hard at this business, and I want to help her as much as I can. You're new to town. I thought maybe you'd be free and looking for something to do besides sitting on base."

"A painting class?" Charlie gave a tight smile. Not only did she have to purchase some new clothes after work, she had to spend time remaking her military ID, file a police report about her stolen purse, and find out if she'd gotten the go-ahead to start looking for off-base housing.

"It'll be fun. I promise." The doctor pressed a warm hand across Charlie's forearm.

If Demarco worried about Dr. Stern's impression of him, it would only make sense for her to take advantage of the woman's friendliness if only to annoy the special agent. Right? "Why not? Sounds like fun." Boy, would Demarco be annoyed if he found out.

Dr. Stern clapped. "Excellent. What's your number, and I'll drop you a pin for the address."

"Think I can Uber it there? I don't have a car."

Dr. Stern's mouth gaped open. "I didn't even think."

"It's okay. I've been saving since Boot Camp to buy something better than the old beater I had in grad school. Just haven't had the time."

"Let me give you a ride."

"Really?"

"Absolutely. I'm the one that invited you to go. I should be the one to help you get there."

"All right. Sounds like a plan, Dr. Stern. What time will you pick me up?"

"You're staying here on base?"

"At the motel."

"How about six fifteen? It'll take us about thirty minutes driving time. The class starts at seven. That way we have time to grab that drink I promised."

"Sure. Fine." Was this really happening? A paint-and-sip girls' night out with a scientist from work? She never imagined something like this happening when she arrived at her new assignment. Surreal.

"Add yourself as a contact." The doctor handed her cell phone to Charlie. "Let me send you a text. That'll make it easier to connect."

The young linguist typed in her number and handed the phone back.

"Perfect." The doctor stood, and as she made her way out of the conference room, she turned and said, "And call me Abigail."

Charlie sat dumbstruck in the conference room. Did that actually happen? Did Dr. Stern—no, Abigail—ask her to attend a painting class? Seemed there was a new surprise every day at A Group. What was a 'regular' work day like in the office?

———

Although the tug of the Voynich manuscript was strong, Charlie couldn't dismiss her curiosity. As she returned to her desk, she kept an eye on the window into Orr's office. Both the commander and the doctor had been talking for a while. Had Dr. Stern told them everything she knew about the evidence they'd gathered? In a world of secrets and clearances, it wasn't hard to imagine only knowing one portion of the story. Demarco and Kellerman both had provided snippets of information without context.

Maybe her outing with Dr. Stern would give her the opportunity to forge a friendship that might help her in her work life. The doctor had been interested in her translation work after all.

Sitting down at her desk and opening up the Voynich translation work in its secure and password-protected folder, Charlie held onto her own secrets. Why divulge everything she'd discovered when her A Group teammates withheld their own details?

In this world, information was power. Considering how adrift she'd felt over the last few years, to finally encounter a place where her skills were needed and her knowledge wanted, she was in no rush to give that up until she knew more.

CHAPTER 16

HOURS LATER, Charlie had made headway on her translation of both the manuscript and the pod fragments. Deep in her work, she'd managed to connect the fuller sentence structure of the manuscript to the short text pieces found in the pod.

Forward. Backward. Right. Left. Up. Down. Locked. Unlocked.

These terms were the first pod terms she uncovered.

The instructions inside the manuscript were written centuries ago. If some creature could create a pod, what was its purpose? Return to space? Did an alien land on earth and somehow manage to blend in with humans? That said a lot about the appearance of these aliens and made her rethink the strange footprints on the sand in North Dakota.

Loathe to make another embarrassing mistake in front of her peers, she weighed the idea of holding on to the information she had until she could present everything in full. Maybe she should make an appointment to meet with Commander Orr to present her findings in private.

She clicked over to her calendar to set up an appointment request for next Monday morning. That would give her the time she needed to type up something clear for a non-linguistics expert to understand. Basic English anyone could grasp. She could dumb it down. She wasn't sure the commander would believe her, so simplicity was paramount.

After selecting an available time slot on his calendar, she sent the request.

Next, she built a dictionary using a simple spreadsheet—one column for the picture of each phoneme, the transliteration of it, and the English translation. Transliteration had been a battle. The symbols had a bit of a relationship to English in her view. Could be coincidence or her own mind playing tricks on her. But she'd built an 'alphabet' of sorts and tied it to the English alphabet, which made pronunciation and reading possible.

Most of the phonemes were swirly and compared most closely to a few letters of the alphabet. She began there. What looked like an 's' or a 't' would become an 's' or a 't' in her transliteration alphabet. Most of the vowels were similar to the vowels 'o,' 'a,' and 'e.'

When she tried voicing the strange 'words' aloud, they sounded quite odd. As if they were two steps removed from a known language, yet was complete nonsense to anyone who heard it.

She whispered one particularly long and difficult 'word' as Demarco walked past her desk toward the coffee.

"I didn't notice," he said.

"Excuse me?"

He stumbled and caught himself. "I thought you asked me a question."

"What question?" She spun her chair to face him.

His gaze jumped from her to her computer screen and back again. "About the weather," he said cautiously.

She held back a laugh. "You promise you won't tell?" It wouldn't hurt to let Demarco in on a little bit of her work, would it? She'd had to keep her best discoveries to herself, just until she was solid on her findings, before sharing any of it. But maybe Demarco wouldn't spill.

He raised his eyebrows and approached her cubicle. "I'm listening."

She turned back to her computer and enlarged the spreadsheet she'd created so far. "I was trying to read some of the

Voynich text." She pointed to the word he'd heard her pronounce as he'd walked by and spoke it aloud again, "Ca-low-dit-y." As she said it, she realized it could sound like 'cloudy.'

His eyes widened. "Wait, you've cracked it?" He knelt next to her chair and stared at the spreadsheet. "Did you tell the commander?"

She could let him look at a little of what she'd done. Couldn't she? "I don't know if I'd say I cracked it, but I'm able to craft my own little dictionary of sorts, and it makes it much easier to talk about the symbols if we can give voice to them. I'm trying to assign each phoneme—a little piece of text—a sound. Like our own alphabet. Makes it easier to think of the symbols as real text, as a real language."

"And the translations?" he asked. "Have you figured any of it out? What does the manuscript say? Who wrote it? Why?"

The barrage of questions surprised her. She had no idea Demarco had been so interested in the Voynich manuscript. He'd been kind to her yesterday after Orr had criticized her, but she didn't think he had real interest in the text. Who knew he almost equaled her enthusiasm? "I've been able to figure out almost all of the text from the pod. The picture where the symbols were the clearest, at least."

"Show me." He leaned in. His breath warm on her bare arm.

She shivered.

"All right." Although her intention had been to present her findings in private with Commander Orr to avoid another embarrassing outburst and ensure he was pleased with her discovery, Demarco's focused interest lifted her spirits. "I went for a swim last night, and that's when things clicked."

"You went swimming at nine o'clock at night? After I walked you back to the motel?"

"Shh." Charlie swept her gaze around the vicinity of her cubicle praying nobody else heard she and Demarco had spent time together outside work. If Stormy heard, she'd be clucking her tongue in disappointment. The office lothario and Charlie alone together? Bad news.

"Not the safest thing to do," he said in a quieter tone.

Why did she have to bristle at his concern? The chiding nature of his comment set her off. "It was perfectly safe. In fact, the commander was there."

"Was he?"

"Never mind about that. You asked about my discovery. Still interested?"

"Yes." He clasped his hands behind his back and remained kneeling next to her computer screen. "Please, I want to know more."

Clicking in her research folder, she brought up a picture of two pages in the manuscript. "The deciphering of the text inside the pods reminded me of a certain spot in the manuscript where I'd been stuck during graduate school." She pointed to a series of phonemes on the displayed pages. "This combination of phonemes didn't appear anywhere else in the manuscript. They were an isolated series of 'words' that didn't match anything else on the other pages. When I'd been doing my research and attempting a translation, these pages disrupted everything I thought I'd uncovered."

"How so?" A wrinkle appeared in the special agent's broad forehead.

How to explain to someone without her background? "Earlier, when you thought I was asking you about the weather? I was reading the Voynich 'words' using my transliteration alphabet."

He gave a quizzical look.

She clicked on the minimized spreadsheet she'd been developing. "To crack a linguistic code, you first need to separate out the phonemes. Each individual phoneme is a sound that makes up the language. For example, this one." She highlighted one of the bits of text from the manuscript. "It also appears in some of the photos we took at Devils Lake." She opened up the photos she'd categorized and labeled. "See?" She used her cursor to circle around the faded text inside the pod. "It's the same phoneme."

"Yes, I see. It's a similar chunk of script."

"Exactly." She clicked back to her spreadsheet. "I first tried to find phonemes on the photos that matched my previous work,

which also helped me figure out the meaning of the words themselves. The pod 'words' were connected to travel, motion—"

"Right, you presented that idea in the All Hands meeting."

"Yes, but what I didn't have time to do before that meeting was
to go back to the manuscript and see if I could find these same
'words.' And last night when I was swimming, it came to me where
I had seen these pod words in the manuscript." Her heart raced,
remembering the moment she'd made the connection. "These two
pages. The ones I couldn't fit in with the rest of the manuscript.
The two pages that eluded me, that tortured me. Why were these
pages here, buried in a book mostly about plants and herbs?"

Demarco stared at her screen, the two manuscript pages maxi-
mized. "What is it? What did you find?"

She pointed out each similar word, "Here and here and here.
Forward. Backward. Up. Down. Stop. Start." Her breath caught in
her throat. She could hardly say the words aloud. "These are
instructions for operating a machine—a machine that travels."

Demarco's face turned ashen.

Did he feel the same excitement as she? "And then when I
thought about the rest of these pages in the manuscript, why the
detail about so many plants?" She brought up another snapshot of
two different pages in the manuscript. "It has been long surmised
that the manuscript contained chemistry details. Primitive chemistry, yes, but chemistry concepts nonetheless. The pods are
organic in nature. They contain no metallic or plastic or any other
non-organic materials." She took a deep breath. "The Voynich
Manuscript is an instruction manual for building a traveling
machine. Someone in fifteenth century Italy wrote the instructions to build a pod."

Demarco brought a hand to his mouth. A pained expression
marred his features.

That wasn't the reaction Charlie had been expecting. He
seemed horrified by her analysis. But why?

"You're certain?" he choked out the words. "You're absolutely
certain about this?"

She focused her attention on her computer screen. "That's

what I've been focusing on today—when we're not being interrupted by visitors."

"I'm very sorry to have interrupted your work, Petty Officer." Dr. Stern appeared.

Charlie's face heated. The older woman had been so kind to her with her invitation, and now she'd mucked it up. "I didn't mean—it was wonderful to have you stop by and let us know what's going on with the samples we collected."

The doctor smiled broadly. "It's all right, Charlie. I can call you Charlie, can't I?" She stole a glance down the row of cubicles. "The commander can't make me use all of that formality he insists on in your office. Isn't that right, Agent Demarco?"

Charlie held back a grin at the doctor's remark.

Demarco stood and cleared his throat. "If you'll excuse me, I need to prepare for my meeting with Commander Orr."

"Of course." Dr. Stern stepped aside.

He headed toward his desk at the other end of the aisle.

"He's a mystery that one," Abigail Stern said as she watched his departure. "Warm one minute, cold the next."

"Yes." Why did he behave so oddly when she'd shared her discovery? She'd made the mistake of bringing him in on her secret only to instantly regret it. Although he'd appeared enthusiastic to learn more about her translations, his reaction had been negative. Did she put her research at risk by telling him too much too soon?

"But sometimes mysteries are fun to solve." Dr. Stern eyes shone. "I'll see you tomorrow evening, Charlie. I'm looking forward to it."

Charlie smiled and nodded, but a cold sensation invaded her gut. Demarco made her doubt, once again, trusting anyone in the office with her discoveries.

———

Charlie grabbed a red leather purse off her bed. It had been an impulse buy at the Px yesterday after work. She opened it and dropped in her brand new military ID and a wad of cash, unsure what one needed to bring to a paint-and-sip event.

Thank goodness Abigail Stern had offered to drive. After cancelling her stolen credit and bank cards, she wouldn't have had the means to pay an Uber driver. At least the Navy Credit Union on base had let her write herself a check for cash while she waited for replacement cards.

She checked her watch. Early yet. But she could wait in the lobby.

As she decided what to wear from her limited wardrobe, her brother texted her. She'd settled on a pair of jeans and a sleeveless print blouse she'd picked up on her quick shopping spree. Comfortable and casual. She slipped into some plain white running shoes, headed out the door, and read her brother's text.

> Hey, sister. Heard you're in DC. Where are you staying?

She paused in the hall and quickly answered him.

> Washington Navy Yard. The base motel. Waiting for okay to rent apt.

Three little dots appeared showing her brother was composing a response text.

Skipping down the stairs, she exited into the lobby of the motel. A tall young man with sandy blond hair stood with his back to her.

"Chad!" She'd recognize that wiry build anywhere. Opening her arms wide, she gave her slightly-younger-than-her brother a big hug.

"Surprise," he said. "Mom told me about your orders."

"It's been a whirlwind, to say the least." She stood back and gave him the once over. "Looking good, Ensign Cutter."

And he did. His face had thinned out since she saw him last—more than three years ago at his Naval Academy graduation—and the lanky body of a young man had solidified into a sturdy, muscled physique.

"It's Lieutenant JG now."

Did he blush?

"Wow." Hard to believe her brother had achieved so much in such a short period of time. His career in military intelligence was buzzing along, while hers had stalled. But she didn't begrudge him his success. He'd known what he wanted: the Navy career their father had hoped for both of them. "I didn't even realize. When?"

"Last year, when you were in Boot Camp."

She nodded. That had been a trying period in her life. She'd joined as an enlisted person without telling anyone in her family. To admit to her hard-nosed father she'd failed in graduate school had been too much to face. "I'm sorry I missed the ceremony."

"That's okay."

She pulled a face.

"No, really. It's not that big of a deal."

She rolled her eyes. "Yeah, right." She punched him in the shoulder. "Wait a minute, what are you doing in DC? I thought you'd been assigned to Rota."

Naval Station Rota in Spain provided support for U.S. and NATO ships along with Navy and Air Force flights and passengers, and also provided cargo, fuel, and ammunition to units in the region. Even some linguists were stationed there. Her Intelligence Officer brother had received the plum assignment only a few months previous.

"I ship out in a couple of weeks. Thought I'd come see you before I got wrapped up in the move." He scanned her figure. "Looks like you have a night out planned, though."

Her stomach dropped. Why did she have to agree to Dr. Stern's invite? If only she'd known her brother would make a visit, she would've cancelled. She glanced at her watch. "My ride's going to be here in about five minutes. I'm sorry."

"Don't be worry about it. If my sister has a hot date on a Saturday night, I'm not going to get in the way."

"It's not a date."

Dr. Abigail Stern entered the lobby. "Ah, now I see why you didn't answer my text." She held up her phone. "This young fella's a lot more interesting than a boring old woman like me."

Charlie noticed the text had lit up her phone screen. "I'm sorry, Dr. Stern."

"Abigail, remember?"

"Abigail. Yes." She gestured at her brother. "I'd like you to meet my brother, Chad. He's a Lieutenant JG."

Dr. Stern nodded approvingly. "Your brother?" She squinted at them. "Yes, I can see the resemblance. Older? Younger?" She reached out and shook his hand.

"Younger," Charlie answered before her brother could open his mouth.

"By three minutes," he retorted.

"Twins. Wow." Dr. Stern studied Chad's face. "I'm kind of into DNA and the nature versus nurture argument. But I don't know if any of the remarkable similarities of identical twins—beyond shared genetics—translates to fraternal twins."

"Only if you count both of us having an allergy to strawberries," her brother said.

"I'm not sure that's really what she meant, Chad." Charlie shook her head.

"Well, it was very nice to meet you." Dr. Stern smiled and then turned to Charlie. "Shall we go then? Iris has our spots ready near the back of the class. That way we can gossip about other people's painting skills or lack thereof."

Chad raised a brow.

"We're going to a paint-and-sip thing in Fairfax." It sounded ridiculous to her own ears. When had she ever been into art?

Her brother held back a laugh. "Oh, okay." He stepped away from the two women and headed toward the door. "It was good seeing you, sis. Maybe we can find a time for dinner before I ship out."

"Absolutely." Although she'd rather spend the evening catching up with her brother, she couldn't break off her promise to the doctor.

"Excellent." He gave her a double thumbs up.

She longingly watched Chad walk out into the parking lot.

Abigail Stern linked arms with Charlie. "Let's go have some fun, shall we?"

Charlie plastered on a smile and decided to make the best of it. If nothing else, she could build up a rapport with someone important to her career, and that was worth it...wasn't it?

CHAPTER 17

DR. ABIGAIL STERN drove a late model BMW X3. As they headed down 395 south across the Potomac toward Fairfax, the interior of the luxury SUV remained whisper quiet. Charlie stroked the soft brown leather seats absentmindedly. Quite a difference from the variety of low-end used vehicles she'd driven since high school.

"Do you and your brother get along?" Dr. Stern asked.

"We're pretty close." A twin, even a fraternal one, had a relationship difficult to describe to outsiders. "My mom claims we had a secret language when we were little."

Dr. Stern turned on her blinker and expertly changed lanes to miss a traffic slowdown. "Fascinating."

"Honestly, I think we were toddlers babbling nonsense. I don't remember any of it." The memory of a proud mother exclaiming her children's brilliance to another mother at a school event flashed in her mind. "But I do enjoy languages, so who knows?"

"Both you and your brother ended up in the military, how did that come about?"

Charlie let out a breath, glanced out the window at the jam of cars, and carefully answered, "My dad is in the Navy, too. Sort of a family tradition, I guess." Her stomach tightened. Why did she feel irritable every time the topic of her father came up?

"The Navy sent you to school to learn linguistics?" the doctor asked.

"No." If only Dr. Stern knew how much she'd tried to avoid a military career. "I had other plans before I joined the Navy."

"I see. That's not uncommon." She applied the brake, checked her mirrors, and maneuvered around an old panel van that refused to keep up with the flow of cars on the highway. "Some of us take time to find what our gifts are and how best to use them."

Charlie nodded. But the way her current job lined up perfectly with her deep interest in the manuscript, she believed more in fate than choices made. "How did you end up on the team?"

"Commander Orr and I go back a ways."

"Oh?" The more she learned about NCIS-A, the more surprises she uncovered.

"We've both had an interest in astrobiology. We met at a Department of Defense conference years ago in Las Vegas. I was a guest speaker in a symposium about Unidentified Objects and the possibility of life in outer space. David—Commander Orr—introduced himself afterwards. His father had been involved in some sort of project." She tapped her fingers on the steering wheel. "What was it called? I can't remember now. He was quite vague, considering we were in an open forum."

Charlie understood the need for secrecy. "His father was also military?"

"Yes, some higher up muckety-muck. He was killed in a military exercise out in the desert just as David was graduating from the Naval Academy. A real tragedy."

"How awful." Charlie's perspective of her new boss changed with that piece of information. As much as she and her father clashed, she couldn't imagine him no longer in her life.

"I had a feeling his deep connection to alien theory was related to his father's unexpected passing. He asked me all kinds of questions about remnants of meteorites and some reports about alien bacteria found by the astronauts on the International Space Station. We had a very pleasant lunch, and I gave him my card. Who knew years later, he would contact me about joining his team?"

"The commander seems to be able to track down almost anyone."

Abigail Stern laughed. "True." She took the turn off to 495 at Springfield and changed topics. "Thanks again for agreeing to come with me. It really means a lot to my cousin."

"Of course." Charlie listed things in her mind she'd rather be doing on a Saturday night: streaming a movie, doing laundry, polishing her shoes. "I'm sure it will be fun." Did she sound convincing?

"Joyce divorced a few years ago and had to start over. She'd been a stay-at-home mom for a long time. Hadn't worked since before her kids. She was an art teacher and always thought she'd go back to it, but never did."

"I'm sorry to hear that."

"About the divorce?" the doctor asked. "She couldn't be happier, really. She plowed her half of their home equity into the paint-and-sip and has loved every second of it."

"Well, I hope she's good at teaching. I'm hopeless when it comes to artistic talents."

"You've seen the paintings in my lab, right?" Dr. Stern burst into laughter.

Charlie couldn't help but join in. "I didn't want to be insulting—"

The response drove the middle-aged woman to snort in between laughs. "Honey, it'd be very hard to insult me. Trust me, you're in good hands with Joyce."

———

Fifteen minutes later, the two women pulled up in front of a well-lit two-story building with apartments for rent above and businesses below. A sign above one of the storefronts read "Some Enchanted Painting."

Cute.

Dr. Stern completed a perfect parallel parking job, clapped her hands together and said, "Let's order that first glass, shall we? I think I owe you."

Any signs of a serious scientist had disappeared on the drive from DC to Fairfax. Who knew Charlie could have such a lovely night out with a colleague? "I think I'll have a shiraz."

"Excellent choice. I'm more of a white wine drinker myself."

They entered the studio together and were the first to arrive.

A tall, elegant woman with a gorgeous riot of black curly hair and wearing a paint-splattered white smock greeted them with a smile. "Abby, you made it." She enveloped her cousin in a hug. "And you brought a friend." She touched Charlie on the shoulder and squeezed. "I'm Joyce. Welcome. I reserved Abby's favorite spot in the back."

"This is Charlie Cutter. She's a new co-worker."

"How nice." Joyce led them to the last row of tables, which stood closest to the floor-to-ceiling window that faced the sidewalk. "You can put your things here and then we can chat over a glass while we wait for the rest of the students."

Charlie set her red purse next to a table-sized easel that held an empty canvas. Two brushes, a cup of water, a blank palette, and a few paper towels lay on the table in front of the easel.

The three women made their way to the back of the studio. Dozens of paintings lined the walls from waist-high to the ceiling —animals, landscapes, fantasy worlds, farms, city views.

Charlie recognized a few that she'd seen in Dr. Stern's lab. "Where do you come up with all of your ideas? This is amazing."

Joyce slipped behind the small bar in one corner and set three glasses on the counter. "Some I come up with on my own. Others are ideas I find on the internet." She shrugged. "I know Abby wants a white. What's your preference, Charlie?"

"A shiraz?" Charlie scanned the bottles lining the wall on a cabinet behind Joyce.

"Absolutely." Joyce picked up a bottle and poured. "This one's from Australia."

The door jingled.

"I'll be right with you," Joyce greeted the newly arrived students and finished filling Charlie's glass. "Guess we'll have to have that chat later. Excuse me."

Joyce headed to the front of the studio to engage with her customers.

Dr. Stern turned to take a gander at who would be in their class for the evening. "Well, this is a surprise." She nudged Charlie. "Angel, when did he become interested in art?"

Charlie choked on her first sip of wine. It couldn't be.

Angel Demarco ushered a beautiful brunette into the studio. When he caught sight of Charlie, his smile wavered. "Cutter?"

Joyce raised a brow, "You all know each other?"

Dr. Stern stepped forward and reached out a hand, "Angel is also part of our team, but I don't believe I've met you, miss—?"

Demarco's date accepted the hand shake. "You can call me Clarissa." She spoke with a honeyed Southern accent and wore a slinky blue dress more suited to a nightclub than a painting class.

"Wonderful. I'm Abigail, and this is Charlie." The doctor grabbed Charlie by the elbow and drew her forward.

The shiraz in her glass threatened to slosh over the rim. "Hello." She waved and knew her smile probably appeared fake because it felt fake.

Demarco's mouth turned down. "I didn't realize you would be here."

"And I'm surprised to see you here," said the doctor. "You'd made it clear a while ago that my art didn't interest you."

Did he turn red? His ears certainly did.

"Angel told me he couldn't wait for our date and said he was going to take me some place special," Clarissa gushed and clutched his bicep. "I wasn't quite expecting this." She gestured at the art-strewn walls. "I don't think he knew how much I've always wanted to do one of these silly little classes."

Joyce's eyes widened at the slight. "Let me show you where you'll be sitting. My assistant will be here in a minute to serve you your drinks." With incredible grace, Joyce showed her customers to their seats.

Dr. Stern excused herself to use the ladies' room.

Clarissa claimed a seat in the front row near the middle. Joyce handed her a utilitarian smock, and the elegantly dressed woman appeared at a loss.

As Joyce helped her don the smock to protect her clothing, Demarco took the opportunity to speak to Charlie. "What are you doing here?"

"Dr. Stern invited me." Charlie took a sip of her wine. "What are you doing here?" she lobbed back at him. Why did Clarissa's appearance annoy her so?

His mouth set in a line. "Excuse me, but I'd like to go back to my date." He left Charlie standing in the aisle.

Although he'd avoided answering her question, she had an inkling why Demarco might've shown up, and her name was Abigail Stern. He'd do almost anything to win her over. The thought of it made her hold back a laugh. He had no interest in painting. Dr. Stern knew it, and now he was stuck here with his date for the next two hours.

Dr, Stern retrieved her wine glass from the bar and rejoined Charlie. "We might as well take our seats. Class is going to start in a little bit. Not sure how many other students are signed up, but yesterday I'd only seen two registered, and I guess we know who made that reservation."

Charlie snickered.

Dr. Stern shook her head. "He's been acting this way ever since the screw up last year."

"The lost evidence?"

They took their seats at the back of the classroom.

"Yes. He'd only been with the team for a few months, and we had no security procedures in place for our specific circumstances." Dr. Stern tied on her smock. "He still thinks I blame him for the loss."

"Do you?"

The door opened, interrupting their conversation.

"Welcome," Joyce said, greeting the next couple who entered. "I'm Joyce, and I'll be your teacher this evening."

———

An hour into the class, Charlie admitted defeat. "I give up." Why did her owl look more like a chicken? She didn't have a light touch for the finer details or maybe the second glass of shiraz had something to do with it.

"It's not so bad." The doctor, who Charlie had gotten more comfortable calling Abigail, consoled her. "I'll have to show you some of my first paintings. Atrocious." She switched her gaze to Demarco and his date. "I think Angel created a crime scene on his canvas."

Charlie held back a laugh. "Think he'll hang it in the office?"

"I'll bet you a dollar he doesn't."

"That's a bet I won't take." It was easier to make jokes about Demarco then to deal with her feelings. Every time he leaned his head toward Clarissa or touched her arm or her leg, an uncomfortable burn built in her chest.

As Joyce moved to the next step in the instructions, the two women dabbed and daubed, attempting to recreate the example.

At the exact same moment, two cell phones in the studio chimed.

Charlie thrust her hand into her purse.

Demarco pulled his flip phone out of his pants pocket.

She read the text that popped up in their encrypted messaging app.

ALERT: Radar signature detected. Coordinates
to follow.

Her pulse quickened. Another pod.

"Abigail, I'm so sorry, but I have to go." She untied the smock and then touched the Uber app on her phone.

"Come on, Cutter. Let's go." Demarco already stood by the door. "I can give you a ride."

His date, in shock, sat frozen with her mouth open and a paintbrush in her hand.

CHAPTER 18

"THE COORDINATES ARE COMING IN." Charlie gripped her new iPhone and stared at the three dots in the text chat.

"Doesn't make much of a difference. We need to get back to HQ." Demarco turned onto the 495 on-ramp headed his vintage Landcruiser back to DC. "Hope you put your go-bag together. Mine's in the trunk."

Her thoughts fluttered to her cramped motel room and the pile of new clothes stacked on her bed. "It'll take me five minutes. I swear."

"That's what every woman says," he mumbled.

"Hold on. They sent a pin." She pressed on the link in the message. "I'd at least like to know if I need to grab my passport."

"You don't keep it in that red monstrosity?" He gestured at the purse in her lap. "You could fit a small horse in there."

The map appeared.

What were the odds?

"We don't need to go to the meet-up location." Her nerve endings tingled.

"What are you talking about?" As they approached a highway sign, he pointed. "This is our exit. 395."

"The pod. It landed not too far from us." She expanded her map with her two fingers. "Near Colchester. In the Occoquan River."

"Shit." Instantly, his demeanor changed. "I need to take you back to Dr. Stern."

"What?" Her mouth dropped open. "A pod is about to land. Are you crazy?"

They neared the exit.

"I'm the security expert. It's too dangerous for you."

How dare he imply she couldn't handle the risks involved with her job.

"Screw that." She held up the map so he could see the pin location. "Switch lanes." She pointed at his last opportunity to merge onto the correct exit ramp heading south.

The special agent glanced at the map. "Dammit, Cutter."

He poured on the gas, and the 1970s gas guzzler picked up speed. The Prius next to him in the correct exit lane refused to move. Laying on the horn, Demarco sped up. An opportunity to squeeze in front of the electric vehicle was closing quickly. The separate exit lanes split in fifty yards. Orange barrels filled the triangle between them.

"You have to move over." Charlie checked over her shoulder. "Maybe if you slow down—"

"I'm not fucking slowing down."

The engine throttled. He leaned forward. The Prius matched him in speed. He met the gaze of the young woman driver with short green hair and a pair of purple-rimmed glasses.

"If you don't slow down, we're going to crash." Charlie braced herself. Would the seatbelts in this old thing work?

The lanes split. They rushed toward the orange barrels.

Charlie held her breath.

Demarco milked a little more speed out of the Landcruiser. He turned the wheel and slid the vehicle right between the surprised Prius owner and the oblivious Ford Focus ahead.

"Hell yes!" He slammed his hand on the dash. "I knew this baby wouldn't let me down."

Her nerves jangled. She hid her trembling, empty hand under her thigh and tightly clenched her phone with the other. "Can we please reach the coordinates in one piece?"

He breathed heavily for a few seconds. "If I let you come with me—"

"If? What are you going to do? Drop me off on a dark street corner and hope an Uber finds me before I get mugged?" He was unbelievable. "We're part of a team. I can't believe you are even suggesting such a thing."

He gripped the steering wheel more tightly. "I swear, Cutter, sometimes you make me want to throttle you."

"Why? Because I question your decisions? Demand to be treated with respect?"

"I'm only trying to keep you safe," he spat out.

"Safe from what? The aliens? The pods?" If they weren't traveling seventy miles an hour down the highway, she'd slap him. "I'm here because Commander Orr wanted me on the team. He thought I could handle it—why don't you?"

Demarco's phone rang and cut through the tension. "Hey, Commander Orr. I'm about—" He snapped his fingers to get her attention and pointed at her phone.

Unbelievable.

She held up the map.

He smiled. "—thirty minutes out from the location. Meet you there."

He snapped the phone shut.

Her annoyance boiled over. "You will not be dropping me off anywhere."

"Fine." He kept his eyes on the road.

"Good."

"But you will follow orders."

"I'm not your subordinate."

He talked over her protest, "Until I can ensure the site is secure."

She crossed her arms. "Let's just get there."

The sun had set, and the only view she had was the headlights from the opposite lane.

"That's what I'm trying to do," he said.

"And I'm trying to do my job, too."

He sighed. "Let's meet in the middle, jettison the feelings, and be professional."

"That's all I ever wanted." Maybe one of these days he'd overcome whatever problem he had with her. Would he treat Stormy like this?

He let a few beats pass. "Think the doc will drive Clarissa home?"

An image of the attractive brunette popped into her head. "Why wouldn't she?"

"I don't know." He ran a hand through his short hair. "That woman hates me."

"Dr. Stern doesn't hate you."

"You only met her a few days ago," he said changing lanes to follow the faster traffic. "How would you know?"

"She's been nothing but kind to me."

"Exactly." He emphasized his declaration with a pointed finger. "I knew she'd like you."

"Why do you say that?" She studied the map.

He glanced at her quickly before directing his gaze at the highway. "You're smart, driven, educated."

Her cheeks heated at his description.

"You're a lot like her."

How did he expect her to respond? One minute he found her irritating, the next minute he tossed out compliments.

He sighed. "What exit am I looking for?"

"One sixty one." She followed the route further south. "Then we'll be on Route 1. We need to find Frenchman's Point, where the river feeds into Belmont Bay."

"Deeper water?"

"Could be."

Deeper water meant the pod could disintegrate within minutes, and all opportunities to collect samples—or encounter a passenger—would be lost.

"Does this thing go any faster?" She glanced at his speedometer.

Demarco pressed the gas pedal to the floor. "We're going to find out."

———

The streets had narrowed quickly after they'd left the main road. Modest homes on several acres dotted the area. Demarco slowed the Landcruiser to a crawl. "Are you sure we're going the right way?"

"Turn here. Bell Avenue. It goes right to the water."

After he made the turn, the woods surrounded them on all sides. Not a house in sight.

"Maybe that's why no one called anything in," Charlie said.

She'd been texting with the group and giving them regular updates on their location to the object. Stormy, camping near Deep Creek Lake with her family for the weekend, had been given the task of monitoring the news and social media sites for any unusual reports. So far, so good. It would take her two hours longer than everyone else to reach the location of the pod.

"Dead end." Demarco parked on the shoulder.

Only a single large mansion sat at the end of the road. The place appeared abandoned. No lights. No vehicles in the long semi-circular driveway.

She opened the passenger door. "Summer home?" The dead silence chilled her.

"Maybe." Demarco climbed out and opened the trunk.

A warm wind blew through the trees, and branches rubbed together. Charlie shook off an unsettling feeling.

"Cutter, get back in the rig." He closed the lid of trunk and tucked a gun in his waistband.

She stepped back. "Whoa, is that necessary?"

"Security, remember?" He opened the passenger side door for her. "You stay here. I'm going to do a perimeter check."

The last time she held a gun, she'd been in Boot Camp and a bundle of nerves. "I don't like this."

"Didn't we agree to meet in the middle?" he reminded her. "I'm going first. Once I make sure everything is safe, I'll give you a signal."

"What kind of signal?" Reluctantly, she reclaimed her seat inside the Toyota.

"Three flashes." He showed her using the Maglite he held. "Like this."

Demarco headed toward the driveway. "Don't move until I give the signal."

Charlie sank in her seat. The special agent crept toward the house and the blackness beyond. Her stomach didn't appreciate the stress as it flip-flopped with every twitch of a branch, every unidentified shadow.

———

Five long minutes later, no signal from Demarco. The hair rose on the back of her neck. Where was he? Did she miss his signal?

She scanned from the house to her left all the way across the side yard to her right, which led to the Occoquan River. Although it was a clear night, the moon hadn't yet risen in the sky. A few lights across the river winked on—other large mansions who shared the same stretch of water.

Then, in the opposite direction Demarco had headed, Charlie spied a strange green glow in the middle of the river. The weird light drew her gaze, and she fixated on the spot. Did any of the pod reports indicate a light had been seen?

As her eyes grew accustomed to the dark, the green glow revealed the curve of a sphere, half-sunk in the deep water between the mansion at the end of Bell Avenue and the lighted mansion on the opposite shore.

The pod!

It could slip beneath the water at any moment.

She burst out of the vehicle and headed toward the shore. Stupid Demarco and his 'security' crap might very well leave an alien being to drown. Why in the hell did he think a gun was necessary?

The mansion had been built on a rocky, unforgiving stretch of beach. A deck ran the length of the back of the house with a wide set of steps that led to a rather ugly water line. A rotting dock about twenty feet in length slumped in the Occoquan River— perhaps a leftover from the house that stood here before the mansion had been built.

To the east of the rotting dock a series of brand new posts had been embedded in the river bottom. A floating crane was tied up next to them. In a few days a brand new dock would be in place. Maybe the mansion wasn't empty after all.

Charlie glanced over her shoulder to ensure none of the lights were on inside the large home and to make one last attempt to spy Demarco. Where the hell was he?

Well beyond the rotting dock and the brand new posts, the eerie glow lit up the dark water at the mouth of the bay. It emanated from a single spot and flickered as the water sloshed against the now visible soft green exterior.

Charlie kicked off her running shoes.

No way was an alien going to die on her watch. Security or not.

"Hey, Cutter, what do you think you're doing?" Demarco called from the deck of the mansion.

"I'm going to swim for it," she yelled back.

She shimmied out of her jeans, and the cool evening air hit her bare legs. If he wasn't going to do anything, she would. "This might be our only chance to see who's inside. An alien species. I have to save him." She picked her way to the water.

"Wait!" His voice came from deep in his chest. "Don't!"

Warning? Or fearful?

"I can make it." She eyed the distance a second time. A few lengths of the pool at most.

"It's too dangerous. Stop!"

The greenish glow flickered.

"We don't have much time," she whispered.

Before Demarco could stop her, she walked into the river up to her waist. Ahead, in the dark, the flickering glow called to her. Inside, she imagined a foreign creature, perhaps millions of lightyears away from its home, struggling to survive.

With strong strokes she swam toward the pod. Distantly, she could hear Demarco yelling something at her. His words were lost to the breeze and the sound of the water lapping against her body. As her legs kicked and her arms fell into a rhythm, her mind turned to the pages of the Voynich manuscript, the strange writing, the formula to build a pod, and the many questions she had for this traveler.

Her fingers touched a softness. Abruptly, she lifted her face from the water. An eight-foot-wide pod bobbed in the river, its hull gooey and with a dent in its top. The glow grew fainter. How much time did she have left before it sank beneath the surface?

She paddled around the object searching for a way in. A door. A hatch. Even a crack. She encountered nothing but green mushy smoothness.

From within she heard a muffled cry. A long sad wail.

It tore at her heart.

An alien arrived to earth only to choke to death in foreign waters.

"Hello?" she called out. "I'm here. How do I get in?" Although she knew the alien couldn't possibly understand her words, she wanted the creature to know he wasn't alone.

The crying stopped.

"Mama?" a little voice said.

Slowly, a hatched opened. Water rushed in.

Charlie swam toward it, unafraid at what she might encounter. Driven by pity and an odd lightness of being, she reached the hatch.

A small creature, three feet in height, dressed crudely in a tunic made of a rough material stood before her. He lost his footing as the pod dipped further under the surface of the river.

"Mama," he said again. "Mama."

The creature leapt into the water and clung to her. Unable to paddle with both arms, Charlie fought to keep her head above water with a forceful tread of her legs.

And it was then Charlie realized she had not rescued an alien being. She'd rescued a little boy.

Continued in Decryption...

THE **GENESIS MACHINE**

DECRYPTION

BOOK TWO

K. J. GILLENWATER

CHAPTER 1

1498. Val Camonica, Northern Italy.

RISA SQUEEZED her son's hand. Crouching in the bushes on the edge of the woods in the dark would frighten any little boy. Being chased by a fearful mob multiplied that feeling times ten, times one hundred.

One times ten is ten.

Two times ten is twenty.

Three times ten is thirty.

Her mind latched on to the things that comforted her: numbers, logic, science.

Things a woman shouldn't know.

Things a woman could be killed for.

Things that not only she could be killed for, but her child. Her innocent child. It was as if an invisible hand squeezed her heart.

She could not lose her son to this mob of witch hunters.

Voices shouted nearby. Lantern light shot through the dark. Dozens of lanterns.

They'd never make it.

How much further to go?

As she pushed through the shrubs, she dragged her exhausted child with her.

"Mama," he wailed.

She clamped a hand over his mouth. "*Tranquillo*, little one." She knelt on the soft grass and gathered him in her arms. "We are almost there. I need you to be very brave for me. Can you do that?"

The boy nodded and clutched her tightly around the neck. "*Ho paura*, Mama."

She whispered into his blond hair, "I know, *caro*." She stood and held his hand tightly. "Come, we're almost there, and then we'll be safe. I promise. *Promesso*."

But she didn't know if her promise would come to fruition. She'd only finished crafting the machines in the last few days. The first one had been an abject failure. It had turned into a pile of green mush within moments. The formula was not quite the same as she'd remembered.

Her experiments had caught the notice of the wrong people. Not the friendly nuns who'd taken her in—a lost, pregnant woman with no husband. But the religious fanatics who increasingly feared the dark arts and blamed innocent women as the perpetrators. In the last year, their fears reached a fever pitch, and focus turned toward the *donna strana* at the nunnery.

Who was she? Where had she come from? Why did she speak a foreign tongue? Why was she seen late at night in the woods near the river? Was her child a child of the devil?

Although the nuns had welcomed her into their community years ago, they'd questioned her strange clothing and mysterious arrival. But when they'd learned of her ability to read and write, they'd found her quite useful. So despite the suspicions of those outside the cloister, they had given her very much needed sanctuary. For within her mind resided the secret to returning to her life and the father of her child.

"*Lei è andata così!*" one of her accusers bellowed.

They were mere steps behind her and her son. The pounding of her heart filled her ears until she could hear nothing else. Branches scratched at her face and tore at her rough woolen dress and the kirtle underneath.

Ahead, she saw the machines lurking in a copse of trees, blending in with their green leaves. She dropped her son's hand, leaving him in a marshy meadow dotted with moonlight, and raced toward them. In the soft hull she pressed a hidden button to expose a hatch.

"Come, *caro*, come. You must get inside." Risa beckoned her child forward.

The rumble of the mob crashing through the woods made her breath hitch in her throat. She'd seen what they'd done to others accused of being witches: torture, burning, horrible things. But a child? What would they do to an innocent child? The horror was too much for her mind.

"*Non voglio*," he said, planting his feet. "No."

There was no time to waste. No time to cajole. Her voice grew sharp, and she hated herself for it. "Inside. *Ora!*" She grabbed him by the arm and dragged him into the machine.

He was afraid of the dark, and the machine appeared to be a black hole.

"No, Mama! No!" Her son fought against her.

"Sit." She shoved him into the single seat inside the machine and strapped him in. The soft flexible safety harness melded with it as if it had always been a part of it.

"Mama!" The boy cried and struggled in the tight restraint.

She wished she'd had time to explain to him what was happening, where he was going, and why. Risa thought she would have had more time. In fact, she wasn't even sure the machines would function properly. The original machine she'd arrived in had failed miserably. She was so off course and had no idea why. A fault of design? A bad program?

"*Eccola!*" the mob entered into the meadow. "*E anche il suo bambino diavolo!*"

"Lord help us," she whispered. She'd never let them take her son. Never.

She fiddled with the controls and set it as best she could remember. It had been years since she'd been inside a machine. Would Byron be on the other side waiting for his son? Would someone make sure he was reunited with his father?

No time to waste. She had no choice. She entered the last of the data.

"I will see you there, my son. Do not fear." She touched his tear-stained cheek and then kissed him on the forehead. "*Ti amo figlio mio.*"

Rough hands pulled her out of the machine.

The boy cried and struggled in the seat. "Mama!"

"My son!" she cried. These animals might kill her, but they would not touch her child.

She raged against the arms that held her. Stinking, dirty, soulless humans. The same kind of men who'd destroyed her world. The same kind of men who'd forced her to flee for her life and her child's life once before. She screamed and bit at her captors' hands. Flailing like a wild cat, she broke free and lunged for the shell of the machine. The meat of her palm pressed the hidden button a second time.

As the hatch closed, a wave of relief filled her. He would be safe. No matter what happened to her, he would be safe.

A heavy object landed with a crack on her skull. Warm blood poured out and ran down her face. It was too late. The other machine would remain unused and disintegrate in the next heavy downpour. But as she lost consciousness and fell into the arms of the men who surrounded her, she smiled as the machine began to spin and spin and spin. Faster and faster until it turned into a blur of motion and green.

"My son," she whispered one last time.

The machine disappeared, and the men fell back in fear.

CHAPTER 2

THE CHILD CLUNG so tightly to her neck, Charlie thought she might go under. Although she didn't want to frighten the poor thing even more, she plunged underwater. The shock of the action forced the child to release his grip.

She surfaced, sputtering. Then she scooped under the dark water, found the boy, and hauled him up. After snaking an arm across his chest, she snugged him to her side.

"You're going to be all right." Did the boy even understand her? Where did he come from? Why was he in the pod all alone? "I've got you."

With a strong side stroke, Charlie towed the child back to shore. After the dunking he received, he calmed down and laid limply in the water—too scared or too tired to fight her.

The pod's green glow flickered out as it sank further into the river. The open hatch sped up the process. As her feet hit the bottom near the shoreline, the final curve of the pod disappeared into the black water. Any opportunity to study it was lost to the river and the dark.

"Cutter!" Demarco rushed toward her, gun in hand. "Are you all right?"

She emerged from the water with the small child on her hip. Her legs trembled, and her whole body shivered. "Didn't think the water would be so cold."

The special agent reeled back at the sight of the boy. His forehead wrinkled. "Who's that?"

"Put that away." She pointed at the gun. "You're scaring him."

The boy's rounded eyes reminded her of the Starry Night Owl painting she'd abandoned in Fairfax.

"I don't understand." Demarco's shoulders slumped. He looked out over the river. "I saw you swim to the pod...and then...but how—?"

Charlie reached his position on the shore. "This little guy was inside the pod all by himself." The boy hid his face in her neck, and a maternal feeling awoke inside her. She wrapped an arm across his thin back in an act of comfort. "I hope the commander shows up soon. What the hell is going on here?"

"It can't be." Demarco's mouth slackened, and he backed away. "It's impossible. I don't understand."

"Where are you going? This boy needs our help." How could Demarco fail to help a little boy so clearly in distress? "Do you have a blanket in your car? We're freezing."

Her scolding snapped him out of it. "Yes, wait, I think I do. Stay there. I'll be right back."

He trotted toward the parked vehicle.

"*Dov'è mia madre?*" asked the child in a whisper.

Without even thinking, Charlie replied, "*Non lo so, ma la troveremo.*" She hugged him tight. "We will find your mother, I promise."

She found a weathered Adirondack chair and huddled with the boy in her lap. His tunic felt rough under her fingers and appeared to be hand sewn. He had deep brown eyes and a thin face, which made him appear malnourished. As they rested there, she combed her fingers through his long locks in a soothing gesture.

"Looks like you made a new friend, Petty Officer." Commander Orr arrived and handed her a silver emergency blanket.

"Am I happy to see you, sir. Thank you." She wrapped the boy in it and set him in the chair. "*Aspetta qui.*"

"No!" The child reached for her.

She disentangled her arm from his grasp. "I left my clothes over there, sir." The sleeveless blouse she'd chosen to wear provided little cover, and now that she'd recovered some from the shock of what had happened, she wanted to be a little more presentable before the rest of the team arrived.

The commander nodded. "Go ahead. I can take care of the little tyke." He kept his gaze on the child and ignored her state of undress.

"Let me grab your clothes," Demarco offered. "Here, you can put this on." He handed her a plaid shirt. "From my go-bag."

The wind picked up and blew against her naked legs. "Thank you." She slipped into the shirt, which covered her to mid-thigh.

"So Demarco told me the boy was inside the pod? Is that correct?" The commander tucked the blanket around the child who seemed fascinated by its shiny, silver exterior.

"I saw the pod in the river and swam out to it. I thought if it had just landed there could be a chance a live alien might be inside." She relived the moment the boy had appeared in the open hatch. "Instead, it was him." She rubbed her temples. "I don't understand, sir. I thought we were seeking aliens and alien tech. But he's no alien. He's a human boy."

"I'm trying to wrap my mind around it, too, Petty Officer," said the commander. "Everything we've learned so far led us to believe these were unidentified objects—things not of this world. The samples we've collected, the writing—"

"Here." Demarco returned with her shoes and jeans. His demeanor had cooled.

"Thanks." She quickly donned her pants and slipped on her shoes.

The boy, fascinated, watched her dress.

"You said something to him earlier...what language was that?" Demarco asked.

"When you went to your car he asked me, *'Dov'è mia madre.'* It's Italian for 'Where's my mother.'"

"You know Russian and Italian?" Commander Orr asked.

"I was a linguistics major, so I learned a little bit of everything, really."

The commander put his hands on his hips. "So what is an Italian boy doing in an alien pod in the middle of the Occoquan River?"

———

"The pod. It's gone," Lieutenant Kellerman said as he approached the rest of the team unaware of the passenger they tended to. "Dammit. I thought this time we'd collect some really good samples."

"We found something better than the pod," Charlie said, kneeling next to the boy. She ruffled his drying hair. "This little bugger."

Orr had found a small tin of mints in his pocket and had handed it to the child, who liked to slide the box open and closed more than he liked the mints inside. He leaned his head against Charlie's leg as she stood next to the chair.

Kellerman stopped dead in his tracks. "Someone going to explain what's going on?"

"I'd love to hear the story, too," Chief Ricard said, the next of the team to arrive. "I left my wife stranded at the movies. She practically smacked me when I told her I had to leave. I don't see a pod." He threw up his hands. "Shit. Was it a false alarm?"

Demarco paced on the rocky shore.

Why did he seem so aggravated? The discovery of the boy opened up a whole new track of exploration.

"Petty Officer Cutter, can you please tell everyone what happened? Then we can decide what our next steps should be. Theories. Ideas. I'll take any of it."

"Theories?" Cole Kellerman raised a brow. "What happened?"

"When Demarco and I arrived—"

"Wait," interrupted Ricard, "you and Demarco came together?" He shifted his gaze from Charlie to the special agent. "I think I'd rather hear that story first."

"Chief, that's a most inappropriate comment," Orr scolded. "Please, Petty Officer, continue."

Great. The last thing she needed was gossip going around the office about her and Demarco. Ugh. "As I was saying, we reached the end of the road, and I could see a pod glowing in the distance. Quite deep in the water at the mouth of the bay." She pointed in the direction of the pod location. "So I swam for it."

"Wow." Kellerman's eyes widened and his mouth went slack.

"She's a hot dog in the pool," the commander added. "Saw it for myself."

Charlie cleared her throat. "Anyway, I swam out there thinking an alien could be inside and might need help. A hatch opened and out he came." She knelt beside the boy.

The child pulled his attention away from the tin of mints and smiled at her. *"Grazie, signora."*

"Wait a second." The chief gave his head a shake. "You're telling me this kid—" He pointed at the little boy dwarfed by the large chair. "—came out of a pod?"

For a few beats no one spoke.

He walked over to the commander. "You've got to be shitting me if you believe this story, sir."

Charlie stood. "Hey, are you calling me a liar?" She crossed to the two men. "That boy was inside the pod. Whatever we are dealing with here, it's not aliens. That's what I know. He's a human boy inside a pod. Whoever told you that these things were from outer space is wrong. Dead wrong. The whole thing didn't make a lot of sense to me from the beginning, but I was brought on the team to do a job."

Chief Ricard met her with equal emotion. "So you're telling me this whole time you knew it wasn't aliens, but never said anything? You've been with A Group for a week, and now you think you have all the answers." He stepped between her and Orr to block the commander's view of Cutter. "She's lying to you, sir. I don't know what her angle is, but she's lying. We've been on this shit since last year, and some of the data we have defies explanation. This has to be alien tech...maybe she wants some sort of attention or something. I don't get it. But I don't believe one word of it."

Kellerman approached and stood abreast of Charlie. "I believe her." He gave her a reassuring smile.

"Thanks, Cole."

"Does it really matter if you believe her or not, Chief?" Kellerman said. "The pod sank. There's nothing to collect. All we have is Petty Officer Cutter's story and a child with no parents. Shouldn't we at least give Dr. Stern a call and ask her to meet us at the office? The boy is the only evidence we have to test."

Charlie felt a tug on her pants. She looked down, and the boy had left the chair. The emergency blanket twisted around his small body. "*Signora?*"

Charlie threw a harsh gaze at the scowling chief and knelt so she would be at the boy's eye level. "*Sí?*"

"Where's Mama?" he said in perfect unaccented English.

Commander Orr jerked his head back. "Yes, I'll give Dr. Stern a call." He pulled out his cell. "Maybe she'll know what we're dealing with here." He stared mystified at the bilingual boy who'd landed in their care and then wandered away from the group to talk to the doctor.

"Did he just speak in English?" Demarco rejoined the group.

Guess he'd played out his temper tantrum by the river and came back to his senses. Would've been nice if he'd backed up her story instead of letting the chief beat her up.

"Yes, he did." Charlie hugged the thin child to her side.

Chief Ricard followed Orr. After implying some kind of unseemly relationship between Demarco and Charlie, he clearly was avoiding a confrontation with the special agent. Plus, he seemed to have no interest in the child.

The mysterious boy gave her a shy smile. "You are pretty. *Carina.* Like Mama." He touched her hair with his tiny fingers.

Her heart warmed, and she couldn't help but grab his little hand in hers and kiss the back of it. "Thank you."

The boy laughed and quickly tucked his hand inside the emergency blanket, as if she'd tickled him.

"What's your name? My name is Charlie." She touched her chest with her palm.

"Armas," he said, pounding his little chest in response. "*Mi chiamo Armas.*"

Demarco noticeably stiffened.

Odd.

"Very pleased to meet you, Armas," Kellerman said, leaning down to shake the boy's hand in a very formal fashion. "My name is Cole."

Armas laughed and did a little dance as he shook the lieutenant's hand in an exaggerated fashion.

"We need to find his parents," Demarco said, his expression unreadable.

"Don't tell me you think I'm lying, too." What a bastard. He'd witnessed practically the whole rescue, and instead of supporting her story, he wanted to agree with Chief Ricard's view?

"Until Dr. Stern can examine him and do some tests, I think we can agree we have no idea where this boy came from or who he belongs to."

Kellerman let out a snort. "You're just as bad as the chief. We all know a pod landed here. We have the radar signal to prove it. Did you see a pod or didn't you?"

"I did," admitted Demarco.

Kellerman took a step toward the special agent. "Did you see her swim out there and come back with the boy?"

"Yes, I saw her swim out and then return with the child in her arms." He let out a sigh. "Against my orders, by the way."

Charlie scooped up Armas and held him close. He looped an arm around her neck as if he'd done it a million times before. "Why don't you ask Armas where he came from? Wouldn't that settle it for you?"

Demarco crossed his arms. "He's maybe four years old. He probably can't even tell us what cartoon he watched this morning."

How infuriating that Mr. Security himself couldn't admit what he saw with his own eyes. Armas had come out of the pod.

"Team!" Commander Orr interrupted the dispute. "Dr. Stern will meet us at our office with the necessary equipment for the tests she wants to run. Can someone please get in touch with Stormy and let her know the change of plans?"

Kellerman tapped on his phone. "On it, sir."

Chief already was heading to his vehicle in the cul-de-sac.

Thank God she didn't have to hear his blathering anymore. Dr. Stern would prove to him the truth of her story.

"Agent Demarco, you and Petty Officer Cutter take the boy with you." He smiled at Armas. "He seems to have taken a shine to our newest team member."

Drive back with Demarco? Crap. "Sir, couldn't I go with Kellerman?"

The special agent tilted his chin down and frowned.

"Why, do you have a problem with Demarco?" His placed his hands on his hips.

That had been a mistake.

"No, sir," she said. "That's fine with me. No problem at all."

Orr turned to the special agent. "And you?"

"No problem, sir."

"Perfect. We're on the same page then. See you at HQ." The commander turned on his heel and crunched down the gravel path to his vehicle.

"You trying to get me in trouble?" Demarco said in a harsh whisper.

"You did it to yourself," Charlie said as she headed toward the Landcruiser. She adjusted the young boy on her hip. "Armas, let's find out where you came from. How does that sound? *Buona idea?*"

"*Si,*" Armas said.

Demarco jogged to catch up to the two of them. "You are being unreasonable."

"Am I?" Charlie focused her attention on the road ahead.

"We don't know a thing about this boy."

"Armas. His name is Armas."

"Armas!" The boy clapped his hands together.

The special agent let out a sigh. "I know his name."

She paused at the top of the rise near the curb and faced him. "I thought we had decided to work together."

"We did."

"Working together means trusting your partner." Did he already forget? "When we arrived, you made me wait in the car."

"Right. It was too dangerous—"

"We were the first people on the scene." She touched the boy's bare knee, exposed by the short tunic. "We almost lost our opportunity to save little Armas."

"What if it had been a full-grown man in that pod?" He took in her blank expression. Then he closed his eyes and pinched his nose. "I don't think I did anything wrong here. We didn't know what we were walking into."

"Second, when the chief accused me of making up a story, where were you? Pacing the beach in your own little world. You hung me out to dry." Couldn't he see how he'd undermined her back there? "Not only that, you sided with him. After witnessing the whole thing for yourself."

"I didn't see everything," he mumbled.

"You saw enough." She jutted out her hip to hold the weight of the boy more comfortably. "Look, let's go back to the office, do what we need to do, and call it a night. I'm tired."

"Excellent idea."

In silence they walked side-by-side to the Landcruiser. The rest of the crew had already left.

As they approached the vehicle, Armas gasped. "*Cos'è?*"

"What?" Demarco asked. "What did he say?"

"*Cos'è quella cosa*, Charlie?" Armas struggled in her arms. "Down, down."

She set him on the pavement. "He wants to know what that is."

"What?" Demarco asked.

Armas ran up to the Landcruiser and pounded on the bumper "*Cos'è quella cosa*, Charlie? *Cos'è quella cosa?*"

"Your car." Charlie couldn't keep the shock out of her voice.

Where did this boy come from?

CHAPTER 3

ARMAS RAN a hand along the smooth side of Demarco's Landcruiser. "Car," he said. His eyes rounded, and his little mouth formed an 'o.'

The special agent hung back, frowned, and tilted his head to one side.

Charlie approached the boy who touched every surface he could reach: the bumper, the door, the handle, the side view mirror. "Yes, it's called a car. We go places in it."

Armas paused and faced her. "Go?"

"*Andiamo.*" Charlie touched the hood of the Toyota. "*Andiamo in macchina.* We go in the car."

"*Macchina?*" He pressed his elbows into his sides and curved his shoulders inward. "*Non voglio andare in macchina.*"

"What's wrong with him?" Demarco's eyes narrowed.

"Hey, hey, it's okay." Charlie knelt and gave the trembling boy a hug. "You don't need to be scared. We'll take care of you. *Ci prenderemo cura di te.*"

Armas clung to her neck and hid his face.

"He's terrified," Charlie said, glancing at the special agent.

"Well, he's going to have to get over it." Demarco placed his hands on his hips. "This is how we take him back to the office. He needs to get in the rig."

Why did Demarco have to be so impatient? Armas had

plopped down, alone, in a pod that came from who knows where. The plummet to Earth must have been frightening to a boy so young.

"Just relax," she said to Demarco. The special agent likely scared Armas even more with his harsh tone. "I'll convince him. Give me a little bit of time, would you?"

"Fine." Demarco gave both woman and boy a wide berth as he passed in front of the vehicle and unlocked the driver's side door. "I'll give you five minutes before I make him get in."

What an emotionless jerk. No sympathy for a small child? Everything was about him all the time.

Gently, she held Armas by the shoulders and tipped up his chin. "Don't be afraid. I'll sit with you. *Mi siederò con te.* I will make sure you are safe."

His wide brown eyes shone with tears. "Charlie, you will sit with me?" He cracked a broad smile revealing a missing tooth in the bottom front row of teeth.

"Yes. I will sit right next to you." She squeezed his narrow shoulders. "I think you might like it."

Armas looked up at the Landcruiser and touched its painted exterior once more. "We go in the car."

"That's right." Charlie stood and locked eyes with Demarco who sat behind the wheel. She gave him a little nod.

"How? How do we go in the car?" Armas pushed against the side panel with all his might.

"Not like that, Armas." She caught one of his hands and pulled him away. If the boy left a dent in his classic Toyota, Demarco would kill her. "Here."

Charlie pulled the handle on the door to the back seat and opened it.

The child gasped.

She scooped him up and placed him on the black vinyl seats.

Immediately, Armas stood up in his sandy, muddy bare feet and marred the clean vinyl. "Go, car, go!"

"Sit down." Demarco turned his body half way around to growl at him.

The boy's lower lip trembled.

"It's all right, Armas. Come here." She grabbed the boy and sat him in her lap. "Let's sit down, and you can look out the window. *Finestra*."

She shot Demarco what she hoped was a look of death.

He shrugged and started the engine.

The boy trembled at the loud noise.

Charlie whispered soothing words in his ear in Italian, and his body relaxed.

By the time they'd reached the end of the cul-de-sac, Armas was excitedly pointing at random lights glowing in the yards of each house they passed.

"*La luce!*"

If Armas marveled at a car and electric lights, what would he think when they arrived in D.C.?

"*Gli uomini con le luci stanno arrivando,*" the boy whispered in her ear.

"*Gli uomini?*" she asked. "What men?"

"The men who hurt my mama. They had many lights." Armas balled up in her lap. "*Dov'è mia madre?*"

Distressed by the child's deep seated fear, Charlie soothed him by running her hand across his head. "We will find her, Armas. I promise you."

But as Demarco drove them ever closer to D.C. Charlie wondered about her promise. After what she'd seen and experienced tonight, doubts set in about being able to locate the child's parents. Little Armas seemed to be a boy with no past, no home, and no knowledge of the world he'd landed in. How very strange.

"Where is this child?" Dr. Stern asked as soon as Charlie and Demarco entered the office.

"Shh." Charlie carried the sleeping boy in her arms. He'd fallen into a deep sleep about ten minutes into their trip. Exhausted from everything probably. "He's asleep."

Stormy rushed around the cubicle walls to meet them. "The commander told us you found a child in the pod." She scanned

Armas from head to bare feet, and her face softened. "He's so young."

No surprise the young mother would have instant sympathy. The rest of the team stood back, as if Armas had a communicable disease.

Her mind raced.

Wait, what if he did? What if he brought some kind of virus or contaminant with him?

Too late for her now. She'd been exposed to anything he may have brought with him.

Dr. Stern approached on cat feet. "He really came out of the pod?" Her slender fingers stopped centimeters short of touching the boy's hair.

"Yes. Despite what some may have told you." Charlie didn't even want to look at Chief Ricard right now, but she hoped he heard her words.

"His clothes," the doctor said. "He was wearing this?"

"Yes, I'm not sure what it's made of, but it looks hand sewn."

Dr. Stern carefully fingered the hem of the garment. "Home-spun wool. Undyed." She nodded. "Primitive."

"I didn't know you knew so much about fabrics."

"In another life, I used to sew." She let go of the tunic. "When I had time."

Stormy hovered. "I think my pea coat is hanging in the closet. Maybe we can make a little bed for him in the conference room?"

Charlie nodded. Who knew a little boy could be so heavy?

"Seems cruel to wake him up just so I can poke and prod him," said Dr. Stern. "Maybe in the morning?"

"We need those samples analyzed immediately," Commander Orr said.

"I'll set up everything here." Dr. Stern sat a hard case of equipment on an empty desk.

Stormy made her way to the conference room with her pea coat retrieved from the coat closet next to the copy machine.

Demarco stood by the commander. "He had no idea what a car was, electric lights, and you should've seen him when we reached the highway."

Chief Ricard snorted. "Ridiculous. Look, you don't need me here. Until the doctor does her exam and has some results, I think my job is done." He yawned. " Nancy's pissed. I'd rather be asleep at home right now."

Orr swept an invisible fleck of lint off the sleeve of his blue Henley shirt. "Fine, Chief. Go." He checked his watch. "But I want you back here at 0800."

"On a Sunday?" Ricard blinked rapidly. "For this kid?"

"If you'd let me finish my thought, Chief Ricard, perhaps you'd understand," Orr intoned.

Chief's face turned redder than normal.

"I'd like for you to review the radar signature of this latest pod. When did it appear? How long was it tracked? From which direction? Altitude?" The commander ticked off on his fingers. "Since we don't have a pod to analyze, we use the data we have. Kellerman will help you."

"Where is Kellerman?" Ricard crossed his arms.

"He probably stopped for gas," Orr said. "So, tomorrow at 0800? I'll text the lieutenant."

"Yes, sir." Chief turned on his heel and headed to the door. "Nancy isn't going to like this," he muttered on the way past Charlie.

"Demarco," the commander said. "You can help Dr. Stern with her sample collection."

"Can't he rest for a little while?" Charlie held the sleeping boy just outside the conference room.

Orr worried his lip for a few seconds. "Fine. Thirty minutes. Then, we need to wake him."

"Okay." Charlie looked to Demarco. "Could you bring me my sweater? It's on the back on my chair. Since we don't have a blanket—"

"No problem." The special agent scooped up her sweater and brought it to her. "Here." He peered down at Armas. "All tuckered out."

From distant to concerned. Demarco made zero sense sometimes. "I can't even imagine what this little guy's been through."

As she carried him into the dark conference room where

Stormy had crafted a bed out of her coat, Demarco leaned against the door frame. "I hope tomorrow he can answer our questions, once he's settled and rested."

Charlie lay the boy on the coat and covered him with her sweater. He sighed and rolled onto his side.

As she watched the boy sleep, the evening played out in her mind. His strange arrival, his lack of knowledge about modern things, and his clothing. Somewhere in the Voynich manuscript there had to be answers. A four-year-old boy could only explain so much.

"Yes," she said. "Tomorrow."

———

"Mama!"

Stormy and Charlie rushed into the conference room. Armas had only managed to sleep for twenty minutes.

Stormy flipped on the lights.

The boy screamed.

Armas crawled under the conference table.

"The lights, turn off the lights." Maybe Chief Ricard didn't believe her and Demarco, but Armas seemed to lack knowledge of the most regular of things—like electricity and lights.

"I'm sorry." Stormy plunged the room into darkness once more. "The poor little thing had a nightmare."

Charlie got down on her hands and knees. "Your mother isn't here, baby."

The boy rubbed at his eyes. "Where's Mama?"

She sat back on her heels. "Come here, Armas." Oh, that face. So awful. How could she help him in such an impossible situation?

He crawled toward her and climbed in her lap. "Charlie, *ho paura*."

"I know you're scared, but I'm here." She turned so Armas could see Stormy's shadowed figure standing behind them. "Stormy is here. We all want to help you."

He sniffed a few times and then rested his head on her shoulder.

"Maybe I should ask Dr. Stern to come in?" Stormy asked.

Charlie nodded. "Might as well. Then we can figure out what the next steps are. He can't live in the office."

"Right." Stormy cleared her throat and played with a fine gold chain around her neck. "Let me go round up Dr. Stern."

Charlie rearranged herself so she sat cross legged on the floor and lifted Armas into a more forward-facing position. "*La dottoressa vuole vederti.*"

"*Dottoressa?*"

"Yes, the doctor. Dr. Stern." She leaned forward and whispered in his ear. "She's very nice."

Abigail Stern entered the room with Stormy right behind her. "I hear someone is awake." She focused her gaze on Charlie. "Stormy said he speaks English."

"Yes." Charlie gave the boy a gentle squeeze. "Although he seems to prefer Italian."

"All right." The doctor opened her case and took out small plastic baggies and a pair of scissors. "I'd like to take some samples of his clothing: the fabric, the stitching. Once we have something else for him to wear, we can analyze the entire piece, but a small sample should get the ball rolling."

Armas stared at the shiny scissors.

"It's a little dark in here," Dr. Stern said. "Can we bring him closer to the doorway? Stormy said he was afraid of the lights, but it will be hard to take my samples without a little more light."

Charlie stood the boy up and then wriggled her way to the door.

Armas laughed at her unusual maneuver.

Score one for Auntie Charlie.

Dr. Stern knelt and quickly snipped off two pieces of the boy's tunic. One piece included a length of stitching.

Armas stared as she placed each cutting into its own individual evidence baggie.

"Now for the DNA sample." Dr. Stern held a cotton swab and touched the boy's forearm with it. "See? Soft."

Armas giggled.

"He really likes your evidence bags. Could he play with one?" Charlie asked. She settled her hands around the boys hips to hold him steady and keep him from hiding under the table again. "That might be a good distraction."

"Excellent idea." Dr. Stern put several cotton swabs into a large evidence bag and handed them to Armas. "For you."

He smiled and clutched the bag in a fist, while tapping the ends of the cotton swabs that stuck out of the bag.

"Can you open your mouth for me?" Dr. Stern asked.

The boy shook his head and squished his lips together.

Charlie plucked one of the swabs out of the baggie and touched him playfully on the cheeks. *"Un, due, tre."* She tapped him once on the nose, once on the ear, and once on his lips.

Armas laughed.

Dr. Stern quickly inserted the swab in his mouth and swept along the inner cheek.

Armas bit down on the swab with a grunt.

"Armas!" scolded Charlie "Open your mouth."

He shook his head.

Dr. Stern smiled. "It's okay, Charlie. But too bad, because I had something for Armas." She stuck her hand in her coat pocket and pulled out a wrapped butterscotch candy.

Charlie grinned at her cleverness. *"Caramella,"* she explained.

The boy's frown melted away. *"Cos'è?"* he mumbled with the swab sticking out of his mouth.

Dr. Stern took the opportunity to pull out the swab, stick it in an evidence bag, and hold out the candy to him. "Here."

He touched the plastic wrapper. *"Cos'è?"*

"Caramella." Charlie took the candy and unwrapped it so Armas could watch. *"Lo mangi."*

Without hesitation, the boy opened his mouth. Charlie popped the candy into it, and a wide smile broke out on his face.

"Caramella," he said. *"Adoro le caramelle."*

What little boy didn't love candy?

"Do you think you retrieved a good enough sample?" Commander Orr stood next to Stormy.

Dr. Stern placed the sample baggies in her case and snapped

it shut. "I think so. I'll send these to the lab at NSA in the morning."

Commander Orr observed the boy as he sucked on his butterscotch. "Please ask them to do a compare to the sample we collected at Devils Lake."

"Do you think the boy could be connected?" Dr. Stern stood and joined Orr in the office beyond the darkened conference room.

"At this point, I don't know what to believe, but it's all I've got." He yawned. "Maybe there will be a connection, or maybe I'm crazy."

"True. I'll let the lab know." Dr. Stern took a glance at Charlie and Armas. "Where will you take him this late?"

"Until we have those results, he should be kept out of sight," Orr said. "I'm not risking exposure by contacting Child Protective Services. He should be with one of us."

Stormy stepped forward. "I'll take him."

Charlie's heart pounded. Why did the idea of giving up Armas to someone else bother her so?

The married petty officer smiled at the boy. "He should be in a family home. I have clothes for him. Owen's a couple of years older than he is, and his old stuff should fit him."

"Excellent, Petty Officer Storm." Orr nodded. "I know it's a little unusual, but your main job, until we know more about those test results, will be to keep an eye on him. Stay indoors. No visitors until we have a better grasp on this."

"Will do, sir."

Charlie hugged the little boy to her chest. "If you need help, please let me know." Why did it feel as if she were giving up her own child?

"Of course I will." Stormy approached the boy and knelt in front of him, a warm smile on her face. "I'll take care of him as if he were mine."

CHAPTER 4

CHARLIE SAT AT HER DESK. Why did she feel so bereft? Stormy had carried Armas away, and now her arms were empty. Although she knew Stormy would do right by the orphaned child, she couldn't shake the strange feeling that washed over her when she handed him off.

Odd how close she felt to a boy she'd only met a few hours ago.

Only she, Demarco, and Orr remained in the office. The clock on the wall quietly ticked the moments away. To go back to her motel room and try to sleep seemed impossible. Her mind worked a million miles a minute.

"Tired?" Special Agent Demarco asked. He stood a few feet distant in his usual rigid pose.

Commander Orr had holed up in his office talking with someone on the phone, his back turned.

"Not anymore." She turned on her computer screen and navigated to her protected folder with her Voynich translations.

"You aren't seriously going to work on that now, right?" He crossed his arms.

"If it bothers you, no, I'm not working on it." She clicked open the PDF of the manuscript and searched for the pages she remembered.

"Yes, you are." He snorted what sounded like a laugh. "I'm standing right here. I can see you."

Demarco was so annoying. "Why do you care?" Why didn't he just go home and leave her to her work?

He casually closed in on her cubical. "Touchy, touchy."

She paused and faced him. "Aren't you the least bit curious about Armas? The pod? What exactly is going on?"

"Of course I am." His defensive wall cracked open a few centimeters, and his shoulders relaxed.

"Then why aren't you asking questions? Why aren't you digging for more information?" She couldn't stop the emotions from flowing freely and concluded with her true issue. "Why did you let Chief jump down my throat out there when you knew my story was the truth?"

He paused before answering. "I need more evidence."

Right. Of course. Even though she'd swam back to shore with the boy in her arms, he needed even more evidence. His own eyes weren't good enough. Good God, he was infuriating.

"Evidence of what? Armas is no alien. He's a human boy who speaks Italian and English. Let's just start there. And remember, the manuscript has connections to Rome."

"I thought you said in your presentation the origins were unknown." He cocked his head.

"Voynich claimed the manuscript had its origins in southern Europe, and last time I checked Italy would be considered southern Europe."

Demarco's brow knit together. "Just spit it out already."

"Spit what out?"

"Clearly, you want me to come to some conclusion. You claim to wonder about the boy, then prod me for answers to questions you already have answered in your own head. Sorry, but I'm not that good at mind reading, Cutter."

Charlie bit her tongue. Why was he being such a...such a...ugh. Why did he have to be right? "Fine. I'll tell you what I think is in the manuscript that might connect to Armas and what's really going on here."

"Finally."

She narrowed her eyes then turned back to her computer screen. "Remember yesterday I told you that someone in the ancient past was building pods? Machines out of organic materials?"

She scrolled past the page where she'd partially translated the symbols that led her to that conclusion. "Well, there's more. And after what happened tonight, I think we need to reanalyze the purpose of this office and our team."

"Go on." Commander Orr joined them.

Charlie's heart sped up and her palms grew sweaty. She'd set up a meeting with Orr for Monday morning, but now it seemed as if she might as well go for it. Either they'd think she was crazy, or maybe they'd see what she did in the ancient text.

"I'd started translating this section, but it didn't make a whole lot of sense until tonight." She'd scrolled to a page that had the chronological year drawn in a circle. "These notes here." She pointed to a corner of the page.

"What does it say?" Orr asked quietly.

Did he already know what she was going to tell them?

"'Calculate arrival year.'" She hadn't translated everything on the page. She pointed to another clump of text. "And here, 'five hundred years in total.'"

Both men stood silently.

The next bit might freak them out.

"And then here, next to this picture of a pod." She pointed to a small drawing on the opposite page with script underneath. "He is not safe here."

Demarco's face turned ashen. He took a step back.

Orr took a quick glance at his head of security. "Well, Petty Officer? Fill in the gaps please."

"The pod wasn't an alien spacecraft. It never was." Charlie took a deep breath to calm herself before she spoke. Would these men think her insane? "The pod is a time machine. Armas traveled through time."

Orr stroked his jaw and had a blank stare. "How is that even possible?"

Demarco paced the aisle between the cubicles. Each exhale escaped his nose in a loud gust of air as if he were a bull waiting on the bullfighter's approach in the ring.

What kept Charlie sane and able to speak was the text in front of her. Focusing on the translations and the written word grounded her in something real. Something believable. Even when it was completely unbelievable. "It's a lot to grasp. I know. But Armas is living proof these translations are correct. Everything about him convinces me he came from the fifteenth century."

The door opened and Kellerman entered. "Sorry about that. I had a little bit of a delay." He scanned the room for a moment. "Hey, where'd everybody go?"

"It's only the three of us," Charlie said. Demarco's silence weighed on her. What did he think about her statement? For some reason, she really wanted his support of her theory. His buy-in would mean he trusted her, he believed her.

Kellerman frowned.

"Lieutenant," Orr said. "We need you caught up with the latest information. I want to hear your input on Petty Officer Cutter's theory. Please, join us."

Maybe she'd made a mistake announcing her idea to the two men. She'd been burned in the past with her declarations and even became so frustrated with her work, she'd quit it altogether. In her head, she knew she was right. But she'd needed the validation of the text to support her idea. The minute Armas had exited the pod, she knew this boy was not of the modern world, and surely wasn't an alien. When he'd leapt into her arms a connection was made. A connection unlike any other she'd ever experienced. It was as if she knew Armas on some deep level. A déjà vu. Something about him had been familiar and unfamiliar all at the same time. And if she had confessed such things on the shore of the Occoquan River, her whole team would have thought her crazy.

She stared across the aisle at Demarco. He wouldn't meet her gaze. Why?

"A theory?" Kellerman approached the small group. "Did Dr. Stern gather her samples already?"

"Yes, she's going to have them compare the boy's DNA sample to the earlier pod samples," the commander said. "Dr. Stern told me the clothing can be analyzed immediately. A report should be available Monday. Petty Officer Storm took charge of the boy. Until we know more, he'll remain in her care."

Kellerman nodded. "So what's this about a theory?" He shifted his gaze to Charlie.

Why did she wish she could present her work in the conference room to the entire team, rather than late at night to only a few? Some rest and a bit of perspective might be warranted before delving too deeply into the topic.

She swallowed. "I was just explaining that after Armas's arrival, I thought again about some of the translations I'd worked on yesterday, and how I think we have this all wrong. These aren't alien pods. These are ancient time machines we've been chasing—from the time period when the manuscript was written."

Kellerman laughed. "What?"

Out of all of the people on the team, she didn't expect that from serious, nerdy Kellerman. Why did his response bother her so much? Worse than when Chief accused her of lying about Armas.

"Hey, give her some respect, Cole." Demarco broke his silence and stepped forward.

Charlie locked eyes with Demarco, and a shiver ran through her.

Without looking away, he continued, "What I witnessed tonight makes no sense. At least Cutter has an explanation for it. I still want results from Dr. Stern's tests, but at the very least, we must accept all theories this team produces until evidence proves one of them wrong."

Thank you, Charlie mouthed.

Demarco answered with a small nod.

"A time machine. That's literally impossible." Kellerman took a wide stance and crossed his arms. "I'm supposed to believe someone in the fifteenth century figured something out that nobody in the twenty-first century has even come close to creating?"

"For now, yes," Orr said. "I'll admit the possibility has my mind reeling. I have to reset my thinking and build up a new plan." He snapped his fingers. "Kellerman, I told Chief he'd be working with you tomorrow on the radar signature data. Wouldn't that give us some information about whether or not this new theory has any legs?"

Kellerman had visible tension in his neck and shoulders. He rubbed his brow. "It might."

"An alien craft should have a full trajectory that we can plot through the atmosphere. I'd like to know if we have a complete signature or a partial signature. When and where did these pods appear on our radar?"

"Right." Kellerman avoided eye contact with Charlie. "Chief and I can do that."

"Tomorrow at 0800," the commander said. "I wish I could ask more about your translation work, Cutter. But I know it's late, and we all need some sort of rest before tomorrow. Is this what you wanted to talk to me about on Monday?"

"Yes, sir. I know you wanted me to translate the pod writings first, but—"

He waved a hand. "We're past that now. Clearly, you have proven to me the manuscript has more clues for us to follow. A time machine—" He covered his mouth with his hand. "Unbelievable."

"Can we go, sir?" asked Kellerman.

"Yes, please. We'll all be back in the morning to discuss further. Stormy will stay home with the boy. Now he has much more significance than I originally thought." Commander Orr eyes glowed. "Truly something miraculous."

As the team prepared to leave, Demarco remained by Charlie's desk.

She picked up her purse and slipped on her dark navy cardigan over her sleeveless top. Why was he hovering there?

"I'd like to walk you to your room." He erased the distance between them.

Kellerman and Orr had already left the office.

Her heart fluttered in her chest. "That's not necessary."

"I need to talk to you."

He touched her arm, and it seared like a hot coal against her skin.

———

Demarco and Cutter strolled side by side toward the base motel under the glaring street lights. The Washington Navy Yard was devoid of life with the exception of two cars, which drove toward the barracks at a crawl.

How different her life would've been if she'd kept her original orders after graduating from DLI. She thought fleetingly of her roommate, a quiet girl from North Carolina who'd been a Persian-Farsi linguist. She'd probably be graduating soon and headed to Bahrain.

The cars parked and several sailors emptied out. All young men. All drunk. They stumbled along singing a Lady Gaga song and laughing at each other.

A different life entirely.

"Idiots." Demarco had noticed them, too. "Life is short, and that's how they want to spend it?"

"What are you? A hundred years old?" She continued to watch the drunk men. If only she had friends who would laugh with her the same way. "They're only having some fun."

"There's more important things to do." He turned away from the revelry.

She sighed. Of course, boring Demarco only wanted to hang out with his plants and impress Dr. Stern. Anything else was a waste of time. "So, what did you want to talk to me about?"

He slowed his pace. "About your theory."

She glanced around. "Out here?"

"Nobody can hear us." He gestured at the empty streets.

"So it's okay to break the rules when Demarco says it's okay. Got it." Could he hear the sarcasm in her voice?

"Angel. When we're not in the office, I'd like you to call me that."

Her breath quickened. "What? Why?"

He stopped by a bench for the base bus and gestured at her to take a seat. "Do you mind?"

The hard crusty exterior she'd always imagined surrounded Demarco—no, Angel—had vanished. "I guess not." She sat at the very end of the bench leaving plenty of room.

Angel sat so close to her their thighs touched.

She moved one inch to the left. His presence overwhelmed her in a very confusing way. Her mind whizzed through all of the Demarcos she'd encountered in her first week at her new job: angry, kind, distant, polite, annoyed, and now—?

"I want to be able to trust you, Charlie." He turned slightly so their eyes met.

"We all need to trust each other on the team." She shifted uncomfortably in her seat as his dark eyes softened.

He shook his head. "That's not what I mean. I haven't been able to find anyone I felt I could confide in for a long time."

Her breathing grew shallow, and her ears rang. What did he mean? "Clarissa, your date, she seemed nice." Beautiful slinky Clarissa in the blue dress. He so clearly preferred that kind of woman over someone like her. "I'm nobody. I'm nothing."

"You're not nothing."

"What could you possibly need to tell me that you couldn't tell Stormy or the commander or Kellerman?"

"Kellerman?" He snorted. "I'd never confide in that pompous ass."

Charlie's mind raced. What was happening here? "My theory. You wanted to discuss it. Well?"

"Right." He leaned back and faced the street, breaking the intense eye contact. "After what we experienced tonight, I think we both know your theory is the correct one."

Well, that was an unexpected admission from the dour and doubtful Angel Demarco. He thought her idea had merit?

"I thought you wanted to wait for Dr. Stern to do her tests?" she asked. "You made that very clear to Chief Ricard anyway."

"I'm sorry about that, Charlie," he said. "I was still in shock. But when I took a closer look at the boy, saw his reactions, and then the translations...well, I'm convinced. I know what Dr. Stern's tests are going to say."

"You believe me?" She studied the pleasing outline of his face in the harsh glare of the bright streetlights.

"Yes."

"You don't think it's crazy or that I'm being silly?"

"No."

Her mouth gaped at his answer. "I don't even know what to say."

"Can I ask you more about the manuscript?" He faced her. "What else have you translated? Any other clues about the machine, the boy, anything at all?"

The directness of his gaze made her glance away. "Well, it's a pretty large manuscript, and I've only begun to create the transliterations and do the comparisons."

He cupped her chin and gently tipped up her face. "I'm interested. I'd really like to know, Charlie."

Their faces were inches apart. A slight breeze blew her hair across her eyes. He swept away the strands and leaned in.

Was he going to kiss her?

CHAPTER 5

NOBODY else besides maybe her advisor in grad school had ever shown much interest in the manuscript translation. And, here, in front of her was an attractive, interested man who truly appeared to want to know more.

Whose mouth hovered above hers.

How could she resist?

"I wish tonight I could've spent more time explaining—" God, could she not stop talking? As weird as it seemed, an odd thrill ran through her at the thought of Angel Demarco kissing her on a bus bench.

"Shh—"

His mouth descended on hers, taking the very breath from her.

So unexpected, so surprising, and so...wow...thrilling.

He pulled her closer and their bodies met. His hard chest against hers. She knew the solid muscle that existed beneath the dress shirt, and her hands were eager to touch. Instead, she curled her hands around his waist.

She wanted to pause time and stay in the moment forever.

How was it possible the man had such soft lips? Everything about him was hard: his clipped speech, his stare, his judgment, his body.

The kiss deepened and became more wild, more uncontrolled.

Why did they have to kiss out here? In the open?

They should be in a private place, in the dark, where they could explore everything. Where she could shift his hands from caressing her jaw to removing her clothes.

Without reason or warning, Angel ended it.

He pushed gently on her shoulders. "I shouldn't have done that." He breathed heavily.

She nodded absentmindedly. "Right." Her lips burned. She wanted more. She didn't want him to stop, which made her mind spin in circles.

His cheeks were flushed, and his pupils were dilated. "Definitely not," he whispered.

"What would Clarissa think?" she blurted out. Why was she unable to shut off the rush of heat to her center? He said he'd made a mistake. He was right. She hated him...well, hate was a strong word...she found him irritating and cold and...dammit so ridiculously sexy.

He stroked a thumb down her cheek. "We can't do this."

"Angel—"

Her saying his name seemed to hit him like a physical blow.

Letting out a grunt, he stood. "I can't do this. Everything about it is wrong." He stroked his jaw. "Shit. Shit. Shit."

He paced along the edge of the sidewalk.

"It was only a kiss." She clamped down on her body's responses. Willed them away. It had been too long since a man had touched her like that. She was starved for affection, that had to be it. It wasn't Angel she was attracted to, but the idea of anyone being attracted to her.

"I'll never do that again. I apologize Petty Officer Cutter." He kept his gaze angled away.

"Okay." How could she hide the disappointment in her voice? He'd unlocked feelings inside her she didn't know she had.

He kicked the bus stop pole full force. "Fuck."

Charlie shrunk back. "Let's forget it ever happened."

He met her gaze. "I never expected this...you don't understand." His posture stiffened and muscles grew rigid.

"The best thing to do then is drop it." Everything in her

screamed 'no,' but his reaction had been so desperate and angry, what else could she do? "I'll never bring it up again."

Her throat choked up. Why was this so hard for her?

He nodded. His warm brown eyes cooled within seconds.

"You wanted to ask me more about the manuscript?" She shivered in the cooling air. Earlier tonight he'd offered her his shirt, but chivalry like that probably would end.

"Yes." He made no move to join her on the bench again.

"Then ask away." The excitement that had taken flight when the special agent showed interest in her discoveries had just had its wings clipped.

———

Angel Demarco remained standing a distance away from Charlie and cleared this throat. "Explain it to me. The translations you're working on."

She lifted her chin to meet his gaze. Although her stomach hardened after his rejection, she wasn't about to let him think he'd hurt her. He was a jerk. A player. A heartbreaker. She'd narrowly avoided being another of his conquests.

"I noticed right away an emphasis on time in the manuscript drawings. The celestial calendar." Better to focus on her work. Facts over feelings. If he was interested in the manuscript, at least they could have that in common. "The depiction of the cycles of the moon, the movement of the constellations across the sky, the shift of the Earth throughout the seasons. Not every page, but many of them."

He broke eye contact.

As she spoke, she was able to tamp down her hurt. Translation work was her passion. Her life. It could fill any hole she had...especially one created by Demarco. "That led me to wonder why. Why so much about the passage of time and seasons? And then when I crafted the transliteration alphabet and decoded what I could, I knew these pods had been built using some kind of formula. An organic machine made without electronics, at least electronics we'd recognize in the modern era. Bioelectric, perhaps?

The science part of it isn't my area. We'd need the help of Kellerman to maybe make sense of it."

He paced in front of her. "And you knew humans created these pods?"

"Not right away. No. When I arrived, I was told we were hunting aliens, so, of course, I assumed this was built off of proof, evidence, factual information that I had yet to see for myself. I trusted the team."

He nodded. The rigidity she'd grown used to seeing in his posture had returned.

Why couldn't she stop thinking about the lightness of his touch on her cheek? The feel of his body against hers?

Dammit. Focus, Charlie. Focus. He doesn't want you.

"When Armas came out of the pod, that's when I knew." Her heart softened at the memory. Poor little thing. "That's when I understood that everything I'd been told about the pods had been wrong. The Voynich manuscript was written by a human hand over five hundred years ago. These time machines were built by human beings. There are no aliens."

He bit his lip. "Is there a name in the manuscript? Any indication of who wrote it?"

Interesting questions he had.

"I don't know. There are dozens of pages to translate. I focused on the ones that had the most relatable phonemes to the writing found in the pods, and those were all related to movement and flight. But now that we have Armas...and we know for sure we are dealing with a human in the past who wrote this text, I hope I can find more. Someone built a pod for Armas. For some reason he was in danger."

"Yes. True." His voice trailed off, and he rubbed his forehead. "I wonder why?"

"I don't know, but if I was his mother, I wouldn't want to send him into a future alone." How could any mother who loved her child send him in a pod into the unknown? Her mind shifted to the one that had exploded in Idaho. If that had been Armas? A pain hit the back of her throat.

"His mother—" He covered his mouth and turned away from her.

"I suppose it could be his father who put him in the pod." The focus on the manuscript helped improve her mindset, center herself on her work. "But since he asked for his mother the whole time, I guess I made an assumption."

"Right. That makes sense." He paused in his pacing and stared into the distance. "Should we keep walking?"

Yes, the whole purpose was to walk her safely back to her room. Whatever his original intent had been, the electricity between them earlier had faded.

She stood and wrapped her arms around her body. The air had cooled, and the humidity made everything damp. They walked side by side with two feet of space between them.

"But it might help if I can translate more of the text, so I can figure out exactly why Armas was the only person in the pod," Charlie said.

"We've never encountered a pod with more than one occupant."

"I thought we'd never reached a pod soon enough to know how many occupants were inside." She stopped in her tracks. How had she forgotten? "Oh my God. I've been so focused on Armas, I didn't think about the other pods. Last summer one landed. Then the one in Idaho, which exploded." The thought of it made her shiver.

"And then the one at Devils Lake in North Dakota."

"You never did tell me what happened in the woods after Kellerman and the chief were attacked."

"Nothing happened." He threw up his hands "I thought I saw a figure far ahead in the trees. But it turned out to be nothing."

"Someone hit the chief."

"True."

"We need to go back." With this new knowledge, how could they do anything less?

"To North Dakota?"

"Yes, now that we know these are human beings. Time travelers. Can you even imagine someone dealing with a modern world?" As she thought more deeply about it, her steps slowed. "It would be a huge shock. For a child, maybe easier. It's been a week. Maybe there's been an encounter. Eventually, this traveler will need food, water, shelter."

"We can bring it up to the commander tomorrow. See what he thinks."

"I want Armas to have his parents with him." How sad for the boy to have no one. Not a parent, not a relative, not a friend. Only A Group. They were his family now. "I want him to feel safe again. I want him to have someone in this world who cares about him."

"You care about him," Demarco said softly.

Why did he have to be so kind? It would be easier to deny her attraction if he would be cold and distant Demarco. "He's only a little boy. Anyone would feel the way I do."

"Would they?" He drew closer to her. "I know you feel responsible for him. That's understandable. You rescued him from drowning alone in the river."

She shuddered. "The poor little thing."

"If the pod in North Dakota connects to Armas, we need to know."

He had closed the gap between them, so much so she could feel the heat of his body. How was she going to work with him, if she couldn't rid herself of these stupid feelings?

She took a breath, and steadied her mind. They were work colleagues only. The kiss had been a mistake. "What if that person is the author of the manuscript? I have so many questions."

"We all do."

They reached her temporary living quarters.

"Guess this is where I say 'Good night.'" His dark eyes glittered in the exterior lights near the motel entrance.

A rush of nervous energy filled her. "You could come up?" Why did she want to make a fool of herself?

His skin flushed, and his hands clenched briefly. He opened his mouth to speak. "Yes." Angel Demarco's demeanor shifted almost imperceptibly.

But Charlie recognized it. She'd been paired up with this man in enough situations that she could see it. The softening around the mouth. The relaxation of his shoulders. The hesitant step toward her.

Had she misjudged him?

"Yes?" she whispered. Mostly to herself because she still couldn't believe she asked him to come up to her room after his flat out rejection. She expected a derisive laugh. A cutting remark. Who was this man? How could the most difficult person she'd ever encountered intrigue her so much?

He guided her by the elbow through the main entrance. "You've seen my apartment, I think I deserve to see yours."

The heat of his hand through the thin cardigan was welcome. But was this merely a friendly visit? Or something more? "I see. Turnabout is fair play?" Easier to make a joke than confront the strong feelings she had for him.

The night clerk watched from his position behind the front desk as they crossed through the lobby. He glanced from Charlie to Angel, read the situation, and returned to the paperback book he had in his hands.

Charlie's heart pounded.

They navigated to the bank of elevators in silence.

Demarco pressed the 'up' button. "We aren't enemies, Charlie."

The low rumble of his voice caused goose bumps to rise on her flesh. What was this game he was playing with her?

She said nothing.

The display above them showed an elevator descending from the third floor.

In a few moments, the door of Elevator 1 opened, and he helped her inside. The doors closed with a whoosh.

Standing in the quiet compartment away from any prying eyes made her bolder in her words. "I don't understand you." She shook off his grasp. "One minute you're annoyed with me, the next you're kissing me. What did I do to make you treat me that way?" Clarissa had been his date for the evening. That was the type she'd assumed he'd go for. Gorgeous. Perfect in every way. Feminine. "Am I not good enough for you? Pretty enough? Smart enough?"

He pressed his hand against her stomach and forced her back to the wall. His gaze burned into her. "You're all of those things and more, Charlie."

Warmth rushed to her center.

His mouth hovered over hers. Breath light on her face. "Why can't I get you out of my head?"

Her mouth parted. "I don't know."

His kiss was harder the second time. Needier.

She looped her arms around his neck and drew him to her. Closer. Closer. Closer.

Their bodies pressed together as if melded together by heat alone.

Charlie drew in his scent, fresh yet masculine. Green like the jungle of plants in his apartment. Who was this strange man who'd despised her on day one? Criticized her?

She didn't care.

He kissed down her neck and mumbled her name.

The elevator dinged.

They broke apart and stared for a moment at the open door. Her floor. Her room. Only twenty feet away.

Angel threw out an arm to block the door from closing. "What do you want to do?"

They stood in a tight embrace.

Charlie didn't want to let go.

He stared down at her. Fire in his eyes.

Her hands slid up his neck and cupped his jaw. "This is what I want to do." She kissed him slowly, gently.

When she finished the kiss, their foreheads touched. Angel breathed heavily.

The door attempted to close.

"God help me." He grunted, scooped her up in solid arms, and carried her into the hall. "Which room is yours?"

CHAPTER 6

THE VIBRATION of her phone on the nightstand woke her. A text had come in.

She stretched, and her bare leg touched the warm body of Angel Demarco. Naked. In her bed. And she wasn't regretful.

She rolled over, taking the sheet with her, and read the text from her brother, Chad:

> Family dinner. Tonight at mom and dad's. Six o'clock?

"Anyone ever tell you that you're a bed hog?"

The deep rumble of Angel Demarco's morning voice caused a flush across her body. "No." She smiled to herself. "It's cold in here. You want me to freeze?"

His arm curled across her middle, and he pulled her to him. "I'll keep you warm."

She shivered and set the phone down. "It's seven o'clock." It would be nearly impossible to think straight at the office after last night, but what choice did she have? "We have an hour to get to work."

"Do you think he'd notice if we showed up late?" He trailed light kisses down her exposed shoulder.

Her breath hitched in her throat.

How were they going to hide this from their co-workers?

Damn. "I wish we had time to talk about last night—" Was it a one-time thing? Did he have feelings for her beyond a night in bed? "But we have a lot to discuss today. I want to know how Armas is doing. And if the commander is open to our idea of going back to North Dakota."

Demarco rolled onto his back. "All business with you, huh?" He let out a heavy sigh. "Got it. Back to work. Let's do this."

She reached for him as he climbed out of bed. "I didn't mean work is more important than what happened." A tingling swept up the back of her neck and across her face. Everything about last night was incredible, unexpected, and supremely satisfying. Did he think they were going to go back to normal after that?

"Is it all right if I take a shower?" He stood naked and perfect in front of her.

She swallowed. "Yes. Absolutely." Her gaze jumped to his face.

He offered a bemused smile. "Glad to know I made an impression."

"We need to talk."

He crossed the room to the bathroom. "Talk. Is that what you call it?"

As he closed the door behind him, she could hear him chuckle.

Once he turned on the shower, she picked up her phone. Staring at the request from her brother, a lump formed in her throat. Everything inside her said to beg off a family dinner. A very attractive, very interesting man was in her shower. She'd rather explore that further after work rather than defend her life choices at the dinner table. But she found herself texting back:

> Can you pick me up at five? I need a ride.

Would Chad be able to read her when he walked in the door? Probably. Even though most of the world believed it was only identical twins who had a special connection, she and Chad had considered their twin-ness as unique. The day Charlie had decided to drop out of her master's program, Chad had called her. Out of the blue. They hadn't spoken in weeks. In fact, they hadn't spoken since Christmas when he'd gifted her with a word origin dictionary. Only Chad seemed to understand her obsession with languages and words.

Until Demarco.

Her pulse quickened.

Her phone pinged.

Yes. See you at five.

Yeah, Chad would know. She might as well start practicing her story right now. How they met. Why this guy. Could Chad meet him. All the awful stuff that was way too early to think about, but totally necessary because it was her brother.

"Don't you have any normal soap?" Angel's muffled voice interrupted her thoughts.

"Normal?"

"Like a bar of soap. You know, soap?"

"The body gel. That's soap."

"That's not soap."

"Yes, it is. Just put it on the pouf and—" She giggled. Would burly, manly Angel actually pour lavender body gel onto a bright pink puff?

"Forget it. I'm just going to use the shampoo."

"Hurry up." Charlie checked the time on her phone. Seven fifteen. Shit. "We can't show up at the same time."

"Why not?"

The shower shut off.

"Then everyone will know." Why did she have to explain this to him? Was he that incapable of thinking about the implications at the office?

The bathroom door opened. "So?"

She gulped. He'd wrapped a towel around his waist. Somehow that made him even more attractive than when he had been one-hundred percent naked only a few minutes earlier. "Well, wouldn't that be wrong or illegal or something?"

"It's not illegal to date someone in the office."

They were dating? Okay. Not a one-night thing. Good. Or bad? What if Stormy had been right about Angel? "Right."

"Your turn." He nodded at the open bathroom door, and his eyes lit up. "I can help if you want."

"I think I've got it." How in the world was she going to handle this? She had important, life-changing work to do. She had to find a way to keep her love life from interfering with possibly the most amazing discovery in history.

First work. Then dinner with her messed up family. Then maybe time to ponder the implications of having sex with Angel Demarco.

———

Impossible though it seemed, Angel and Charlie had arrived at the office together at five minutes before eight o'clock and nobody batted an eye. He'd headed straight for the coffee at the back of the room, and she'd taken up where she'd left off with her translation work.

Although for the first five or ten minutes, she'd had a difficult time shaking off memories of last night, the familiar loops and whorls of the Voynich text soon took over. The translations were coming faster now, which seemed impossible. Scholars spent their whole careers on this text and had come up with nothing. She'd discovered a few clues from a pod, and now she was whisking through the pages and uncovering the true meaning of the manuscript. An impossibility in graduate school, yet here she was succeeding with the support of her team.

And yet she wouldn't be able to share that success with her family tonight. Although they knew she'd been brought on for her linguistics background and that she'd requested her Voynich work, that's as far as she could take it. Her work was classified, and so was her accomplishment. If only she could explain to her father, maybe he'd finally be proud of her, like her brother Chad.

Why did she have to care so much about what her father thought of her and her career? Inside, she burned with the desire to bring him into the fold and tell him everything about what they discovered. The pods. The translations. Armas. The ancient time machine. All of it. Oh, what a fantastic conversation they could have. Two adults working in the world of classified material. What had he seen and experienced all of those years in the NSA? She'd never asked, but now she understood better the burden he must carry.

"So while I wait for Chief to show up, walk me through these translations of yours." Kellerman stood a few feet from her cubicle. "Chief didn't seem so keen on your story about Armas, and if you catch me up on what you've uncovered, maybe I can advocate for you. He's pretty stubborn, if you haven't figured it out already."

"Stubborn?" Charlie spun in her chair to face the lieutenant. "He was rude and condescending. He accused me of being a liar."

Kellerman tucked his hands under his armpits and leaned against the cubicle wall opposite her. "It's all about rank to him. He's an E-7, you're an E-4. You made him look bad in front of Commander Orr."

She let out a laugh. "How did I make him look bad?" The egos of some of the military men she'd encountered were ridiculous.

"Chief's been on this team since the beginning, and he has yet to encounter a pod landing right in front of his eyes—"

"It had already landed."

"Or being the first on the scene."

"I just happened to be in the vicinity." She shrugged. "He should be made of tougher stuff than that."

"You don't want to be on Chief's bad side," Kellerman warned. "He's a good guy, if you give him a chance."

"I did nothing to deserve being on his 'bad side.'"

The door opened and Chief Ricard walked in. "Good morning, everyone."

Charlie turned back to her computer screen. "Maybe you should move along and do that radar work the commander wanted the two of you to focus on."

"Is there a problem here?" Demarco strolled down the aisle, a mug of coffee in each hand.

Oh, God, not now Angel. Not now.

"No, no problem," Kellerman said straightening up.

"Good." The special agent set a mug of coffee right next to

Charlie's keyboard. "Thought you could use an extra cup this morning."

Shit.

Kellerman raised a brow, noting the gesture. "Hey, weren't you wearing that shirt last night?" he asked Demarco.

Why didn't Angel stop at his Landcruiser and swap shirts with one in his go-bag, like she'd suggested on their walk to work?

Angel looked down at his shirt and then glanced at Charlie. "I like this shirt. Something wrong with wearing it two days in a row?" He winked at her when Kellerman wasn't looking.

Lieutenant Kellerman said nothing for a couple of beats.

Charlie could feel his stare weighing her down, judging her. He knew. He absolutely knew. And he'd asked her out only a couple of days ago. Her stomach roiled. Why did she put herself in this position? She should've left Angel standing outside her motel room last night. This mess was all of her own doing.

"LT," said Chief in a booming voice that was far too loud for eight o'clock on a Sunday morning. "Let's get cracking on the data."

"There's a rank system here, Petty Officer, even if you don't like it," Kellerman said. "No matter what someone else might tell you." He stared daggers at Demarco as he joined the chief on the other side of the small office.

Angel stepped closer to her cubicle. "What's his problem?"

Charlie sipped on the hot coffee he'd brought her. "Did you really have to do that?"

"Do what?"

"You know."

"Why don't you explain it to me tonight at dinner?" His eyes shone.

The same low rumble he'd spoken with that morning returned melting her insides.

"I can't."

He lifted his chin, and his body stiffened into the Demarco she'd known before last night. "Oh?"

"Team," Commander Orr announced from the entrance to his office. "Looks like we're all here. Let's meet in the conference room and discuss next steps and bring the chief up to speed on last night's discovery, shall we?"

Angel frowned.

"Let's talk later?" she offered.

"Sure," he said coolly and headed toward the conference room.

———

Commander Orr stood behind the podium. "Before we launch into last night, I heard from Petty Officer Storm a little while ago."

Charlie leaned forward in her seat.

Demarco sat to her left with his arms crossed.

"Armas is doing well. Despite the strange circumstances of his arrival, he's eating, he slept well, and he's playing with her two children."

"Did you call CPS?" Chief asked.

"No, Chief," Orr said. "We decided until we hear back from Dr. Stern, we should keep the boy under wraps."

Ricard snorted, but said nothing more. He knew when he was outranked. Orr had the say for how Armas would be treated.

"Next, I wanted to let all of you know Kellerman will be heading out on special assignment later today."

Charlie stared across the conference table at the lieutenant. What was this all about?

Orr held up his hands. "I know this comes out of left field, as we are supposed to act as a team. But last night's discovery, Petty Officer Cutter's translation work, and other information has led me to believe we need to go back to North Dakota."

Could it be possible Orr came to the same conclusion as she? That if Armas came from the past, then the other pod most likely held another human from the past? Maybe Armas's mother?

"Sir," Demarco said. "Why Kellerman? He has no training in tracking or investigations of this sort." His brow furrowed.

"Last night, Kellerman met with a contact."

Charlie thought back to last night when Kellerman arrived later to the office than everyone else, and Orr had mentioned he'd maybe stopped for gas or something. "Who?"

"I'll let Kellerman share that with you." The commander gestured at him. "Lieutenant?"

The young officer stood, straightening his khaki uniform pants. Typically, he wore civilian clothes, so it was notable he'd chosen to wear his uniform on a Sunday trip to the office. "Thank you, sir."

Negative vibes rolled off of Demarco, as if his skin were covered with visible prickles.

How easily she could read him now. Has she been able to do that before they'd had sex? Or was this a new ability she'd acquired?

"This is a huge mistake," the special agent said.

"Angel." Charlie touched his arm and instantly regretted it.

Chief's eyes narrowed, and his gaze shifted from Demarco to Charlie and back again.

"Agent Demarco," the commander said with clipped speech. "You will give the lieutenant some respect. Back off." The older man stood to the side of the podium to let Kellerman approach.

In his uniform khakis the lieutenant appeared older and more mature. He braced his hands on either side of the podium and connected his gaze with each person in the room. "We weren't the only agency tracking the pod last night. As everyone knows, I transferred here from an assignment at the Nevada Test and Training Range in Nevada at Groom Lake or Area 51." Kellerman used air quotes when he spoke the well-known nickname. "Although I cannot divulge the work I participated in at that facility, I still have contacts there. The radar signature data was collected through the NGA, or National Geospatial-Intelligence Agency, and that data is shared throughout the Department of Defense."

"What does any of this have to do with you needing to go to North Dakota by yourself?" Demarco spat out.

"Patience, Special Agent." Orr gave him a pointed look.

"My contact also tracked the landing in Devils Lake for their own purposes. They've run into a situation that needs my assistance."

"Situation?" Charlie asked. Did someone find a passenger from the earlier pod?

"They've recovered a body from the area near the landing site. My contact was aware of our office and thought we should have access to samples."

Why did she feel so nauseated all of a sudden? A body? In what condition?

"Why did this contact believe the body was connected to the pod?" Demarco asked.

"It wasn't until I came back to the office and heard about Cutter's translation work that I realized how important that body could be," explained Kellerman. "It was found maybe a hundred yards from where the chief and I were attacked. And one other unusual thing." Kellerman picked up the iPad he usually carried. "The body had a strange deformity."

He tapped on the screen to bring up a photo.

When he turned the iPad to show them, Charlie gasped.

Deformed feet with a single big toe and a split like a vee with another malformed toe splitting off in the other direction.

Just like the footprints she'd seen in the sand.

The footprints Demarco had convinced her didn't exist.

What was going on?

CHAPTER 7

"WHAT IN THE FUCK?" Chief declared at the sight of the photo on the iPad. "What is that?"

"A strange deformation of the feet," Kellerman said. "Genetic problem of some kind."

Demarco slumped in his seat.

Why did Angel try to convince her the footprints she'd seen hadn't been real? "I saw footprints like that on the beach, near the woods," she confessed.

"Why didn't you document this?" asked the commander.

She lifted her chin. "Special Agent Demarco told me I was seeing things." How could she do anything less than tell the truth? They all needed to know what she'd witnessed that day. Those strange feet had to have been the ones to make those footprints. "I'm quite sure the body connects to the pod. That has to be the passenger."

Angel tilted away from her.

Everything they'd shared last night in her motel room disappeared, and it was as if they were back at square one. That first day rushed back to her mind. How annoyed he'd been with her. How certain he was that she was a burden on the team and not an asset.

"Demarco, I'd like to meet with you later in my office," the commander said.

Angel barely nodded. His gaze turned inward, and it was as if he checked out completely from the team.

Any intimacy they shared faded.

"Tell me more, Petty Officer Cutter," Orr said.

"After Chief and the lieutenant arrived at the pod crash site, Special Agent Demarco had made his way down the beach. I assumed he was following tracks of some kind or some sort of evidence." Why did her insides feel as if they were on fire? She only wanted to share what she knew, so that they could figure out more about Armas, the pods, the whole mystery. But each word tore at her. She didn't want to hurt Angel, but what else could she do? He'd lied to her. "He'd left me with the pod, so I thought it was important, and I followed him. That's when I saw the tracks leading into the woods."

"This is significant. I wish we had evidence of what you saw, but since we have the body, the lieutenant will be able to retrieve it and bring it back to Dr. Stern for a thorough exam." Commander Orr stood with his feet planted solidly apart. "Kellerman, do you have any more information you'd like to share before you leave this afternoon?"

"The body found is that of a male, and he had been hit with a blunt object. Perhaps a rock or other item on the scene. They're in the middle of a storm cycle, so it will be hard to identify the murder weapon."

"Murder?" Charlie gasped.

Kellerman nodded. "Someone attacked this person. We might never know who did it or why, but at least we have the body to examine."

Dr. Stern entered the room. "A body?" She held a locked, zippered case in her hands.

"Doctor, I'm so glad you're here," Orr said. "We were about to discuss Cutter's discoveries in her translation work."

"I listened to your voicemail a little while ago. Time travel? I couldn't believe it. I want to know more." Her eyes lit up. "Since I was on my way here with my preliminary analysis of the boy's tunic, I didn't return your call." She set the case on the end of the table near the door. "But a body? Could it be another time traveler? Tell me more."

"Time travel?" Chief gawked. "Would someone like to clue me in? When did we decide on that theory?"

Orr held up a hand. "Sorry, Chief, a lot has happened since you went home last night. We'll get to that explanation in a minute."

Ricard crossed his arms, and his brows knit together. "You've got to be kidding me. You've all lost your minds. I can't wait to hear what made you all come to that conclusion."

Charlie gritted her teeth, struggling to contain her irritation at Ricard's dismissive words. First, he didn't believe Armas came out of the pod, now he pushed aside the time travel theory without even listening to her evidence.

"We'll get to that in a minute, Chief." Orr quickly summarized the discovery, "Kellerman is traveling to North Dakota today to retrieve a body that was found near the pod we investigated last week."

Dr. Stern's mouth formed an 'o.' She pulled out a chair and sat. "Incredible. You think it's related to the pod?"

Orr looked at Charlie before answering. "Yes, there seems to be a pretty solid connection between the location of the pod, the body, and some footprints discovered near the scene."

"Sounds like we're going to keep the NSA lab busy," remarked Dr. Stern. "I'm very interested in making comparisons between the blood that was recovered by Petty Officer Cutter, the body, and the boy."

How awful if the man found in North Dakota was related to Armas. Although it would answer some questions, it would leave the boy an orphan in a strange world.

"It also appears the person in the woods had been attacked and died from his wounds," Kellerman added.

Charlie's stomach soured. Demarco had run off into the woods, leaving her to tend to an unconscious Chief and a wounded Kellerman. He'd told her later he hadn't encountered anything, but now her mind turned over the new information and doubt grew like a noxious weed. Could she trust him? He'd lied to her about the footprints and now a dead body turned up.

"Despite this astounding new discovery," began Dr. Stern. "I wanted to share with you my early analysis of the boy's clothing."

"I wasn't expecting anything so quickly, doctor," said Orr.

"I couldn't sleep much last night. All that excitement," Dr. Stern explained. "I woke up around four-thirty and have been in my lab since five o'clock."

Why couldn't Charlie focus on Dr. Stern's words? Since she'd made her claim last night that Armas had traveled through time, she had been anxious for physical evidence to support it. But the revelation about the body, the footprints, and Demarco's strange words and behavior filled her mind.

Could Demarco be the one who murdered the man in the woods?

DR. STERN TOOK the podium and unlocked her case. "Now that we might have additional evidence coming from North Dakota, we will be able to do some comparisons." She removed the two plastic baggies she'd filled with small bits of the boy's clothing and held them up for everyone to see. "I was able to look at the fibers under a microscope earlier this morning. It is most certainly wool. The sample, however, was a coarse wool, not the finer wools we see from merino sheep or even goats. That would be mohair or cashmere. This was a rougher wool. Less processed. The fibers were coarse and the weave rather loose. I made comparisons to some wool items I had at home. The tunic has a very rough texture and appearance. It also appeared to be undyed."

"But you couldn't tell the age of the wool?" asked the chief. His posture was rigid, and his mouth formed a tight line. "For example, did anything about your investigation give you a date? A time in history? Did this come from some other time period or whatever Cutter is claiming?"

Charlie flinched. Why did his accusations sting to much?

"No, I could not age the piece, Chief," Dr. Stern said. "But, if we are accepting that the child travelled through time, the age would not match the amount of time between the fifteenth century and the twenty-first. Armas skipped right over six centuries and so did his clothing."

. . .

"The fifteenth century? That's what she's claiming?" Chief Ricard's gaze looked away, and he crossed his arms. "This is nonsense."

"Let's continue, shall we?" Commander Orr said.

"The other aspect of his tunic I examined was the stitching. I wanted to know the quality of the thread, the type of stitching used." Dr. Stern displayed a baggie, which held a one-inch clip of thread. "The thread is wool, handspun. The quality was not very fine, and it was clear that it had been made by hand. I brought a sample of modern thread for the team to examine." She handed Demarco and Kellerman spools of thread. They sat on opposite sides near the head of the conference table. "I will pass around the sample so you can see for yourselves. The difference can be seen with the naked eye, but I can send you my photos when it was under the microscope."

Everyone examined the thread and made a comparison to the sample, except Chief, who slid it across the table to Charlie with an eye roll.

"The only conclusions I can make from my examination is that these are handmade items—the wool cloth used to make the tunic, and the thread used to stitch it together. However, I would need to consult a fibers expert to see if this tunic could be an item from the past. Perhaps a DNA-level test of the wool or an x-ray, which has been used to date fabrics in recent years."

"Thank you, Dr. Stern." Commander Orr took the front of the room once more. "Really we are no further along in determining where—and when—Armas came from." He looked pointedly at Charlie. "However, I think Kellerman's trip to North Dakota might be the very thing we need to prove Petty Officer Cutter's translations of the text are accurate."

Chief snorted.

"Will someone be investigating who murdered this person?" Charlie asked. Why did her voice tremble so? "Everything we learned so far points to foul play."

Demarco repositioned himself in his chair.

Did he have anything to do with it? Her blood ran cold at the thought. The man she'd been with last night bore no resemblance to a ruthless killer. But she had to admit, Angel could be distant, could be sullen. What did she really know about his background? His capabilities?

"I think we are setting the cart before the horse," the commander said. "I'm more interested in the possible connection of the body to the pod at Devils Lake and then the connection to Armas. Once we do those tests, maybe we can talk about why he died or if he was killed."

Didn't he care that someone may have been murdered?

Charlie opened her mouth to speak.

Demarco touched her arm.

She jumped at the unexpected touch. Their gazes met. He had a pained expression on his face, and his eyebrows drew in.

What was he trying to tell her?

Dr. Stern spoke, "I agree with Commander Orr. Let's examine the body, test the DNA, see what we can link together. We can't even begin to think about the how of this person's death before we know who he is."

"I'll make sure I bring everything back, ready to test," Kellerman said. "My contact said the body has been put into a body bag and will be on ice at Minot when I arrive."

"Make sure you take the time to interview the people who found the body." The commander paced at the front of the room. "I want you physically on the scene. Take as many photos as you can. I'd rather have too much to examine, than too little."

"I'd like to request one last time to go with the lieutenant," Demarco said quietly. "I thought this is why you brought me on the team."

"As I recall, you wormed your way onto this team last year, Agent," Orr snapped. "Enough already. We have our assignments." The commander scooped up a sheaf of papers on the table and left the podium. "Petty Officer Cutter, would you like to give your presentation now? Kellerman is wheels up in two hours, and I want to give him time to prepare for his flight."

———

After explaining her theories to the group, everyone except Chief Ricard agreed Charlie's translations coupled with the arrival of Armas supported her theory. The meeting wrapped up, and everyone began to exit the conference room to return to their work.

Chief and Kellerman followed behind Orr.

Dr. Stern carefully packed the baggies into the case.

Charlie had questions for Angel, not the least of which was Orr's accusations about how Angel ended up in A Group, but couldn't ask them freely with the doctor in the room.

Demarco pushed his chair back.

"Wait," Charlie said. "Can you give me five minutes?"

Dr. Stern glanced at them from her position behind the podium. "I'm sorry, am I in the middle of something between you two?"

"There's nothing between us," Demarco said. His fingers drummed out a rhythm on the edge of the conference table.

Charlie froze.

The doctor raised a brow. "Clarissa is a very sweet young lady. If you want to know, I delivered her safely back to her condo last night. She has your painting and told me she was sure you'd be in touch." She snapped her case shut.

He rubbed the back of his neck. "Right. Thanks. That was very kind of you."

Charlie's stomach soured at the reminder. How serious was he about her? He'd left one woman in the middle of a date, and managed to end up in her bed by midnight. A player. Just like Stormy had warned. But, to be honest, she hadn't cared last night either. The attraction between them had been too magnetic. Her curiosity—and her libido—had gotten the better of her.

Dr. Stern glanced past Demarco. "Charlie, I have your painting in my trunk. If you want, you can follow me out to the parking lot, and I can give it to you."

As much as she wanted a few minutes alone with Angel to dig for some answers, she didn't want to be rude. "I suppose I can scoot out for a few minutes."

"Great." The older woman smiled. "That way I hit two birds

with one stone this morning. Give me a moment to chat with the commander. I'll meet you out in the lobby."

Demarco remained seated.

As soon as the doctor left, Charlie unloaded. "What is going on, Angel? You said you never saw anyone in the woods, that those footprints were bogus. Why did you lie to me?"

"I don't want to lie to you." His neck muscles jumped under his skin. So much tension beneath the exterior.

"So you admit that you did." Her thoughts went spinning. "I don't understand. If I am part of the team, if Commander Orr is in charge of this office, why are you keeping information hidden? How can I be so sure you didn't have something to do with the death of the man they found in the woods?" If only she could go back to last night, when they were in bed together. Nothing between them. He would've told her just about anything she asked.

"I didn't murder anyone." He flinched as he said the words. "Do you really believe that?"

She pushed up the sleeves of the hoodie she wore. "I don't want to believe it, but the evidence isn't looking good."

"Charlie—" He leaned toward her and touched her knees.

She couldn't keep her gaze off his hands. The warmth burned through her jeans. "Why did you lie to me about the footprints? Let's start there."

"I didn't know if I could trust you." His eyes were a crisp, clear brown.

"Trust me with what?" She bit her thumbnail. "What aren't you telling me?"

Angel rose from his chair and quietly closed the door to the conference room. He leaned against it for a few seconds. "I know who was in the pod."

"What?" A fluttery feeling hit her stomach. "How could you know who was in that pod?" Everything she thought she knew about Angel, who he was, where he came from, what his motives were, were shot down like clay pigeons in a target shoot. "I don't understand you. You aren't making any sense."

His gaze met hers. "I want to tell you everything, I do. But you have to understand, I'm used to being alone, staying in my own head."

The Voynich text returned to her mind. The unbelievable truth she'd found in that manuscript had somehow been easy to accept. It had made sense in a swirl of confusing events and impossible theories. If she had been willing to accept the facts she'd uncovered in the translations, she had to be willing to trust what Angel had to offer. That seemed the fair and right thing to do.

"You can trust me," Charlie said.

His forehead wrinkled. "I'll try."

Charlie sucked in a breath, held it a few seconds, and let it go. Give him a chance to explain. Give him the benefit of the doubt. "How did you know this person?"

"There's so much to tell, Charlie." He rubbed his forehead. "So much."

"That's okay."

"Is it?" In the fluorescent lights, his brown eyes sharpened. He hung back keeping a void between them. "Once I start down this path, there's no turning back. Are you sure you really want the truth?"

CHAPTER 9

CHARLIE AND ANGEL sat silently staring at each other. Was she ready to find out what Angel had been hiding from her—and from the team?

"Yesterday, I wasn't sure anyone would believe my translations nor the fact that I thought Armas had traveled from the past." His support of her theory had buoyed her. How many times had she felt alone translating with no one willing to accept her work? "You trusted me then, so I have to trust you now. Yes, I want the truth, Angel. I need the truth. I want to help you. You don't need to carry this alone anymore."

He closed his eyes. As if an invisible weight had been lifted from his shoulders, the tight muscles in his neck relaxed. "I know who the man was in the pod, because I've seen him before. During an operation gone bad. One that put me in my current position."

"Where did you see him? I don't understand." Orr had indicated Angel had forced himself into A Group. Why? What kind of work had he been doing before last summer?

"I was the lead on a team in charge of tracking down fugitives who had begun experimental work that was dangerous to mankind."

"Experimental?"

"Altering DNA. Human DNA. They wanted to create a superior human being. We couldn't let them."

"Who is 'we'? The federal government? The CIA?"

"The Purists." He stumbled over the words. "We had to stop them."

"I've never heard of that group before...the Purists?" Charlie ran through recent news stories about terrorists and enemies abroad. The name didn't ring a bell.

"There is so much to explain and not enough time. The rest of the team will wonder why we are still in here together." He glanced at the closed door. "But you have to believe I didn't kill that man. I only wanted to track him down and ask him questions. He wasn't someone to fear, but there is another."

"But, Angel, the pods. They're time machines. I still don't understand how you could recognize this person. What are you saying?"

His chest rose and fell. He bit his lip.

Her mind raced. Could Demarco really be the same as Armas? The same as the man in the pod from Devils Lake?

Dr. Stern popped her head inside the room. "Ready to come pick up your painting, Charlie?" A friendly smile lit up her face.

Her stomach churned. She wanted to ask more questions. She wanted more information. Her mind filled in the gaps, and the reality choked her. How was that possible?

"Charlie?" the doctor's question had a lilt of confusion in it.

She snapped back to the normal world. A world where people went to Saturday night painting classes and drank glasses of wine. A world where a daughter fretted over a family dinner she didn't wish to attend, but knew she should. A world where people were born, lived, and died without having any clue about time travel or its implications on world events.

Charlie squeezed Angel's hand. "We need to talk more—later."

He nodded. "I trust you, Charlie."

"I know." She gave him a smile before joining Dr. Stern outside the conference room.

"Looks like you two are getting cozy." The doctor poked Charlie gently in the ribs with her elbow.

Charlie's face grew warm. "Could be." If the doctor only knew the truth of how cozy, which went well beyond the realm of the physical. How soon could she and Angel find time alone for him to share more? An endless supply of questions popped into her mind.

Dr. Stern smiled. "I thought you might be good for him. A man shouldn't be so alone. It's not healthy."

They exited into the hall and headed to the elevators.

"There's a lot more to Angel than I knew." Charlie pushed the 'up' button.

"He's definitely a man of many mysteries." The two women stood shoulder to shoulder waiting on the elevator. "The strong but silent type. Though I'll miss pushing his buttons."

"Why would you stop?" Charlie grinned.

"I like you too much." The doctor patted her on the back. "He's made a good choice for once, and I'm not going to get in the middle of it."

"That's kind of you to say."

They entered the elevator and, as they rose to the lobby, Charlie wondered who exactly she'd fallen for and what other secrets he had to tell.

They strolled in amicable silence through the lobby and outside toward the parking lot.

Dr. Stern knew Commander Orr well and had joined A Group at the beginning. Could she perhaps present a different view of Angel? It might provide her a foundation for when she found time to question him more thoroughly.

"So how well do you know him?" Good softball question.

"Angel?" Dr. Stern slowed her steps and smiled to herself. "I remember the first day he showed up in the office. He wasn't as confident as he is now. Seemed a little befuddled by some of the office equipment. I thought maybe he'd been out in the field so long that he'd gotten out of the habit. You know the type: all brawn and no brain?"

Charlie nodded. If she interrupted, Abigail might stop talking, and she needed her to keep talking and reveal everything she could about the man.

"Well, he caught on pretty quick, as I recall. Anyway, he and the commander did bump heads a few times. Guess David—Commander Orr—didn't request him for the team. Was surprised when he showed up."

"Oh? How strange."

Dr. Stern shrugged. "People get assigned and reassigned to things all the time in a cleared setting. You know how it goes." She pointed her key fob at her parked vehicle to unlock it. "But he had the paper work, the clearance docs, everything. After a few weeks of working together, David accepted it. And it's worked out rather well. Except for the lost samples—"

"When did that happen?"

The doctor popped the trunk. "Ah, here we are."

Charlie's partially completed painting lay on top of a gym bag. All she'd managed to finish was the basic parts of the owl. Its massive round eyes stared back as if watching her every move.

"I think you did rather well for your first painting class," Abigail remarked. She lifted out the canvas and handed it to Charlie. "My cousin hopes you'll come back for another one, and maybe finish it next time."

Could she imagine herself sitting on a stool painting another garish example of art-gone-wrong? "That would be lovely." She clutched the canvas. Where would she stow it once she returned to the office? "You were saying...about the lost samples?"

Dr. Stern closed the trunk. "Yes, that was really unfortunate. We still don't know what happened to them. David blamed Angel, as he was supposed to be the one in charge of any evidence gathered. It caused a pretty good rift between them for a few weeks. That's sort of why Angel is scared of me." She shook her head. "He knows my relationship with David goes back quite a few years. And because David bumped heads with him at the very start, Angel assumed I would take David's side in everything. I suppose I shouldn't have teased him about things, knowing his view, but it was easy to do. He can be so rigid sometimes, you know? I wanted him to loosen up. Looks like it might've backfired on me."

"Right." Charlie stood awkwardly holding the canvas to her chest. "Well, I guess I need to head back. I have a lot of work ahead of me today. Everything has ramped up so quickly since last night. And with Kellerman heading back to North Dakota—"

Abigail lowered her voice to a whisper and scanned the parking lot. "Can't wait for him to come back with a whole body." She rubbed her hands together. "I'll be buried with work the next few days, too. Just how I like it."

Charlie took a few steps backward. "Thanks again for the canvas."

"My pleasure." The older woman opened the driver's side door and then stopped herself from climbing in. "One more thing, Charlie."

"Yes?" Her stomach fluttered uncomfortably.

"Angel really seems to like you. Different than the other women I've seen him with."

Charlie's cheeks heated.

"Give him a chance. I think there's someone really special under all of that bravado."

Charlie shifted her gaze to a small dent in Abigail's bumper. A ghost of last night crossed through her mind—her body entangled with Angel's. Her heart picked up speed. "I'll keep that in mind."

How could she think of a relationship with a man who'd practically confessed he, too, may have time travelled? Who was Angel Demarco? And where did he come from?

———

When Charlie returned to the office with her owl painting in tow, she spied Angel in the commander's office deep in conversation. She'd have to find a later opportunity to pull him aside and answer more of her questions. On the solitary walk through the parking lot, she'd thought of many new ones.

Kellerman had departed for his flight to North Dakota, and Chief Ricard looked to be knee deep in a pile of radar data from the last twelve months, to ensure they hadn't missed any additional pods.

Charlie sat at her desk and contemplated the possibility Angel had come from a different time. Her mind could barely comprehend it. How could someone from the fifteenth century blend into the twenty-first with almost no one suspecting a thing? He hadn't confessed to it, but he'd implied it with some of what he'd revealed to her earlier. Could he be found in the Voynich text? Or some evidence he was connected to it?

She opened up her work. The colorful pages were familiar yet she saw them in a new light with the recent revelations about Armas and Angel's possible connections to it. She dove into translating every page—from the beginning. A need to understand everything about the text grabbed hold of her like a magnet did an iron filing. The answers were in here somewhere. She knew it. All she needed now was time and focus.

———

Charlie paused in her analysis. Her eyes burned from staring too long at her computer screen. Tipping her head from one shoulder to the other, she waited for a pain-relieving crack.

"Let me help." Angel gently massaged her neck.

How long had he been behind her?

A flood of heat hit her at the touch of his warm hands. "Wow, you're good at that." Her tight muscles relaxed as he kneaded with his thumbs.

What would her co-workers think about such intimacy between them? But Angel's hands were working miracles on her neck, so why did she care? She closed her eyes and a long sigh escaped her lips.

He leaned down and whispered in her ear, "There's only three of us. Kellerman's gone, Chief finished his analysis, and Orr's making phone calls to Minot."

Her eyes snapped open. Although she wanted to let him continue his massage, which had developed into more of a caress, she had too many questions in her head. She covered one of his hands with hers. "I need more answers."

His hands stilled. "I know."

Did she detect a tremor in his voice? "You said you trusted me. I want to help, but I need to know more."

Her phone vibrated on her desk. A text from her brother.

Crap. What poor timing.

Glancing at the time on her desktop, she knew Angel's story would have to wait. "I have this family dinner to go to." She scooped up her phone.

> Beep, beep! I'm outside.

"My brother's picking me up, and it looks as if he's early." She flashed her phone screen so he could see the text.

Angel's unblinking gaze unnerved her. Then he slowly nodded. "Right. Family. I understand."

No way was she going to give Angel the chance to clam up. She'd finally gotten him talking, and a family dinner wasn't going to get in the way of finding out the answers she needed. "How about we meet tonight when I get back? Before we're back in the office with interruptions and assignments and—" She glanced at Orr still busy in his office. "Other people."

He bit his lip and searched her face. "All right. Tonight. I'll pick you up?"

She nodded. "I'll text you when my brother drops me off."

He gave her a slight smile and took a few steps back. "Okay. I'll explain everything. Tonight. I promise."

"If I can handle pods falling from the sky and a time traveling boy, I'm sure anything you have to tell me can't be any worse."

Angel gestured at her phone. "You'd better answer him before he starts wondering where you are."

"Right." She tapped on the phone screen and quickly texted Chad to wait a few minutes.

Angel retreated, heading toward the door.

"Wait, I wanted to share something with you." How could she forget? He'd been so interested in her translation work and what else she might find. Although a majority of the deciphering revealed mysterious formulas and plant biology, she'd uncovered something intriguing.

He approached her desk.

"I think I found another name." She clicked through the Voynich pages she'd been working on. "Right here. A signature, I think."

"Show me." Angel's voice shook.

She enlarged the page with a few clicks. "See here? Ree-sa. A name. Do you think this could be Armas's mother?"

In a daze, Angel knelt next to her and touched the name on the screen. "Risa. Oh, my God. It can't be true."

CHAPTER 10

CHARLIE'S BODY TENSED. "You know that name?"

Angel scrubbed a hand over his face. "I imagined it was possible, but I hoped I was wrong." He stared down at his lap. "I never should have done it. Never."

"Done what? Who's Risa?" She grew lightheaded. Thoughts swirled in her mind. None of this made any sense. How could she leave to meet her brother when Angel had just confessed he knew the name she'd uncovered?

He winced. "I'll explain everything, Charlie. I will." His usual resonant voice weakened to a thin whisper.

Commander Orr's booming voice interrupted them both. "It's five o'clock. I think we've done enough for today. I'd like to lock up."

"Right. Five o'clock." Angel stood and stepped away from Charlie as if in a daze. "You need to go meet your brother, Cutter."

"You have plans, Petty Officer?" Orr ignored the strange actions of his security specialist and focused in on Charlie.

"Just a family dinner." How could she possibly set aside what she'd learned about Risa and Angel and pretend everything was normal at her parents' house? The idea of it was ridiculous. Impossible. Not doable.

"Delightful. Families are important, wouldn't you agree, Demarco?" Orr clapped him on the back.

Angel's shoulders curved inward. "Yes, sir, very important." He couldn't meet Charlie's eyes.

"Well, let's skedaddle then. I'll lock up behind you." Orr pointed at Charlie's computer. "Shut that down, and let's go."

"Yes, sir." Charlie saved her work and turned off her desktop.

The two men made their way to the door. To anyone who didn't know him, Angel appeared steady, quiet, and thoughtful. But Charlie noticed the stumble in his step, the weakness in his profile. As if all the bravado and rigidity had been sucked out of him.

After she shut off her monitor, she followed them into the hall. Her questions would have to wait.

———

Chad honked on his horn three times in a row when he saw his sister approaching.

She jumped at the noise, her mind still buried in thought.

Her brother leaned across the passenger's seat and popped open the door. "Hurry up! We're going to be late."

"Sorry." Charlie slid in and closed the door of her brother's Honda. "I had to work today."

"Work?" He scanned her casual outfit. "Since when do Navy linguists wear civvies to the office?"

"It's Sunday."

"So?"

"We're a mixed office—some civilian, some military. It has a different dress code."

"If I were the Officer-in-Charge—"

"You're not, okay? Commander Orr is in charge, and what he says goes. He has zero problems with me wearing this." Why did she let her temper get the best of her? Chad didn't know the bizarre details of her job and her personal life and how they were mixing together in a very uncomfortable and confusing way, but he could sometimes be a bit of an annoyance.

The good brother. The obedient brother. He was the boy her

father always wanted; she was the girl her father always butted heads with.

Tonight's dinner at her parent's house was to celebrate Chad's new orders, his career taking off, the amazing responsibilities he'd have...and no one would know anything about what she was working on, nor how important it was. Regular military life seemed so boring and trite in comparison to the truths she encountered in merely one week at her new assignment. Pods, time travelers, a boyfriend who may be a time traveler...who may even be connected to the death of another time traveler.

Chad snapped his fingers in front of her eyes. "Hey, sis, where did you go? I thought you were about to give me a royal thrashing, and you just disappeared there. Hello! Earth to Charlene."

She slapped his hand away. "It's been a long week, okay? Let's go. If you're so worried about being late, let's drive. The traffic can't be that terrible on a Sunday afternoon, can it?"

Chad let his hand drop. "Fine." He drove toward the beltway and their parent's place in Columbia, a high-end suburb between Baltimore and Washington D.C.

Charlie had only visited once before. Halfway through her second year of grad school, her mother had bought her a plane ticket for Christmas. Her father had received new orders from Texas to the National Security Agency on Fort Meade twelve months earlier. Not exactly a family home to her. But most military brats lived similarly—constantly on the move, always starting over, unpacking, repacking. Lather, rinse, repeat.

"Have you found out yet whether you can live off-base?" Chad smoothly transitioned to a different topic. If he ever got married, he'd know exactly how to handle a wife in a prickly mood.

"Should find out soon." She stared out the car window at the stuttering traffic—stop, go, stop, go. The traffic in D.C. never seemed to improve no matter what time of day or night. "Rumor has it they don't have any space in the barracks for another female sailor."

"Hope you can find a decent apartment. Pricey around there." Chad flicked on his signal for a few seconds and merged like Jeff Gordon on the Talledega Speedway to make the exit ramp for 95.

Charlie gripped her seat. "I'd like to make it to Mom and Dad's in one piece, please."

He snorted. "Everyone drives like that around here."

Her mind flashed to last night when Angel had almost run them into the orange barrels on the way to the pod. How similar these two men were. "Are we really in that much of a hurry for Mom's meatloaf?"

"She making ham." Chad ran a hand through his short, brown hair. "I know Dad can get under your skin, but can I ask you to just lay off tonight?"

"He doesn't get under my skin."

Her brother gave her the side eye. "Yeah, right." He sped up to pass a minivan that had slowed down for a merging vehicle. "For Mom's sake, let's keep the topic of conversation on easy stuff."

"Like?"

"The food, the weather, her latest knitting project—"

"Mom's knitting again?" Charlie had a hard time holding back a laugh.

"Yeah," Chad said with a smile. "Prepare for all of your Christmas presents this year to be 'handmade' yarn nightmares. She's been taking a class at some yarn shop near their house."

She could do this. She could forget for a few hours the weight of the knowledge she held. Chad was right. Talk about easy stuff. Silly stuff. Things that didn't matter. Anything but Angel Demarco and his mysterious background.

Charlie fiddled with the radio finding nothing but cheesy pop music, bro country, or static. Light conversation had dropped off. Any minute her brother was going to ask about it. She could sense it. Just like she always could. Almost as if she could hear the gears of Chad's mind cranking through his questions and curiosities about her. When had there been a time in her life without this odd twin connection? She couldn't remember.

"Shut that thing off, would you?" Chad brushed her hand away from the dial. "If you really want to listen to something decent, I have loads of good music." He paired his phone with the car stereo system, and the interior filled with an acoustic guitar cover of 'Hungry Like the Wolf.'

Settling in the passenger's seat, she stared out the window at the lush green shrubbery that lined the freeway. "I feel as if I'm being hijacked."

"Hijacked?" Chad's brows came together. "If you don't like my music, that's fine. We can drive in complete stupid silence for thirty minutes." He tapped on his phone's screen.

"That's not what I meant." Crap, a few days before her brother would be heading to Europe, and she had to step in it. "The dinner. Mom and Dad—"

"This isn't about them. You can't BS me, Char. You've always butted heads with Dad. What's really bugging you?" He poked her side. "What is it you don't want Mom and Dad to know?"

Charlie shrugged. Damn, Chad, and his spidey senses.

He mocked a shocked face—round eyes, open mouth, a hand to his cheek. "Wait, are you seeing someone?"

Her whole body flushed. "Maybe." Her mind already skipped ahead to later that night, a rendezvous with the sexy agent, and a chance to question him more deeply about his past. How did Demarco manage to equally attract and fascinate her?

"Who's the lucky guy?" he asked.

They drove right by the exit for Fort Meade. A sign read: NSA Restricted Entrance. The National Security Agency lay less than a mile from 95. A regular-looking office building stood surrounded by trees and, ever since 9/11, a very solid infrastructure of fences and gates and guarded access points.

Her heart thumped in her chest. Their samples were somewhere inside that facility. Right now, people were possibly analyzing the blood taken from the North Dakota pod site. So tantalizingly close to answers about Armas, the body in the woods, and more.

"Well?" Chad prompted her.

She snapped back to the conversation. "A co-worker."

"God, I hope he's not an officer," he muttered.

Of course that would be his biggest concern: an enlisted

person dating an officer. Chad rigidly adhered to military rules and standards without question. When had he not followed every directive ever given to him by parent, teacher, or coach? "No worries, Chad, I'm not dating one of your peers. You're safe from scrutiny."

"That's not what I—" His shoulders bunched up. "I've just seen some really bad outcomes when you cross ranks like that. It's not worth it. No matter how great the guy is. It's a mess not worth getting into."

The tone of his voice made her wonder if perhaps Chad was not such a rigid rules follower after all. A personal experience with an enlisted woman, perhaps? Something to ponder.

"I'll take that into consideration if the opportunity ever comes my way." She carefully controlled her voice to correct him, "His name is Angel Demarco. He's the head of security in our office. Non-military. Which would make you happy, I would think."

"Angel, huh? Sounds like a movie star name."

She chuckled—although the special agent did have the body of a leading man. "He's different."

Chad chewed on that description for a few moments. "So he's not a quiet, librarian type who hangs on your every word?"

"What?"

"Every guy you've ever dated has been such a wimp. Like, absolute loser material."

"And your girlfriends have been perfect?" A few of the women he dated ran through her mind. "Remember Erin? Tall, brunette, and bratty."

"Bratty?" he said with a laugh.

"A girl knows—" Erin had been annoying and clingy and horrible. When her brother had ended that relationship a few years ago, Charlie had let out a joyous shout at the dinner table—when her brother had been ripped to shreds over the break-up. "And I'm sorry she dumped you."

"She didn't dump me."

"Yes, she did. She specifically texted you those words: I, Erin, dump you, Chad."

"I don't remember it quite like that." He stared ahead at the road.

"She broke up with you in a text. That part is true."

"Okay, how did you turn this around on me?" he asked. "I am supposed to be grilling you about your angelic boyfriend."

"His name is Angel. He can't help what his name is." Or could he? If it was true that he was a time traveler, would he have been able to use his given name? Or would he have to take on a new identity to blend into modern society? She sobered at the thoughts that ran through her head. Who was Angel really?

Chad took an exit off of 95 toward their parents' home. "You have exactly five minutes to tell me everything about him or I'll let Mom know."

His teasing took her mind off her speculations. "You wouldn't."

"Do you really want to risk finding out?" He waggled his eyebrows.

She crossed her arms in faux outrage. "Fine." Didn't she deep down want to tell someone about Angel? He was one part mystery, one part hunk. A man who challenged her, confounded her, and attracted her. A dangerous combination. "I'll tell you about him. But no mention of him at Mom and Dad's."

Chad raised a hand. "I swear."

———

"Sweetheart!" Angela Cutter enveloped her daughter in a warm hug. She smelled like fresh-baked bread and merlot. "You're wasting away to nothing." With a firm grip, she held her daughter a foot away to examine her head to toe. "Are you eating three meals a day?"

"Yes, mom, I'm eating." Charlie didn't tell her mother she also was obsessively swimming in the evenings to burn off nervous energy and clear her head. "You rearranged the living room."

"That was months ago." Her mother stepped away to give her brother a similar greeting. "Tall, dark, and handsome. I'm sure all the girls have googly eyes for you, honey."

"Mom." Chad's face reddened. "I'm almost twenty-six. You make it sound as if I'm still in the seventh grade."

Angela shook off the criticism and locked arms with her twin children. "Harrison, the kids are here. Time to be social."

Daisy, the aging and prickly family cat, rubbed against Charlie's legs and meowed.

Charlie's mother marched her and her brother into the dining room and pointed to a seat on the left side of the table. "You sit here, Charlie."

A decorative ceramic platter filled the middle of the table laden with steaming roast beef.

"I thought you said we were having ham?" Charlie shot an accusatory look at her brother who took his seat opposite her.

"Ham?" Her mother trilled her usual high pitched laugh. "Your father hates ham. Too salty or something. I can never remember."

As much as Charlie loved her happy-go-lucky, absentminded mother, her inattention to detail sometimes landed her in hot water with her husband and her children.

Captain Harrison Cutter entered from the opposite doorway. "I love ham. I can't stand lamb. Ham, lamb. Hmmm." He kissed his wife on the cheek before taking a seat at the head of the table.

"That's right." Angela stamped her foot. "Ah, but everyone loves roast beef. I can never go wrong with a roast." She sat in the last empty chair opposite her husband.

"Charlene, you are looking well." Her father eyed her up and down before pouring himself a glass of the merlot on the table.

Her mother must have decided to take a nip before dinner.

"Thanks." She waited for the criticisms to begin. One compliment was typically followed by a barrage of comments that made her feel worse than when she walked in the door.

Chad, perhaps wanting to avoid the usual arguments, interrupted, "Let's eat. I'm starving. Everything looks delicious."

Their mother beamed. "It's only the usual stuff. I'm sure they feed you well in the officer's mess."

Chad took a heaping serving of carved roast beef and then passed the platter to their father. "The food's okay, but I'm going to miss home cooking."

"Rota. You must be excited about that assignment." Harrison

Cutter scooped out mashed potatoes on his plate. "I always hoped to go back overseas."

"Sweetheart," said Angela. "For the kids' sake I'm so glad you were able to stay stateside for the most part." She poured herself a fresh glass of wine.

Wasn't that quite of bit of drinking for her mother? In the past, the woman couldn't finish half a glass.

Her mother redirected the conversation, "Charlie, can you tell us anything about your change in orders? That was so sudden and unusual, wouldn't you say, dear?" She gave her husband a pointed look from across the table.

"I don't know, Mom." Her stomach dipped. Why did she feel so uncomfortable discussing the topic? Anticipating negativity?

"Well, you needed your research, so they must've found out about your studies. Is that it?" Her mother forked a slice of beef and set it on her plate. "That weird manuscript you gave up on."

"I didn't give up." Charlie stopped mid-bite, a spoonful of peas in the air.

"Well, you quit the program," her father said. "Not sure how else we are supposed to perceive that except 'giving up.'"

"Right," Charlie snapped. "I'm a quitter and a failure, I forgot."

"I never said—" Her father raised his voice.

Chad held up a hand. "Can we eat in peace, please? My God, you two ruin every nice meal with this shit."

"Chad, your language," Angela Cutter admonished.

"Sorry, Mom, but how can you stand it?" When he set down his fork, it clanged against the china plate. "I wanted one nice night with all of you before I ship out for the next three years, and they couldn't do it. Not for me. Not even for you, Mom."

Charlie lowered her eyes and pushed her peas around her plate. Why couldn't she control her temper? She had mentally fortified herself for tonight and had failed miserably. "Sorry, Chad."

"I never said you were a failure." Her father quietly cut into a slice of beef. "But something made you leave school and join the Navy without telling us anything. I wish you would've asked for some input."

"Harrison," her mother hissed.

Spots of color appeared in Chad's face. He pushed back from the table. "Just stop it. I don't know why the two of you always go at it like rabid dogs, but I'm sick of it. Dad: Charlie is an adult and can make decisions without your input. Charlie: Dad is only worried about you and wants the best for you." He gripped the back of his chair until his knuckles turned white. "There. Can we move on?"

"Honey, please, sit down." Angela Cutter's eyes grew watery, and she reached for her son. "Please." Her posture crumpled.

Harrison Cutter stood up from the table and set his napkin on his plate, "I've lost my appetite."

"Dad, come on," Chad said.

Their father lifted a hand to wave off his son's plea and retreated to his office at the back of the house.

Angela Cutter dropped her chin. "He loves you so much, Charlie."

"Oh, Mom." What was it about her father that set her off so much? Although she desperately wanted his approval, she never seemed to be able to live up to his expectations. Every choice a mistake. Every opinion wrong.

"You're just too much alike." Her mother took a drink of wine. "That's what I've always said." As she stared out the front window behind her husband's chair, her gaze blurred.

Chad walked over to his mother and put an arm around her shoulders. "That's it, Mom. And they both can't see it." He locked eyes with Charlie and nodded his head.

She gulped. She knew what he meant, and because she loved her mother and hated to see her so distraught, she said, "I'm dating someone, Mom."

Her mother sniffed a few times, squeezed her son's hand, and lifted her head. "Oh? Tell me about him. Is he handsome?"

CHAPTER 11

"HARRY, THE KIDS LEFT." Angela stood in the doorway of her husband's study. "I wish you'd joined us for dessert."

He sat in his favorite chair next to a side table with a single reading lamp lit and a book in his lap. "Charlene knows." How that was possible he didn't know, but deep inside he'd felt it for a while. "We should've told them a long time ago."

"No." Angela's reply was sharp and tinged with fear. "That's not true. She was only annoyed with you, as per usual. Ever since high school, you two have butted heads. This is nothing different. When two people are so much alike—"

He slammed the book shut. "Stop it, Angie. Just stop it. Why do you insist on that kind of nonsense?" With a flourish, he whipped off his reading glasses and knit his brows.

His wife shrank back. "I only meant that you both have so much in common: stubborn, smart, determined."

"Yes, Charlene's always been smart. Too smart for her own good." He smiled at the memory of his daughter as a young girl winning every science fair and spelling bee she entered. But his heart sank at the adult Charlene. Slipping away from them. Becoming someone he didn't recognize. "And she knows that something isn't right about this family."

Angela's eyes grew wet. "How dare you say that, Harrison."

He rose from his chair and placed his book back on the wall of bookshelves behind his desk. "I didn't say that to hurt you, Angie."

"Our family is just as normal as anyone else's."

With tender hands, he gripped his wife's narrow shoulders. "Of course it is, sweetheart. But someday we will have to tell them. And I'd rather choose that moment than have Charlene figure it out by herself. That would be so much worse."

Angela looked up at him. "Can't it wait a little while longer?" Her face grew red and splotchy. "She was opening up to me out there. Telling me about a man she's dating. I don't want to drive her away." She wiped the back of her hand across her nose.

Her pleading words drove a knife into his heart. How could he hurt his beautiful wife? How could he ruin the relationship she had with her twin children by confessing their deepest secrets? Secrets husband and wife had promised to keep between them forever?

But neither one of them had known when they'd looked down at baby Charlene and baby Chad snuggled together in a single crib that someday those babies would grow up and have minds of their own. That they might wonder about things that didn't add up. Questions people asked. Timelines that didn't quite match up with the dates.

He pointed to a framed photograph on the wall of his study. "Remember when they were little? It was so much easier then."

Angela turned to view the photo of Charlene and Chad as toddlers washing their old German Shepherd, Duke, with the hose in the backyard of their base housing in Texas. Charlene had a thousand-watt smile on her face and held the hose, while Chad scrubbed the dog down with a sponge he'd found in the laundry room.

His wife smiled, but the smile didn't reach her eyes. "I sent that to you when you were on TDY in Germany."

"I wish I'd been there for that."

"I know." She put her arm around her husband's waist. "You've been a good father to them. A good provider."

He kissed his wife on the top of her head. Oh, how he wished he'd been there for all the little things. His heart squeezed painfully. "At least I got that part right."

"Maybe we can take a trip to Spain to see Chad when he's all settled in."

Casually, the conversation had shifted away from his desires to be honest with his children to his wife's need to live in her fantasy world a little longer. Where her daughter and son came over for family dinners, and they pretended all was normal, all was fine. And that no secrets existed. How many more years could he remain silent?

As Charlene drifted further away, he had an urgency to confess. He loved his daughter, but the lies were eating at him a little bit at a time. The arguments, the abrasive responses, all a means to protect himself when Charlene found out everything. Would she see him in a different light? A negative light? Would she want to have nothing to do with him? The thought of it was frightening, as she and Chad were his only children, but he knew his daughter sensed it. Deep inside she knew something wasn't right.

"Sure, we can go to Spain after my retirement. In fact, we can go anywhere you've ever wanted to travel, Angie." He drew her into his arms and rested his chin on her head. "All those years you sat at home and waited for me to be free of my obligations? Now it's your turn."

"Harry, I love you so very much." His wife whispered into his chest. "What would I have done without you?"

"I love you, too, Angie."

Without him wanting it to, doubt crept into his mind. Would his wife have chosen him if things had been different? Even after twenty-five years, the idea still plagued him. Would she really?

He tamped down the thought for the millionth time and hugged his wife closer.

CHAPTER 12

CHARLIE WAVED at her brother as he sat idling his car on the curb near Angel's apartment. Although she was grateful he'd agreed to drop her off at the special agent's home, the protective brother thing needed to end. Guess he wasn't going to leave until he saw her safely enter the building. If her brother could see her face, he'd notice the most exaggerated eye roll in the history of eye rolls.

How embarrassing. As if Chad were her father, and she was going on a date to prom.

Before she could knock, Angel opened the door wearing a loose pair of athletic pants and a gray t-shirt that clung to his well-developed chest and shoulders.

"Is that your brother?" Angel stood barefoot on the stoop and squinted at the dark vehicle lurking on the street.

Charlie shielded her eyes and looked down at the concrete path in front of his apartment. "Is he still there?" Why did her ears feel so hot?

He gently grasped her by the shoulders and moved her three inches to his right. "Yes. Should I ask him to come in?"

"God, no." Her heart skipped a beat.

He chuckled. "I'm kidding, Charlie." Instead of approaching her brother's car, Angel gave a quick wave at the tinted windows.

Chad sped off.

"Thank God." She drew a deep breath through her nose. "Dinner was brutal."

"Oh?" He guided her inside. "Tell me more."

The air smelled of wet potting soil and fertilizer. Could it be possible Angel had added another three or four plants to his collection since her first visit?

"My mother knows all about you, which means—" She checked the time on her cell phone. "So does my father by now. Expect to be asked to some sort of awkward dinner at a chain restaurant in the near future with Angela and Harrison. My mother loves the Olive Garden. I pre-apologize."

He raised a brow. "Sounds interesting."

Angel spun her to face him in the foyer. Their gazes met.

"Hello," she breathed. His brown eyes glowed and held a warmth she'd only recently noticed.

"Hello," he whispered.

While his hands clasped her waist, he kissed her slowly.

After the stressful evening at her parent's home, the close contact soothed her and brought down the tension inside. Could she forget about the questions she had and, instead, spend the evening in his arms? Vivid memories of the previous night filled her mind. Wouldn't be so bad to experience a repeat performance.

They broke apart.

He swept a hand across her brow. "You are so beautiful."

Heat crept into her cheeks. They were getting way off track. "Thanks." She pulled out of his grasp.

"Something wrong?" His hands remained suspended in the air, as if he held a ghost Charlie in them.

Crap. She'd messed up.

"I'm sorry, I didn't mean to be so abrupt." She rubbed a hand over her lips. "I have so many questions for you, and I didn't want us to get—you know—*distracted*."

He nodded his head slowly. "You're right. You're right." His gaze roved her figure. I just can't help myself." He slipped past her, touching her hip, and headed to the kitchen. "Do you want a drink? Tea? Coffee?"

She took a seat in the brown armchair. "Some coffee would be great."

"You got it."

As he searched in his cupboard for coffee and a filter, Charlie made light conversation as a warm up to the harder questions she wanted to ask. "I wish I had a green thumb like you. I had a cactus once, a gift from a friend, and I managed to kill it in one semester. Something about too much water, or not enough water? Wait, don't cactus like no water? I can't remember."

"Cactuses need water, but not very much." Angel filled the reservoir of the coffeemaker with fresh water from the tap. "I grew up around plants. I guess it's rote for me now. I don't even think about it. I put them on a watering schedule, fertilizer, and those lights up there." He pointed at several can lights that were mounted in the ceiling above her. "Full-spectrum day bulbs. Whenever I go to work, I turn them on."

"Quite the set up. I probably couldn't handle more than one."

"I could point you in the right direction, if you really wanted to try again. Although you wouldn't think it, orchids are very easy to care for." He pointed at a cluster of blooming orchids in one corner of the room—pink, white, yellow. "Especially in such a humid climate. They love humidity. We didn't have orchids where I grew up. It was one of the first plants I acquired when I moved in here. So delicate and special. My mother would've loved them." His gaze grew unfocused, and his posture relaxed.

"Tell me more about where you grew up." The tenderness in his voice surprised her. "And when you grew up. I want to know everything."

"One thing at a time, Charlie. One thing at a time." He pressed the 'on' button on the coffeemaker and then joined her in the living room, choosing a padded wooden bench surrounded by flora of all kinds for his seat. "Let's start with the life I used to live. A life that I probably will never return to." He stared down at his hands for a few moments, as if gathering the courage to speak.

Charlie held her breath and leaned forward. At last, the real story about Angel Demarco and who he really was. "Please," Charlie urged. "Tell me more. I want to know."

Angel looked at his hands and then stroked his chin. "This is hard for me, I want you to understand that."

"You can trust me."

He locked eyes with her and nodded. "There's so much to explain. And a lot of it probably will make no sense."

Charlie clasped her hands together in her lap. "I know you traveled through time and that you had to have traveled in a pod. I know that sometimes you blend in perfectly with everyone around you, and then suddenly you don't. I know that something painful happened and it would feel better if you shared that pain with someone."

He winced. "I don't even know where to start."

"Start at the beginning," she said as calmly as she could.

"The beginning. Yes, the beginning." He let out a sigh. "The truth is, Charlie, I don't know 'when' I grew up, because our idea of time and years have changed over the centuries. But I do know this: I am from a future time. A time well beyond the one we live in now."

"Wait, the future?" Not the answer she had expected. The manuscript, the instructions to build the machine, the arrival of Armas—she'd assumed all of it had occurred hundreds of years ago. She shook her head. "I don't understand. How—?"

"Where I come from, we don't live like you do. All of those gadgets and screens and things."

"But you said you are from a future time." She frowned. "How could that be?"

"We lost knowledge. I didn't realize how much knowledge until I found myself here. And it was overwhelming." His eyes widened before he reasserted control. "The amount of information that zips across the world in a matter of moments. I still sometimes have trouble grasping the concept."

"How was knowledge lost?" She tilted her head to one side.

"We called it the 'Zhadan.' Hundreds of years before my birth." He gestured with his hands, an invisible ball between them, that suddenly flew apart. "A massive weapon of some kind that destroyed all knowledge. All electronics. The whole of the world was knocked down to its knees."

"Who would do such a thing?" She recoiled at the thought.

"We didn't know." He shook his head. "We lived in the aftermath, and life was different for us than our ancestors. We had stories passed down from one generation to the next, and a new written record, but very little survived."

How could that be possible? The millions of texts and journals and newspapers, the learning built upon centuries of tradition and accumulated knowledge. "But you had books, surely, historical texts to rely on."

"No. The books you have on your shelves, the libraries? Before the Zhadan everything had been moved into electronic form after an academic purge sparked by out-of-control mobs. Those in academia and the government decided knowledge was safer in electronic form. They thought they were helping knowledge survive, instead they made it more vulnerable. Only a few books remained as historical pieces for display. Why spend the time and money to print more books when everyone gathered knowledge from electronic sources?"

"How far into the future was this?" Charlie mused.

"I'm not sure." He shrugged. "It could be five hundred years; it could be a thousand. But the exact number doesn't matter, does it?"

"No, I suppose it doesn't."

"So as a result of this disjointed understanding of history, I grew up in a world where electronics were shunned. It was a weakness that had been exploited in the past and returned us to primitive living. We worked hard for everything we had. I grew up in a farming community. We raised pigs and cows and sheep. We ate what we grew. Any attempt to improve our standard of living created fear among the older generations. They'd been raised to maintain a simple lifestyle to avoid a second Zhadan. We couldn't survive another. Great fear surrounded that possibility. We do not know who destroyed the world, so there was fear it could easily happen again."

"Zhadan," Charlie mused. "That sounds familiar." She tucked it away in her mind for further contemplation at a later time. As a logophile, she couldn't turn off that part of her brain. "But how did you travel here if your culture didn't allow for such projects? A machine that travels through time would be more than an 'improvement.' It would require great knowledge and skill."

"Like the mysterious person in the fifteenth century?" he posited.

"Yes. True." As she contemplated the connection between the future and the past, she had a feeling Angel would connect these two things for her if only she could be patient. So much to learn. So much to comprehend. "Another time period with no modern knowledge, yet someone achieved an unheard of marvel."

"Charlie, I mentioned how I lived, how I grew up. As time went on, not everyone accepted our way of life."

"Oh?" Her pulse quickened.

"Most of us wished for humanity to remain pure, unadulterated by unnatural things."

"Like computers, the internet, electricity, even?"

"Yes."

"That sounds so primitive."

"But it worked for us," Angel explained. "We lived a simple life, and though it was hard and sometimes we suffered through difficult times, we persevered as a people."

"It sounds like the Pilgrims."

"By what I have read over the years, it would be similar to the lives of American in the Wild West. Wagon trains, raising cattle, growing crops."

"And who were the other people who wanted to live differently?"

"Eventually they became known as the Genesis Project."

———

Charlie found herself fascinated by the story Angel told. He was from the future, but yet the future was not the world she anticipated it would be. "Why was the Genesis Project different?"

"The Genesis Project began with noble intentions. We'd lost what you'd call 'modern science' after the Zhadan. Many died after that event. Humans had become so dependent on machines and electronics that when they were wiped out, so was everything on which life had been built. Including medical knowledge and scientific advancements. The Genesis Project was a group of our most curious, our most intelligent men and women who grew tired of being held back by our elders and the ruling classes who would not allow for a return to how people before us had once lived."

She couldn't shut off her curious mind from wanting more of an explanation about what had happened to send human beings back to an agrarian lifestyle. Only one thing kept popping up in her mind. "The Zhadan sounds as if it was possibly an EMP—an electromagnetic pulse."

Angel nodded. "I have run across that term since I arrived here, and it does seem to match up with the stories we were told."

"That would fry everything...even down to the components in your car." Charlie considered the implications. "We would definitely be reduced to a primitive state." Factories, power production, trucks, ships, planes—everything upon which the world depended had ended overnight. Her mind reeled at the idea.

"When I was nineteen or twenty, we had an incredibly hard winter." Angel paused here. His shoulders drooped. "Most of our animals died. And because we lost our animals, we had trouble planting crops. There was talk of starvation and difficult times ahead." He stared at nothing, his eyes blank of expression. He crossed his arms as if warding off a terrible memory. "A man came to our village, his name was Byron Allwood. He was part of the Genesis Project. He wanted to recruit more to his cause. He wanted to build an even better world than what existed before the Zhadan. He even spoke of avoiding the mistakes of the past. Many of us were swayed by his arguments." He spat out the last sentence. "When you are cold, hungry, and broken, you can easily be manipulated by words. He urged us to come to a speech he would make the following night in a village not far from us. Both my younger sister and I decided to attend. My parents wouldn't have let us go if they'd known—we were barely out of our teens."

"You have a sister?"

"Yes, I did." He scrubbed a hand over his face. "And I wish I'd never taken her with me. Things would be so different now."

Angel left the bench and returned to the kitchen to pour them each a cup of coffee. He handed her a steaming mug, and Charlie sipped it slowly contemplating the unbelievable story he told. If she hadn't translated the text and seen Armas arrive in a pod with her own eyes, she'd think he was crazy. She wanted to know how this story of the future and his life there tied into the pods and into their research, but needed more details about this mysterious rudimentary existence that awaited mankind many centuries in the future.

"Tell me about the speech," she prompted.

"Allwood explained his plan and the experiments the Genesis Project had been conducting in secret. All animal cells and human cells maintain a small electric charge in order to communicate within the body...brain cells, nerve cells, a whole host of cells. Byron posited that the way to protect the future from another Zhadan would be to create biologic systems using the same principles. Such small electric impulses could not be as easily disrupted. His theories made a lot of sense based off of what we knew about the past. Although my parents hadn't attended his speech, several elders from our village had been curious. The Genesis Project had begun to distill the idea into a working concept, which would rebuild the world to the modern, advanced place it used to be without the risk."

"So did the Genesis Project convince people?" Charlie leaned forward. "Did they have a viable solution?"

"Many of us believed so. Byron Allwood was a convincing speaker. He recruited able bodied men and women to join the work they were involved in. He promised we would all benefit from the discoveries being made. We believed in him—or most of us did. My sister more strongly than myself." His chin dipped to his chest.

Something bad had happened to his sister. She could sense it in his words and body language, but she didn't want to ask. Not yet. She had to let the story play out.

"When the elders found out what Byron and his followers were planning, they were frightened," he continued. "They were worried what this meant for the tenuous existence of human beings in the world. We were facing a bad year with little food, and it was believed wasting time and energy on risky experiments threatened everyone. It used precious resources we didn't have. And that is when the split occurred."

"A split?"

"Between those who wanted a purity of nature, and those who wanted to enhance nature and build an even better world and a better mankind to go with it. Byron called us 'The Purists,' as if it was a dirty name."

"I can understand why many were scared of trying something new."

"Not only trying something new," Angel's voice cranked up a few notches. "We 'Purists' feared altering nature would damage the earth, human beings, animals. We wanted laws in place to stop the Genesis Project devotees from conducting their experiments."

"But how could these experiments be so harmful? Biological circuits? It doesn't sound harmful."

Angel curled his lip. "This is where you are wrong, Charlie. It wasn't merely about recreating circuitry and electronics. I wish it were. But, to convince others their work was good for the world, the Genesis Project began using their new knowledge to experiment genetically on human beings who were considered 'mistakes'—the deformed, the diseased, the insane."

"What kinds of genetic experiments?"

"They hated to see suffering. Disease, physical ailments, injuries. One of these Genesis Project followers managed to find an old medical textbook, long thought lost to time and the elements. It became their Bible. They began to learn from it and had a desire to fix what they saw as needless pain, needless death. And I have to say I think at the beginning, they thought they had a noble cause. But then the Genesis Project followers began experiments we considered going against nature itself. They wanted to be able to correct the 'defects' of humans."

"What defects?"

"Whatever they deemed to be 'wrong' about someone...their appearance, their imperfections."

"I see."

"We Purists saw every human being as worthy and special—

from the youngest to the oldest, from the sickest to the healthiest. All had worth and value and were made as they should be."

"But what if you could fix a physical problem with a little bit of knowledge?"

"We didn't see it that way. We all took care of one another, no matter the difficulty. We all cared for each other the same. The Genesis Project made people feel as if they were damaged, unworthy, in need of correction. And eventually they went beyond merely 'fixing' what was broken. They thought they could make human beings even better."

"Better how?"

CHAPTER 13

ANGEL COULDN'T KEEP STILL. He set his mug on the bench and began to pace the living room, rubbing a hand on the back of his neck. "His work went beyond the norms of humanity...if one person ran fast, Allwood wanted him to run faster. If one person was quick at learning, Allwood wanted to make him even smarter."

"All using genetics? DNA?" Charlie's gaze followed his movements. "But how? You said you had been reduced to a simplistic life. That everything we see around us in the twenty-first century was alien to you and unbelievable."

"These were secrets Allwood kept close to the vest." Angel shrugged. "But we saw the results of his experimentation—the physical and mental ruination of vulnerable human beings, and to what end? Who was this improvement for? Beyond trying to improve how we lived our lives, Allwood seemed bent on an improved human."

"That sounds horrific." Images of the Nazis and their medical experiments on Jews and others in their clutches ran through her mind. History repeating itself, even hundreds of years into the future.

"Some in my village actually sought him out for help with their own ailments or perceived imperfections. He had an ability to hone in on people's weaknesses and convince them he could help." He paused his steps and stared down at his empty hands. "One morning I woke to do my chores in the barn, when it was discovered my own sister had run off to join the Genesis Project."

A sudden coldness hit her core.

Gently, between his fingers, he rubbed a leaf on a rubber plant beside the bench. His voice dropped several notches. "I had no idea Risa had been swayed by Allwood's speeches."

"Risa—" She lifted a hand to her mouth. It couldn't be. His sister?

"She bought into his ideas and had kept it from me, her own brother." His gaze became unfocused. "I thought we had been close. That we shared everything. I was the one who encouraged her to go to his speech in the first place. But he had a hold over her, and I had no idea how strong." He tore the leaf off the rubber plant and crushed it in his fingers.

She sat quietly, but her mind raced to make connections, to understand what he was telling her.

"I found the notes after she'd run off. She'd been corresponding with Allwood." He scooped up his coffee mug and dropped it into the sink. "God, why didn't I stop her?" White knuckled hands gripped the porcelain edge.

Charlie joined him in the kitchen, set her mug in the sink next to his, and settled a hand on his back. "She was a grown woman. She could make up her own mind."

"But I'm her brother." He shrugged off her touch. "I should've kept her safe from that madman."

"You couldn't have known—" Her hand hung in the air. How could she comfort him? Bring peace to his tortured mind?

"Yes, I could have, Charlie." He whipped open the dishwasher and flung both mugs into it, slammed it shut, and then whirled to face her. "I was her older brother. I was supposed to protect her, keep her safe, and I utterly failed."

"Risa." Her breath hitched in her throat. "That's your sister's name?"

"Yes." He scrubbed a hand over his face, and his eyebrows gathered in. "Now you understand why I needed to know who wrote that manuscript. Why I suspected...but couldn't reveal...I thought it might be her. Dreaded it might be her." He squeezed his eyes shut. "I've lost her, Charlie. She was trapped in time, and I lost her. My only sister, dead centuries ago."

And Charlie's work on the Voynich manuscript had been the thing allowing him to piece it together. No wonder he had so much interest in her work. No wonder his actions and words flashed hot and cold. He'd known all this time NCIS-A was seeking out time machines, not alien spaceships. And every one that landed, each pod they'd discovered, he imagined his sister could be in it. Even the one that had exploded in Idaho.

My God. How horrific.

"Is that how you ended up in this time, Angel?" If only he would look at her. "Were you trying to find your sister?"

"I had to stop them, Charlie, don't you see?" He backed away from her. "The Genesis Project. Not only were they breaking the laws of nature, they had stolen my sister away with their lies. With Allwood's lies. He lured her away with promises—"

She furrowed her brow. "Did she fall in love with him?"

After putting the coffee filters away, he slammed the cupboard door. "That wasn't love. Allwood used her. He wanted her mind, her intelligence."

"Oh?" She needed to tread carefully.

"My sister, although raised in the simple lifestyle of our village, had a mind for science and mathematics." He leaned against the counter, and his tense body relaxed as he remembered happier times.

"I thought everything had been lost centuries before," she prompted. A young woman with an interest in science and math, but living an agrarian life? Impressive. "She must've been very bright."

He nodded, and a faint smile played across his lips. "My sister —she was unlike any other child in our village. She thrived on learning. Yes, most knowledge had been lost, but the basics of education: reading, writing, math. Those remained. We still had schools and learning. While most girls cared for the animals and worked in the kitchens, my sister grew experiments in the barn." His eyes brightened at the memories. "My father indulged her because he loved his only daughter. Growing weird mushrooms or strange bacteria or whatever she was interested in."

If only Charlie could've met his sister. What a fascinating woman she must have been.

He swept his arm, gesturing at the multitude of flora that filled his apartment. "The plants you see everywhere? Why do I have them? They remind me of her. Her bedroom used to be full of plants and vines and shrubs. Foundations for many of her experiments." He leaned in to smell a purple orchid that sat on the edge of the counter. "I thought, by having these around me, I'd miss her less. I'd be able to hold on to her somehow. I really believed one day I would find her. But your translations—"

"I'm sorry, Angel." She swallowed the lump in her throat. Why did she push him for these painful details? "I didn't know—"

"How could you know? I couldn't tell anyone where I came from. Why I was here. I couldn't ask questions about anything. I had to figure it out and quickly. You have no idea how confusing it was for me when I arrived."

Charlie studied him from the opposite side of the kitchen. How strange was it for him to arrive in their time with no friends, no family, no information? She had so many questions.

"So Risa, she ran off to work for Allwood?"

"He lured her away. He was dishonest and stole her from us." He crossed his arms and a dark look took over his face. "Who knows what he did to her once she fell into his hands."

"Do you think he did any experiments on her?" she asked as gently as she could. "Any of those genetic experiments?"

His brow wrinkled. "He played into her self-doubts about her intelligence, her physical characteristics, and he promised her just about anything to make sure he had what he needed to pursue the plans of the Genesis Project. Which went much further than anyone knew."

"Was there any attempt to stop him?"

"We tried." He stared at the floor, and his shoulders slumped. "I joined up with a team to stop him. When we felt things had gone too far. He had to be purged. They all had to be purged...every single one of his followers." He spat out the last sentence.

"Including your sister?"

Angel didn't answer her. He scrubbed a hand over his face as he distanced himself from her and sat at the small table beyond the island.

As Charlie stood in Angel's kitchen, surrounded by plants, listening to his story, pieces of the puzzle came together. "Armas could be your nephew."

Spots of color entered his cheeks. "No."

"Why would you say that?"

He raised his voice. "Impossible."

"I think you have to consider the possibility—" Why would Angel be so negative toward the idea? Armas, who had no one, could possibly have someone. An uncle. Angel could be his uncle.

"Stop, Charlie." He held his head in his hands. "Stop, please."

"I'm sorry, Angel." In a fluid motion, she rounded the island and knelt at his feet. She'd have to keep these kinds of thoughts to herself for the time being. It was all too hurtful for him. "Everything you told me? It's a lot to comprehend." The two of them alone couldn't tackle the situation revealed by his story. What if they included someone on the team? "We need to share this with Commander Orr. He could help you."

"No." He lifted his head and looked her in the eye.

"But why not?" Her brows came together.

"You think this was easy for me?" He clasped her hand in his. "To tell you the truth of who I am?"

"Of course not." She pulled her hand free and sat in the empty chair at the table.

"You are the first living soul I have told since I arrived here." His dark gaze burned into her. "Just you. And there's a reason for that."

"You have to trust someone else besides me, Angel." Why couldn't he see how helpless she was? Having all of this knowledge and then having no real way to do anything? It gnawed at her. "I don't have any power. Orr could provide all kinds of resources—"

"If I trusted Orr, I would've told him all of this months ago. I have to be careful, Charlie. If the wrong person found out I was from the future, that I traveled in a pod—"

Any scenario she ran through her mind ended badly.

She nodded. "You're right. I'd never see you again, would I?"

"I doubt it. I'd be locked away and prodded and poked. Turned into a living specimen—a freak from the future. No one can know, Charlie. Only you."

Under the table, she touched his knee. "I want to help."

"I know you do." He gripped her hand. "Would you find it odd to know that I was working on the translations myself? Before I came to this time?"

"The manuscript?"

"No, the manuscript was a new discovery to me and likely lost to time—my future time, that is." He played with her fingers. "The Genesis Project learned to hide their actions in coded documents. We still aren't sure who created the code, but it began to appear in correspondence we intercepted. A way for Allwood to hide his true intentions, the true goals of his organization."

The writing wasn't hundreds of years old, it was a futuristic code carried to the fifteenth century. "And your sister took it with her to the past." Her mind opened and processed the new information like a hungry blue jay cracking into a peanut.

"Yes."

"Were you able to decipher any of it?"

A faint smile played at his lips. "I thought I made some headway, but unlike you I don't have a degree in linguistics."

"I never finished my degree."

"Charlie, you are so unaware of your capabilities." His gaze grew heated. "That's one of the things that drew me to you—so talented, so intelligent, but you hide it behind this façade of innocence."

For a moment she wanted to return to the night before, when she knew nothing about Angel's connection to the pods and time travel. Things had been so much simpler when they were together without all of these complex and troubling details. Her mind was overwhelmed with new data.

With one final squeeze of her hand, he sighed. "I'm tired, Charlie. So tired." Then he tugged her toward him. "Would you stay here with me tonight? I've been alone for so long—"

Without hesitation, she slid from her chair to his lap. How could she resist? "And those other women, Stormy told me about?"

He wrapped an arm around her waist. "I hate to admit that I followed my baser instincts. When you've spent years sharing yourself with no one—living in isolation among crowds—you'll do anything to grab a few minutes of normalcy. Pretend normalcy, but normalcy nonetheless. And those—connections—let me forget for a little while where I was, when I was."

She bent her head to touch his. How awful it would be to live without roots, without connections, without hope. A stranger transported to the past who had nothing. How did he do it? How did he survive?

"I never thought I could have something like this, Charlie."

Their lips met in a fiery kiss. As if the very act of revealing himself to her shed invisible barriers between them. Charlie wrapped her arms around his neck. Angel rose, lifting her in his arms, and headed toward his bedroom.

"I'll stay," Charlie whispered.

CHAPTER 14

Minot Air Force Base, North Dakota

LTJG COLE KELLERMAN powered down the iPad that had kept him entertained for most of the flight from Andrews Air Force Base and switched on his cell phone.

He opened his encrypted texting app to type in a message:

> We've landed. Will make contact soon.

The C-17 taxied to the hangar where they'd deplane. Although night had settled, at least it wasn't raining this trip. Besides picking up the body, he had some investigative work to do, and it would make it much easier to conduct in dry conditions.

"Pretty rough landing, eh?" A middle-aged representative, whose name Kellerman had forgotten promptly upon introduction, had wandered down the aisle. "But I'll guess you do a lot of these jump flights."

Why did people assume he wanted to have banal conversations? These politicians were really something else. He'd chosen the second to last row in the dozen or so rows of seats for a reason. Too many words tired him out.

"Yes, sir." Kellerman's Officer Candidate School training kicked in. Traveling in uniform on these flights, though required, annoyed the crap out of him. Every Tom, Dick, and Harry from

DC who wanted a free flight shared the space and forced him to socialize so they could pretend they cared about those who served. The less said, the better.

"I'd rather be landing in North Dakota in August than in January." The politician smiled the fake smile that probably won him his seat. "But I'll bet you're a tough kid."

"Yes, sir." Kellerman stared at the front of the fuselage willing the door to spring open to make his escape.

His phone blinged.

Shit.

What bad timing for a text reply. He wished he were somewhere more private.

The older man's eyebrows shot up. "Right, we can switch out of airplane mode." He fumbled for the inner pocket of his gray suit jacket. "I'm waiting to find out how the vote went this afternoon. I had to catch this flight for a townhall in Bismarck tomorrow morning, so I couldn't stick around to find out the end result."

Kellerman nodded dumbly. His thumb itched to unlock his phone.

"Excuse me, Lieutenant." The representative's gaze focused on his phone screen. "I have a few voicemails I need to listen to before I head to the hotel." With a sigh, he held it to his ear and headed back to his seat near the front of the fuselage.

Thank God.

Need those samples ASAP.

Kellerman replied in the affirmative.

Nothing new added to his list of tasks. Good.

As he waited for the door to open, he absentmindedly scrolled through his photos. Pausing on one, he expanded it with his forefinger and thumb for a close up view. Cutter and Demarco sitting at a bus stop.

Strange to see them casually chatting after hours when they seemed to constantly be at odds. What was up? He'd made it his business to keep tabs on his co-workers. Since Cutter had arrived, the power balance in the office had changed. Any attempts at friendliness with the new recruit hadn't worked out well.

Demarco, typically cold and standoffish, had changed his tune when Cutter entered the picture. Why?

He scrolled through the series of photos of the same scene. If that drunk idiot hadn't stumbled across his hiding place behind the bushes near the barracks, he would've maybe uncovered more about their interaction. Instead, he had to scramble around the corner to remain unseen, losing his view of the bench.

Were they discussing work outside of the SCIF?

Cutter was fresh out of language school. Usually that meant a stickler for the rules. NCIS hammered the fear of God into newbies after granting them a Top Secret clearance. And Stick-Up-His-Ass Demarco? That didn't jibe.

The exit door opened with a whoosh. Passengers worked their way forward.

Kellerman slipped his phone and iPad into his military-issue duffel bag. He'd have to return to those photos and his thoughts later. Right now, he had a contact to meet and a job to do. Two jobs, actually.

Thank God Orr trusted him enough to not ask too many questions. With more people to keep track of, increased information to parse through, it grew harder and harder to stick to his orders.

As he exited the plane, he scanned the dark runway next to the hangar. A limo waited for the representative and his cronies, who'd nabbed seats as well—all courtesy of the US taxpayer. A couple of airmen disappeared into the night, probably returning to their home base after some sort of TDY travel. Off to the left of the limo stood a dark figure: his contact.

Kellerman headed straight past the limo. No time to waste. He needed to return to the office as soon as possible to keep tabs on anything else that might be revealed in his absence.

His thoughts skipped to the boy.

What to make of him? Maybe Dr. Stern's test would uncover something he could share. Was it a link? Or merely a distraction from the goal?

A solidly built airman in her late 20s with dark hair stuffed neatly under her flight cap saluted Kellerman. "Welcome, Lieutenant."

He returned her salute and read off her nametag, "Thank you, Airman Fletcher."

"Sir." Fletcher handed him a manila folder. "These are the documents you requested for the body transfer. It's late, so I'm to drive you to your quarters for the evening. Tomorrow I'll accompany you to the site where the body was discovered."

He took the folder, and she hefted his duffel bag. Although he wanted to protest, the muscular airman carried it without much effort.

They walked side by side to a white sedan parked on the west side of the hangar. A single light affixed over a door lit up the parking area. A host of moths fluttered around the yellow bulb.

"My intentions are to return to Andrews Tuesday. I've heard there's a flight scheduled."

Fletcher set the bag on the pavement by the trunk, then opened the rear door on the passenger's side of the vehicle, as if Kellerman were a dignitary who required a chauffeur. Laughable. He was reminded daily at the office that Commander Orr outranked him by several steps.

"I'll sit up here if you don't mind." He chose the front seat and skirted around the young airman.

Even five years into his life as a Navy officer, he had not adjusted to the privileges of rank. Probably because every place he'd been assigned involved combining forces with civilians and other branches. At some point, it all became a wash and distinct rank differences grew foggy. His degree and intelligence had vaulted him ahead of his peers, which had been recognized by his civilian boss at Area 51.

"Of course, sir." A strong wind kicked up, and Fletcher adjusted the collar of her shirt, which had flipped up. She took position next to the passenger door.

"I think I can manage." Kellerman pulled the door closed without assistance.

The airman scurried behind the car, opened the trunk, and made short work of his bag. The wind gusted again, and she pressed her flight cap to her head. She slid into the driver's seat with hands noticeably trembling.

"Let's forget about rank in here, okay? We have to work together for the next day or two. I need someone who can do as I ask without any questions and keep me on a schedule so I don't miss the flight back."

"Yes, sir." She took a deep breath and let it out before starting the car and backing up. "I can do that, sir."

As she drove away from the hangar, he took the opportunity to ask a few questions. "First escort assignment?"

"Yes, sir." Sweat beaded her brow.

No matter how much he wanted her to relax, she only seemed to grow more nervous with each passing minute.

"You'll do fine. Mostly driving duty."

"What about the body, sir?"

He confined a laugh to a snort. "Never helped transport a corpse before?"

When he said the word 'corpse' her lips pressed into a straight line and, if it weren't so dark in the vehicle, he guessed her face turned a few shades paler.

"No, sir."

"If it makes you feel any better, I haven't done it either." Whatever it took to calm her nerves. Did she really need to know the truth? "We'll figure it out together."

"But collecting samples, sir." She followed a long, straight road past a chain link fence topped with three rows of barbed wire.

"You only need to hand me the vials and labels. I can do the rest."

"Okay, okay." She took a few deep breaths. "As long as I don't have to look at it—him—again." The airman slid a quick glance his way.

"Oh." So she wasn't quite as uninvolved as he'd been told. The text he'd received earlier in the day alluded to an assistant who wouldn't ask questions and wouldn't have a clue as to his purpose. "I didn't realize you were part of the recovery crew."

She nodded and turned the vehicle toward a collection of buildings opposite the main runway. "I was on watch yesterday when the call came in from Devils Lake. Me and Airman Quintana. The captain on duty assigned me to the crew. Quintana stayed behind." The car's headlights lit up the sign for the Visiting Officer's Quarters. "He owes me," she muttered under her breath.

Quintana and an unnamed captain also involved? He made a mental note to find out the officer's name. Just in case.

"They're expecting you inside, sir. I'll retrieve your bag." She reached for the door handle.

"Pop the trunk. I can handle my own bag, Airman."

As the young woman pulled a lever near her knee to open it, Kellerman thought ahead to the tasks he needed to accomplish tomorrow. Fletcher was eager to please, which should help in collecting two identical sets of samples. One for NCIS-A and Dr. Stern's lab, and one for the professor.

———

In the morgue exam room of the base hospital Kellerman stood over a zipped body bag.

Fletcher's face had turned the color of an unripe banana, and she white knuckled the edge of the gurney.

"Are you going to be sick, Airman?" The lieutenant pushed his glasses up his nose with a nitrile-gloved finger.

"No, sir." She gulped while staring at the unopened bag. "Can I get a drink of water?" Her gaze wandered to a sink along one wall with a stack of paper cups next to it.

"Go for it." The young lieutenant suppressed a grin. He could manage the samples alone if he had to. Why was she selected as his assistant anyway? "What's your connection to the professor?"

Before answering, she filled a cup with water and drank half of it. "Groom Lake."

"I don't remember seeing you there." Although he didn't have the best memory for faces, he had been stationed at Area 51 almost three years.

She crunched her cup into a ball and tossed it in the garbage can next to the door. "Well, I don't remember you."

"Touché." He chuckled. "Feeling better now? I could do this myself, but it would go a lot faster if you could label the vials. Start by adding today's date."

He opened up the hard case he'd traveled with and handed her a permanent marker and a sheet of labels.

The airman pawed through the case of supplies. "How many vials do you need? I still have to drive you out to the scene before it gets too late."

"In a hurry?" This far north summer days were long, and he'd been promised assistance for all data collection—including gathering samples at the scene.

With bent head, she filled out each label in perfect script. "Since they found the body, they've been closing the gate early at Camp Grafton." She held up the sheet with the first row completed. "How's this?"

"Perfect. I'll call out the rest of the label as I collect the sample. You hold it for me while I add the material."

Did her face pale again at the word 'material'?

"Yes, sir."

Kellerman unzipped the body bag. The smell of decomposition filled his nostrils, which immediately turned his stomach. The body had been outside for a week after all. What else did he expect? He raised his arm and pressed it up against his nose.

Fletcher gagged.

He swallowed the bile that bubbled up in his throat. "First vial: blood, head wound." He swabbed at the congealed blood around a gaping wound on the corpse's scalp. Probably the killing blow.

"Vial, please."

Fletcher scrambled to complete the label, stick it to the vial, and hold it for Kellerman to add the sample collected on the end of a cotton swab.

Dr. Stern had given him a crash course in evidence collection a few months back when he'd first arrived at NCIS-A. Such a small team needed cross training in other work. Who knew he'd have to put it to use so quickly?

To encounter a pod traveler's body had been a hope when he'd received his new orders. The professor had been pleased his application to join the team had been accepted. A glowing reference from his commanding officer probably helped. But Kellerman had been a steadfast believer in the professor's pursuits. He stood behind his goals and wanted to support them in any way he could.

No need for Commander Orr to know he'd been sending samples back to Nevada, too. Cutter had almost caught him snatching a few samples out of the bus last week on their trip to North Dakota. After that incident, he realized he'd grown a little sloppy.

But what did it hurt? Different agencies withheld classified information from each other all the time. Just because one small office had its own mission and its own compartmented source of information, didn't mean another office for another agency didn't pursue a similar line of information. Kellerman had clearance for both, so no conflict in his mind.

He continued his sample collection and, after thirty minutes, the smell no longer bothered him.

"Are we almost done, sir?" Fletcher had dutifully labeled and handed him vials, capping them off once the evidence had been collected and placing them carefully in the case.

"I think this is the last one." With a pair of tweezers, he had removed skin samples from around the head wound and collected hair samples. He hadn't received specific orders about what to collect, so he made an educated guess: blood, hair, skin. He'd also found some lingering green goo under the man's fingernails. With careful precision, he scraped the goo with an orange stick in his case and added it to the samples. The professor would be most interested in that vial.

He surveyed the strange figure in the body bag one last time and unzipped it further to expose it in its entirety. The bizarre foot deformation fascinated him. If this was the person who'd attacked him and the Chief, he sure moved quickly on those awkward things.

"What was wrong with him?" Fletcher asked, gaping at the deformed feet.

The lieutenant zipped up the body bag. "Some sort of birth defect."

Fletcher chewed on her lip and processed the answer.

"Weird." She scanned the two dozen vials. "Did we collect everything he wanted?"

"I think so." He removed his gloves, being careful to turn them
inside out, and then tossed them in the bin marked 'biohazard
infectious waste.' "Why don't we grab some lunch at the chow hall
before the drive out to Devils Lake?"

"You have an appetite after all of that?" Fletcher snapped the
case shut.

"Yeah, I do." Perhaps this kind of work suited him after all.

THE CAUTION TAPE sagged between the branches where it had been strung. Weighted down with rain from a summer storm, it was easy for Kellerman to step over.

"Are you sure it's okay for us to be in here?" The young airman hung back with her hands on her hips.

As the lieutenant surveyed the scene, he noticed small orange flags marking an area on the other side of a fallen log. "I think they found the body over here." He picked his way through sodden leaves, sticks, and mud. "The authorities who were here before us were looking for different things." With a long stick, he poked around the location where the body had been.

Fletcher crept up behind him. "What are we looking for?"

Every few pokes, he lifted the end of the stick and examined it. "Organic material."

"What kind of material?"

His focus sharpened on the tip. "Do you have a flashlight?"

"I think so. Why?" Fletcher dug through the backpack she'd brought with her. It was full of all kinds of useful things besides evidence collection materials from snacks to bottles of water to, hopefully, a flashlight.

"If it's the right material, it should fluoresce in the light."

"Got it." She pulled out the flashlight, triumphant.

"Shine it on the stick."

With a quick flick of her finger, she snapped on the flashlight.

A warm breeze blew through the elms. Even though it was mid-afternoon, the thick canopy of trees above kept the sun from breaking through.

She played the light across the tip of the stick.

It glowed a weak green.

"Wow."

The lieutenant smiled, then snapped his fingers. "I need a vial. Quick."

Fletcher grabbed a handful of glass vials and uncapped one. "Here."

From his pocket, he pulled out a packaged cotton swab. Then he snapped open the wrapper, wiped at the glowing goo, and dropped the swab into the vial. "Perfect."

Fletcher capped it. "How should I label this one, sir?" She'd prepped the vials ahead of time with the blank labels showing only the date.

"Sample 1."

"That's it?"

"That's it." Kellerman focused in on a pile of leaves right next to one of the orange flags. "Hold on, we might get lucky again." He prodded the spot with his stick. "Flashlight?" He lifted the pile with it.

Fletcher played the flashlight across the exposed detritus underneath. More glowing green light. Brighter this time.

"Jackpot!" Kellerman shook a fist. "I hoped we might find some that hadn't been destroyed by the rainstorm."

The airman prepped a few more vials and handed them, in turn, to the lieutenant for him to add the swabs. "Will we need samples for NCIS-A?"

Kellerman popped the last swab into a vial. "Nope. The commander gave me orders about the body, not these." He gestured at the half dozen vials Fletcher secreted in her backpack. "But he did want photos of the crime scene." He tossed his stick into the woods.

"Didn't we just trample all over the crime scene?" Fletcher looked down at her feet. Orange flags surrounded them.

"The authorities trampled it before we ever got here." The lieutenant took his phone out of his rear pocket. "The light's shit right here." He looked up at the sky blocked out by the branches above them. "Oh, well."

For a few minutes he took snapshots of every flag, the depressed area where the body lay, and, once they'd stepped outside the caution tape, the whole scene.

"Enough?" the airman asked. "They close the gate in thirty."

Kellerman nodded. "The body is more important than these pictures, really."

They headed back. A mile walk back to the duty van should mean they'd squeak out of Camp Grafton with a few minutes to spare.

Fletcher, a mere five-foot-two to Kellerman's towering height, trotted alongside to keep up with his pace. "So did you work with the professor on his project?"

"Yep." Kellerman took purposeful strides down the trail that led to the parking lot.

"Is this green stuff going to help him with it?"

"Yep."

The airman followed a few steps behind him now. "Before I received my orders to Minot, there were rumors flying around about what he was building in the warehouse." She shifted the heavy backpack to her other shoulder.

"People like to gossip."

"Do you know what he's building in there?" She raised her eyebrows. "I never had a chance to go inside. It must be something really amazing."

"Uh-uh."

The parking lot came into view.

"You aren't going to tell me anything are you?" Her mouth flattened into a line.

"What made you think I would?"

"We both have the same clearances," she pointed out.

"Do we?" He stopped abruptly and faced her.

"I couldn't walk into your NCIS-A office. But the professor's work? You think he'd have me help you, if he didn't trust me?"

He crossed his arms and snorted. "If he trusted you that much, wouldn't he have told you about the project in the warehouse?"

She gave an exaggerated sigh.

Fletcher looked over her shoulder toward the scene that now was invisible behind a layer of trees and shrubs. "Wonder who that guy was."

———

On the return trip to DC, Kellerman was glad to see he had the plane mostly to himself. No highbrow DC politicians or lobbyists on this trip.

A pair of airmen sat toward the front—as far away from the cargo area as possible.

They'd seen the gurney roll in with the coffin-like container used to transport the body.

Although it had been on ice since they'd found it on Camp Grafton, the flight back had no refrigerated compartment. The box stamped "Handle With Extreme Care" held the body bag and the remains of the unknown man. Dr. Stern would be meeting him at Andrews to take ownership of everything.

Before the plane took off and they lost their wi-fi signal, Kellerman sent a text:

It's done.

Three dots appeared and flashed across his encrypted texting app indicating a response was incoming.

The plane began to taxi down the runway.

He stared at his phone. With this job complete and the samples acquired, what were his next steps?

I have a new assignment.

He blinked his eyes rapidly. He typed back:

I'm listening.

Kellerman's pulse quickened. To have the trust of someone he admired so much pleased him more than he expected.

The sound of the engines roared in his ears, and the plane accelerated.

He needed an answer.

How he could help? How could he further support the important work being done? He believed in the project now more than ever. And with Cutter on the verge of uncovering the correct formulas from that old manuscript, he knew he could produce results quickly once he returned to the office. In fact, he was itching to be back.

A new text popped up on the screen.

Not the response he had expected.

Shit.

He answered in the affirmative and shut off his phone for the duration of the flight. Over the next several hours, he had a lot to think about.

CHAPTER 16

THE PROFESSOR FINISHED TEXTING and set his phone on his desk. He pinched his bottom lip. Kellerman had come through with the samples despite many obstacles and at great risk to himself. He could trust him with this next request.

He spun his chair around and approached the large window that looked out over the warehouse floor below. From this vantage point, the project he'd obsessed over for more than twenty years sprawled before him. Finally.

Clear plastic sheeting protected the delicate work from the elements. Too much moisture and the material would disintegrate. Too dry and the circuitry wouldn't work properly.

Workers were split among four separate sectors: material recovery, testing, replication, and application. Rather than keep each group separate and in the dark about the ultimate goal, the professor had built the laboratory as an interactive space. Knowing the why of one's work usually produced better results. It had been a hard fought battle with the security folks who loved their regulations and compartmented information. But since he came from outside that world and had brought his knowledge and techniques with him, the military had been eager to please him and keep his work moving forward.

They understood the potential.

The last thing they wanted to do was upset him and tempt him to end his experiment.

Especially now that his team was so close.

He knew this day would come.

He only had to have some patience.

Someone knocked on his office door.

Pressing a button on a small, black remote, the blinds automatically closed over the window, blocking a visitor's view of the warehouse activity.

"Enter." He rolled down his sleeves and buttoned the cuffs.

One of the many flag officers, this one naval, who loved to stop by and pretend he had a hand in his project, crossed the threshold. "Professor, I have a VIP guest on base today. Thought you could give her the grand tour."

Slipping his hands into his pockets, he kept his distance from the Rear Admiral. "A tour?"

The Rear Admiral closed the door and sat in one of the leather armchairs that flanked the desk. "May I?"

Considering he'd already made himself at home, the question was belated. "Be my guest. What kind of tour? You know we're doing delicate work here."

The buttons of the officer's jacket strained against the middle-age man's gut. "You've done tours before."

"For a select few. And those few were in charge of funds that would keep my work afloat." A necessary evil, he'd learned, in the world of military science experiments. "Who is this VIP?"

"Senator Hargraves. She's on a tour of some of the bases out West."

The name meant nothing. Politics were of no interest to him. The only thing that interested him was enough money, enough people, and enough equipment to see the project through. And he was almost there.

"No."

The officer leaned forward with mouth agape. "What do you mean, no? She's a senator. A very important one."

"I don't care."

The Rear Admiral's face turned bright red. "Who do you think pays for that shit down there, Allwood? The federal government.

That's goddamn who." He leapt up from his chair. "You will give this woman a tour. She'll be stopping by in the next hour. Either you explain the project to her, or I'll do it."

The professor flexed his fingers. Every fiber of his being wanted to lash out physically at this stupid buffoon of a man. Who was he to command anything? "This is my project. My expertise. You will not bring an unauthorized person into my lab. Perhaps you need to speak with the Base Commander?" He picked up the phone receiver and punched a button.

The officer's nostrils flared and his eyes bugged out. "I will take this up with the Base Commander personally."

The professor hung up the phone. "Be my guest."

After the irate Rear Admiral left, Byron Allwood wondered how much longer he could bully these military officers before they finally followed through on their threats. He sensed he didn't have much time left before he'd lose control. For years they'd seen his work as 'promising' and 'interesting' enough to fund at low levels. But as his work had sped up in recent years, expectations had risen along with the funding.

He couldn't give up now, not when he was so close. Everything depended on his success.

CHAPTER 17

RESTLESS IN HER SLEEP, Charlie rolled over. Her elbow jabbed Angel's prone form.

He groaned and shifted on the mattress.

It had been a fitful night. Not only was she in an unknown bed, her mind wouldn't turn off. After Angel's confession about being from the future—and what the future held for mankind—should she really be so surprised she had trouble sleeping?

Her mind shifted to the manuscript.

She sat alone in an empty library with shelves all around and tables covered in stacks of books. In front of her the Voynich manuscript sat open. She attempted to translate one of its mysterious pages with drawings of plants and instructions. As she stared at the pages, however, the symbols rose into the air and floated in front of her like holograms. They spun faster and faster until they transformed into words in English that she could read.

Her heart sped up.

She reached toward the floating symbols. When her fingers were about to touch them, her leg jolted, and she awoke.

Charlie looked at her watch.

Five in the morning.

She sat up, a strong need to continue her translation work pushing her.

As she slipped out of bed, naked, and picked up her clothes

from the floor, Angel mumbled something. She tiptoed to the bathroom.

Turning on the shower, she waited for the water to heat up. She brought up the notes option on her phone and began typing out what she'd seen in her dream.

Despite the lack of sleep, her mind was clear and focused. Somehow she knew she'd be able to read the manuscript with native fluency.

But why now? Was it the pod examples? Was it truly as simple as that?

Angel knocked on the door. "Come back to bed. What are you doing?"

"I'm taking a shower." She stepped under the showerhead and the too-hot spray.

"I figured that part out. Where are you going?"

"Work."

"Orr won't be there for two hours," he reminded her.

"Will you unlock it for me?" Only Orr and Angel had the combination to retrieve the key for the lock on the door.

"Come back to bed, Charlie."

The tone of his voice ran shivers down her spine. "I can't."

"Yes, you can."

She shampooed her hair. "Something clicked. I think I can read the manuscript."

He said nothing.

"I don't need to work on translation anymore. Somehow my mind must've worked it out. I can read it." She rinsed her hair, soaped up her body, and quickly finished showering. "We can find out what your sister wrote, Angel."

Grabbing a towel off the bar, she wrapped it around herself and opened the door.

Steam bled into the hall.

"How is that possible?" Angel's brow furrowed.

"I can read the manuscript. I know I can."

"But how?"

"I don't know. In my dreams something told me I can. Maybe I've internalized things in my subconscious without even realizing." A feeling of weightlessness filled her. "I'm surprised you aren't rushing me over there."

"If what you say is true, what if something in the manuscript exposes me?"

"I don't have to tell anyone else. Not right away. We can decide together."

He hesitated and pressed his lips together.

"I would never risk exposing your secret, Angel. You have to know that."

He crossed his arms. "I know I said I trust you, but understand how hard this is for me. I've hidden my past for so long."

She reached for him. "It will be all right. I promise." Why was he so distrustful of her? He'd shared so much. Why did he put up another wall? "We'll have time in the office alone before anyone else shows up. Now's the time to take advantage of the opportunity."

He closed his eyes and took a deep breath. "You're right."

She brushed a hand up and down his arm. "The manuscript contains everything we need to know about the pods. Maybe it will even tell us what happened to Allwood or more about Armas."

He drew away from her. "Armas."

Why did the boy make him so uncomfortable? Hard to believe he wouldn't be happy to find a connection to his sister—a nephew.

———

When Charlie looked at him like that, he wanted to tell her everything. By admitting where he came from, the time travel, the Purists, and the Genesis Project, he'd already risked a lot. But, God, he'd wanted her. Despite all of his attempts to push her away, treat her badly, ignore her—he couldn't fight the attraction any more. It had been worth it to give up some of his secrets if he could have her.

Even now, as she stood a few feet away, wrapped in a towel, he'd confess more if she'd follow him back to the bedroom. Her intelligent gaze penetrated him.

But she wouldn't forgive some of the things he'd done, some of the things he still had to do. His mission was tantamount, and it was the only reason he was stuck in this bizarre time. To protect her, she didn't need to know all the details. Did she?

How could she possibly understand the hatred that burned inside for Allwood? The seething dark side of him that could be brutal when necessary. She didn't need to know that part. Never needed to know. Only he knew the truth of what he'd done, and it would stay that way.

He'd arrived in this time alone, and now the manuscript had proven true what he dreaded—although many had traveled from his time via the pods, not everyone arrived in the same time. His heart hurt thinking about his sister. He'd never contemplated the idea she could have traveled so far back that it would be too late for him to rescue her from Allwood. And the boy? The last time he saw his sister she hadn't looked pregnant.

He shuddered at the possibilities.

Risa.

Why didn't she escape when she had the chance?

CHAPTER 18

Many years in the future...

ANGEL DEMARCO CROUCHED outside the crumbling structure. A leftover chunk of concrete and metal from The Before. The sun set behind the hills, and a chill filled the air.

A lantern flickered on and off in the distance.

The signal he'd been waiting for.

One of their reconnaissance men had tracked a follower of Allwood's from the market to this long abandoned structure. The farming communities shunned the old cities and the remnants of the way people used to live with their odd metal fragments and broken bits and pieces that held no meaning hundreds of years later. The old ways of living had been dangerous. That's what they'd learned. The old ways had caused massive destruction, starvation, sickness. No one in their right mind would want to recreate The Before. It was madness that would end with death.

Everyone knew it.

Why did Allwood think he knew better than the elders of the community? The ones who carried the stories and passed on the community memories of the troubles.

He scrambled low to the ground and headed for a dark doorway half sunken into the ground. The small team had split up in order to enter the rumored test facility from all directions. The Purists wanted no one to escape. The experiments the Genesis Project had been conducting were an abomination. The whole place needed to be burned to the ground, destroyed. And the Genesis Project followers?

His heart ached.

Although Angel had originally joined the strike team after his sister, Risa, had disappeared from the family farm over a year ago, the evidence he'd encountered in that time solidified his hatred of Byron Allwood and his sick experiments.

How could his sweet, innocent sister be drawn to such a person?

Allwood must've tricked her. He had charisma, Angel could admit that much. But he thought Risa was smarter than that.

He needed to find her before the team decimated them all. His fellow Purists didn't believe any of Allwood's followers could be rehabilitated. The knowledge they'd acquired was dangerous. And once someone has learned something, how can one unlearn it? The knowledge must be destroyed, down to the very last convert.

"Go, go, go," a dark figure to his left gave the command to enter. All were in position.

Armed with farm implements and bows and arrows, each member rushed the hide-out. Demarco gripped his scythe, freshly sharpened that morning.

He raced inside, determined to find his sister before any of the others. He couldn't let her die because she had been tricked. She deserved a second chance. And, as her brother, he vowed to protect her despite his loyalty to the Purists.

Strange green lights, strung together by what looked like vines, lit the interior. One of the Genesis Project's contraptions. Their organic circuits and wiring had been built into the structure. The intel had been correct. A Genesis Project lab had been hidden in an ancient ruin.

Distantly, he heard screams and loud thuds. The fighting had begun.

His throat constricted.

He had to find Risa. The others on the team would have no mercy.

"Brother?" a familiar voice said from the shadows.

A rush of adrenaline tingled through his body.

At the appearance of his sister, Angel's thoughts were jumbled. "Risa, come with me." He reached out for her. After almost a year with no contact, no information about his only sibling, he wanted nothing more than to touch her, make sure she was real. "We need to leave this place."

"No." Risa, dark hair loose around her shoulders and wearing a long green gown threaded with silver, stood her ground.

He scraped a hand over his face. "We're about to burn this place to the ground with everyone and everything in it." Couldn't she see it was over? The Genesis Project had been cornered, and it was only a matter of time before Allwood's grip on his followers was broken.

"Why, Angel?" Her features were smooth and expressionless, and her body had an unnatural stillness. "Why would you do that to me?"

Yelling and the clashing of metal on metal echoed from deeper in the structure.

"I'm not doing it to you, I'm doing it for you." How could she not understand why he looked for her? Why he was here now? "Allwood has messed with your head. Convinced you of lies."

"They aren't lies." Her voice waivered, and her gaze shifted to the dark place from which she had emerged.

He gritted his teeth. "Allwood will destroy everything we've built. You've heard the stories your whole life. You want to go back to all of that?"

"Byron isn't a destroyer." Risa stepped from the shadows into the dim green light. Her appearance had changed since he last saw her a year ago. "He's a builder. A healer."

"What has he done to you?" For a split second his breathing suspended. "My God, Risa, did you let him experiment on you?"

His sister flashed a sad smile. "You thought I was so perfect, Angel. You thought I had nothing that needed to be fixed. But you have no idea how I've suffered with my imperfections." She ran a hand down her cheek. "I knew I could be so much more. Byron was right."

"Oh, sister." He wanted to touch her face, to make sure it was still really her. Her brown eyes had turned a milky blue, her face more gaunt and oddly angular. "Why?"

"All of my work on the farm?" she scoffed. "I could only go so far with my ideas. My dreams of what was possible."

The clashing and crashing grew louder. Screams bounced off the crumbling concrete walls.

He glanced down the hall. When would his team appear, demanding Risa be killed for her part in all of this? "We have to leave. I told our parents I wouldn't come back without you."

She took several steps back. "I'm not leaving."

"You'll die here."

Smoke billowed into the space. Tongues of fire licked the edges of a doorway down a distant hall.

Angel's eyes began to sting.

A handful of Allwood's followers, in clothes similar to what Risa wore, ran past.

Angel gripped his scythe.

He coughed and covered his mouth with his arm. "Risa?" Her last opportunity to join him before it was too late

Silence.

His lips pressed together in a grimace. He couldn't leave without her.

A female follower caught sight of him and backed away with a scream.

He'd almost forgotten his purpose. Turning away from his sister, he lofted his scythe in the air. These evil people must be destroyed. All of them. Every last one. Angel slammed the blade into a man's back as he ran past, and he bellowed in pain.

Blood gushed from his wound, and he crumpled to the ground.

Angel swung again and the scythe cut cleanly across another man's neck. More blood.

The dead man's young female companion took several steps backward, her face white even in the dim lighting. Without hesitation Angel spun and caught the woman in her abdomen. Her belly ripped open, and her guts burst out like pus from an infected wound.

Risa covered her mouth, stepped back, and disappeared into the dark where she'd come from.

An older woman appeared in the doorway, noticing the three dead bodies blocking her passage, her eyes became as round as ration coins.

Angel wiped a spatter of blood from his face and regripped the scythe.

The woman saw her opportunity and scrambled away.

The smoke grew thicker. It became harder to breathe. Fewer Allwood followers emerged from the interior.

Blood dripped from his scythe. He surveyed the carnage at his feet. A wave of revulsion, bitter and tainted, interrupted his duty. He blinked and stumbled back. What had he done? Risa never should've been a witness to this.

He stood alone.

Where had Risa gone?

The cries and screams grew louder. His fellow Purists were following through on the plan. It would only be a matter of time before they turned their hatchets and other sharp weapons on his sister.

He had to save her. If she didn't come willingly, he'd have to drag her out of there. He'd promised his parents. He'd made a vow to himself.

Plunging into the hidden doorway after his sister, Angel found himself in a pitch black tunnel that sloped downward. He dug a match out of his pocket and lit it. It threw out minimal light in the space, but it was enough to see.

How did Risa navigate the darkness without any light? Although the tunnel followed a straight path, he could see no evidence of anyone ahead of him. Was she doing it all by feel? Or had she really gotten that far ahead of him in moments? Or was it true Allwood had given his followers enhanced vision?

He'd heard rumors of people with super human abilities. But he'd dismissed them as more of Allwood's lies to recruit more to his cause. All he'd been witness to were the failed experiments who wandered back to town. The people who'd trusted Allwood and ended up catatonic, missing limbs, huge scars on their heads, or worse. Horrific things no human should be subject to. It was wrong. It was disturbing. It was evil.

Why would Risa think she needed to be part of it? The idea disgusted him. That his innocent sister would choose Allwood over her family. Allwood over humanity. Allwood over everything and everyone else.

As he trotted deeper into the tunnel, the smoke cleared. The sounds of battle from the structure above grew fainter and fainter. How large was this place? How far down did it go?

The tunnel abruptly ended at a small alcove. A string of the strange green lights drew him closer. He expected a door, but instead he found an open archway to a massive space. As he passed through it, a strange electric charge ran through him with a sharp, explosive pain.

ANGEL AWOKE in a cage made of some kind of organic material, tough and slimy. Through the bars he scanned the dimly lit interior of the huge space he'd entered at the end of the corridor.

What had happened to him when he'd passed through the archway?

His body still tingled.

Was it a defense weapon of some kind? An alarm he triggered?

At the far end of the vast room, which was nearly twenty feet high and several hundred feet long, sat a series of large, green pods. At least several dozen. All lined up along a track. A group of Genesis Project followers had gathered at the far end of the string. He recognized Risa among them, her dark hair rippling down her back.

"He's awake!" a teenage boy cried out.

Angel had failed to notice he had a guard.

The call caught the attention of a tall man mixed in among the followers.

Byron Allwood.

He stood out among the rest due to his height—at least six-foot-three—and also his physique. His arms were thin and a little too long, his legs the same. With narrow shoulders and a long neck, he appeared taller than he was. He'd shaved his head and even in the dim green lighting, his scalp shone.

"Thank you, Neil." The leader of the Genesis Project said a few more words to the people surrounding him, and then headed toward Angel's cage.

In the background, Risa ignored her brother as if he weren't even there. As if they hadn't even talked only a few minutes earlier. He felt invisible. Was he nothing to her?

His heart hurt.

He and Risa used to be close. Spending every summer day out by the stream, swimming in the pond their father had built, doing chores. Rise together early, go to sleep late. Only a year apart in age, Angel still had shouldered the duty of an older brother to a younger sister. He stood up for her when other children teased her for her quirky habits and strange experiments. He'd protected her when their father wanted her work to end—saying it was a distraction from the farm, from his sister's future as a contributing member of the community.

Angel gripped the bizarre organic bars and seethed at the man who approached him. The man who'd destroyed his family and stolen his sister. He wanted to rip the cage apart with his bare hands. If only he still had his scythe by his side, he'd take great joy in slicing this man in half, his guts spilling out. He'd tear all of these abominations apart. Every single one of them.

They were no longer human. They were no longer the same.

These followers were in a cult of death. A cult of inhuman experiments and unnatural existence.

He couldn't let them get away with it. He couldn't let them continue. It wasn't right. It wasn't moral. It wasn't natural.

A deep cry forced its way out of his throat. If he died here, his sister would be lost forever. He would have failed. For the first time, he would've let his family down.

"You are Risa's brother, no?" Allwood stared down at Angel. A jagged scar ran from the top of his head down past one ear. "She told me why you are here."

Risa glanced across the room at them both and then quickly

looked away. One of the pods had opened, and a follower climbed inside.

What was happening here?

"Let me go, Allwood," Angel snarled. "They'll find you down here. You can't get away. You're surrounded. They're burning the place down."

Allwood held his shoulders back and chin high. "I think you'll find out you are mistaken. You should've left while you had the chance. Now I'll have to leave you down here. We can't have you interfering." He smiled a knowing smile.

Angel wanted to wipe it off his face. Rip him to shreds. Punch him over and over and over until he was bloody and senseless. "Let me out. Or are you a coward?"

Risa helped another follower into a different pod. The people lined up and casually entered, as if there was no raid going on above them, no fire, no killing.

"I am the opposite of a coward. You are the coward." Allwood crossed his arms. "You are blind to the benefits of my work and why we must be allowed to continue."

"Today it ends. Up there?" Angel pointed toward the ceiling. "Your research is being destroyed, your followers are being put to death for their crimes."

The tall man arched a brow. "Believe what you want. I don't have time for you. We need to complete our journey, and then there won't be anyone to stop us."

Rage poured out of Angel in waves. He couldn't let this madman get away with his sister.

Allwood shrugged and returned to his flock as they mindlessly climbed into the pods.

"Go ahead." Allwood signaled to two women who stood near a panel of controls. "We haven't much time before they come looking for their man."

One of the women pushed a glowing green button and the chain of pods moved forward with a lurch. The pod at the far end of the line began to spin, faster and faster and faster.

The neat line of followers watched open-mouthed with unbridled excitement in their eyes, as the pod spun so quickly it turned into a blur of green and motion.

What was happening? What were these mysterious things?

The two women at the panel stepped away and joined the end of the line.

The spinning pod made an explosive sound, like the booming of a cannon, and then shimmered and disappeared altogether.

The followers gasped and then clapped.

Angel felt sick.

What had he witnessed? What sort of experiments had Allwood been conducting?

"Risa's your sister? She's a genius." The young guard, Neil, returned to his post with a tall metal staff in his hand. "She hoped you'd join the Project. You still can, you know."

"What?" Angel barely paid attention to the boy's words as he tested each slimy bar that made up his cage. One of them had to be weaker than the others, didn't it? No way would he let an organic cage made of green slime hold him.

"The machines." Neil relaxed and leaned against a wooden crate next to the cage, not even noticing Angel's actions. "Risa made them."

That caught his attention. "What do you mean, she made them? What are they for?"

Another follower climbed into a pod, and it spun into nothingness. The line grew shorter.

Angel's gut clenched. Something was very wrong here.

"It's our escape plan." The guard poked at the bottom of the cage with his staff. "I thought you knew what she'd been working on before she joined us."

He thought back to the experiments his sister had spent so much time on. She'd never explained to him what she was attempting. He had indulged her and protected her from their father's irritation with her work, because he loved her. Not because he understood what she was doing. He remembered plants of all types in the barn, in her bedroom, and a special pair of glasses with magnifying lenses she'd had the doctor craft for her from discarded eyewear. Oh, and a book in which she kept her notes.

"I don't know anything." He continued testing each bar. Was that one softer and more pliable than the other? "What are these machines?"

The guard stopped poking at the cage. "I probably shouldn't tell you then." He looked up and locked his gaze on Allwood and Risa, who stood close together.

Angel followed the boy's gaze. He ground his teeth together, and a headache pounded at the back of his skull. Probably from all the smoke he'd inhaled upstairs or maybe the electric zap he'd been given. Allwood wouldn't get away with his. Not after everything Angel had sacrificed to track him down, destroy his enclave, and decimate his followers. No way would such a coward escape in some crazy orb and flee for a new community where he'd wreak havoc among innocent, hard-working people.

No.

It had to stop here.

He had to end it.

Without Allwood there to lead, the Genesis Project would quickly fall apart.

Just look at them. The people waiting in line. Their pitiful figures dressed in ridiculous matching outfits. Like a cult. Even if they were worth saving, the Purists could never allow them to mingle with regular human beings. Their DNA had been tainted. The unknown experiments could cause harm to any children these others—*these abominations*—might produce.

When his gaze landed on his sister, a pain pricked his heart. She, too, was tainted. She, too, had been altered. He couldn't let any more of them escape. Especially Allwood. If he could stop Allwood—kill Allwood—this whole nightmare might end right here.

The guard, enthralled by the accelerating pods that disappeared every few minutes, crept closer to the line.

Angel redoubled his efforts to find a weakness in his green prison. He stretched and pulled at the weakest bars using all of his strength.

Neil leaned his staff against a crate and joined up with a few younger followers who lingered near the back of the line.

Angel had to act quickly.

He grunted as he forced the green goo apart. It stretched into a thinner, lighter green bar. The force he'd put on the material seemed to be weakening it little by little.

The staff slipped from its leaning position, fell to the floor with a clang, and rolled toward the cage.

Angel winced at the sound. Expecting Neil or Allwood or some other follower to notice and see exactly what he was up to. But nobody did. The sound of the spinning pods filled the large space with enough echoing sound that the metallic clang blended in.

Able to extend his arm all the way to his shoulder through the stretched opening he'd created, he reached for the staff. If he could grab it, he could use it as leverage against the green material.

The remaining followers disappeared into the pods.

Distant shouting echoed from the hallway where he'd entered into the space earlier.

His team. They'd found the hidden passage.

If not for the strange alarm system he'd encountered earlier that had immobilized him, the Purists would've had a chance to end the Genesis Project according to plan.

An emptiness filled him. He had to do this alone.

Angel had only moments to escape before Allwood climbed into a pod and disappeared. He reached once more for the staff, managed to grab the very tip, and pulled it into the cage.

Only a few followers remained, and the line of pods had been reduced to a handful.

Angel angled the staff between the bars and leaned his whole body against it. The thick green strands, already weakened by his brute strength, turned light green under the stress of the metal staff. He grunted, exerting even more force on it.

Now only three pods were left and two people: Allwood and Risa.

Angel leaned on the metal staff one last time. The stretched bar snapped apart and created a head-sized opening in the cage. Not large enough.

He chose another bar next to the opening and began the stretching process all over again.

Sweat stung his eyes. His strength was flagging.

In the distance Risa whispered something into Allwood's ear. Allwood smiled and touched the small of her back. The touch of a lover.

The thought made Angel's stomach heave.

He hooked his elbows under the staff and pulled with every fiber in his body.

How could she stand Allwood's hands on her?

Allwood helped her up to one of the few remaining pods.

The bar of the cage exploded in a burst of green goo.

Angel forced his body through the hole. Would it be large enough?

The strange green material stretched to accommodate his shoulders. He landed on the floor with a grunt, staff in hand. Where was his scythe?

The motion caught Allwood's attention. His eyes widened at Angel Demarco's successful escape.

"Risa, wait," Angel yelled. Could she even hear him above the noise of the pod conveyor? He scrambled to his feet and sprinted toward them.

Allwood rushed to load Risa into a pod.

As Angel emerged from the shadows at the edge of the room, he spied his scythe next to a stack of wooden crates. He traded the staff for his sharpened farm implement.

"Stop!" The cry came out of his mouth in an agonized moan. "Don't do it, Risa."

But the door to Risa's pod was already closing.

He caught a final glimpse of her face. She had an empty stare, and her mouth turned down at the corners.

The pod slowly began to spin.

He had only moments to act.

Allwood leaped into his. The door closed.

Angel reached the conveyor and wielded his scythe. Every bit of anger, regret, and sadness surged into his blade. The scythe sliced at Allwood's pod, cutting partway through the gooey green exterior and leaving behind a jagged scar. The tip of his scythe accidentally caught the edge of Risa's swirling pod. It moved so quickly, it was hard to tell if it had been damaged. And, for a fleeting moment, he didn't care.

Allwood must be stopped. Allwood must die. Allwood destroyed his family and now he would pay for it.

Angel regripped the scythe to swing again. One more cut, and he might slice through and reach the psychotic Allwood. End him right then and there.

Risa's pod spun into nothing.

Gone.

In moments.

To where, he did not know.

The very act of it disappearing with his sister inside gutted him. The forward motion of his scythe lost its arc, and the blade bounced off the conveyor throwing out sparks.

Before he could swing for a third time, Allwood's damaged pod continued to spin. It spun so quickly, Angel could no longer see the damage he'd inflicted on it.

His final swipe at it ran through empty air. Allwood's also disappeared.

"No!" Angel tossed away his scythe and bared his teeth. Rage boiled over. He'd missed his opportunity and now both Allwood and his sister were gone.

The last pod in line ratcheted forward. The door opened with a green misty hiss. The dark opening called to him.

It may be the only way to find his sister. They could be on the other side of the earth by now. Far enough away he'd never find them again.

"Demarco!" A member of his team had made it to the doorway. "What is this place? Have you seen Allwood?"

Lost in his anger, Angel ignored the question. He climbed up the steps.

"Demarco!"

Angel entered the dark green maw. The door automatically

closed behind him.

The pod slowly began to spin.

CHAPTER 20

CHARLIE'S EYES GLAZED OVER. For the last few days her life had been focused on manuscript translation while they waited for any news about the body and the samples Kellerman brought back from North Dakota. She rubbed her eyes to give them a break

The transition from aliens to time travel had been swift and almost seamless. All attention focused on three things: the manuscript translation, the arrival of any new pods, and the evidence gathered from the pod traveler's body. They had an All Hands meeting in a few minutes to discuss any updates to their assigned areas.

"I heard you were approved for off-base housing."

Charlie opened her eyes. Kellerman hovered near her desk. He'd returned from North Dakota more talkative than normal.

"Yep." She peeked at her coffee mug, noticed it was empty, and frowned. "The paper work was waiting for me last night when I returned to my room. I put a deposit down on a one-bedroom not too far off-base."

"Nice." He tucked his hands in his armpits. "If you need any help moving, let me know."

"Probably will need more help furnishing the place than moving in. But my stuff arrives Saturday, and I can't even remember what the movers packed."

He nodded. "Been there."

"At least I have a mattress, a couch, and a table and chairs."

"You're halfway to fully furnished." He smirked.

"Let's go, folks." Commander Orr clapped his hands. "Meeting time."

"Yes, sir." Charlie popped up. She had a new presentation completed and waiting. She'd had to walk a fine line between doing her duty and protecting Angel.

Demarco appeared in a back hallway that led to a storage area and their file room. He caught Charlie's eye, and her body instantly flushed with the memory of the last night they were together in his apartment.

Be professional, Charlie.

———

Charlie stood at the front of the briefing room, one of her slides projected on the screen behind her. "After Armas's arrival and connecting the dots, my translation work moved more quickly. It became obvious that, yes, we are dealing with time traveling pods."

She clicked to the next slide where she displayed the translation of several pages she'd decoded over the last few days.

Chief Ricard let out a sigh.

His stubbornness knew no bounds. The older enlisted man reluctantly accepted the newest view of the pods.

"Do you have a question, Chief?" Charlie asked.

"I do." He leaned back in his chair, laced his fingers, and slid them behind his neck. "What specifically have you found in the manuscript that says: time machine?"

"I will admit, those specific words do not appear in the text—at least I haven't found them so far. I based my judgment on the drawings, the clues, and the formula."

"What formula?" Commander Orr sat up in his chair.

"It's on my next slide." Charlie clicked to a slide, which was a snapshot of a page she'd translated late yesterday. "Although I don't have a background in science, it was clear to me that this page is some kind of formula for an organic compound. Likely the compound that makes up the pod."

"The formula we've been trying to figure out since this whole project began." Orr rubbed his hands together. "Dr. Stern will want to hear about this."

"I invited her to the meeting, but she declined. I think she's busy with the samples the LT brought back from North Dakota."

Kellerman nodded.

"She needs to be here." Orr leapt to his feet. "Let me give her a call."

"Already here, Commander." Dr. Stern stepped into the conference room. "Did I hear you say something about a formula?" Her dark brown eyes lit up with an interested fire as she took in the slide projected on the screen. "Hm, intriguing. It looks incomplete."

Charlie clicked to the next slide. "Yes, unfortunately this part of the page was either damaged or faded by the sun. I wasn't sure if the formula even followed modern scientific notation." What she didn't say is that she knew this was written by a woman from the future who had learned science completely separate from the modern education system. Was Risa using her own made-up notation? Or did it bear any resemblance to a formula Dr. Stern could understand?

"I really didn't intend to stop by for your meeting." Dr. Stern stepped further into the darkened room. "I have so much work in the lab, but I wanted to grab a few minutes to update you on my preliminary findings." She fixated on the screen. "But I find this incredibly fascinating. Charlie, I should have time near the end of my day to meet with you about this formula. See if we can figure it out together with your translation capabilities and my medical degree."

"Sounds good." A thrill ran through her at the acknowledgement of her latest work being of use to the group and of interest to the doctor.

Demarco flicked his gaze her way.

He looked worried.

Charlie hoped he could read the positive signals she was trying to send his way. She would never reveal what she knew about Risa or about Angel. She'd sworn it. Didn't he trust her to keep his secret?

Dr. Stern took up the podium as Charlie returned to her seat. "I've come across some interesting findings in the early tests I've done on the new samples."

All eyes focused on the doctor as she explained her discovery.

Commander Orr snapped on the lights.

The room transformed into the sterile, government office that surrounded the team every day. The reveal of the manuscript translation and the incredible information within seemed less magic under the harsh fluorescent lighting.

Dr. Stern blinked. "The samples recovered from the body by Cole have been incredibly enlightening. Especially with our new view of the pods. I've found minute cellular level damage that could indicate time travel does not leave the body unharmed."

Charlie sucked in her breath and shifted her gaze to Angel. What kind of damage? This sounded bad.

Angel kept his focus on Dr. Stern and crossed his arms. He was expert at hiding his emotions.

"Have you compared this finding to the samples taken from Armas?" Orr asked as he returned to his seat at the end of the long table.

The doctor nodded. "I see the same damage, which is what led me to this conclusion. Although the child had less noticeable signs of cellular abnormalities, he, too, has experienced the same as our unidentified man."

Charlie's throat thickened. Her attachment to the boy had been so instant and strong. The idea he could have been harmed by a journey he hadn't chosen for himself was hard to comprehend. "Will Armas be all right? Should we contact Stormy? Maybe he should have a more thorough medical exam. The poor thing."

Kellerman, who had taken the seat next to hers, scratched his jaw. "Charlie's right. We should bring him back to the office. Dr. Stern, what would be a sign of damage? And is there risk to the child's life?"

Dr. Stern held up a hand. "I knew this would cause concern.

The damage is noticeable, but I don't think in the short-term it's something to be worried about. As I said, Armas had even fewer signs in the samples I reviewed. But it's something to keep in mind as we continue forward. We know other pods have landed. If there were survivors from those pods, this cell-level sign of time travel could come in useful."

Orr cleared his throat. "Could this be a determinative way to perhaps locate others who arrived before our team came into being? We don't know how many pods exist nor how many arrived."

"Could we use DNA data from the federal database as a starting point?" Angel asked. "Then maybe reach out to companies processing customer DNA for family ancestry?" He sat at the edge of his chair, and his back stiffened into a straight line. "We have to find them all. Every single one of them. This could be detrimental to the gene pool."

Charlie bit her lip. Angel's eyes glowed, and his rapid-fire questions were unlike his usual, thoughtful and serious approach. Would the team notice the change?

Dr. Stern held up both hands. "Whoa, wait a minute. I only mentioned similar, traceable damage because it gives us another clue, another piece of evidence that connects them. I wouldn't say that means there is a danger to us if for some reason these time travelers mix into our society. You are taking a few big leaps with your analysis, Agent Demarco."

Angel's gaze shifted from the front of the room to the commander. "Shouldn't we be searching for more of these —people?"

He ground out the last word between his teeth. When his gaze fell on Charlie, she attempted a little shake of her head.

For God's sake, Angel. Stop.

"When do you expect the more detailed DNA analysis from NSA, doctor?" the commander asked.

"Any day now."

"Before we take off on what could be a wild goose chase, Demarco, let's wait to find out what the NSA experts find. We only have so much money in our budget." Orr tapped his pen on the table. "What you're suggesting could end up costing us more than we're willing to spend. It would be like finding a needle in a haystack. As far as we know only a scant few of these pods landed. I want Chief and Kellerman to finish their research into the radar signals first. That would give us a better idea of numbers and how many time travelers are here."

Angel tucked his chin to his chest.

Maybe later Charlie could coax more out of him and give him an outlet for his irritation before someone grew suspicious.

"Besides the cellular evidence," the doctor began. "I also wanted to update you on my findings regarding the cause of death for our North Dakota traveler."

The room settled.

Kellerman's foot jittered against the floor.

"Although the man had a large gash on his head, which led to an assumption about an assailant—"

Although Angel had sworn he did not kill the man, something inside Charlie still wondered about the truth of what happened in the woods.

Dr. Stern continued, "—I believe his death was caused by the violent landing of his pod."

Charlie let out a deliberately quiet exhale. Why did she think the doctor was about to say the man was murdered?

She sneaked a peek at Angel. He stared straight ahead. Not shaken one bit by the news.

An unexpected release of tension made Charlie realize how insecure she had been about Angel's involvement. She shifted in her seat. The one niggling thing in the back of her mind about him had now been removed. While Angel had trusted her so completely that he'd confessed his true origins, she'd been holding back.

No more.

The last shred of suspicion melted away.

"What led you to that conclusion?" Kellerman asked. "When I retrieved the samples, the blow to his head looked pretty severe."

"The organic material you retrieved from the body also was

present inside his head wound. The only way that could've happened is with a massive force as the injury was made. I know when we have encountered these pods they appear to be soft and flexible, but to withstand the energy that must be released when these pods travel through time, they also must be incredibly strong." Dr. Stern grasped the podium with both hands. "His wound was more of a crushing injury that cracked open his skull. I'm surprised he managed to escape from the pod after it landed, much less run into the woods and attack both the Lieutenant and the Chief." She lifted an eyebrow. "He must've been impacted by adrenaline and flight-or-fight reflexes. A very strong man despite his genetic abnormalities."

Commander Orr nodded in agreement. "I suppose little Armas is lucky he came out of his pod in one piece."

"Well, the boy's weight made a huge difference in the forces applied," the doctor replied.

"Could it be the restraint came loose?" Charlie asked. "The seat inside the pod was equipped with a restraining device. Almost like a seatbelt." How lucky Armas didn't suffer any injuries when he plummeted into the river.

Dr. Stern weighed this information. "Perhaps."

"I guess I'm glad to know we aren't dealing with a murderer on the loose," Orr said. "That would add another level of complexity to our work. We have a body. We know he traveled from the future. And now we have solid evidence that connects the manuscript to the pods and to the body."

"Correct." The doctor bounced on her toes. "I'd like to return to my work. There is so much more to test...decomposition rates, blood work ups, an x-ray, dental exam." She waved her hand as if clearing away her mental list. "I won't bore you with the details. His clothing was distinctly different from the boy's. So we have that angle, too. Was he also from the past?"

"I didn't consider that." Orr sat up in his chair. "Since the manuscript has been dated, shouldn't we assume any pod came from the same time frame?"

"Not necessarily." Dr. Stern tapped her fingers on the podium. "The clothing analysis and dental exam might tell us a lot more about time differences. We also have no idea who was writing this manuscript and why."

"The formula might tell us something," Kellerman said.

"Right, the formula." Dr. Stern tilted her head to the side. "Charlie, let's chat after this meeting. I'm dying to find out more. Can we discuss it in my lab?"

"Sure. I'll send you the page scans with the notations and then meet you there in ten?"

"Perfect."

Kellerman abruptly stood. His chair making a loud squeak across the floor. "I have work to do."

Commander Orr snapped to attention. "Yes, we all have assignments. I want to know how many pod signatures you can find ASAP."

Kellerman nodded and Chief followed him out the door.

Angel and Charlie met at the far end of the table.

"They don't understand the danger," he whispered.

Danger? From cell damage? From the pods?

He gripped her arm as he walked past.

"What's wrong with him today?" Dr. Stern asked with a smile.

Charlie shook her head. "Nothing. Just the usual Demarco stuff."

"I'm not so sure," the doctor said as Angel exited the room.

DR. STERN, sitting at her desk in her cluttered lab, clicked open the electronic images of the Voynich manuscript pages in question. "To me, this looks like gobbledygook." She expanded the size of one of the images so that the symbols dominated the screen.

Charlie scooted her chair closer to the older woman. "If you open up the text file included with the images, I'll show you what I've come up with so far."

As the doctor navigated to the correct file, Charlie looked up and eyed the stainless steel table covered with a blue sheet. Were body parts under there? Dr. Stern had mentioned the work she'd been doing since Kellerman had returned from his trip. Surely the doctor would need a refrigerated space to keep a body from decomposing?

Her stomach rolled at sight of unidentified lumps and bumps under the sheet. She swallowed to keep the nausea from building and returned her attention to the screen.

Ignore it.

The body must be somewhere else.

Nothing was under the sheet.

Her imagination was working overtime.

Dr. Stern read the translation file, ignorant of the shift in Charlie's demeanor. "This isn't like any formula I would know. I suppose these are elements here." She pointed to clusters of letters connected with lines. "And it does have a similarity to organic chemistry notation, but nothing I recognize. These letters could represent anything, and unless I knew what those letters meant, these sketches don't tell us much."

Charlie clasped her hands in her lap. "I really hoped we'd be able to crack it together."

"Maybe I could run it through a comparison program that might be able to find similarities to known compounds?"

"Would that work?"

"It might." The doctor stared at the translation once more. "Kellerman didn't retrieve any additional organic material with the exception of what I found inside the wound itself, which was a very degraded sample. If you believe this may be a formula for how to create the substance used to create the pods, maybe I can piece it together."

"Do you think so?" A jolt ran through her body at the thought she might help solve the puzzle of the pods. What would Angel think? Would that be a good discovery or a bad one? She couldn't be sure. His sister had transported herself to a much more distant time than he'd found himself in. What if A Group could build its own pod? What if he could be reunited with Risa? Would he take the risk? And where would that leave her?

She bit the inside of her cheek.

"Perhaps. I'll see what I can do and keep the team updated." Dr. Stern minimized the translation page and refocused on the image. "Can you really read this language?"

"Before I came to A Group, I'd spent a lot of time on the manuscript." Charlie briefly closed her eyes to refocus her mind. "I think it maybe took some time to sink into my brain before I could understand it."

"But haven't other linguists and experts been trying to translate this for a couple of centuries?"

"Yes."

Dr. Stern sat back. "Wow. That's pretty amazing. You must have a real knack for this. I should introduce you to some of my friends at the NSA. They're codebreakers of a different kind. They might find your abilities very useful."

"I'm not sure about that." What would her father think if she showed up at his place of work? Embarrassed? His enlisted daughter consorting with his co-workers? "Besides, I like our little team."

Chad had driven them past Fort Meade—the location of the National Security Agency. The size of the building even from the highway had been imposing with an endless sea of reflective windows and fencing all around.

No, such a place would not be for her. She liked the intimacy of A Group's office, the camaraderie with Orr, Stormy, Kellerman, and even the grumpy Chief. Not to mention her budding relationship with Angel.

"Well, if you ever want me to introduce you, I'd be happy to." Dr. Stern spun her chair and turned away from her computer. "I might have mentioned your name. I hope that's okay."

"Oh?" Mentioned her name to whom? "I guess so."

"I was thinking more about your military career. A lot of agencies will be fighting over you once the news breaks. A translator with a clearance and your skill level? Something to think about. You'll be up for a new duty station in a few years. It might be a good idea to mingle and let the intel world know about your capabilities. Better than letting BUPERS send you off to Hawaii and just being another body in a linguist's chair."

Charlie hadn't even thought about her life beyond A Group and the work they were doing. Considering another station, another job, another opportunity with the same level of excitement and satisfaction? Almost hard to believe somewhere else could surpass her current assignment.

"I do appreciate the advice, but for now I'm glad the commander found me."

Dr. Stern nodded. "That's understandable."

Her desk phone rang.

"Hello?"

Charlie stood and strolled past a wall full of paintings. Dr. Stern's version of the Starry Night Owl had been added to the gallery. She smiled at the memory of the paint-and-sip class.

"No, don't take him to the hospital."

The serious tone in the doctor's voice made Charlie turn around.

Dr. Stern's forehead wrinkled. "Bring him here to my lab. We need to know what we're dealing with."

Charlie wrapped her arms around her middle. Something was terribly wrong.

The doctor hung up the phone.

"What happened? Who's coming to the lab?"

"Armas is very sick." The doctor hurried about the room searching in drawers and cupboards for various medical equipment and bottles of unidentifiable medications. "Stormy found him unconscious this morning."

ARMAS, pale and small, lay on a gurney covered with the quilt he'd been wrapped in when he arrived.

Stormy, Commander Orr, and Charlie circled around him while Dr. Stern took the child's blood pressure.

"I found him like this. He sleeps in my son's bunk bed—the top bunk. When I called the kids for breakfast, Armas didn't show." She sniffed and wiped the tears from her eyes. "I knew something was wrong. He eats like a horse." The young mother gave a wan smile.

Charlie curved an arm around her shoulders. "He'll be okay, won't he Dr. Stern?" But why did her stomach drop at the sight of the lifeless boy when he'd arrived? He'd been bright-eyed and curious when she'd seen him last. The child in front of her looked nothing like the little boy she remembered. What was wrong?

"His blood pressure is very low, his heart rate quite high, and his temperature is concerning." The doctor slipped off the blood pressure cuff. "Did you give him anything for the fever?"

Stormy shook her head. "I couldn't wake him. That's when I called Commander Orr." She clutched her purse in a claw-like grip. "Why didn't I think to give him some medicine?"

"How would that be possible if he was unconscious?" Charlie asked. "Bringing him here was the right thing to do."

"I agree," Orr said. "The boy is special and in our care. Until we know more about him, our duty is to keep him safe and keep him outside of the public eye. A hospital or urgent care would've asked too many questions you couldn't answer. You absolutely did the right thing calling me."

Charlie picked up the boy's limp hand and squeezed. Why did she think that might bring Armas to consciousness? "Is there any possibility this could be linked to the cell damage you discovered?"

"Cell damage?" Stormy asked, her eyes red and watery.

In less than a week, the petty officer seemed to have made quite an attachment to Armas.

"Let's not get ahead of ourselves, Petty Officer Cutter," Orr said. "Could be it's just a run-of-the-mill flu or something. Right, doc?"

"Were any of your children ill, Stormy?" Dr. Stern palpated the boy's abdomen. "Even something small like the sniffles?"

"No, nothing like that."

"Did he complain about any pain or feeling sick?"

"He said he had a headache last night, but I thought he was just overly tired."

"Hm." She touched the back of her hand to his cheek. "We need to bring down his fever. Once we do that, I'll feel better and we can do some tests."

"Tests?" Stormy asked.

"See if he has infection." The doctor rushed to the sink and filled a container with water. "Charlie can you go get me some ice from the break room down the hall?"

"Yes." She'd rather be active and doing something useful than merely watch Armas suffer.

"Thanks." She handed Charlie a plastic bag. "Fill this up." Then she opened a cupboard, unfolded a rag, dipped it in the tap water, and laid it across the boy's burning brow.

Charlie dashed for the door and ran down the hall toward a room labeled 'Staff Lounge' near the elevators.

What if Armas couldn't handle modern germs? What if he'd been living in some kind of isolation and had never been exposed to common diseases?

Charlie shook her head. That didn't make sense. Infancy and childhood hundreds of years ago had weeded out the weak and sick. Without inoculations or other modern medicine, children who made it past the first few years of life would have had a very robust immune system. Wouldn't they?

The break room was empty.

She pressed her hand against the lever, and ice dumped into the open plastic bag.

Her mind ran through the possibilities: meningitis? measles? something worse?

When the bag filled, she dashed back to Dr. Stern's office. Near the elevator she ran into a thirty-something soldier in fatigues. Ice spilled out of the bag onto the tile floor

"Hey, watch where you're going," he snapped.

She'd kicked the ice to one side and tossed an apology over her shoulder.

Armas needed her.

She didn't have time to slow down.

When she opened the door, Armas's body arced upward off the gurney.

She stopped short.

What was happening?

"Bring me the ice, Charlie!" Dr. Stern yelled. She held the boy by a wrist and an ankle.

Stormy had thrown her body across his torso. "What's wrong with him? My God. What's wrong?"

"We can't take him to a hospital." Orr held a cell phone limply in his hand and stared at the disturbing scene in front of him.

"We might have to." Dr. Stern's eyes sunk into her head. "I think this might be tetanus."

"Can't we give him medicine?" the commander asked.

"If we don't get him help now, he could die."

The boy's body relaxed.

Stormy wept and stroked Armas's sweaty brow.

Charlie handed over the bag of ice and fainted.

———

"Charlie?"

She heard her name being called from a far distance. Her brain was foggy, muddled. She couldn't remember what happened nor where she was.

"Wake up, Charlie."

Someone cradled her head in their lap.

With a sharp intake of breath, she came to full consciousness. Her eyes snapped open. Angel stared down at her with concern in his eyes.

"Where's Armas?" She struggled to sit up.

"Hey, calm down," he soothed. With a firm grip he held her still. "You gave the commander and the others quite a scare. They asked me to keep an eye on you while they took the boy to Walter Reed."

"We have to go to him." How did she end up on the gurney? How long had she been passed out?

"You need to relax." His hand pressed her down gently. "You fainted."

"I don't faint."

His mouth quirked into a half-smile. "Well, you did, so I guess you do."

His making light of the situation riled her. "There's nothing wrong with me. I'm fine." She shrugged off his hands and swung her legs over the side of the gurney. "But Armas. He's so sick. We can't lose him."

The last thing she remembered was Armas's thin little body wracked in pain.

"Let the hospital and the doctors take care of him." Angel sat back on a stool. "There's nothing you can do."

"How can you say that?" A washcloth slipped off her forehead and onto the tile floor. "You're his uncle."

"Stop it, Charlie." His posture grew rigid. "Slow down and relax for a minute."

Her gaze penetrated him. "You are the only family that boy has in the world. How can you be so callous?"

"I'm not callous." He raised an eyebrow, picked up the fallen washcloth, and set it on the gurney next to her.

"You hate him, don't you?"

With a sigh, Angel straightened up. "I don't hate him."

Had she hit too close to the truth? Any mention of Risa and Byron being lovers, and he shut her down. Maybe it was something too horrible for him to admit. "Do you hate him because you think he might be Byron Allwood's child?"

"Charlie—" He flinched and jerked back.

"Why won't you open up to me?" She rose to her feet and brushed out imaginary wrinkles from her clothes. "You tell me everything else about you, where you came from, you trust me with everything, but not this." As she confronted him about her suspicions, she folded the quilt into a neat square and fluffed the pillow. "Why do you hate an innocent child?"

"I don't owe you an explanation."

"Is that what it is now?" She paused with pillow in hand and turned to face him. "You draw me into your secrets, because you need someone to listen, but when I have questions about what you've told me, I'm just supposed to forget about them?" Using the pillow as a shield, she clutched it to her middle. "Believe you unconditionally with no doubts?"

"Wait, you don't believe me?" He thrust out his chest. "You think I'm making up stories?"

"That's not what I said." How did they go from a passionate night in bed where everything between them was exposed, to this? She'd done nothing but trust him. Why was he holding back?

"You said you have doubts about what I told you. Do think I'm a liar, Charlie?"

"Well, you kept the truth from Commander Orr and others on this team." If he wanted help, why was he so reluctant to ask the very people who could give it?

"I told you why I had to do that. I thought you understood why." His brown gaze clouded. "They'd never leave me alone if they knew where I came from."

"And you think they'll leave Armas alone? He doesn't have anybody to stand up for him, anybody to protect his interests. Don't you think he could end up being poked and prodded the rest of his life?" She imagined Armas, even now, in the hands of the doctors at the hospital. His life depended on their help. What if they discovered the truth? "Everything you fear about yourself could happen to him. And now that he's at Walter Reed all bets are off about A Group keeping that secret."

"I'm not sure what you think I can do." His empty hands spread apart in a pleading gesture.

"We have to protect him." She gripped his hands in hers and squeezed. "We have to keep him safe." At her very core, she knew it to be true. The boy was special.

CHAPTER 23

ANGEL TILTED his head to one side. "Why does it matter so much to you?"

How could she explain the connection she felt between her and Armas? The minute he'd appeared in the doorway of the sinking pod, she'd worried about him, wanted to protect him. A little boy all alone with no one to care about him? Her heart had immediately opened up for the child. A connection maybe no one else would understand.

"He needs us, Angel."

He pulled his hands away and avoided eye contact. "Sorry, but I have my own problems. I don't need a kid to worry about, too."

Would he be mad at her if she gave him a reason? She had to try. "Risa would want you to care for her son."

He clenched his jaw. "We don't know this is Risa's child."

Did he know how obvious it was that he was lying? "The first time you saw him on the lake shore...you knew, didn't you?"

"What?" He widened his eyes.

"Something about him reminds you of Risa." Why couldn't he admit it? "Is it his face? His hair? Why are you so cold to your sister's child?"

"Any child of Allwood's would be an abomination," he spat out between his teeth.

"How can you say that?" She swallowed hard at the admission.

"You want to know why I don't care, why I don't want to have anything to do with that kid?" His eyes, which were normally a warm brown when they were together, hardened into flint. "Because he's tainted. He's not one of us."

A sudden cold hit her core. "What do you mean he's 'not one of us'?"

"Allwood's experiments changed them. They aren't human."

"Of course Armas is human." What was he saying? What sort of lunacy had taken over his mind? "You're crazy."

"I'm not crazy, Charlie." He stood and kicked the stool out of his way. It crashed to the floor and knocked over a trash can.

She flinched.

"I saw my sister before she disappeared into the past. I saw what he'd done to her. She wasn't the same. He'd changed her—physically, mentally." His eyes reddened. "The woman I saw that day was not the same person I'd grown up with. Allwood killed the sister I used to know." His hands clenched into fists. "And this boy? The one you worry so much about? He's just like her—something different, something wrong, something inhuman and impure."

"Impure?" she whispered.

"I don't help *things* like him."

She gasped. How dare he. "Get out."

"What?" He blinked rapidly.

"I can't believe what you're saying about a little boy. An innocent child." She couldn't keep the disgust off her face. He must see it. The horror she felt at his use of the word 'thing.' "Even if he is the product of Allwood's experiments, is it his fault he was born?" Her body temperature rose. "I want you to leave. I'll drive to Walter Reed by myself. I don't need you."

"Charlie, please." He grasped her elbow.

"Let me go." Her whole body shook with emotion. How could he say such awful things?

"You didn't see what I did. You didn't live the horror of what Allwood's people did." A pained expression came across his face. "If you had, you'd be on my side."

"I didn't choose any side, Angel. I only see a little boy who needs someone to make sure he's safe, make sure he's okay. Because nobody else will."

Without glancing back, she burst out of the lab into the hall, tears rolling down her cheeks.

———

"Did you and Dr. Stern figure it out?" Kellerman asked as he hovered outside of Charlie's cubicle. "The formula?"

The young petty officer, focused only on Armas, snatched her purse from her desk and shut down her computer. "Can you drive me to Walter Reed?" Her whole body twitched.

He jerked his head back. "What?"

"Walter Reed. It's about a thirty-minute drive from here. I already looked it up on my phone in the hall." She showed him the map on her cell.

He rubbed his forehead. "Why do you need to go to Walter Reed? What's going on?" Kellerman raised his head and scanned across the desks in the small office. "Where's the commander? And Demarco?"

Charlie forced her arms into her cardigan sweater. Did anyone else notice the chill in the air? "Didn't anyone tell you? Armas is very sick."

"The boy is here?"

"Stormy brought him to the lab, but they've rushed him to the hospital. Dr. Stern thinks it could be tetanus. I guess I never thought about a child from the past being vulnerable in a modern world." Her vision blurred. Why did she think it would be an easy transition for a boy from the fifteenth century to blend in with the twenty-first?

"Of course I can take you. Let me tell the Chief. We were wrapping up our data project."

"Thanks." She forced a smile. "I really need to buy a car."

Kellerman hesitated. "That's okay. You seem pretty upset. I wouldn't want you driving alone."

"Thanks, Cole."

He smiled warmly. "No problem. I'm glad he has someone so

concerned about his well-being." He quirked his lips and stared into the distance, as if remembering something. "I've never been around little kids before, but you seem like a natural."

"You would feel the same if you'd seen him in the pod."

"Did he say anything to you?" He tilted his head to the side.

"What? When he was out on the river?"

"Yeah." He edged closer to her desk. "I know he was speaking mostly Italian. Did he mention anything significant?"

What an odd question for him to ask. "I'm not sure what you're getting at."

He shrugged. "We know he's a time traveler from the past, so I thought maybe you're reanalyzing what he may have told you. People, places. Did he tell you who put him in the pod? Who made it?"

"If I had those answers, you think I'd still be translating the manuscript?" Her head began to ache. "He's just a little boy. He was frightened and alone. He only wanted someone to care for him."

"That makes sense. I was just curious."

Although there was something weird about Kellerman's questions, Charlie shrugged them off. She didn't have time to delve any deeper. Armas needed her. "Can we leave now?" Purse clutched to her side and cover in hand, she met his gaze.

Kellerman cleared his throat. "Right. Yes. The chief." He held up his hands. "Give me two minutes." He dashed for a quiet corner of the office where he and the chief had set up camp to conduct the analysis.

Chief popped up. "The poor kid's sick?" His brow wrinkled.

That was the first sympathetic thing he'd said about Armas. Some progress had been made.

"Yes. He's headed to the hospital. Did you want to come?" Even though she hoped he'd say no, it was only polite to ask.

Chief Ricard tapped a finger on the edge of the cubicle wall. "We're about to wrap up our analysis. I'd like to finish the report for the commander. Demarco and I can handle things here."

Demarco.

Hearing his name caused an uncomfortable feeling in her

chest. He could appear in the office at any minute, and she wanted to leave before that happened. Whatever his problem was, she didn't want to hear about his ludicrous suggestions regarding Armas. For whatever inane reason, Angel had condemned the boy merely for his parentage. The thought of it horrified her and made her question her feelings for him. No matter what he'd experienced in a future time, it didn't excuse what he'd said. Not in her mind. An innocent child had nothing to do with the crimes of a future time.

Maybe he was merely emotionally reacting to his feelings about Allwood, which made sense if she were to put herself in Angel's shoes. But a child? What did a child have to do with any of it?

"Charlie?" Kellerman prompted. "I said, are you ready to go?"

"Yes, right." She gave a quick shake of the head. "Let's go."

As they headed out the door together, Angel stepped out of their way.

Charlie's stomach dropped, and she waited for a confrontation.

He merely side-stepped them, his eyes dark hollows in his face.

Was he regretting his words in Dr. Stern's lab?

Kellerman touched her elbow, and she followed him toward the elevators. She'd have to save her questions for later. Armas needed her.

———

In an open waiting area on one of the many floors of the expansive hospital, Charlie and Kellerman waited on a bench. She was surprised they even managed to find where Armas had been taken. Stormy and Commander Orr weren't answering their texts, and the building was a maze of specialties, patients, rooms, and floors that seemed to go on for days. Huge signs hung over hallways directing military men and women to the correct department. But where was the department for little boys who needed emergency treatment?

"Ask him again." Charlie nudged Kellerman in the side and pointed at the male nurse behind the counter at the emergency department. They'd been waiting for thirty minutes for someone to help them, to no avail. Everything was hidden behind military IDs and regulations. Nobody seemed to know anything about a boy brought in for tetanus. You'd think in this modern age that kind of diagnosis would stick out like a sore thumb, but no, everyone they'd encountered hardly made eye contact or wanted to tell them a thing and even mentioning Commander Orr didn't make the needle move.

"I thought rank was everything. Especially here. Why don't you use it?" Was her voice sharper than normal? Everything that had happened today had set her on edge, and now she was taking it out on Kellerman. She chewed her lip. "I'm sorry. I'm just worried about Armas is all."

"I know." His deep voice soothed her. "You're aware in DC there are probably more generals and admirals than O-2s, right? I'm nobody around here."

Even as he said the words, Charlie looked up and watched a female captain with four gold bars on her shoulder boards walk past. Kellerman was right, high ranking officers were a dime a dozen in one of the most prestigious hospitals in the country. Name dropping wouldn't help them much.

"I'm going to try texting Stormy again." She picked up her cell phone.

"Hey." Kellerman pointed at two figures emerging from a closed door. "There they are."

Commander Orr had his arm around Stormy's shoulders.

Not good.

Charlie's throat constricted.

She and the lieutenant rushed to their co-workers.

Orr had downcast eyes. "It's not good, guys."

"It's all my fault," choked out Stormy. "I should've been keeping a better eye on him."

"The doctor said there was nothing you could've done differently," Orr said gently. "He brought the infection with him."

The petty officer shook her head. "I saw the wound on his

shoulder when I gave him a bath. It looked bad, but I thought cleaning it and putting on some antibacterial cream would do the trick." She scanned the familiar faces surrounding her. "Like I would do with my kids. I've never...they've never—" Tears welled up in her eyes, and she hid her face in the commander's shoulder.

"I'm sure he'll be fine." Kellerman stood with feet apart and arms crossed.

"Let me take Petty Officer Storm over to the waiting area," Orr said. "She doesn't need to hear the details all over again."

As Orr slowly walked the emotional Stormy to the rows of chairs, Kellerman turned his attention on Charlie.

She gave him a quick update. "I was hoping Dr. Stern had been wrong about the diagnosis." The memory of the little boy's body spasming and wracked with pain haunted her.

"Tetanus." Kellerman stared across the room at Stormy who bowed her head and prayed. "Who gets that anymore?"

"A child from the fifteenth century." Glancing at her distraught co-worker, she feared what Orr might have to say. Could she handle bad news about Armas? The boy without a family? The boy who'd traveled alone through time?

"I'm sure the doctors here can fix him." Despite the confident words, Kellerman's brow wrinkled.

But as Commander Orr rejoined them, the deepening frown on his face suggested a different outcome.

She clasped her hands together, nails digging into her palms. If Armas died, she would never forgive Angel for acting so callously toward his own nephew. Never.

CHAPTER 24

"DR. STERN, ANYTHING NEW?" Commander Orr greeted the doctor as she exited from the exam room entrance.

The usually cheerful and upbeat Dr. Abigail Stern wore a grimace and shook her head.

Charlie blinked back tears.

As the doctor joined them in their tight huddle, she clasped her hands together. "They are doing the best they can right now. They've given him a sedative to control the muscle spasms and an antibiotic to combat the infection. But they've had to intubate him for the time being as his respiratory muscles were affected."

How could it be only days ago Armas was walking and talking and now he was hooked up to all kinds of machinery to keep him alive? "But he'll get better, right?" Charlie had to hold out hope. She couldn't bear to think of the boy never waking again.

Dr. Stern let out a breath. "I won't lie to you, this is a very serious illness. Right now it's hard to tell if he'll be able to pull through. We don't know how long the toxin has been circulating in his bloodstream. There is an anti-toxin treatment available that they'll give him later today, but without knowing how long ago he was exposed, the effectiveness of the treatment may be marginal."

A rapid stream of thoughts ran through Charlie's mind. "How long will he have to be intubated?"

"Most likely? A few weeks. That's how long it might take

before he is able to breathe on his own." Dr. Stern's mouth flattened into a line. "If he can make it through the first few days, I think he has a good shot at beating this. But for the next forty-eight to seventy-two hours, I'd say a lot of prayers."

Commander Orr ran a hand through his hair. "Will he be safe here, doc? I mean, the doctors, they asked us some pretty tough questions, and I'm not sure they bought our story."

"I'll stay here twenty-four seven if that's what it takes. Let me keep an eye on him. The staff know I'm a doctor, know I have a clearance. They've been pretty open about sharing treatment options for Armas. I think they trust me. Plus, I'll know what's good news and what's bad news. That way, none of you have to worry." Dr. Stern shifted her gaze to Stormy's bent head in the waiting area. "Can someone take her home and let her know everything will be all right?"

Kellerman lifted a finger. "I can do it."

"Thank you, LT," Orr said. "I can drive Petty Officer Cutter back to the office so we can update the rest of the crew."

Angel.

Charlie's stomach hardened.

Could she bear being in the same office with him? Would the commander notice her change of attitude toward the special agent? Maybe she should share what Angel told her about his own time travel, the probable parentage of Armas, and everything else.

As their group split apart and headed in different directions, the commander's phone blinged. Then Charlie's. Then Kellerman's. Stormy dug her phone out of her purse. Dr. Stern cocked her head to one side and scanned the group.

Oh, God. Not another one.

Orr read the message off his phone. "Lake Havasu. A new radar signature's been detected."

Another pod?

"Andrews then?" At least she wouldn't have to be alone with Angel now. They'd be whisked away to Arizona and be busy with tracking down another pod. This time, with the knowledge of a time traveler being aboard. A fluttery feeling blossomed in her stomach.

Orr nodded. "I'll text the chief and Demarco to let them know we'll head straight there."

"And Stormy?" Charlie glanced at the emotional woman. "Is she really in the right frame of mind?"

Orr took a beat. "Kellerman, can you call her husband? Have him come pick her up. Dr. Stern can keep an eye on her. "Doctor?" He raised an eyebrow.

Dr. Stern turned on her heel and changed direction to head toward the waiting area. "No problem. You three go." She shooed them toward the elevators. "I want my samples this time."

Orr gave a whisper of a smile. "We'll do our best."

"Do we have time to stop at the base motel?" Charlie asked. "My go-bag is in my room."

"Lieutenant." Orr snapped his fingers. "Drive Petty Officer to her room. I'll meet you on the runway."

Kellerman touched Stormy on the shoulder, said something to her, and then caught up to the commander and Charlie.

"Let me run to the head first," the lieutenant said. "Can you wait with Stormy?"

"Sure."

Orr gave a quick nod and left the scene.

As Charlie approached Dr. Stern and Stormy, a dark cloud seemed to hang over both women. Would prayers be enough to save Armas?

CHAPTER 25

KELLERMAN LEFT Charlie with the doctor and Stormy and sought out the closest restroom. After a few tries down the wrong hallway, he stumbled across the men's room, which was located just past an enclosed glass atrium with well-trimmed hedges in the center and carefully arranged pavers. It created an oasis amidst the stark, medicinal feel of the rest of the hospital.

He entered the restroom and scanned the space for occupants.

No one at the urinals.

He bent down and took a peek for any feet under the stall walls.

Empty.

He slipped into the furthest stall, pulled out his phone, and selected his encrypted messaging app.

Lake Havasu. New arrival.

As he waited for a reply, he leaned against the wall. With Armas in the hospital how could he possibly fulfill Allwood's earlier assignment? Maybe this new information would mean updated orders.

He expanded his lungs and took a deep, satisfied breath.

Hard to believe only a few years ago he was dealing with unruly sailors, and his biggest concern had been conducting enlisted uniform inspections and signing off on leave requests. As an officer in the intelligence field, he'd assumed his work life would be exciting and important. But a low-ranking officer in any designation started out doing the crap jobs. The menial management tasks an O-4 thought was beneath him. Mostly paper work. Boring paper work.

But would he ever have believed a few years later he'd be living a double life and working on the most fascinating scientific discovery in modern times?

His luck had improved when he'd been assigned to the professor's office. Something about Allwood's confidence, his energy, excited the newly minted Lieutenant Junior Grade. Allwood didn't take any crap and seemed able to intimidate even the most high-ranking officers on base. It was how the man managed to turn a ridiculous idea—time travel—into a believable reality over the last two decades.

How did he do it? And could Kellerman learn something from him?

His phone buzzed.

A new message.

Will meet you there.

Wait? What? Never before had the professor wanted to be present at a pod landing. What had changed?

Kellerman quickly pulled up a mapping app to figure out the distance between Groom Lake and Lake Havasu.

Less than a four-hour drive.

Maybe that was the difference? Location? Was Allwood eager to collect samples for himself? Or did he have other intentions, since he'd arrive well before A Group could?

He texted back.

Got it. What about assignment?

Three dots appeared to indicate Allwood was typing a response.

The restroom door opened, and two men chatted about preseason football.

> Sounds like delay. There will be another
> opportunity.

Kellerman closed the app and slipped his phone into his pocket. He flushed the toilet and exited the stall.

The two men, army officers in BDUs, stood side-by-side in front of the urinals continuing their discussion about NFL teams and their favorite players.

Kellerman quickly washed his hands and grabbed for a paper towel.

One of the officers finished, zipped his pants, and joined Kellerman at the sink. "What do you think? Do the Colts have a chance this year?" He jacked a thumb toward his buddy. "This guy thinks it's their year. I think he's crazy."

Kellerman gave the officer a blank stare.

The army officer raised a brow. "Not into sports, I take it?"

He dried his hands with the paper towel. "I have better things to spend my time on."

The other officer joined his friend at the sink and whistled. "Guess we're just a couple of dumb jocks, huh?"

It was then Kellerman noticed they outranked him by a couple of bars. If the professor were here, he'd know how to put these two in their place. Who cared about football when there were so many more interesting things to focus one's brain on?

Heat crept across his cheeks, and he gritted his teeth.

Why couldn't he think of a good comeback?

His phone rang, startling him.

One of the officers snorted a laugh. "Looks like your old lady has you on a short leash. Better pick up before she makes you sleep on the couch."

"H-hello?" Kellerman answered and backed away from the two jerks at the sink.

"Where are you?" Charlie asked. "We need to get going or we won't have time to grab my stuff."

"I'm on my way." He avoided eye contact and exited from the men's room.

The echo of the officers' derisive laughter following him down the hall.

CHAPTER 26

THE C-17 SPED down the runway a few hours after the radar alert.

Charlie, seated next to Kellerman, kept her distance from Angel. She needed time to process her feelings and figure out how to move forward. His view of Armas was completely unacceptable. Disgusting, even. He was not the man she thought she'd come to know. His carefully controlled exterior hid many things. Perhaps her first read of him—arrogant and cold—had been the correct assessment that very first day on the job.

Angel seemed content to sit alone at the rear of the plane, arms crossed, with an empty stare.

Fine.

That suited her.

Ignore her. Ignore the team.

Go ahead and shut yourself off, Angel. Nobody cares.

Should she find time to meet with the commander while on this trip and tell him what Angel had confessed to her? What she'd translated fully in the manuscript? And the fact that the author of the document was none other than Angel's own sister?

Her stomach burned.

Could she betray Angel's trust? Was keeping secrets from her boss worth it? Recent events told her, no, it was not. The truth was more important now. Her feelings no longer would get in the way of her assignment—they never should have. Look what a mess she'd put herself in.

At the soonest opportunity, she'd pull Commander Orr aside and tell him everything she knew. Angel would have to cough up the truth. Not her problem anymore.

Chief Ricard, sitting closer to the front of the cabin, bent over with an old man grunt and picked up a container of mint gum that had slid off his lap. He looked around to see if anyone had heard and locked eyes with Charlie. His ears turned red.

She glanced away.

He still thought her nuts for suggesting the time travel theory. She didn't need another reason for him to dislike her.

As soon as the plane reached altitude and leveled out, the commander stood and walked to the front. "Chief, would you please take a moment to update everyone about your radar research? And thank you to the LT for tag teaming on this one. Incredible data. Just incredible."

Both Charlie and Cole focused their attention on the Chief. Demarco kept his rigid posture and appeared to be lost in his own head.

Ricard popped a square of gum into his mouth and tapped on an iPad. "Sure, sir." He swiped several times and then raised the tablet for everyone to see a chart he'd created. "After several days of compiling data and inputting radar signatures from various sources, I was able to find some surprising information." He pointed at Kellerman. "Thanks, LT, for writing that program, it saved me a ton of time."

"No problem, Chief." The lieutenant pushed up his glasses and leaned forward in his seat.

Charlie forgot about brooding Angel for a moment. How many pods had arrived? And how many time travelers were roaming the modern world unbeknownst to anyone?

"At first, I was working with the timeline given to me, sir." Ricard directed his words at the commander. "But as more data came in, and the lieutenant's program sorted through the information, I was surprised to see similar radar signatures going back more than ten years."

A shuffling caught Charlie's attention. She snapped her gaze toward the back of the plane. Angel had shifted his body to face forward.

"How many pods?" the special agent asked. His dark eyes snapped with fire. "How many did you find?"

Did Angel know how many time travelers existed? They had never discussed how or why he'd managed to climb inside a pod and travel back in time.

Commander Orr held up a hand. "Let's hold off on the questions for a minute. This is where it gets really interesting."

Chief Ricard swiped and another chart appeared. "By happenstance, the Defense Intelligence Agency sent us thirty years of data instead of the time period we'd asked for. Without the lieutenant's program, I couldn't have parsed through so much in such a short period of time. But I'm glad we were able to because look at what we found." The chief expanded one area of the graph to encompass the nineteen nineties. "We have pod signatures going back more than twenty-five years."

"Twenty-five?" Angel said.

His face was ashen.

Did only Charlie notice the intensity in Angel's voice?

"Yep, let me show you." Chief scanned the plane, gave a satisfied smile, and whisked to the next graphic. "Here's the first instance of the signature in the data I received: nineteen ninety-six." With a finger he drew a red circle around that year. Only a single blip appeared on his chart in the nineties.

Demarco bounced a foot.

No doubt he wanted to interrupt and ask more questions, as did Charlie, but the commander had asked them to wait until the presentation was complete.

"From nineteen ninety-six through the present, I was able to count in excess of thirty pod landings all over the world, with the majority in North America." Ricard swiped to a world map showing each pod landing location marked with a yellow dot. "We've even had several—besides the landing last week—in the DC area." He expanded the view of DC-Virginia-Maryland to reveal more yellow dots, including Armas's pod.

One of those pods must've been Angel.

Charlie's heart beat more rapidly.

Did Angel ever tell her how long ago he'd arrived? Did he know others had landed in the same vicinity?

"The international landings may be difficult to investigate, as some of the locations are in political hot zones or so remote as to make travel nearly impossible. Besides, we all know how quickly the pods deteriorate. A pod that landed years ago? The best we could probably do is question the locals about any atmospheric phenomena on the day in question. But to track down if there are any survivors?" The chief shrugged. "I recommend that we ask for additional data to see if there are any signatures recorded even earlier."

The chief tapped on the screen to shut everything down and returned to his seat.

The commander took his place at the front of the plane. "Thank you, Chief. There is so much more to know about these pods and the people—yes, people—within them. We know that now. These are human beings we are dealing with. From what time period have they traveled? The assumption made at this time is that these time travelers are from the same era as the manuscript. Which should make these people stand out. They wouldn't have an understanding of the modern world. Perhaps this could make our jobs easier as we explore each of the landings."

"We're going to investigate more than thirty landings over twenty-five years?" Kellerman asked. "We only have six people on our team—seven if you count Dr. Stern."

"We count Dr. Stern." Commander Orr folded his arms across his chest. "I have no problem adding more people to the team, if that's what's required. I think what I'd like to do is split up the work. Someone take the recent landings—let's say the last five years. Someone take the middle range, five to ten years ago. And a third person can investigate the oldest cases. There aren't as many of those. A single landing in nineteen ninety-six. A scattered few in the early two thousands. Any volunteers?"

Demarco raised a hand. "I'll take the oldest ones."

Commander Orr raised a brow. "You sure you're ready for the challenge? I know you don't love doing a lot of research."

The special agent gave a curt nod. "Was assuming a lot of it would be interview work, travel, tracking down pre-internet sourcing for the most part."

Of course Angel would want the older cases: there were fewer of them and an absence of online information. Perfect for his background.

"Fine. That works for me," the commander said. "Anyone object?"

Kellerman spoke up next. "I'll take the newest ones. The last five years."

Orr nodded. "You got it." He rubbed his hands together. "Chief, that leaves you with the middle chunk. I want Petty Officer Cutter to focus on her translations. Stormy, when she's feeling better, will log your findings and create a repository on the intranet."

"Commander?" Demarco asked. "One thing I'd like to know: where was that very first landing? The one in nineteen ninety-six?"

Chief Ricard answered without even looking up from his iPad, "Corpus Christi Bay. Near the Naval Air Station."

A slight chill ran through Charlie. Her father had been stationed at NAS Corpus Christi in the nineties. She and her brother had been born at the military hospital there. She kept her eyes in her lap.

What an odd coincidence.

CHAPTER 27

SEVERAL HOURS INTO THE FLIGHT, Charlie approached Orr about her translation work. With nervous energy, she crossed and uncrossed her legs while contemplating her choices. Although she wanted to bring him in on the secrets Demarco had shared with her, what would her boss's perception of her be once he found out she'd withheld vital information from the team? And how would the special agent be viewed once she revealed who he was?

"Sir." Charlie slid into a seat next to her boss. "I'd like to update you on my translations."

Orr had his head down scrolling through texts on his phone. "Better than trying to figure out what's going on back at Walter Reed. Dr. Stern needs to learn how to dumb down what she sends me about Armas and his condition."

She bit her lip. "Does she think he'll pull through?"

"If I'm reading between the lines correctly, I think they've started him on a treatment plan." He flipped his phone upside down and set it in his lap. "But that isn't why you sat down. What new information do you have on your work?" He swept a hand down his uniform slacks to brush off imaginary crumbs.

She took a quick glance at Angel who chatted with the Chief about something—probably the radar data. Her chest grew tight. Breaking his confidence had not been her intention, but perhaps she'd put too much faith in him and his reasons for hiding the truth.

"I hope you can forgive me, sir."

"Forgive you? For what?"

Charlie cleared her throat. "Agent Demarco divulged to me a personal connection to the pods, which I've kept to myself. I shouldn't have done that."

He scanned her face, and his expression grew serious. "What personal connection?" For a quick moment, his gaze shifted to the special agent. Then, he twisted his body to face Charlie and to turn his back to Angel. "Petty Officer Cutter, I'm sure you understand that if you know anything that would be of value to our office and our investigation, I want to know about it. No matter who is involved; no matter who asked you to keep things a secret. That's not how A Group operates."

"I understand, sir, and it was wrong of me not to say something sooner." Her stomach soured.

"Did he threaten you?"

"What? No." Her palms grew sweaty. "We developed a—" How could she explain this without sounding crude? "—personal relationship outside of work."

Orr raised an eyebrow. "I see."

The confession caused her face to heat. "He confided in me and asked that I not tell anyone." Charlie's gaze settled into her lap. "I didn't want to break that trust. I didn't think—didn't know what he'd tell me had such a close connection to the work we are doing."

Commander Orr tugged at an ear and lowered his voice. "Should we wait for a more private opportunity?"

Chief Ricard walked past them and headed for the small bathroom at the front of the plane right outside the cockpit.

Charlie eyed him as he walked by. Perhaps the commander was right. She wanted to unload the information inside her before it ate her up, but maybe this was not the right place. "Yes. Maybe once we arrive at our hotel?"

He nodded. "Let's do that." Then, he reached out and touched her shoulder briefly. "Thank you for coming forward, Petty Officer. I'm sure that wasn't easy to do as the newest member of our office."

"I also have some updated information on the manuscript translations." The two went hand in hand—Risa and Angel, the past and the future. And she still had questions for Angel. If only she could stomach the thought of continuing their relationship. She could ask those questions. Dig for more answers. Find out exactly why he'd traveled back in time, how he had done it, what his plans were. She straightened her posture.

"Oh?" Commander Orr asked. "Then I look forward to our discussion."

Her thoughts turned to Armas and his suffering. That little boy deserved better in his short life. He deserved safety and love and happiness. His only living relative viewed him as less-than-human, worthy of hatred and scorn. She'd be damned if she'd let someone like Angel interfere with giving the boy a better life.

———

Returning to her seat, Charlie felt a lightness of being that had evaded her ever since she'd joined A Group. She was meshing well with most of the team and finding satisfaction in her work. To build a solid relationship with her boss had transformed her view of her job. Why did she think she only had loyalty to Angel?

She glanced down the aisle.

The special agent had crossed his arms, stretched out his legs, and had fallen asleep. His handsome features relaxed making him appear less intimidating. For a fleeting moment, he reminded her of her father napping on the couch after watching a football game. She'd grown up thinking he was supportive and loving and everything a dad should be, only to find out if she veered off the carefully created path he'd made for her, his love was conditional.

Similar vibes came off of Angel. The dark look he'd had in his eye when he spoke of the Genesis Project followers worried her. It seemed only those of pure, unmanipulated DNA were 'real' humans to him. The thought he could see others, even Armas, as non-human nauseated her.

Was he only involved in A Group to track down these 'abominations,' as he called them, in order to eradicate them? He'd implied as much. And what did that mean for Armas's safety?

When they landed, she needed to keep a watchful eye on Angel's actions. And what better way to do so then slip right back into the role of 'girlfriend'? Could she do it?

What would be the fastest way to find out more about the time travelers? Get close to a time traveler. As of now, the only one they knew of who was alive and well and within their reach was Demarco.

Satisfied with her plan, she picked up the iPad Chief Ricard had issued her for the trip, and navigated to the manuscript file she downloaded to it before they'd left Andrews Air Force Base. Her notes and translations might be classified, but the manuscript was open source and available to all via the internet. No classification needed. Now that she could fluently read and translate the text in her head, her notes and the key she'd built were no longer necessary.

Would anyone on her team believe she could have achieved this level of fluency in two weeks' time? She could maybe convince them some of the ease with which she translated the document was due to her graduate work. However, she knew differently. Something strange had happened when she'd opened up the manuscript and started over with her translations. It was as if a switch had been turned on in her brain allowing her to gulp up the symbols and spit out the meaning. Much like that night in the swimming pool when the symbols had floated in her head, where she could visualize them as if they were words on a white board.

Her high school friends had thought her 'weird' when she spoke of how she could visualize math problems, science experiments, and other academic work without the need to take notes or study very much. The information was locked inside her head and waited to be accessed. That's why foreign language had come so easily to her, especially. Once she'd learned grammar rules for one language, she could easily apply them to another and another. Then, it was only a matter of learning the vocabulary and plugging it in.

The manuscript translation had worked the same. Once she'd figured out the phonemes that made up each word, the rest fell into place somehow. Too hard to explain to someone outside her own mind—but she was used to people not understanding and finding her strange. Even her own father had been shocked at her and her brother's innate abilities in school. Not much effort, but incredible results. Her mother? Not as surprised. Maybe similar traits ran on her mother's side of the family. She'd never really asked.

Charlie scrolled through the manuscript starting on the very first page. One line at a time, she read it slowly but fluently as if she'd known how to read this symbolic code her whole life. Science concepts, bits and pieces of Risa's life in fifteenth century Italy, and even the birth of Armas leapt off the page. It was clear to her now the manuscript wasn't merely a place for Risa to record her experiments, but a place for her to pour out her heart and soul in a world where nobody understood her, where she came from, or what she'd experienced.

Oh, the poor woman.

A person of great intellect and amazing talent banished to a past where educated women were not the norm and had little power or control over their lives. How did she manage to conduct her experiments and produce a working pod that transported her son to a future time? And why would she do so?

She turned the page.

Armas and I must leave this place.

Her gaze focused on the words that followed.

It is too dangerous to remain. I must finish my work.

Charlie touched a finger to that section of the manuscript. All Risa wanted was safety for her son. How could she not want to help this poor young mother with her quest? Two women who cared for Armas, who wanted nothing more than love and safety, separated by centuries.

Yes, Charlie would do anything to save Risa's child—even betray Angel.

Continued in Revelation...

THE GENESIS MACHINE

REVELATION

BOOK THREE

K. J. GILLENWATER

CHAPTER 1

THE C-17 TOUCHED down at Nellis Air Force Base. Charlie stared out the window at the dry desert that stretched out for miles in all directions ending abruptly at some distant brown mountains. Base housing and a golf course stood out in sharp green contrast against the natural surroundings beyond the base's perimeter.

She'd come to grips with her plan during the last hour of the flight. As soon as they arrived at their hotel, she and Orr had agreed to meet and discuss more about what she'd revealed.

Angel's confessions had made her feel closer to him and stoked her attraction for him. What woman wouldn't feel flattered if a handsome man chose her to be his confidante? But now she realized her mistake in keeping his secrets, the truth bubbled up inside. She needed to unburden herself. The sooner, the better.

Gathering their go-bags and stepping out into the early evening sun, the team exited the plane in silence.

Kellerman shielded his eyes and scanned the runway. "I have a work colleague who'll be meeting up with us."

"Work colleague?" Orr made a face.

"Yes, my old boss. I guess he caught wind of the same radar signal." He hefted his bag onto his opposite shoulder. "I don't see him here. He didn't really give me a lot of information."

Strange.

Charlie didn't know Kellerman kept in touch with his previous office. Wouldn't it be difficult with so many levels of security keeping individual research and information compartmented?

"What?" Orr forcefully tucked his shirt into his jeans. "Who are you talking about? Someone from Area 51?"

"Groom Lake," Kellerman corrected.

"How would they know about our radar signal?"

"It's not really *our* radar signal," Charlie offered.

The commander shot her a sharp look.

Kellerman shrugged. "I don't know any more than you do, sir. The professor texted that he'd see me once we'd arrived. I didn't know if he meant Nellis or Lake Havasu. I thought I'd better explain before he showed up. Might look weird."

"You bet it looks 'weird.'" Orr's tone turned harsh. "What kind of work were you doing for this professor?"

The team reached a black Ford Excursion. Wordlessly, Angel opened the back and hefted his bag inside. He took the chief's proffered duffel and did the same. Both men remained silent as the conversation continued.

The entire team knew Area 51 research was rumored to include extraterrestrial life and UFOs, but nobody said a thing.

"You know I can't talk about that, sir." Kellerman's face turned red. "I thought you should know is all. Sorry I even brought it up."

Orr caught the young lieutenant's arm before he could head to the back of the vehicle. "This is highly irregular. If I find out you leaked information—"

"I didn't leak anything." A sheen of sweat appeared on Kellerman's brow.

Was he nervous or merely overheated? Although the early September desert heat felt hotter than DC, the faint evening breeze seemed to be reducing the outdoor air temperature.

Orr let go of Kellerman and crossed his arms. "Then you'll introduce me to him tomorrow when we drive out to Lake Havasu. I'll ask him personally what turned him on to our radar signal. Let's see what he has to say."

Kellerman gave a curt nod and loaded his bag into the back of the Excursion.

It would be interesting to see how that played out. Charlie had to admit her own curiosity about Kellerman's former boss.

"Sir, where are we staying tonight?" She'd assumed they'd be heading to Lake Havasu upon landing, but his comment had her wondering.

"Don't get too excited, Petty Officer, but we're booked here in Las Vegas."

"Now that's what I'm talking about," Chief Ricard said as he opened the driver's side door. "Who wants to hang with me at the poker tables?" He pointed a finger at Angel, then Kellerman, noticeably skipping over both her and the commander.

"Calm down, Chief, we're way off the strip." Orr's hackles had settled, and he grinned.

"Vegas is Vegas, sir."

The team climbed into the vehicle and headed off base into the setting sun.

———

Charlie's armpits were sweaty. She had been standing outside Commander Orr's hotel room door for five minutes trying to work up the courage to knock.

Did she really want to tell her boss everything? What if it blew up in her face?

Just as she was about to rap on the door, it flew open.

"Sir!" she choked out.

Commander Orr's eyes widened at the surprise guest. "Petty Officer Cutter. To what do I have the pleasure?"

"Would now be a good time to talk?" After finding her room, she'd changed into more comfortable clothing—a pair of jeans and a sleeveless top.

The commander opened his door in invitation. "Please, come in."

Although a little uncomfortable being alone in her boss's hotel room, they needed privacy for what she was about to tell him.

"Thanks." She rolled her shoulders to loosen the tightness that had settled there. "I'll try to keep this brief."

"Nonsense. I was only heading out to grab a burger." He closed the door and gestured to a loveseat near the window. "I'm not much of a gambler. Vegas is a bit too gaudy for me."

She sat in the proffered seat. "I know what you mean." On her way through the lobby she'd seen no less than three scantily clad Vegas showgirls wearing large feather headdresses and handing out invitations for a nightly show at a theater down the block. The chief had grinned, Kellerman's ears had reddened, and Angel hadn't even noticed.

"So you mentioned you had more detail on your translations you wanted to share, along with something about Demarco's connection to the pods?" He sat in an office chair, which he had rolled out from under a small desk. "I have to say I was a little surprised when you brought that up." He flashed a quick grin.

"It will make more sense when I explain."

He leaned forward to rest his elbows on his knees. "Please. Explain."

She bit her lip and clasped her hands together. "Special Agent Demarco isn't who you think he is."

The commander's eyebrows shot up.

"I'm not sure if you are aware, but Demarco and I have been—" She cleared her throat.

"Dating?" Orr said. "Yes, I think most of us noticed something had changed between the two of you recently."

Her face heated. Although she thought they'd done a good job of keeping their relationship a secret, clearly that wasn't the case. "Um, yes." She crossed and re-crossed her legs. This was more difficult than she imagined it would be. "As we got to know each other better, he felt comfortable opening up to me. Told me some things about his past."

"Did something happen between you two and now you're hoping I'm going to punish him for some sort of lover's spat?"

"It's not a lover's spat, sir. I wouldn't be here to discuss something so trivial." This wasn't going well. "It's difficult to explain."

"Maybe get to the point." He glanced at his watch.

She was losing him. In a matter of seconds he'd send her back to her room. "Right. The translations, the research, our office." Where had her determination gone? "The whole reason Demarco wanted to join our team in the first place is because he is one of the people you are looking for."

"What do you mean?" The commander looked perplexed.

"He's a time traveler, sir. He told me so."

He leaned back. "You're joking."

"I'm not joking, sir."

"Angel Demarco is from the fifteenth century? This is ridiculous." His cheeks puffed out as he released a big breath.

"No, sir. That's just it. The translations, the work I've done on them, it lines up with Angel's—Demarco's story. Risa, the woman who wrote the manuscript, who is Armas's mother—Risa is his sister. They are both from the future, sir."

"I don't understand." He rubbed at an eyelid.

"It's true." What if he didn't believe her? "He was worried if anyone found out the truth, he'd be turned into a lab rat."

Charlie explained everything she'd learned about Angel, his origins, the Purists and the Genesis Project, the goals of Byron Allwood, and how his sister fit into everything. She then revealed Angel's view of Allwood's followers—even his own nephew—as impure and against the laws of nature. The commander had been quiet and respectful as she threw out wild details. At any moment, she expected him to laugh and accuse her of playing a joke.

"What else does he know about the pods? Has he explained exactly how he arrived here?" The commander had a pinched expression. "There are so many questions I want answered."

"If he knows what I told you, I don't know what he'd do. He might disappear. He might act on some of his impulses. I'm worried for Armas. I'm not sure what he has in store for him or any other travelers we might encounter."

"His dislike of tech makes a lot of sense now," Orr mused.

Charlie nodded. Was he slowly coming around to the truth? Would he work with her to keep Angel in check and find out as much as they could about the pods and the people inside them?

"Keep this between you and me for now. I need to think through the implications."

She rose from the loveseat. "What will happen to Demarco?"

"Let me worry about that." The commander ushered her to the door. "Be cautious."

She nodded.

"I'll be the one who decides when and to whom to reveal this information." His hand grasped the doorknob. "Your translation work? No more reporting to the team. We'll keep it between you and me. If you must share with Demarco, do it. I don't want him suspecting anything. Otherwise, the chief, the lieutenant, and Petty Officer Storm? Keep them in the dark."

He opened the door.

"Yes, sir." Charlie stepped into the hall.

"Tomorrow at Lake Havasu, let's keep an eye on Demarco. See what he does."

Charlie nodded in agreement, but inside her stomach hardened like a rock.

———

The next morning, the team gathered near the elevators before the two-and-a-half hour drive to Lake Havasu. Charlie stood next to Angel, hoping he'd noticed her change in demeanor. Maybe he'd think their argument was over and everything was back to normal. He didn't seem unhappy she'd approached him.

"Team," said the commander. "We have a bit of a drive this morning, but should be arriving at our destination before noon. I know some of you think we should've pushed on to the location after our flight yesterday, but new information has come to light."

Chief and Kellerman exchanged glances.

Angel touched her hand.

The warmth of his fingers affected her more than she cared to admit.

"I'll share it with you once we're enroute."

The team wended their way from the elevators to the lobby. Even at eight in the morning, gamblers sat on stools in front of clanging and chiming slot machines and drank the free, watered-down drinks from the bar maids. Maybe they should call Vegas the 'city that never sleeps.'

They headed out the automatic doors and into the glaring desert sun.

Brutal.

Charlie held up an arm to block the light. Was the sun brighter in Nevada somehow? Commander Orr donned a pair of sunglasses. Chief pulled his baseball cap lower on his forehead. Demarco and Kellerman squinted.

They all climbed into the waiting black SUV they'd arrived in the night before. Kellerman took the wheel.

As they headed to the highway, Charlie leaned forward to ask the commander a question. "Any update on Armas?"

"Nothing new, I'm afraid. But he's stable, so that's a good sign." Orr slid his sunglasses down his nose to meet her gaze. "Dr. Stern swears she will make sure he pulls through, and if anything changes, she said she'll call. No worries, Petty Officer Cutter, he's in good hands."

Charlie nodded and sat back. She couldn't relax until Armas was out of the woods.

Angel sat next to her, and the chief had selected the back row of seats. Probably because there was a cooler full of drinks and snacks on the floor next to him.

"What's the new information you were going to share, Commander?" asked Demarco.

Orr turned sideways to face the rest of the team. "The pod we're tracking had a pretty rough landing. Instead of hitting the water, which seems typical for the pods, it scraped the top of London Bridge and then skipped across the surface and landed on the shore."

"So a useless trip, then?" Demarco asked.

"Not useless. The local police quickly cordoned off the area after a citizen called it in, and they have someone in custody."

"Someone?" Shivers ran down Charlie's spine. A live time traveler? She sneaked a peek at Angel who had a furrowed brow and hands closed into fists.

"Man? Woman?" the special agent asked.

"A woman. She was injured, confused, so they took her to the local hospital. They say she's spouting crazy things and think she's got some mental problems."

Orr's gaze locked with Charlie's.

She sucked in her breath.

"So we'll be stopping at the hospital as our first order of business. Lieutenant Kellerman and Chief Ricard, you can drop us off and then head to the crash location to see if you can recover any samples."

"Sir, did they get a name from this woman?" Demarco asked.

Did she detect a tremor in his voice?

"All I know is, she was speaking in gibberish. If she's a time traveler and survived that wreck, she could have some head injuries or otherwise that could be affecting her mind."

Kellerman spoke into his phone to correct their destination on his mapping app. "We're about ninety minutes out, sir."

"Thank you." The commander scanned Demarco's figure for a moment and then turned back around.

The special agent stared out the window, his mind elsewhere.

Charlie scooted closer to him and took one of his hands in hers. Despite her misgivings about his view of the Genesis Project and its followers, she knew what must be running through his mind. "We don't know that it's her," she whispered. "The manuscript only documents one attempt at traveling forward in time."

"Maybe she didn't record everything she did, everything she was thinking." He looked around to make sure no one heard him but Charlie.

"I'll read more of the text. See if there's anything else I can find." It wasn't easy to turn off her sympathetic nature. She couldn't even begin to imagine the pain she'd feel if Chad had disappeared to another time, never to be heard from again.

"Are you still angry with me?" Angel asked with a bitter twinge to his voice.

She shook her head, but her stomach dipped at the lie. "I only want to help, Angel." Until Commander Orr figured out how to handle Angel, she had to stick close to him, make sure he didn't act on his negative feelings toward Allwood's followers.

He smiled briefly and then turned his face toward the window again, as if he wasn't quite certain of her answer.

CHAPTER 2

THE BARE BROWN desert that had surrounded them for two hours changed dramatically as they neared Lake Havasu City. A large swath of deep blue, startling it its size, appeared like a mirage on the horizon. But each mile closer they drove, it became clearer that Lake Havasu was not a mirage, but very real, and very different than the hot, dry country surrounding it.

"The hospital is only a few miles from London Bridge. So close to the crash site," Kellerman said looking down at his phone.

"Keep your eyes on the road, LT," Commander Orr barked from the passenger's seat.

"Yes, sir."

The AI voice on Kellerman's cell directed him to turn away from the bridge and toward the city center. To their right the London Bridge blended almost seamlessly with the modern town built around it. Surprising due to the fact it was almost two hundred years old.

"And where's this professor going to be meeting you?" Orr asked. He popped a top to a diet soda and took several long sips before setting it in the cup holder between the driver's and passenger's seats.

"He's not meeting me sir." Kellerman checked his mirrors and changed lanes. "He happened to be coming to the same coordinates based on his own research."

"Right. You said something similar yesterday." Orr's tone indicated doubt. "Has he contacted you today?"

"No, sir."

Orr stretched his legs out. "And you won't be sharing with him any additional details, such as the possibility of a crash survivor?"

"I would never break my oath, sir." The lieutenant gave a quick sideways glance at his commanding officer.

"Never?"

Kellerman's neck turned bright red. "No, sir. I'm offended you think you have to ask me, sir."

"I have to protect the integrity of this group. My job is to ensure security and that includes the details of our investigations. It seems as if you look up to this professor, and maybe want to impress him." Orr turned in his seat. "Chief, you stick to the LT like glue. You hear me? Nobody tells anyone anything about why we're here and what we're investigating."

"Yep, Commander, you got it." Chief choked out from a mouth full of potato chips.

Clearly, he'd found the snacks in the cooler.

"I don't need Chief babysitting me, sir." Kellerman stiffened in the driver's seat.

"Don't think of it as babysitting," Orr said. "Think of it as my insurance policy that you aren't going to fuck up our investigation."

Chief's booming laugh filled the SUV. "I'll keep an eye on him, sir. Keep the baby in the playpen."

Charlie observed Kellerman's profile. His eyebrows lowered over his eyes and, if she looked hard enough, she thought she could see steam coming out of his ears.

"Shut. Up. Chief," Kellerman ground out between his teeth.

Chief snorted, unfazed by the lieutenant's temper flare.

The SUV made a sharp turn to the left. All the passengers, with the exception of Kellerman, grabbed onto whatever they could to maintain their seats. He bounced them into the hospital parking lot. "Here we are."

The vehicle ground to an abrupt halt sending all the passengers forward.

"Thank you, LT." Orr clapped Kellerman on the shoulder and then grabbed his soda. "I'll text you when we're ready for a pick-up."

After Charlie and Angel slid out of the Excursion, Kellerman took off in a squeal of tires.

She wasn't so sure it was a good idea to piss off Kellerman. Who knew what his relationship was with this mysterious professor? Maybe he'd leak details out of spite for the way Chief and Orr had treated him.

A bad feeling entered her bones as they stepped through the entrance of the hospital.

———

Angel and Charlie stood in the waiting area while the commander spoke with the reception desk about locating the room of the crash survivor. Orr flashed his NCIS badge, and the young woman at the desk widened her eyes, picked up a phone, and pressed a number.

"I think she'll cooperate," Angel said with a smile.

"Do you think the time traveler will be someone you know?"

His face clouded. "I'm not sure."

"You never did explain how you ended up in a pod." Charlie couldn't help it. She needed to know, needed to understand. If he hated everything about the Genesis Project, why would he have willingly set foot into one of them?

Angel shifted his gaze. "This isn't really the place for such a conversation," he whispered.

"I want to understand everything." She touched his arm.

He brushed off her hand. "Let's talk more when we go home."

"At your place?" Her stomach clenched at the deceit, but she knew he'd accept. Their physical connection had been very strong from the beginning. For now, she had to fake her feelings. She'd find a way to back out of it before they returned to D.C.

His gaze searched her face. "Yes. My place."

"Let's go you two." The commander gestured for them to join him. "We have an escort coming. She's on a secure wing."

They followed their boss as he led them to the elevators.

A nurse dressed in purple scrubs joined them. "Are you the group from the government?"

"Yes, we're here to talk to the accident survivor," Orr said.

She nodded. "How many government organizations are they going to send?"

"Excuse me?"

"There's someone else talking to her right now. Don't you guys share notes?"

The elevator opened, and the four of them stepped inside. The nurse waved her badge in front of a reader and pressed the fifth floor button.

"What are you talking about? What 'someone else'?" Orr crossed his arms.

The nurse frowned and glanced at each of them, as if looking for an answer. "Didn't they tell you downstairs? That's why I was so confused. We already have a government authority here questioning her. Now you guys, too? She's not a well woman. The doc wants her to have some rest. All of these people trooping in and out? Not good for someone with a mental health issue."

"What government authority?" Angel tugged at his tightly tucked shirt.

The elevator stopped at the fifth floor. The door opened.

"A professor somebody-or-other. I can't remember his name. From some Air Force base in Nevada." The nurse exited the elevator and led them down the hall. "This way, please."

The three A Group representatives exchanged glances, then followed the nurse.

"Do you think that's Kellerman's professor?" asked Charlie.

"Guess we don't have to worry about Kellerman spilling the beans to him at the crash site," Angel said.

"I don't like this." The commander picked up his stride.

The nurse waved her badge in front of a card reader on the patient room door. The door beeped. She opened it. "You have ten minutes. Doctor's orders."

A tall man wearing a crisp gray suit and rimless glasses exited from the men's restroom and passed them in the hall. He nodded at them. When he noticed Angel, his mouth opened slightly and his eyes became steely.

"Allwood?" Angel whispered and turned his head as the man walked by.

Charlie grabbed his arm. "Hey."

Orr had entered the room, and the nurse waited for the two of them to join him.

The tall man picked up his pace and continued down the hall without a word.

"Was that the other government authority you were talking about?" Angel demanded. "The professor? Byron Allwood!" He shook himself free of Charlie's grasp and chased the man down the hall. "Stop!"

"Angel, what are you doing?"

He'd run off after the stranger.

"That's right. Professor Allwood." The nurse replied, as if nothing was wrong with Angel chasing this man through the hospital. "Do you know him?" She gave Charlie a quizzical look.

"Petty Officer Cutter, let's go." Orr beckoned her inside the patient room.

Beyond the door she could see a pale woman lying in the hospital bed wearing restraints. "But sir, Demarco, he—"

"Where is he?" Orr appeared in the doorway.

"He ran off after the professor. He thinks it's Byron Allwood."

"It *is* Byron Allwood," said the nurse.

Charlie's thoughts scrambled to understand. "What should we do?" She didn't know what Angel had in mind for the man he'd hated all of these years. Was Kellerman's former boss the infamous Byron Allwood? How was that possible?

Orr looked down the hall. "Shit." He let out a sigh. "You stay with the patient. I'll take care of this."

Charlie entered the room, her heartbeat racing. Stars filled her vision. To comprehend what was happening took her breath away. How could she focus on the woman lying in the bed when two mortal enemies had crossed paths? What did it mean for Armas? For the team? For Angel?

———

"Byron is that you?" the woman in the bed called out weakly.

Charlie wanted to be out in the hallway with her boss, Angel, and the mysterious Allwood. Not here in the room with a pod crash survivor. She was inconsequential compared to what was happening outside of this room. But her boss had wanted her to meet with the woman, so she would follow orders. "My name is Petty Officer Cutter, I'm from NCIS-A. Did the nurse tell you? We'd like to ask you some questions."

She really didn't have any questions in mind. She'd assumed Orr would take the lead on the conversation, but now that she was alone with her, maybe she could find some of her own answers.

"Where is Byron? He told us we would all be together again." The patient pulled at her restraints. "Where am I?"

Charlie pulled up a chair. "You're in the hospital."

The woman, who was barely out of her teens, had long brown hair, a cherub face, and a snub nose. She turned her head in Charlie's direction. "Are we in paradise?"

"Excuse me?"

The woman blinked. One eye was milky blue, the other a dark brown.

Charlie gasped at the odd appearance.

A large jagged scar was visible down the side of her face from scalp to chin. The woman reached for her hand. "Paradise. He told us we were traveling to paradise. A world without hate and fear."

Charlie clasped the woman's hand in hers. "You are in a safe place. They will take care of you here, I promise. What's your name?"

"Safe. Yes, I want to be safe."

The woman's grip tightened like a vise.

"Ow, you're hurting me." Charlie twisted her arm to break the woman's hold.

"I don't know you. Who are you? Why should I trust you?" The woman's face twisted into a snarl. The soft, child-like features disappeared.

"I want to help you." Charlie managed to free her hand. "Tell me your name, so I can help you."

"You think I haven't seen your tricks? The tricks of the Purists?"

"I'm not here to hurt you."

"Is that right? The last time I saw your kind, I was being chased through the tunnels, attacked for being different, I would've died if it weren't for Risa and Byron." She struggled against her restraints. "They saved us—the most loyal, the most obedient—we were rewarded. I am here in paradise like I was promised."

"This isn't paradise."

"Where is Byron?"

"You traveled through time. You're in the past. The world as it is now is probably no better than the time you came from. We have violence and problems and everything else. Allwood lied to you."

The woman bucked upward. "No! You're a liar. You're Purist scum."

The nurse entered the room. "I'm sorry, your time is up." She fluttered around the agitated patient and adjusted the blankets. "You're safe here, remember? Nothing can hurt you here."

The woman began to relax with the nurse's ministrations and soothing words.

"Did she give you a name?" As she asked the nurse the question, Charlie moved her chair back where she found it by the window.

"No. But she did seem to know that professor your friend chased after." The nurse checked the patient's IV line. "We're hoping we can track down her family, but she didn't have any ID on her."

Suddenly, the patient grabbed at her throat. Her eyes grew wide and panicked.

The nurse rushed to the woman to check her pulse. "What have you done?"

"Nothing." Charlie backed away from the bed. "I only was asking her questions."

The woman's face turned purple.

"She's not breathing." The nurse pushed a button on the control attached to the patient's bed. Then, she quickly released the rail on the side of the bed and removed the pillow from beneath the woman's head. "What did you do?"

Charlie shook her head and skirted the end of the bed, heading for the door. Where was the commander? She shouldn't be in here.

Another nurse burst through the doorway with a crash cart. A doctor seconds behind.

As the team circled the unresponsive patient, Charlie slipped out into the hall. Would she be okay? The woman had seemed perfectly lucid and awake when she'd entered the room. Maybe an undiagnosed injury from the crash? Or her time travel experience?

She reflected on the survivor's appearance—her eyes, the long scar down her face. Maybe Angel was right. Had Allwood been experimenting on innocent people? And what was Allwood's purpose in doing so? Maybe Angel's anger was reasonable. Seeing the crazed woman for herself had given her a different perspective. Was Allwood a caring man who wanted to advance humans for the better? Or some kind of Dr. Frankenstein?

"We're losing her—"

Charlie's stomach dropped.

CHAPTER 3

ANGEL RACED DOWN THE HALLWAY. He couldn't let Allwood slip away. The knowledge that Allwood had been Kellerman's boss at Area 51 made his stomach turn. What kinds of experiments had they let him get away with? And how did he end up working for them anyway?

A nurse stepped into his path. He dodged and spun bouncing off the wall. The woman gasped and reared back. He missed colliding with her by inches.

Allwood sprinted ahead of him. A few more feet, and he would reach the bank of elevators at the end of the hall.

Angel felt for the gun he'd tucked in the back of his pants under his jacket. No one on the team had known he was armed. Even though he held the role of 'security,' the commander discouraged Angel from carrying any weapons. But when Angel heard on the ride to Lake Havasu they had a pod survivor, he was glad he'd done it.

"Allwood!" He was closing the distance.

The older man stumbled, but he caught himself, gripping the wall as he turned a corner—not toward the elevators but following a sign for the stairs.

How many years had Allwood been here? The last time Angel had seen him, he was still a young man. No more than thirty. Now he looked well into middle age—bald, a bit of a paunch, and an uneven gait. Twenty years? Maybe more? The chief's data indicated a pod had landed in the late nineties. Perhaps that had been Allwood's pod.

He rounded the corner. The older man pushed through the stairwell door. Angel was mere steps behind. As he burst through it seconds after Allwood, he took a chance and leapt at his prey. Angel crashed into him as he headed downstairs. Their bodies collided. They tumbled together down the stairs to the landing, and Angel had the air knocked out of him. His gun flew out of his hands and bounced off the wall. They both landed with a hard thud.

Allwood groaned. He'd hit his head on one of the steps and bled freely from a cut on his scalp. Angel balled up his fist and pounded the man in the face. The older man crossed his arms to protect himself from the hail of blows. Over and over Angel punched the man. His mind was a single thought: kill him.

Somehow the smack of his fist against Allwood's chin satisfied a deep seated need in him. A need to punish. A need to destroy. A need to end this man's life right here, right now before he harmed anyone else.

"Demarco!" The commander's voice echoed in the stairwell. "Get the fuck off that man. What in the hell do you think you're doing?" Within seconds, his boss had reached the pair of scuffling men and had Demarco in a headlock.

Orr hauled Demarco off Allwood. Angel was surprised how strong the commander was. He fought him with everything he had, but the choking hold diminished his strength quickly.

Allwood scrambled away from both of them and scooped up the gun.

When Orr saw the weapon, he loosened his grip on Demarco.

"Shit." Angel spat on the tile, hauled himself up, and hurtled toward the now-armed Allwood and barreled into the man with his shoulder.

The gun went off, and a bullet glanced off the stairs above them and buried itself in the tile floor right in front of Orr.

Angel latched onto Allwood's arm with both hands in a struggle for the weapon. "Drop it, Allwood."

Their faces were inches apart. The jagged scar he'd remembered on Allwood's face had faded to a faint white line. "What did you do to her?" the older man asked.

"What did I do to her?" Angel pulled back slightly. His mind raced.

"The pod survivor is just fine," Orr said as he plucked the gun out of Allwood's restrained hand. "I don't know what's going on here." He nodded at Allwood. "But one of you better start talking."

Orr's cell phone rang. He pressed his lips together, looked at the phone screen, sighed, and answered it. "Petty Officer Cutter, this had better be important." As he listened, the commander's face paled.

———

Charlie hung up the phone and leaned against the wall next to the patient room where the pod survivor had died. The host of nurses and doctors who had poured in to save the woman's life had failed. Now A Group would never know more about the time she came from, why she'd willingly gotten into a pod, or how many more of these travelers existed.

The nurse, who had been in the room with Charlie when the patient coded, warned her not to leave, as the doctor would want to speak with her. Why did the nurse think she had something to do with the woman's sudden change in condition? She wiped her sweaty palms on the front of her pants. She needed her boss to step in and fix this. Something wasn't right.

But Orr had sounded breathless on the phone. Had Angel caught up to Allwood? Had Orr managed to stop them both from killing each other? Maybe the commander had his hands full.

"Young lady?" A short Asian man in a doctor's coat approached her. "Are you the one who was with the patient earlier?"

She nodded. "My name is Charlie Cutter. I'm with the government. We were sent here to investigate a crash by the lake. The woman was our witness." She opened her purse and pulled out one of the generic looking business cards Stormy had given her last week.

The doctor took the card and read the face of it. "You're Navy?"

"Yes."

His face softened. "My dad was a Navy Flight Officer. Did twenty-five years. I almost went to the Naval Academy."

Charlie smiled.

"I'm Dr. Phan."

They shook hands.

"What happened to her?" Charlie nodded toward the patient room. "She was totally fine when I first went in there, but then after the nurse arrived—"

He nodded and tapped his pen against his cheek. "The nurse mentioned another visitor before you. Was he part of your investigative team?"

She shook her head. "I was here with my boss, Commander Orr, and another co-worker, Special Agent Demarco. If you know anything about another visitor, we could really use some more information."

The doctor's eyebrows shot up. "I only know there were two requests today for visitors. I gave the okay, as long as they were brief visits. I was hoping someone would be able to help us identify her, and when I heard you were from the government, well, I hoped you knew something we didn't."

"I'm sorry. I can't give you any details about our investigation. I'm sure you understand."

The doctor nodded, but Charlie wasn't certain he truly understood.

"I only wish I knew what happened in there," he said.

"Oh? I thought maybe she had an injury from the crash."

"We did a thorough exam last night when she was admitted—CT, x-rays, blood work. The scans all came back normal. We're still waiting on the blood results. But what we saw in there...well, it almost seems as if–" He trailed off and shrugged.

"As if what?"

"As if she was injected with something. Her condition deteriorated so rapidly."

The hair lifted on the back of her scalp. Had Allwood done something to the woman? The leader of the Genesis Project and supposed 'savior' who brought the survivor to 'paradise'?

Her mind flitted through the possibilities. She'd assumed Allwood had shown up at the hospital to rescue one of his followers, but now it looked as if he was taking her out. Why?

"Dr. Phan, my team will have to take possession of the blood and the results. Can you show me where I can retrieve those?"

"What?" The tapping of his pen against his cheek ceased. "I can't approve that."

"And the body. We'll need to have the body ready to be transported by the end of today." Orr had instructed her very carefully about what she needed to do. Would the doctor listen to her?

"Excuse me, but we have protocols here." Dr. Phan tucked his pen into the breast pocket of his white coat. "An autopsy must be performed, so we can identify cause of death, make sure no foul play was involved."

"Doctor," a familiar voice said, "I'm sorry but this is now a federal case." Commander Orr approached flashing his A Group badge. "We'd appreciate your cooperation."

Charlie bit her lip. "Where's Demarco?" *And Allwood*, she thought.

Her boss let out a sigh. "That's a long story. Let's go pick up the blood work and arrange for the body to be delivered to Nellis, and I'll catch you up."

The doctor stood between them and rubbed at his eyelid.

Orr clapped him on the shoulder. "Thanks, doc, you've been helpful."

———

Allwood, zip cuffs restraining his hands, attempted to stand in the ER waiting room. "You can't keep me here. I'm not a criminal."

Angel grabbed him by the belt and forced him to sit.

A middle-aged nurse with a tired look on her face approached them with a clipboard. "Calm down, sir, I'm sure the officer only wants you to be treated for your injuries."

"He's not an officer." The older man's lip curled. "He's unlawfully restraining me."

Angel flashed his NCIS-A badge. "I'm with the Naval Criminal Investigative Service. He's my detainee and is wanted for questioning. Could you please clean him up, maybe give him a few stitches?"

Allwood jerked his head back when he saw the badge. "How did you manage that one?"

"Same as you managed to convince people you were a professor."

The nurse inspected his head wound and the bruising to his face. "Did you have an accident?"

"This thug tackled me in the stairwell and punched me." Allwood's face reddened. "I want you to call the police."

Angel made eye contact with the nurse and gave a slight shake to his head.

"Let's examine you first and take care of that cut," the nurse soothed. "Then we can decide what to do next. All right?"

Allwood calmed down, and his posture relaxed. "Yes, thank you. At least someone here is listening to me." He announced it to the room as if the other people waiting for emergency medical care had any interest in his situation.

The nurse handed Angel the clipboard. "Please fill in his information for him and any insurance provider."

"I'm not paying for this," Allwood squawked.

"We'll be paying cash," Angel explained as he filled out the form.

"You can bring it with you." The nurse took hold of Allwood's arm. "Come this way. We've got a room for you to wait in. The doctor will be with you shortly."

Although the man towered over the portly nurse, he let himself be led as if he were a small child. Allwood was shifty—pathetic one minute, brutal the next.

Angel's mind veered back to his sister, what had she been

thinking when she joined the Genesis Project? And how had she ended up with this rat?

———

The 'room' was a curtained off area near the back of the emergency department. Angel took the only chair and filled out the form. "I know your name, but what's your address? And how old are you these days, Byron?"

He held the pen over the form and eyed his captive who comfortably lay on the gurney, dried blood marring his brow and a bruise darkening on his chin.

"You think I'm going to give you my address?" Allwood sneered.

"Yes, I do. Because if you won't give it to me, I'll be forced to call the officer in charge back at Area 51 and ask him for your details."

"Groom Lake. Only civilians call it that." He pulled down his jacket sleeve with his handcuffed hands.

Angel slammed the clipboard on the counter next to him. "Enough of this shit, Allwood." He lowered his voice so it wouldn't carry beyond the curtains surrounding them. "I never thought I do it, but I found you. And now your whole scheme is over with."

"What whole scheme exactly?" He crossed his ankles and put his restrained hands behind his head in a relaxed pose.

"The pods, the traveling, your followers. It's over." He leaned toward the older man. "I don't know what you're up to, but it ends here. Today. No more of your sick experiments."

"Aren't we looking for the same thing, Demarco? Haven't we always been since we arrived here?"

His pulse increased. Was Allwood about to reveal some of his secrets? "I don't know what you're talking about."

"Yes, you do." The professor tilted his head from side to side until his neck cracked. "You couldn't stand to let Risa make up her own mind. Choose her own path. She told me about you, you know."

"Shut up." Angel ground his teeth together.

"How you despised her intelligence. Was embarrassed by her. How you never stood up for her."

"That's not true," Angel snorted. "I protected her. My father—"

"Your father. Yes, tell me more about the man who made her life a living hell." Allwood raised an eyebrow. "Squashing her brilliance. Forcing her to live the life of a farmer's daughter."

"She loved our family." A heaviness filled his body. Had Risa really told him that? Had she despised their simple way of living?

Allwood smirked. "If she loved her family so much, why did she seek me out?"

"You're wrong, Allwood." He crossed his arms. All these years of waiting to confront the man who took his sister away and now he was in a battle of words. He had questions he wanted answered, but found himself distracted by strong emotion. "You took advantage of her. She was a young girl. She didn't know what she was doing. You lied to her."

"She was twenty and perfectly capable of making up her own mind." He casually touched his wound with his fingers and looked at the bright red blood on them. "Don't you think?"

A pain hit the back of his throat. "You killed her, and I'll never forgive you for that."

CHAPTER 4

ALLWOOD'S FACE PALED. "What do know about her?"

Angel's body tensed. "You put her in one of those pods, and sent her back to the dark ages. That's what I know. I'm sure you've seen the manuscript. It's your fault."

"You stupid fool." Spots of color entered the older man's cheeks. "You have no idea what part you played, do you? Why I ended up separated from her?" He frowned. "Why didn't you let us leave? We weren't hurting anyone."

"Hurting anyone?" Just as he remembered, Allwood was an arrogant prick who didn't give a fuck about anyone but himself. "You were surgically altering vulnerable people. Promising them cures and a better life. I saw what your 'treatments' did to people." A sour taste filled his mouth.

"They chose that path. I didn't make them do it."

"You made ridiculous promises that were never going to be real," Angel spat out. "You took life and ruined it. You ruined *her* —Risa."

Allwood gaze became unfocused. "She was even more beautiful after I helped her become the person she was supposed to be."

"A monster?"

Allwood snorted and shook his head. "I made her better, smarter. I helped her fulfill her true purpose, her true destiny."

"To die alone in some barbaric time?" Blood pounded in his ears. "Where women were burned at the stake for witchcraft?"

"You were the one who sent her there, Demarco. When you damaged her pod. It was your fault and yours alone. We only wanted to escape where our work could be understood."

How dare Allwood blame him? "Is that what's happening now at Groom Lake? Continuing your work?"

The curtain flew open, and a woman in a white coat entered. "I've heard you need some stitches, Mr. Allwood. I'm Doctor Sala."

Angel found himself standing over Allwood in an aggressive stance. The doctor's arrival made him turn off his anger and resume the role of arresting authority. "I have a transport arriving in a few minutes. Will this take long?"

Dr. Sala approached the patient, donned a clean pair of gloves, and examined the wound. "I'd guess about ten stitches. That's quite a cut. Would you like an ice pack for the bruising?"

"Yes, thank you," said Allwood. "At least someone cares about my injuries."

Angel wanted to punch his bruised face a few more times.

"It shouldn't take more than twenty minutes." The doctor turned her attention back to the patient. "Let's get you all patched up, shall we?"

As Angel watched Dr. Sala stitch up Allwood, he reviewed the facts of what he knew. Allwood and Risa had attempted to escape to the past using pods, which according to Charlie's translation work, had been the scientific work of his sister. And even though Allwood's followers had joined him, Angel was beginning to wonder if that had merely been a way for the two lovers to cover their tracks. What was the true purpose of the pods? To allow the Genesis Project to continue in another time? Or was it a more personal pursuit? What made his sister want to create such a thing?

Even though he thought he understood Risa—after all they were only eighteen months apart in age—had he missed something? He recalled fondly their childhood together on the farm, spending time in the barn with the animals and playing in the hay stacks up in the loft. Yes, she had struggled with the expectations of her family and the community, but he never thought her unhappy.

For Angel, the jump to the past had been a startling one. Something he hadn't anticipated. The sensation of floating and spinning had been odd. He had imagined himself traveling through the air to another part of the earth, and, he had to admit, deep down he found that exciting. He'd lived his whole life in his little village with the same people, the same work, the same future laid out in front of him. But when he'd made the decision to step into the pod and follow his sister, had he been choosing that to rescue her or to save himself?

"There, all done." The doctor wiped away the dried blood and studied her handiwork. "It should heal well and will barely be visible." She touched Allwood's scar that marred the side of his face. "Have you ever thought about plastic surgery for that? Not sure what happened here, but it must've not been a very skilled hand."

Allwood jerked his head away

The doctor lowered her hand. "I'm sorry. I didn't mean to—"

Angel handed her the clipboard. "I told the nurse we'll be paying cash. Is there somewhere where I go to do that?"

The doctor took it and flipped through the pages. "We'll need an address on here, so our accounting department can send you a bill."

Angel pulled a business card out of his shirt pocket. "You can send it here."

The doctor frowned. "Washington D.C.?"

"Come on. Let's go." He hauled up the older man by his elbow.

"He needs his anti-biotics." Dr. Sala slid back the curtain. "The hospital pharmacy is down the hall on the first floor. The prescription should be ready by now."

Angel's phone rang. While holding onto Allwood with one hand, he dug his cell phone out of his pocket with the other. "Hello?"

The doctor handed Allwood a slip of paper with instructions

on it and headed to the patient next to them behind another curtain.

"The pod survivor is dead," the commander said on the other end of the line. "We think Allwood might've given her something. Be careful."

"Got it." Angel eyed the man next to him.

"We're down at the lab collecting her blood samples and test paper work. First floor."

Angel processed the possibility that Allwood had murdered one of his supposed followers. Why would he want to do that? "We have to pick up some medication and then we can meet you there."

"Everything okay?"

"I have it under control." Angel tightened his hold on his captive.

"Wonder what the LT's going to think."

"I don't know, but I think Kellerman has some questions to answer.

CHAPTER 5

DR. STERN RUBBED HER EYES. It had been a long and uncomfortable night sleeping on the cot in the hospital staff lounge, but she hadn't wanted to leave Armas's side until his vitals improved. Only when the night nurse insisted she leave the ICU and get some rest, did the doctor give in to advice.

As she sat on the edge of the cot, she straightened her blouse and slipped on her navy flats. Since no one had called or texted last night, it must mean Armas was still stable.

She wanted to take a moment and let the good news settle in. Yesterday had been touch and go—she hadn't shared with Charlie how close Armas had been to death. The young petty officer had grown so attached to the child in such a short period of time, she couldn't crush her hopes. Plus, Stormy would've fallen apart. Tetanus at this stage even with modern medicine had a low survivability rate. It had been a difficult decision to withhold the facts about Armas, but the team had work to do. More important work than sitting around a hospital while a little boy struggled to survive.

Her cell phone rang. When she picked it up, a fluttery feeling hit her stomach.

Her contact at the NSA lab.

That could mean only one thing...

"Hello, Sam. Do you have news for me?" she asked.

"Good afternoon." The familiar grizzled voice of her old mentor made her smile. "I hope you're not eating your lunch."

She checked her watch, twelve-thirty p.m. She'd slept longer than she'd thought. "No, not at all." She cleared her throat.

"Probably not the news you were expecting."

"Oh?" Goose bumps appeared on her arms. As her brain ran through the possibilities, she rubbed her forearm.

"The elimination DNA you sent."

Her posture perked up. "Just spit it out, Sam." That was Charlie's sample. The one to make sure her DNA didn't mix in with the DNA from the blood on the broken test tubes the team brought back from North Dakota.

"We got a hit."

"What do you mean?"

"A match."

"To what?" Dr. Stern's mind raced. What was Sam talking about?

"The DNA sample you turned in a week later. They're related."

Armas's sample from the night of his arrival? What was going on?

Dr. Stern held her hand against her mouth. "Related how?" Her heart beat a million miles a minute.

"Half-siblings. Different mitochondrial DNA, but similar paternal strands."

Armas and Charlie were half-brother and sister? But how...? "I see." It was nearly impossible to remain calm. This news had massive implications. It made no sense and called into question everything she'd thought she knew about the young woman she'd grown to respect and appreciate.

"And there's more."

"More?" She stared straight out in front of herself, not seeing the room around her. It was as if the walls disappeared, the cots, the curtains, the chair in the corner. A sleepy-looking young intern stumbled into the dimly lit room and grabbed a cot next to her and pulled the curtain shut.

Dr. Stern picked up her cardigan draped across her lap and exited the lounge. Where could she find some privacy?

"On all three samples you sent us, the DNA swabs plus the blood, we saw some identical cellular-level damage."

The same damage she had noticed on the samples Kellerman retrieved on his recent trip to North Dakota? The damage she'd ascribed to time travel? "Did you send the report to NCIS-A?" She needed to compare her results to the lab's.

"I was about to hit send on my email. You were copied on it."

Suddenly, a gaggle of young privates with fresh haircuts and baby faces filled the hall. Their chatter bounced off the hard flooring and surfaces making it hard to hear Sam on the other end of the line.

Dr. Stern stuck a finger in her ear before responding to block out the noise. "Can you give me an hour before you do that?"

The group passed by her laughing at some raunchy joke one of the men shared with his buddies. The smallest of them met her gaze and blushed bright red at the possibility they'd been overheard.

"Is there a problem?" Sam asked.

"No, no problem." She took a deep breath to control the shakiness in her voice. "I need to make a phone call first."

"I suppose I could do that for you, Abigail."

"I appreciate it, Sam." Thank goodness she'd sent the samples to the classified lab where she had a contact. The results would go no further than the SCIF at the National Security Agency. But the copy of the report sent to NCIS-A? The explosive information in that report could shatter the trust that had been built among the team. "You'll destroy the samples, yes?"

"Of course."

"Thanks for everything."

Dr. Stern hung up and thought for a moment before selecting a saved number in her contacts list. A familiar voice on the other end amped up her nerves. "We need to talk. Are you free?"

CHARLIE STOOD next to Commander Orr waiting for the hospital lab to hand over the blood and other samples they took from the time traveler along with her CT scan and x-rays. The body had already been loaded into an ambulance and would be delivered to Nellis for the return flight to DC in a couple of hours.

Orr pounded on the bullet-proof glass that protected the lab staff from any threat that might enter their domain. "Where are my samples? Hello?" Little did they know Orr was more dangerous than any threat they could've imagined. He was on the warpath.

Two white-coated lab techs, one male and one female, whooshed past the counter and disappeared into a lab area protected by a security door. Neither one of them seemed interested in dealing with the irate Navy man with the bulging biceps and a bone to pick.

"This is ridiculous. We have to go back tonight. We don't have time for this shit." He threw up his hands and faced Charlie. "Have you heard anything from Chief or Kellerman?"

"No, sir." By now she understood Orr had serious misgivings about Kellerman's relationship to Allwood. "What about Demarco and Allwood? What did he tell you?"

Orr chewed on his lip before answering. "Sounds as if

Allwood was stitched up, and they'll be joining us here in a few minutes."

"How are you going to handle this, sir?"

"If Allwood killed the survivor, we have some serious questions to ask him. I'm not even going to think about what you told me earlier. That's a whole different ball of wax." He ran a hand through his short hair. "But the fact that the professor came here on behalf of Area 51 could pose some problems."

"How?"

"I'm sort of familiar with the structure at the base. Allwood should be under the purview of the base commander and possibly a division chief. They might be expecting his return with samples or even the woman's body. If we interfere, I'm not certain we'd get very far."

"May I help you?" A brave lab worker stood behind the counter. She must've not gotten the message from the other lab techs about Orr's threatening behavior.

The commander pasted a smile on his face and approached the protected space. "I would like to pick up Jane Doe's samples and test results, please. Commander Orr. NCIS." He slid a card through the narrow space under the bullet-proof glass. "Jane Doe from the fifth floor."

The tech's eyes widened. "Right, yes. Dr. Phan's patient."

At that moment Charlie's phone rang. She looked at the screen. "It's Dr. Stern, Commander. Perhaps she had news about Armas." Her heart thudded. Was the boy all right?

He waved a hand at her, more intent on ensuring they left the hospital with the records he wanted.

Charlie stepped out into the hall where it was quieter. "Abigail, is Armas okay?"

"Listen to me carefully, Charlie."

The serious tone in Dr. Stern's voice worried her. She placed a hand on the wall next to her for support. "I'm listening."

"A report will be delivered shortly to the NCIS-A office. One that has results your co-workers might find shocking."

"What report?" She rubbed her forehead. "What are you talking about?"

"Charlie, I really like you, I do. I'm only letting you know what I found out because I want to understand what's going on. I can't believe you'd lie to me—"

"Lie to you?" Did Dr. Stern know about Demarco and his past? Her blood chilled.

"The lab at NSA called me a few minutes ago. They completed the DNA testing on the blood sample from North Dakota and the testing on Armas." She paused. "I know."

"I don't understand." Her body heat started to rise. "What do you know?"

"I know you and Armas are half-brother and sister."

A roar filled her ears, and her limbs began to shake. "What?" Impossible. There must be some mistake. The lab must've screwed up. There was no way...no possible way...

"Are you a time traveler, too, Charlie? Is that how you ended up on the team? Is that why you were so easily able to translate the manuscript text? Help me understand."

Her grip on her cell phone tightened. How could she and Armas be brother and sister? She had a mother and father who had a house in Columbia and had been married for over two decades. Her only sibling was Chad, her twin. This was madness. "The tests are wrong. I don't know what's going on, but it's not true."

"My friend at the lab wouldn't make that kind of mistake, Charlie."

"It *is* a mistake." A lump formed in her throat. What else could it be? "What you're saying is impossible."

"As soon as you arrive back in DC, the rest of your team will know. You might want to think about trusting me and telling me the truth. I can help you."

Down the hall, Demarco and Allwood in plastic cuffs appeared. Angel's gaze captured hers. A strange feeling ran through her.

"I have to go." The DNA results made no sense, but even if it didn't make sense, the doctor was right—her whole team was about to find out, including Demarco. Her eyelids fluttered. "I'll call you back when I'm free." She felt detached from her body.

How could this be? How could such a mistake be made? She needed to know more, needed to talk to the doctor in private, needed to see the results for herself.

CHAPTER 7

"WHO WAS THAT?" Demarco asked as he approached with his captive.

Charlie slipped her phone into her purse and waved a hand. "It's my brother." As she said the words, it dawned on her that Dr. Stern's reveal connected to her twin brother as well. If she was flagged in that report, her brother would be connected as well—it would only be a matter of time. She chewed on her bottom lip.

Her gaze flicked over to Allwood. According to the data, she and Armas supposedly shared the same father. Her gut tightened. No way could this awful man be her biological father.

"Everything all right?" The special agent's brow wrinkled.

What would happen once the office read the report? Would she be at risk of becoming the 'experiment' Demarco had feared for himself? What about Chad? Too much came at her all at once.

She smiled. It didn't feel like a real smile, but she hoped it passed muster with the two men. "I'm all right. Maybe a little hungry." She checked her watch. "We had breakfast so early this morning."

"When will I be allowed to call my office?" Allwood placed his body between her and Angel. "This is ridiculous. You can't hold me. The lieutenant will set you straight."

"Shut up." Angel shoved the older man aside. "Where's Orr?" he asked Charlie.

The commander, at that very moment, exited the lab with a small Styrofoam cooler. "Samples and tests acquired."

As Orr and Angel discussed the next steps in handling Allwood, Charlie's mind flitted somewhere else. How was it possible Harrison Cutter was not her real father? Had her mother lied to him—and to her and her brother—for the last twenty plus years? She itched to pick up the phone and call her parents. Confront them. It didn't make any sense. She needed to hear from both her mother and father the test results were wrong. Dr. Stern and the NSA had been mistaken. There was no other possible explanation. Unless Chad knew something she didn't—?

"Petty Officer Cutter, are you with us?" Orr snapped his fingers in front of her face. "It seems as if you drifted off there for a moment."

"Yes." Her face heated. "I was wondering if we shouldn't call Kellerman to pick us up, return us to Nellis." Most of her thoughts were focused on her next steps. She had to call Chad. He had a right to know the same information she'd been given. If he knew anything at all, maybe it would give her clarity and a path forward.

"That's what Demarco just said." Orr crossed his arms. "Are you okay? You look a little pale."

She needed time away to think, to process, to analyze. All of this was too much to handle, plus keep her mind on her work and deal with her confused feelings for Angel. Her ears began to ring, and her vision faded to a dark tunnel. "I'm not feeling so well." Her knees buckled under her.

Angel rushed to catch her. "I've got her, sir." His solid arms wrapped around her. "She said she felt hungry earlier. Maybe she didn't have enough to eat this morning. I'll walk her to the cafeteria."

"Ever the gallant hero," scoffed Allwood with a roll of his eyes.

Angel's secure hold comforted her. If only she could confide in him, trust him. But he hated Allwood, and if he got wind of the DNA results his hatred would surely extend to her. "Yes, something to eat," she mumbled.

"Sir," Angel said, "if you can escort Allwood outside, we'll join you as soon as we can."

Charlie found her footing, and Angel curved an arm around her waist. "Lean on me. You'll be all right. I'm sorry. I didn't realize you were feeling that badly."

The commander eyed Charlie's physical state. "We'll wait out in the parking lot in the SUV." Orr hefted the cooler and jerked his chin in the direction of the exit. "Get moving, Allwood."

"Kellerman will know what to do." The professor sneered. "This is completely ridiculous. I didn't kill anyone."

"We'll see what the evidence says," Orr said. The two men walked together down the hall, the commander's free hand tightly gripped the professor's upper arm.

Angel leaned into Charlie's hair and kissed the top of her head. "Let's get you something to eat."

Shivers ran down her arms at the gentle kiss. She didn't want to be attracted to him anymore, but her body betrayed her. Damn him for being so chivalrous. "I'm sure I only need something to drink, and I'll be fine." She pushed out of his grip.

His posture stiffened. "Right. The cafeteria's this way." He led her in the opposite direction of Orr and Allwood.

She didn't care anymore if she hurt his feelings. Her whole life had blown up with one phone call. If those results put her in danger, then they put her brother in danger, too. And heaven forbid anyone touched him. Not on her watch.

CHAPTER 8

"WHERE'S KELLERMAN?" Commander Orr asked the chief when he arrived behind the wheel of the Ford Excursion. "Don't tell me you left him behind because he annoyed you." A believable possibility considering how many times Ricard had complained to him about Kellerman's obnoxious know-it-all attitude.

"He disappeared." Ricard shrugged. "Who's this guy?" He made a face at the sight of Allwood.

"Never mind about him. What do you mean Kellerman disappeared?" Orr gripped Allwood's arm more tightly. "What do you know about this?"

"Nothing. How could I? You've had me tied up for hours." Allwood lifted his plasticuffed wrists and grimaced. "When am I allowed a phone call? The base commander will be angry. We have a visiting senator who expected me this evening for a dinner engagement. The funding she could secure for my project—"

"Shut up." The man was a blowhard. How could the LT stand this guy? "Where is Kellerman?" he asked the chief for a second time.

"The sample collection was a bust, by the way, the city was finishing the clean up as we arrived. Green shit everywhere. Wouldn't let us within ten feet of any of it." The chief heavily stepped out of the SUV, which he'd parked along the curb clearly marked: *Emergency Use Only*. "Anyway, a few minutes later he got a phone call. Didn't want me to hear it. Wandered back up toward the road. And that's the last I saw of him. Thank God I had the spare key."

"What the hell?" Orr knew he never should've trusted the little prick. Always so smug about everything. Even the first day on the job. "Can you track his cell?"

"I'm the equipment guy; the LT was the tech expert." Ricard leaned against the black SUV and then flinched. "Ouch, that's fucking hot. Stupid Arizona."

"So you've lost one of your men, commander." Allwood raised his chin and exposed his longer-than-normal neck. "That's too bad. Now what will we do?"

Orr yanked open the sliding side door. "You are going to sit in here, while the Chief and I talk. And if I find out you and Kellerman were up to something, the NCIS is going to come knocking on your door, senator or no senator." He grabbed the professor by the wrists and forced him into the vehicle. Before the man could protest, Orr slammed the door shut in his face.

"Where's Cutter and Demarco?" Ricard took a wide stance and set his hands on his hips.

"They'll be here shortly." Orr headed to the back of the Excursion, opened the door, set the cooler in the back, and hid Demarco's gun under the rear seat. He'd deal with that later. "I've got lab evidence in there that's going to prove our survivor was murdered."

"What?" Ricard swung his head from Orr to the SUV and back, putting two and two together. "That jerk do it?"

"A high likelihood, yes." How was he going to convince a senator, a base commander, and probably a bunch of other muckety-mucks at Area 51 that their precious professor was a murderer? "He's coming back to DC with us until I can prove it."

"Shit, sir." Ricard rubbed a hand over his short, military-style haircut. "What do we do about Kellerman?"

"Until we can prove otherwise, I consider him an accomplice, and quite possibly the mastermind of this whole thing."

"Kellerman? That dweeb?" Ricard scoffed.

"He managed to fool us for months. Who knows how much

information he's been sharing with Allwood." Orr thought through recent events and when their team might have been betrayed. "I'll bet he shared samples from his North Dakota trip with his pal. Who knows what else."

"So what's this Allwood been up to?"

"I don't know, but I'm sure going to find out."

Demarco and Cutter exited from the hospital.

"We've got six hours before our flight back home," Orr said. "I want the body, the samples, and Allwood loaded and ready to fly before nineteen-hundred. I'll take Demarco and make a plan regarding Kellerman. He might have some ideas about what tools are available to help."

"How will you get back to Nellis?" Chief asked.

"Don't worry. We'll figure something out." The commander turned his attention toward Demarco. "Special Agent, I've got a job for you."

CHAPTER 9

SWEAT RAN down Kellerman's face. Jogging a few blocks from the crash site had him dripping with the stuff. All those hours spent keeping in shape for the bi-annual Navy physical fitness test couldn't overcome the relentless heat of Arizona in late summer. He wiped his brow with the back of his hand and headed into the confusion of streets opposite the bridge.

Chief would notice he'd disappeared any minute. He didn't have much time to work a plan. The distraction of the city employees hosing down the crash area had been the perfect opportunity to slip away.

Allwood had called him well over an hour ago. The necessary task had been done. Although it made Kellerman's stomach roll at the thought, Allwood's explanation made sense: any survivors posed a risk to the professor and his ultimate goal. And Kellerman would do anything to protect that goal. He'd been promised a place at the professor's side. His right-hand man as they traveled through time together, exploring, learning, and dominating the past with advanced knowledge no ancient human could understand. Kellerman's tech expertise combined with the professor's knowledge of the pods and their capabilities would make them a powerful duo.

He stepped into the street.

A horn honked.

"Hey, watch where you're going." A middle aged woman in a compact SUV rolled down her window to scold him. "Do you want to get killed?"

He held up his hand and cleared out of the road. "Sorry."

But could he help it if his mind wandered? He and the professor were on the cusp of completing the formula and building pods that worked. Really worked. After all this time. Incredible.

With the heat beating down, Kellerman slowed to a walk. He checked over his shoulder. Nobody had followed him. He'd managed to slip away without being caught.

He looked at his phone for a text from Allwood. The professor had promised to pick him up after the stop at the hospital and transport him back to the Groom Lake warehouse. His time on the NCIS-A team was coming to a close. With his backdoor access to the office files in DC finally up and running, the professor would have everything he needed to finalize the formula. Charlie's notes on the manuscript, the doctor's data on the samples they'd retrieved—it all brought the professor closer and closer to solving the puzzle of the pods.

A new text appeared in his conversation with Allwood, but it was a garble of letters. Nonsense. What did it mean? Was every-thing under control?

He paused under the shade of a eucalyptus tree and stared at his phone screen. He typed another message in the encrypted app they used:

> Ready for pickup.

As he waited for a response, he noticed he'd received a new email in his secondary account. The one that forwarded any new files placed in the office system.

The subject line of the email read: *DNA Results*. It had come from the NSA lab to which Dr. Stern had sent the samples.

He clicked on the email and opened it.

As he read the results of the DNA comparisons, his stomach hardened.

It couldn't be. Not that bitch. Impossible.

Allwood had never said a thing.

A daughter? Charlie Fucking Cutter was his daughter?

The realization that the boy was Allwood's had been shock enough. An unforeseen wrinkle in his plan to serve by the professor's side. But a boy so young? Allwood wouldn't be interested in exploring time with a toddler. Even though he'd assigned Kellerman the task of retrieving the kid before he'd fallen ill...he didn't seriously think Allwood would bring him along? Would he?

But Charlie?

Pain radiated from his jaw. He had clenched his teeth—hard.

She'd translated the Voynich manuscript.

Allwood had been impressed with the young woman's capabilities and had been overjoyed when Kellerman reported she'd begun to tackle the formula page with the missing text.

After sacrificing everything for Allwood—his relationship with his brother, his oath to adhere to the restrictions of a Top Secret clearance, his career in the Navy—would the professor reward him? Or would Allwood shunt him aside for a newly discovered daughter with incredible capabilities?

Since he was the only one in the office who knew the truth and the only one who had access to the DNA file besides Dr. Stern, perhaps he should keep this information to himself. Why share it? Why jeopardize his place next to Allwood?

With no response to his text, Kellerman mulled over his next steps. Could Allwood have been discovered? Thank God he'd installed a tracking app months ago to make sure the professor stayed true to his promises. Watching his mentor's whereabouts had given him a modicum of peace. And now the app might save the professor's ass if something had gone awry with the plan.

He tapped on it.

Shit.

Allwood's yellow dot glowed brightly on the map—he was outside the hospital in the parking lot. However, the yellow dots of Commander Orr, Charlie, and Chief Ricard were clustered around him. The only person on the team he couldn't track was

Demarco with his low tech flip phone. But if those three were together, he'd bet dollars to donuts Demarco was with them.

Kellerman stroked an eyebrow. The cluster of dots could only mean one thing: Allwood was in trouble.

WHEN THE COMMANDER mentioned he had a job for him, Demarco hesitated. After years of searching for the bastard, he didn't want to let Allwood out of his sight. "What do you need, sir?"

Charlie opened the sliding door to expose the professor seated behind the driver's seat. Instantly, Demarco's anger flared up.

"Kellerman's gone missing, I think our fears he may be leaking information to your friend here have been realized." Orr nodded in Allwood's direction.

The 'professor'—what a joke he'd given himself that moniker—expelled air through his nose. "I had nothing to do with it. My project has the full backing of the United States Government and has for twenty years. The lieutenant was merely another officer in my lab. I barely knew him."

"That's not how he described it to us before we arrived," Orr said.

"The lieutenant is an arrogant man." Allwood raised his eyebrows and gave a glassy stare. "Why do you think I fired him from my office and was glad to see him receive a new assignment?"

"Shut up, already." Demarco stepped menacingly toward the restrained man sitting calmly in the air conditioning. One more word, and he'd feel the need to pummel him again.

"Did you already search him?" The chief, although quite a few inches shorter than the reedy Allwood, outweighed him by fifty pounds easy. He scanned the professor up and down.

Shit. How did he forget to search his pockets? "Things happened kind of quickly."

"He attacked me like a wild animal," Allwood said as Ricard helped him out of the vehicle to pat him down. "I might have to sue."

"A wallet." Ricard tossed it onto the sidewalk.

The commander picked it up.

"A syringe and a cell phone." The chief locked eyes with Orr as he held the capped syringe in his hand. "Sir?"

"Let's put that in the cooler with the lab samples." Carefully, Orr plucked the syringe from Ricard's hand and carried it to the back of the SUV. "Quite possibly he injected the survivor with whatever's in this thing. Dr. Stern is about to have her hands full."

Demarco grabbed the cell phone and turned it over in his hands.

Could be a lot of secrets on this thing. Including what Allwood had been up to all these years. Back in the ER Allwood had accused him of damaging Risa's pod, which sent her too far back in time. Could similar damage he'd inflicted on Allwood's pod have caused him to land far earlier than he intended?

"Charlie, can you unlock this?" He'd adapted relatively well to all the bizarre technology around him, but when stressed, he had trouble being patient. And figuring out how to unlock a cell phone when he wanted to throttle the man being re-loaded into the SUV counted as one of those times.

Charlie took the phone from him. "Sure," she said quietly.

Something was up with her since the minute they'd met up in the hall outside the lab. Was the death of the time traveling woman too much for her? Maybe she was more sensitive than he realized.

He swept her figure. Where did the confident, intelligent woman go? Her posture slumped, and her gaze was fixed on their captive.

"Hold on, Chief," she said. "Could you face me, please?" Her voice was a squeak as she addressed the man in plasticuffs.

Allwood continued climbing into the vehicle as if he hadn't heard her.

"Hey, professor, the lady needs your face." Chief Ricard forced Allwood's head to turn by grabbing his chin.

"Thanks." She held up the phone screen to the man's face, and the facial recognition kicked into gear. "We're in."

Chief loaded Allwood into the SUV for a second time and slammed the door.

"Demarco, we need to track down Kellerman now." Commander Orr redirected focus. "He doesn't have a vehicle, and we know he ran off from the crash site. What should our next steps be?"

"Maybe he called an Uber?" Charlie said as she scrolled through emails and texts. "Most of this is routine communications. I don't see anything here that connects to Kellerman."

"What about encrypted apps?" Orr asked.

A light came on in Charlie's eyes, and she tapped and scrolled on the phone screen.

Demarco looked at his watch. "It's been fifteen or twenty minutes since the LT probably fled the scene. In this heat, he could maybe make it a half-mile." The sun was like a ball of fire. Even in good shape, the temperature would impact a man's stamina.

"Since the crash occurred on the banks of the Lake, we only have one direction he could've run." Orr and Demarco locked eyes. "Let's do a sweep."

Demarco nodded. Lake Havasu was one third retirees, so a young, fit man in his late twenties should stand out on the streets.

"So I'm coming with you?" Charlie asked with a hopeful uptilt to her voice. She stood on the sidewalk making no move to join the chief.

"Ricard needs someone to keep an eye on the prisoner while he drives. Head straight to the base. Chief can secure him in the plane. We'll meet you there." Orr checked his watch. "Kellerman's the priority. He's our leaker and every minute he's out there, our team and our work is in jeopardy of being exposed."

"Right. I'll see you at Nellis." She frowned and then climbed into the passenger seat.

Why was Charlie so reluctant to go with Ricard?

CHAPTER 11

CHIEF RICARD PULLED AWAY from the curb. "I hope they find that piece of shit. They should put Kellerman away for twenty years. Leaking classified materials. I knew he couldn't be trusted. The minute he walked into the office—all pressed and perfect with that stick up his ass."

Charlie nodded, but her mind was elsewhere. The man seated behind her was her birth father. Dr. Stern had told her, so it must be true. The NSA lab likely had some of the best equipment and best scientists in the field. How was she supposed to reconcile this new information and fit it into her life history? Who was Harrison Cutter? Why did her mother lie to her?

She half-turned her body. "We know you arrived in one of the pods, professor."

Ricard flinched and pressed a bit too hard on the gas, causing the SUV to lurch forward onto the street. "What the fuck?"

Charlie ignored him. Who cared what she divulged now? The minute they all returned to the office, everyone would know her DNA tied her to Armas. Everyone would be looking at her. Might as well put all her cards on the table. She wanted to know the truth.

"You mentioned your work goes back twenty years." Her gut twisted. She thought back to the radar data presented to them upon landing in Nellis. "So when did you arrive? 1996? In Texas?"

Her brightly colored memories of her childhood on the Naval Base in Corpus Christi turned faded and gray. Something had happened there. Something before she was born that her mother had kept from her.

"Goddammit, Cutter, what in the hell is going on?" Ricard swung them onto the highway to head back to the Air Force base.

Allwood raised an eyebrow. "So Demarco told you everything?"

"If you two don't tell me what the fuck is happening here, I swear—" Ricard's face turned bright red.

"Our professor is a time traveler," she explained to the chief. "He's been here for years. Demarco figured it out." That was as much as she wanted to say. Maybe Ricard would puzzle the rest out eventually, but for now it was all about learning the truth of her parentage.

"If you have the data, you already know that's when I arrived." Allwood leaned back in his seat. "Why do these questions matter?"

"You mean this shit is real?" Ricard's shoulders relaxed, and his chin dipped. His tough guy demeanor melted away in seconds once he realized the truth: time travel was real. The last one on their team to believe it.

"I want to know what you did when you climbed out of that pod." Her thumb absentmindedly rubbed across the screen of his phone. What was he hiding in the encrypted chat app she'd found? "How did you manage to survive? How did you end up as a respected researcher at Area 51?"

Allwood lifted a shoulder. "I made friends. I'm sure Demarco told you a similar story. You'd be surprised how easy it is to find people sympathetic and willing to help a man in need."

"Friends?" Before her mother met Harrison, what had her story been? Charlie had so few details to build on. The information had been sparse: maybe a job on base or was it a friend on base? If she only had some privacy and a few minutes to call her mother or Chad, maybe she would be able to uncover the truth.

"Why would Demarco have a similar story?" Ricard, although focused on the road ahead, managed to pick up on the slightest of hints.

Allwood's eyes lit up. "Ah, so not everyone knows the truth. I see. Demarco always was a miscreant. Stirring up trouble for no reason. He wouldn't leave me alone. He has some kind of vendetta against me."

"Cutter, you'd better tell me the goddamn truth." Chief's hands gripped the steering wheel so tight his fingers turned white "Who the fuck is Demarco?"

"That's not important right now." Charlie felt the conversation slipping away from her. She'd wanted answers about Allwood, about her, about her family history. These answers couldn't wait. She needed them now. Needed to know if her brother would be in danger.

"Petty Officer Cutter." Chief's sharp tone reminded her that he was still her superior. He outranked her by several steps. "I am demanding you tell me what is going on here. Why is this guy talking about Demarco?"

"Oh my, didn't she tell you?" Allwood chuckled. "Angel Demarco followed me here in one of my machines. He fooled you into believing he's something he's not. That badge you let him carry around? And the lies he probably told to convince you of his background? He's a farmer's son. He barely knows how to tie his own shoes."

Charlie froze. She stared out the window in a daze.

"And he's alone with Commander Orr? Who the fuck is he?" Ricard swerved the SUV across all lanes of traffic to the shoulder. A car behind them honked at the dangerous move. He braked hard, and they jerked to a dead stop on the side of the highway. "Cutter, what did you do?

CHAPTER 12

DEMARCO JOGGED another block over from the hospital. He and Orr had split up to cover more ground. They had to find Kellerman before he slipped away—and maybe it already was too late. That bastard.

Although a breeze kicked up, the sweat dripped from his forehead. It reminded him of haying season back home. Hot, dirty work. But they'd had to keep working until the job was done. Spoiled hay wouldn't feed the horses and cows through the winter.

He couldn't stop until this job was done either. Kellerman had been sharing NCIS-A secrets with Allwood. Maybe even keeping information from them to make their jobs harder. The break-in at the motel in North Dakota had probably been his doing and who knows what he'd shared since then. Translations? Reports? What about the arrival of Armas?

An odd sensation filled his chest when he thought of the boy. But he brushed it off.

He rounded a corner and scanned the street.

The sight of a dark haired man at the end of the block caught his eye.

Could that be Kellerman?

He slowed his jog to a walk so as not to draw attention to himself.

The man had his back to him allowing Demarco the opportunity to close in without fear of being seen. As he drew nearer, his breathing slowed. His target turned so that his profile was visible, and he looked down at his phone.

No mistaking. It was Kellerman.

Demarco paused behind a parked delivery van that provided him some cover, pulled out his phone, and called Orr.

"I've got him. We're on Willow Avenue." He kept his gaze fixated on the lieutenant. "About five blocks down from Emerald Drive."

"I'm on my way. Detain him until I get there."

"Yes, sir." He hung up.

Kellerman turned and looked up the street. Their eyes met.

Shit.

The lieutenant bolted.

Demarco chased after at full speed. His shorter stature and solid body mass slowed him down, compared to the taller, leaner Kellerman.

A gray-haired man walking a dachshund blocked his route. Demarco pushed off the man's shoulder, spun, and barely avoided tangling his legs in the leash.

"Hey!" the surprised dog walker yelled.

But he had no time for apologies. Kellerman had crossed the street and was headed between two houses.

Demarco dug as deep as he could to draw on the last bit of energy he had. His thigh muscles burned. If he'd been fresh off the farm, he would've been able to best the younger man, but years of less physical living had reduced his stamina.

"Fuck!" He rounded the corner of the southwestern style home. Gravel kicked up under his heels.

A motorcycle flew past, practically knocking him to the ground.

Kellerman.

Instinctually, he changed direction to chase after him, but Kellerman sped away toward the highway and disappeared in seconds.

Demarco slowed to a halt and leaned over, resting his hands on his knees to catch his breath. He'd failed. He'd lost him.

"Dammit." They'd never catch him now. Kellerman would be stupid to show his face at their offices or anywhere near the Washington Navy Yard. Even Area 51 should be off limits once they received the news. The whole of the military would be on high alert for Lieutenant Cole Kellerman.

A RAV4 pulled up next to him with a blonde woman in her late forties in the driver's seat. The back passenger window rolled down. Commander Orr's sweaty face appeared. "Get in. We can catch him."

Without saying a word, Demarco skipped around the back of the Toyota and climbed in.

CHAPTER 13

RICARD PICKED up his cell phone from the center console and dialed a number. "I can't believe you left the commander with some impostor." Chief's eyes bulged.

"Demarco's not an impostor." Charlie looked down at her hands in her lap. What did it matter what chief thought of Demarco, of her, of this whole big mess blowing up in their faces? Her whole sense of self had been ripped out from under her. Her mother was a liar, her father wasn't even her father, and her brother? What would he think when he heard the news? He idolized Harrison Cutter. He'd modeled his whole life after their father—correction—stepfather. It would devastate him.

Allwood clucked his tongue. "What a terrible shame your little investigation is falling apart. Your office will be disbanded by morning once I bend the senator's ear. I should've shut you down months ago. I could have you know."

Charlie's heart beat sluggishly. The work she'd abandoned and then rediscovered had brought her so much satisfaction—the Voynich manuscript—now she wished she'd never come across it. If she could only wish herself away from this spot on the side of the highway and instead land in Navy survival school in Maine to pursue her original dream. What would happen to her now? Would she be kicked out of the military for her connection to Allwood? Would she lose her clearance? What implications did this have for her future? In less than twenty-four hours news of her parentage would be revealed to the team. What was her plan?

"Commander, are you with Demarco?" Chief asked. His thumb beat out a nervous rhythm on the steering wheel. He was silent for a few seconds. "What? Where is that little SOB?" Without a word of explanation to Charlie, Chief hopped out of the vehicle.

"Chief?" She leaned forward to catch a glimpse of where he went. What had Orr told him?

"So, Cutter is it?" Allwood's voice sounded as smooth as fresh ice.

Chief stood on the asphalt and scanned the lanes of traffic. Although she was curious what the commander may have told Ricard, this might be her only opportunity alone with Allwood. Should she ask him more questions that might divulge their connection?

She blinked a few times. "Petty Officer Cutter, yes."

"I hear you haven't been with the office very long."

"Kellerman tell you that?"

Allwood didn't answer. "If you still want to have a career when this is all over, you might want to consider your actions going forward."

"Is that a threat?" Her gaze became unfocused.

"I happen to know people in very high places who could be valuable to you."

"I don't need your help." A high pitched buzzing sounded in her ears.

The professor expelled air out his nose. "Everyone needs someone's help. Do you think Demarco was smart enough to get where he is on his own? Even he had to rely on someone."

She tumbled that over in her brain. She didn't want to listen to what Allwood had to say about Angel. She'd heard the story from his side and trusted him far more than a man who would abandon the mother of his children. What kind of heartless, selfish person would do that?

Chief yanked open the door. "Buckle up, we're on a mission."

Before Charlie could check her seatbelt, Ricard pressed on the gas and exploded forward to rejoin the traffic on the highway.

She grabbed the handle on the door to keep from bouncing out of her seat. "What's going on?"

"That little bastard Kellerman stole a motorcycle, and we're gonna catch his ass." Ricard hunched over his steering wheel and checked his mirrors before swerving into the far left lane. "See that yellow and black Suzuki up there?"

She tilted her head until she saw the motorcycle several cars ahead of them and then nodded.

"Kellerman's on the run, and we're going to be the ones to stop him."

"What about taking the prisoner to Nellis and catching our flight home?"

Ricard gunned it, made a quick right into the middle lane, and then cut off a red Honda Civic in the fast lane. "I don't give a flying fuck about missing the goddamn plane, Cutter. This jackass is a criminal, and we need to shut him down. We'll figure out the rest later."

Allwood's silence in the back was notable.

Charlie turned to face him. "Where would he be going, professor?" She pushed out of her mind the fact the man with the maniacal grin on his face and a strange gleam in his eye was her biological father.

The SUV bumped over a pothole. She grabbed the headrest to steady herself, but still managed to bite her tongue.

The professor shrugged. His earlier loquaciousness disappeared.

But it didn't take a genius to figure out Kellerman's destination. "He's headed to the one place he knows, the one place he feels safe."

She and Ricard exchanged glances.

"Area 51," they said simultaneously.

KELLERMAN PUSHED the motorcycle to its limits. Knowing the capabilities of Demarco, he'd find a way to catch up to him. He'd steal a car, hijack a bus—something. He'd learned in the last few months never to underestimate the special agent. As he zipped through traffic, weaving in and out of lanes to put as much distance between him and Lake Havasu as he could, he began to make a mental plan.

Groom Lake was his only option. He could hide there. And, if he was lucky, he could disappear from there, too.

The professor might be ticked, as it deviated from their plan, but he didn't care. The minute he'd seen the news come across his phone about Charlie, he knew he didn't have much time. The way the professor had talked about his long-lost wife, he knew loyalty to family and to his blood would surpass any loyalty he held toward Kellerman. No matter how much he'd sacrificed for the man. Charlie had changed everything. Damn her.

The heat of the midday Arizona sun beat down on his back. He had hours to ride before he'd reach his destination. The base was ninety minutes beyond Nellis. Checking his gas gauge, he mentally calculated if he had enough.

Maybe.

If he were lucky.

———

Demarco sat next to the commander in the back of the hired SUV. "We've got to catch up to him, sir."

"Ricard can handle it."

Their driver, Pam, drove the speed limit down the highway. Demarco wanted to leap into the front, shove her out of the seat, and take over. Kellerman had to be stopped, and he had to ensure Allwood was secured. Too many loose ends. His mind ran into two directions at once. Then there was Charlie. Trapped with a madman. Ricard had no idea of the capabilities Allwood had to deceive, to charm, to draw a victim into his way of thinking.

He'd managed to dupe hundreds of people to give over their lives to him, their very bodies to his experiments. Would he manage to convince Ricard to do his bidding? To let him go? Or something worse?

His stomach churned.

Which was the correct action to take?

"You said to head toward Vegas," Pam said in a bright voice. "I need to be home by supper time. Chester's expecting me. He won't like it if I don't have his food waiting for him when he comes home. Are you going to the airport? A hotel?"

"Take us to Nellis." The commander made his choice. They were going to play the supporting role.

Demarco itched to take control. He was so close to taking down Allwood. So close. And now they were going to sit on their hands at Nellis and do nothing?

"What are we going to do there, sir? You expect Cutter and Ricard to handle the professor *and* chase down Kellerman?"

"You two military?" Pam switched from the middle lane to the slower right lane, as if she were enjoying the ride and didn't want it to end any sooner than it had to. "My Chester's a former Marine. Did two tours somewhere. Maybe Iraq? He doesn't like to talk about it."

Both men ignored Pam's inquiry. "We don't have any choice," said Orr.

"Of course we have a choice." Demarco's mind darkened. Orr was too much of a regulations man. A rules follower. That sort of thinking would destroy any chance he had of attaining his goal. Allwood was within his grasp. If any time was the right time to risk the security of his position, it was now. "Pam, pull over."

"What?" In the rearview mirror, Pam's gaze locked with his.

"I don't want to have to ask again, please." He lowered his voice a few notches. His dangerous voice. The voice he used when he'd killed some of Allwood's men in a time when guns didn't exist. When killing involved sweat and blood and looking into a man's eyes when you sliced his throat. "Pull over."

Commander Orr leaned forward, alarm in his eyes.

Demarco quickly captured the older man in a headlock, his arm tight across Orr's throat. "Don't, sir."

"I don't understand. This is an Uber." Pam's voice trembled and ratcheted up to a higher pitch. "Just tell me where you want to go, and I'll take you there. You said Vegas: where in Vegas?"

The desperation he heard in her words cut him up inside. He wasn't the bad guy here, but she wouldn't understand. The commander wouldn't understand.

Demarco's arm tightened on Orr's windpipe. The man struggled under the unexpected pressure. His eyes bugged out. Disbelief was etched into his features as his trusted security officer choked him into unconsciousness. He clawed at Demarco's solid arm, the elbow bent just enough to prevent the flow of oxygen to his brain.

"I'm sorry, sir." The special agent felt his superior go limp in his arms.

Pam screamed.

Demarco asked one more time, "Pull over, Pam."

Pam turned on her signal and took the off-ramp—a deserted road miles from anywhere. Her whole body shook. "P-please. I don't have any money."

As the car stopped near the overpass, Demarco opened the back door and used his feet to shove Orr out onto the shoulder. "I don't want your money. I want your car."

The blonde woman nodded, tears rolling down her cheeks. "Yes, take it. Whatever you want." She leapt from the vehicle and ran toward the traffic at the other end of the off-ramp.

Demarco stepped over the unconscious body of his boss, climbed into the driver's seat, and sped back onto the highway.

———

Several drivers flipped off Ricard. He'd cut them off making hazardous lane switches and passing slower cars on the right. Every time the SUV came within a few car lengths of Kellerman, the lieutenant managed to zip between cars or even two semi-trucks.

"Shit," Ricard swore under his breath. "When did Kellerman learn to drive a bike like that?"

Allwood sat silently in the back. Charlie relished it. For now, she wanted to focus on making sure Ricard didn't kill them. She didn't need to be distracted by thoughts about her mother, her brother, and her birth father. That would have to wait until later.

"We're hours away from Area 51," she pointed out. "We've got plenty of time to catch him. Maybe he'll run out of gas."

Ricard took a quick glance at the gas gauge. "Dammit."

Charlie covered her mouth with her hand. "Oh, no."

"Oh, fucking, yes. This behemoth gets fifteen miles to the gallon, and we're at a quarter tank." Ricard smacked his hand on the dashboard. "No way in hell we're letting that weasel get away."

She furrowed her brow. "Call the commander."

"You do it."

Charlie nodded, set Allwood's phone on the center console, and dug her own cell out of her purse.

Ricard looked down at the gauge for a second time. "Tell him we've got maybe fifty or sixty more miles and then we're out."

The phone rang and rang. "He's not picking up." She rubbed her free hand on her pant leg. The phone rang two more times. She showed him her phone screen. "He's not answering. Now what?"

"Fuck." Ricard dodged a Toyota Camry that had changed lanes right in front of him. "Gimme that." He snatched her phone away.

The SUV crossed over into another lane. A car honked.

"Keep your eyes on the road." Her adrenaline spiked.

"I got his stupid voicemail." Ricard tossed Charlie's phone at her. It clattered to the floor and landed under her seat.

"Hey. Be careful." She felt around underneath her for the smooth screen of her phone. "Should I try calling Demarco?"

"Yeah." Ricard wiped a sheen of sweat off his brow. "Demarco. They're together. Good thinking, Cutter."

Charlie came into contact with her phone. "Got it." She pressed Demarco's number.

"I see him!" Ricard's eyes lit up. "The fucker. Thought he could get away from me. I don't think so." He hunched over the steering wheel. "Let's see how fast this baby can go."

The SUV's eight-cylinder engine struggled to give Chief the additional power and speed he wanted.

"Not very," Allwood quipped from the back.

"Shut up." Ricard zoomed forward.

The phone rang several times. No answer. Charlie's gut twisted. Not good. Why weren't Orr or Demarco answering?

"Charlie?"

Hearing the familiar voice of the special agent alleviated some of the tension inside her.

"Angel," she breathed.

"You got him?" Ricard asked. "I see Kellerman's pansy-ass. Right up there. Stuck behind a Walmart truck and boxed in by the Ford F-150."

"Yes, he picked up." She glanced at the cars in front of them. Distantly, almost two hundred yards away, she could barely make out the bright yellow motorcycle behind the semi.

"I've got something to do Charlie." Angel's voice had an odd quality to it.

"What are you talking about?"

"Where are you?" he asked.

"We're following Kellerman. That's why I called."

"What road marker are you near?"

"What? I don't know." She felt a tingling in her chest. "Look, Demarco, we tried calling Orr, he didn't pick up. We aren't going to be able to follow Kellerman much longer. We're going to run out of gas. We think he's headed for Area 51. Can you and the Commander catch up to us?"

"Orr's not available right now."

"Okay." What a strange way of wording it. What did he mean by that? "Can you catch up to us?" They passed a green directional sign. "We're right near Exit 141 just past Needles."

"141. Thank you, Charlie."

The line went dead.

DEMARCO ZOOMED THROUGH TRAFFIC. Although he'd landed in a time period with vehicles capable of incredibly high speeds, he'd never driven so quickly. The desert landscape flashed past. He kept his gaze focused on the mile markers, barely comprehending them as he flew past.

A green directional sign above the highway announced Exit 141 to Needles in two miles.

Driving at—he glanced at the speedometer—over one-hundred miles an hour should mean he'd catch up to his team in less than two minutes.

As he thought about what he had to do, a black emptiness filled him.

Charlie was in that car. So was Ricard.

But he had no choice.

Orr and the others on the team weren't taking this seriously. They thought they could arrest Allwood, put him in jail, send him through the ridiculously slow and tainted court system, and end up with a guilty verdict. But he knew better. He knew Allwood would never stop. The minute he was a free man, he'd start up right where he left off. The man was obsessed with perfection. He'd never let go of his twisted vision for the human race: to manipulate and alter them to the point that no one would recognize themselves as human anymore. And Demarco had to stop him.

He swerved around a silver two-door car and spied a large, black SUV in the distance that sped past other vehicles around it. That had to be Ricard.

As the cars passed by the exit for Needles, the traffic thinned and the lanes narrowed down to two.

Just what he needed to pull off a move.

Charlie, I'm sorry.

He approached the team's vehicle from behind. He'd seen a PIT maneuver completed successfully multiple times in online videos. Although he'd intended to learn all he could about law enforcement early in his arrival in order to blend in and play the role he'd chosen as best suited to find Allwood, he never thought he'd actually have to use the maneuver himself.

Done correctly, the target vehicle should safely spin out into the shoulder.

He tightened his hands around the steering wheel and exhaled through his mouth.

It was time.

Demarco pressed on the gas lightly and drove partially onto the shoulder to approach Ricard from the correct side. Before the other vehicle had time to detect his presence, he aligned the front of his car with the rear tires and steered into them.

Shit.

He used more force than he'd intended.

The other vehicle lost traction and began to skid. The SUV turned in front of him.

For a split second, he caught sight of a terrified Charlie in the passenger's seat. He averted his gaze, because he couldn't watch what was about to happen.

He'd hit the vehicle too hard, and instead of slowing to a crooked stop in the shoulder, it tilted up and began to roll down an embankment.

A pain hit the back of his throat.

What had he done?

Envisioning an unconscious and injured Charlie, he slammed on the brakes, left his car running, and raced down the slope toward them. Someone on the highway surely saw what had happened and would be dialing 911 within seconds.

Ricard and Charlie would be fine.

He repeated that over and over in his head as he approached them.

Securing Allwood before the cops showed up was more important.

The SUV lay on its side.

He saw no movement, no attempt from anyone to climb out.

The blazing heat of the desert sun beat down on everything. If the engine caught fire, there could be a serious problem with dried grass and scrub brush everywhere.

"Help me," a faint voice called.

Demarco ran around the back end. Allwood lay twenty feet away from the crash site. He'd been thrown free of the vehicle at some point. Debris littered the ground. Without thinking, he picked up papers and a cardboard box full of vials that must've been in the back of the SUV as he made his way to the injured man.

Where was Charlie? Still inside?

Fuck.

He didn't have time to worry about her. This is why he'd remained alone for seven years. This is why he chose not to make friends or get close to anyone. For this very reason.

Why did he have to fall for her?

He dropped the box and the papers. "Get up."

"I can't," Allwood whined.

The man had a cut on his leg that bled freely and one of his arms looked mangled. Somehow he'd been freed from the plasticuffs in the wreck.

Demarco grabbed his uninjured arm. "Get the fuck up."

Allwood cried out in pain as the special agent forced him to stand. "I can't walk."

"Yes, you can." He twisted the older man's arm behind his back and pushed him toward the highway. "You're coming with me, and you're going to show me everything. Got it?"

"Angel?" Charlie was extricating herself out of the blown out passenger's side window. "What happened?"

Blood ran freely from a head wound, but otherwise Charlie appeared uninjured.

Demarco's chest tightened. "There was an accident." He relaxed his grip on Allwood. "Don't make a move, bastard, or I'll break this arm, too," he spat out.

"Did we hit something?" She sat on the edge of the door and surveyed the ground below.

"Yes," he lied. "I think you blew a tire and swerved off the highway. I have to secure Allwood. Then, I'll come back and help."

Charlie nodded weakly. "Okay. Right." She looked down into the vehicle. "Ricard looks bad, Angel."

"He'll be okay, Charlie. The police will be here any minute." As he said the words, he could hear the faint sound of sirens in the distance. "Stay there. I'll be right back."

But he knew he wouldn't be back, and he hated himself for it.

What would she think when he drove off? That he'd used her? That everything he'd said to her was lies? Probably.

"My head really hurts." She touched a hand to her wound and then looked at the blood on her fingers.

"I know. You'll be okay." He had to ignore the voice inside that told him to stay, to make sure she was okay, to check on Ricard. "Come on, Allwood."

"Where's the commander?" she asked.

His mind flicked to when he'd pushed an unconscious Orr out of the Uber and left the driver running away in fear.

Demarco's grip on Allwood became like iron. "I'll be right back." He couldn't look at her anymore.

He pushed the older man up the slope and to his car at the top. If the cops showed, they'd not only see the damage, but they'd probably run the plate, find out it was stolen, and arrest him. He only had a few minutes to escape.

Charlie would be fine.

Charlie would be just fine.

It would be better for her to hate him, anyway. What could he possibly give her? He was a mess. He wasn't built to handle more than one emotion at a time. And his whole reason for being after finding himself hundreds of years in the past had been to capture this man. This lunatic. This disgusting 'professor' who'd harmed dozens of innocent people. Love? He didn't have space for that in this bizarre life he'd found himself in. She was better off without him.

Opening up the passenger's side door, he flung Allwood inside. He could keep a better eye on him up front.

"You have to take me to the hospital," Allwood complained when Demarco climbed into the driver's seat.

A flush of heat flooded Demarco's body. He snapped his seatbelt, shifted the car into drive, and pressed on the gas. "Shut the hell up. You're going to take me to your lab, show me everything, and then we're going to burn it all down."

Demarco hoped to God he didn't strangle the man before he could achieve all of that. Because his fingers itched to do it. He'd never hated a man so much. A deep, black, ugly hate festered inside him and threatened to consume him.

Allwood sat silently next to him. His captive had realized there was no way out, and the only option was to obey.

In his rearview mirror, Demarco caught sight of red flashing lights. At least two police cars raced to the scene of the accident. Witnesses would probably be able to describe him, Allwood, and his vehicle. So he had to put as much distance between him and the wreck as he could.

Forgive me, Charlie.

A sign overhead read: Las Vegas – 108 miles.

He blasted his brain clear of worry and thoughts of Charlie and focused on his destination.

CHAPTER 16

INJURED AND CONFUSED, Charlie drew a deep breath through her nose at the sight of Angel at the bottom of the embankment. He'd recaptured Allwood and, despite her concerns about his loyalty to the team and his view of Genesis Project followers, was going to rescue her and Ricard. But then he'd dragged Allwood away, hopped in some car, and drove off in a cloud of dust. She couldn't believe it.

He'd abandoned them.

And where was Orr?

The bottom dropped out of her stomach.

Something wasn't right here.

Angel had Allwood in his hands and Kellerman in his sights. The worst possible person to be alone with either man. He had vengeance on his mind.

Before the authorities arrived, she hopped down into the overturned vehicle to check on Ricard's status. What else could she do? Everything she'd been working toward was about to be ripped away—her career, her family, her future.

Allwood was her father. As unbelievable as it sounded, according to Dr. Stern it was the truth. Within days, everyone would be looking at her and her brother. Would she and Chad be lumped into the same category as Allwood and his band of time travelers? Would they be questioned, studied, incarcerated? Her clearance would likely be revoked. His officer candidacy yanked. All because of their DNA.

Not only that, she'd likely be a target of Angel's rage. The very rage she saw on display only a few moments ago. Angel had been willing to abandon his girlfriend and his teammate for a chance at revenge. Would that feeling extend to her once he found out the truth?

Ricard groaned. The front end of the SUV had been crushed when the vehicle had flipped. The engine had been pushed inward, which pinned him under the steering wheel.

"Are you all right, Chief?"

He didn't answer.

She kicked away plastic and metal fragments that littered the interior to clear the view.

"Chief, are you hurt? Can you move?" She planted one foot on the side of the driver's seat and the other on the edge of the dashboard.

Was that her cell phone?

She grabbed it. The screen had a crack in it, but it appeared to be functional.

"Cutter? What happened?" Ricard's labored speech told her his breathing was compromised.

"We've been in an accident."

He struggled to break free of the steering wheel.

"The police are on their way. Try to relax."

She popped her head out the window to check for any approaching police cars. The sirens grew louder and louder. The only way Ricard would make it out of here was with help—serious help. But at least he was talking and alert.

Ricard lay still. "Where's Allwood?"

At least he remembered they had another passenger. "Don't worry about him."

"Where is he, Cutter?" Although his voice lacked its usual power, the demanding tone remained. "He's our responsibility. The commander is counting on us."

"I'll explain later." No point in telling him the truth at this stage. He was in shock. Any increase in his stress levels could be detrimental. "Let's focus on you. Breathe."

Hearing a door slam, she took another look outside. Two uniformed officers trotted down the embankment.

"Help is here." A sudden lightness filled her. "I'm going to let them know what happened and that we need some help getting you out of here."

Charlie pushed herself up and out of the window and sat on the edge.

"Miss," a female officer reached the wreck first. "Are you all right? An ambulance is on its way."

The other officer, tall and dark-haired, spoke into a radio attached to his shoulder.

"I think I'm okay, but my friend is pinned in the driver's seat."

"Phillips, we need fire and rescue," the officer said to her partner. "We've got another occupant trapped inside."

The male officer helped Charlie down to the ground. As the police went into rescue mode, she backed away.

What was the next step? How could she stop Angel?

She looked down at her damaged phone, unlocked it, selected a name from her contacts list, and pressed the call button.

CHARLIE STOOD thirty feet away from the wreck, watching the fire crew bring down the Jaws of Life. As the phone rang on the other end, she bit the inside of her cheek. She'd really been hoping to have this conversation in person, but there was no time to waste.

"Charlie, hello!" Angela Cutter greeted her daughter in a bright voice. "Have you moved into your new place yet? I was thinking about some old curtains I have in the basement somewhere—"

"Mom, I need to ask you something important." Her insides quivered. "And I need you to be honest with me." She couldn't move on to the next step in her plan until she'd taken care of this.

"Honest?" Charlie imagined her mother twisting her wedding ring as she always did when nervous. "What are you talking about, sweetie?"

"My dad. I know."

A firefighter positioned the battery-operated jaws around one of the roof supports and switched on the power to cut through it. The noise made it difficult to hear. Charlie walked up toward the road to put some distance between her and the machine.

"What about your father? I don't understand."

Charlie swallowed. "Harrison Cutter isn't my father."

There was a long pause on the other end. Then, the sound of a door closing.

"Charlene, how dare you say such things." Her mother's voice became a harsh whisper. "Who told you these lies? Who?"

The panic in her mother's words came across loud and clear. Charlie had hit on the truth. Harrison Cutter wasn't her birth father. For some reason, having the fact confirmed made her chest ache.

"Byron Allwood is my real father." An EMT approached Charlie after noticing her injury. She waved him away. The cut on her head would have to wait.

Her mother gasped on the other end.

"You both were in Corpus Christi at the same time. Maybe you met on the base? But what I don't understand is why would you lie to me? To Chad? All these years. I don't understand."

"Chad can never know."

"Chad *will* know, Mom." She stared out at the traffic, wishing with all her might she was a normal person in a car headed home or to Las Vegas or to the airport. She wanted to be anywhere but here. "Why do you think I'm calling you? Why do you think I know? The truth is going to come out whether you like it or not. If you aren't going to explain it to Chad, I will."

"It will crush him, Charlie."

"I know." Charlie's gut twisted. Before she called her mom, she'd been angry, but now she felt only sadness. "But he'll find out whether you want him to or not. Wouldn't it be better to hear it from you?"

"Your father—we made a pact we'd never tell." Angela Cutter quietly cried. "How do I explain it to him?"

"There are DNA results. Indisputable. They found out at work—"

"At work?"

More emergency vehicles arrived, surrounding her on all sides. One police officer set out cones and blocked traffic from passing the scene in the right lane. "I can't tell you more than that, Mom."

"And Byron? He's still alive?"

"Yes."

"You've found him after all this time?" Her mother sounded shocked.

"Yes."

"I thought he was dead. All these years...and knowing I was carrying you two. Why would he do that?"

Her heart hurt for the young mother Angela Cutter had been more than twenty years ago. "I don't know."

"He abandoned me. Pregnant and unmarried. A job at the Px. I couldn't raise twins by myself."

"I'm sorry that happened to you." Tears pricked at her eyes. Her anger at being lied to gave way to sympathy for the loving, kind mother she'd known her whole life. Allwood had used her just like he'd used his followers. It had been all about himself, his needs, his desires, his dreams. Maybe Angel wasn't so wrong about his feelings toward Allwood.

"Your father—Harrison, I mean—he was so kind to me. A customer who befriended me. Somehow it turned into—well, we got married. He promised he would raise you as his own."

"He did, Mom," Charlie said. "You did the right thing. He was a good father."

An EMT rolled a stretcher down the embankment. Maybe Ricard had been freed from the wreck.

"He still is, Charlie. If you'd only let him in."

A large, white pick-up truck emblazoned with a local tow truck service's logo drove down the embankment.

"Right now I'm more worried about Chad." Her scalp prickled. "I don't know how to get a hold of him. I tried texting him, and he's not answering."

"He's on a flight to Spain."

The EMT appeared on the shoulder with Ricard strapped to the gurney. The chief noticed her on the phone and weakly waved. Charlie faked a smile and waved back.

"I thought he was leaving in another couple of weeks?"

"He took some leave, so he could scout out a place to live. Housing is tight on base."

"Dammit." How was she going to protect her brother from five thousand miles away?

"I promise. I'll tell him."

The female police officer who'd been first on the scene approached her with a metal clipboard and a serious look on her face. "I have something I need to do, Mom. You have to make sure he knows. We have maybe a day, possibly less."

"I don't understand," her mother said.

"People might come looking for him. Bad people."

The officer raised her eyebrows.

"What are you saying—?"

Charlie turned away from the officer and whispered into the phone. "Byron Allwood is not a good man. I don't know who he was when you met him, but he's not that man anymore. He's a fugitive. He murdered someone. And I have to make sure he's brought to justice."

"My God." Angela Cutter paused for a few seconds. "And Chad? Why would anyone be after Chad?"

"Because we are his children and that puts us at risk. There are people out there who think we are just as guilty because of our family connection." Charlie took a quick look over her shoulder. The officer wouldn't be patient for long.

"Guilty of what? How could either of you be guilty of a murder someone else committed? I don't understand."

"Please make sure you get a hold of Chad. Explain to him. Tell him he needs to be careful. Have him call me when he can. I need to talk to him."

"I'm sorry, sweetie. I'm sorry I didn't tell you the truth," her mother said.

"It's okay. I know you were only trying to protect us and give us the best life you could."

"And it was a good life?"

"Yes, Mom, it was."

———

After giving the female officer a quick description of the accident and leaving out a few pertinent details, Charlie hoped the woman would sympathize and do as she asked. "Would it be possible for someone to give me a ride?"

With the vehicle towed away and the ambulance carrying Ricard long gone, all that was left of the accident was Charlie and some bits of wreckage. Any evidence they'd carried in the SUV had been destroyed or scattered by the strong afternoon desert winds.

The officer tucked her pen in her shirt pocket and held the clipboard at her side. "Don't you have someone you can call?"

Charlie's mind flicked to Orr, the only remaining team member whose whereabouts were unknown. Did Angel hurt him? "I'm only here visiting. Could I get a lift to Vegas?" From there, she could arrange her own ride somehow to Area 51. No doubt that's exactly where Angel would be headed, too. Kellerman, Angel, and Allwood—all converging on the mysterious lab. She had to stop them. All of them.

The fighting and secrecy needed to end.

Today.

Officer Phillips reached the top of the embankment and handed Charlie another cell phone. "We found this on the ground about fifteen feet from the wreck. Still seems to be working. I'm assuming it belonged to the driver?"

Allwood's phone.

Charlie nodded. "That's right."

"Normally, we'd send it with the ambulance as part of the victim's belongings, but the EMTs have already left. I'm sure it'd be easier for you to take it to your friend rather than have it tied up at the station."

"Right. Sure." Without looking, she slid it into her pocket. "Which hospital?"

Phillips tucked his shirt in and wiped dirt off his pants. "Colorado River."

"Is that nearby?"

"Right off the highway in Needles."

The female officer, with a badge that read Garcia, said, "She's looking for a lift to Vegas."

Phillips nodded. "We can drive you to the hospital, but you'll have to find your own ride from there."

"Right." She couldn't waste time with a trip to the hospital and a long wait in the ER for a chance to talk to Ricard.

Garcia opened the driver's side door of their police vehicle and put the clipboard inside. "Are you coming, then?" She looked to Charlie.

Phillips strode out into the blocked traffic lane and picked up orange cones, handing them to another officer who carried them away.

Charlie shook her head. "I need to go to Vegas. I have a plane to catch."

"What about your friend?" Garcia tilted her head.

"I'll call his wife, and she can take care of him."

The officer's body grew rigid, and she placed her hands on her hips. "Could I have his phone, then?"

A beat-up Ford pick-up pulled onto the shoulder about fifteen feet in front of where Charlie stood. The window rolled down, and a familiar face looked back at her.

"Petty Officer Cutter," Commander Orr said. "Glad I finally found you. Let's go."

Her mouth gaped. She didn't know where he'd been, what had happened between him and Angel, or how he'd gotten a hold of a truck, but she didn't care.

Phillips, noticing the vehicle, stopped collecting cones and approached the driver. "Sir, you can't park here. You'll have to move along."

Despite the protests from Garcia about the cell phone in Charlie's hand, she ran to the other side of the truck and climbed in.

"Just go, sir," she urged.

"Hey!" Phillips put a hand on his holster.

"Go!" Charlie banged on the dash.

Orr pressed on the gas, rear tires swerving, and rocketed onto the highway.

———

As they sped away, Charlie turned to look through the back window at the disappearing crash site. "You arrived just in time, Commander."

Orr appeared disheveled, which was unusual for him. Out of everyone at the office, aside from Angel, the commander never had anything out of place. But today? His hair was mussed, his shirt unbuttoned, and dust blanketed him.

"Where's Allwood and Ricard? What happened back there?"

"We had an accident. Allwood got away." She wasn't ready to spill the whole truth. Although she needed Orr for the ride to Area 51, she didn't want him to get in the way of what she needed to do. Orr was a by-the-book sort of Navy officer. Someone who wouldn't cut corners or break rules. She didn't have time for that.

"And Ricard? Is he all right?"

"I think so. He was awake when I saw him on the gurney."

Orr gave an acknowledging nod.

"What happened to you?" she asked.

With his gaze firmly fixed on the road, Orr's jaw tightened. "Demarco attacked me."

"What?"

"That bastard choked me out and left me for dead on the side of the road."

"My God." Angel had crossed a line she never thought he would.

"I'm going to throttle him with my bare hands when we catch up to him. Where do you think he is? Headed for Nellis?" The commander dodged a pair of Harleys cruising side by side and then the road opened up in front of them. He pressed on the gas, wringing as much power as he could out of the aging vehicle. "The authorities can pick up Kellerman, but Demarco? He's all mine."

Maybe Orr could break the rules after all. As long as she could keep her parentage a secret for today, her boss seemed willing to help in her pursuit.

"I think he's going to Area 51."

"Why do you think that?"

"He has Allwood. I think Angel wants to take him there for some kind of revenge." If Allwood was continuing his work at

Area 51—the genetic modifications and 'improvements' Angel had described, it would make the most sense he'd want to destroy it.

Orr violently swerved the truck into another lane to avoid slamming into a car entering the highway. "How did he get a hold of Allwood?"

She thought a moment. "He hit us."

"Hell, Cutter, why didn't you tell me before?"

"Angel caused the wreck." She averted her gaze. "We spun out and went over the embankment."

"Shit."

"He took Allwood with him, and I'm sure that's where they'll go. Angel hates everything about him and knows he has a lab where the professor might be continuing his experiments."

"Charlie," the Commander said, using her given name for the first time, "we have to stop him."

"I know."

The scenery flew by in a blur. How many things would have to come together in order for her to end everything? She and Orr had no idea where Allwood's lab was located on base. But her gut told her all three of them—Kellerman, Allwood, and Angel would show up there. And they needed to arrive before Angel killed Allwood or destroyed his lab. There were answers she needed, questions she'd wanted to ask. She kicked herself for not having the courage to do it in front of Ricard.

For a long stretch of road, they traveled in silence.

The quiet only made her think more about her brother and the trouble he'd be in once the news broke out. How could she protect him? He needed to know the truth, and Allwood had to give it to her.

"How did you end up with this truck?" she asked.

"Some guy stopped to help me. I offered him cash for it. He accepted."

She tried to imagine someone willing to give up his truck to a stranger. "Did you pay him?"

"Ever heard of Cash App?"

She jerked. "Seriously?"

As the truck ate up the miles, they reviewed the facts about

Angel, Allwood, the human experiments, everything. But she stopped short of admitting her connection to Allwood. Orr would find out in time and telling him now would be a distraction. She was not the enemy here. Angel? He had nothing to lose. His whole focus since he'd traveled back in time had been to track down his number one enemy, Byron Allwood, and find his sister. Risa was lost to him, but Allwood? He was all too real. All too evil. And he'd landed right in Angel's lap. Years of anger, hatred, and frustration were about to be unleashed.

"Sir, we have to make it to Area 51 before he does something."

"Don't worry, Charlie, we will. I promise."

CHAPTER 18

AS KELLERMAN ARRIVED at the warehouse where the professor kept his work, he slowed the motorcycle and parked in the side lot where it would be less visible. The guards at the entrance to the secured area where the most secretive projects were housed let him by with barely a glance at his badge. They recognized him. For three years he'd worked with Allwood and passed through the same gates every morning. Even after he'd taken the transfer to NCIS-A, he made occasional trips to Nevada to report in person about his findings.

The lab would be closed at this time of day. He judged the angle of the sun—maybe two more hours of daylight. But he wouldn't be leaving the facility once he entered.

His stomach fluttered.

He brushed his thumb across his access card. The professor should have confiscated it when the lieutenant had taken on his new assignment. But it had been easier to let him keep it. No questions asked when he returned for one-on-one meetings to transfer intel to Allwood.

He chose an entrance at the back of the facility—closest to the professor's office and nearest the locked room where the experiment in progress lived. The one he'd helped bring to fruition through his sacrifice and cunning. They wouldn't be as far along on it if he hadn't collected samples and crafted some of the software to reveal the formula's building blocks.

Would they have changed the code since he left last year?

He punched in the numbers and hoped.

The metallic click told him the professor had been sloppy in his security procedures. The combination should've been changed every three months. But how many times had he reminded Allwood to do it? The professor didn't care much about rules and regulations. He only wanted to be left alone to continue his work. He'd relied on Kellerman to keep the security auditors out of his hair, but never thought to select a replacement.

His mistake.

The door buzzed. He entered and headed upstairs to the room that held their greatest achievement: a time machine.

After waving his badge in front of the card scanner, Kellerman entered the dark room and flipped on a switch. Fluorescent lights lit up the space. The warmth of the room meant it hadn't been long since Allwood's best scientists had occupied it.

A large organic orb took up half the room. It rested in a metal stand. A wall of floor-to-ceiling plexiglass separated the machine from the row of computers and equipment on the opposite wall. Humidity steamed up the inside of the glass. One of the first things they'd had to figure out was the level of dampness that kept the orb from disintegrating, but also kept the organic material from crumbling. He was sure the last few samples he'd collected from North Dakota helped finalize the formula. No need to wait for the translations any longer. Who cared if Allwood wanted to run a few more simulations?

The lieutenant stood there for a moment staring at the object. When he'd hopped on the motorcycle and zoomed down the highway, he'd had a very focused mind. To reach the machine and disappear to another time—like the professor had promised—had been his only goal. With the reveal that Charlie was his daughter, he'd begun to doubt Allwood would follow through.

But was he really ready to leave everything he knew for life in a time period long past?

He placed his palm on the glass and dipped his head.

What did he have left in this time?

Ricard, Orr, and Charlie knew the truth—he'd been deceiving them. His work at NCIS-A was over. His clearance would be pulled. He'd never be able to work in intelligence again, which meant not even the professor could fix things. With Charlie in the picture, and Armas, too, he was only an assistant who'd aided Allwood in his quest. An easily replaceable assistant.

His hand turned into a fist.

With determination, he headed for the computer that controlled the pod. He knew how to program it, as he'd helped build the code based on instructions from Allwood. According to the professor, his wife had crafted the formula for the original machines, and he had created the inner workings that directed it. With unfamiliar twenty-first century tech at his disposal, the professor had handed over that work to Kellerman and others who came before him and, instead, focused his time on growing his sources of funding for the project.

But with the arrival of Armas in a pod from the past, Kellerman wondered at the truth of Allwood's abilities. How much of the machine was truly the professor's work?

The screen came to life. Kellerman navigated to the command program. With trembling fingers he typed in his time destination —not so far back that he'd be stuck in a primitive time with little hope for survival, but not so modern that he'd ever be tracked down or noticed.

A hatch appeared in the side of the pod and hissed open.

———

Demarco slowed their speed to avoid unwanted attention and kept a careful eye on his prisoner. He wouldn't put it past the man to jump out of a moving vehicle traveling at eighty miles an hour. He'd kept pace with traffic for the last hundred miles or so. The cops were probably already out looking for a stolen vehicle, and who knows what Charlie told the police once help arrived.

His gut twisted.

It couldn't be helped.

He had to choose Allwood over her.

It was always going to be that way.

To bring Charlie into his world and share what he'd seen and suffered because of this man came with risks. She'd been sympathetic, kind, and loving. When he'd climbed into the machine all those years ago, he hadn't expected to have the love of a woman in his life. He'd chosen his path. A lonely one. A path he'd intended only for himself. Then he'd met her.

The temptation had been strong to end his quest and forget about everything: his family, the horrible experiments, the loss of his sister. One part of him longed for it—to have a wife, children, a regular life. The dream reminded him so much of home on the farm his heart ached for it. A time when everything had been simpler. But then he knew he'd never completely forget, and his obsession would always haunt him.

After he eradicated Allwood and his experiments and everything was known, Charlie would loathe him. If she didn't already after the way he'd abandoned her at the accident scene. She must know he was responsible. Perhaps he'd shut the door on his dream the minute he chose to ram the SUV.

"Where are we going?" For tens of miles Allwood had remained silent, but now he'd finally opened up.

The sound of his voice grated on Demarco. If only the man knew the level of hatred inside, he'd stop drawing attention to himself.

Demarco snorted a breath through his nose. The 'professor' didn't deserve an answer.

"My arm, it's broken." The older man held it awkwardly in his lap. "Are you going to do something about it?"

"Shut up." Demarco spied a police car parked under an overpass and slowed the car. "When we drive up to the gates, you're going to act as if everything is normal. I'm your security. That's what you'll tell them."

"They won't let you on base without a badge."

"It's your job to make sure they do."

"I can't make someone break the rules."

"All you've ever done is break the rules, Allwood." Demarco pushed a thumb into the professor's leg wound.

Allwood let out a strangled cry.

"You will get me on that base." He gritted his teeth.

"You're an animal. A lunatic who should've been put down instead of caged. But your sister begged me to spare you." Allwood spat out his words. "Little did she know that decision would ruin our plans and destroy everything we'd built."

The speeding landscape around them blurred. Demarco's vision tunneled. So the only reason he'd lived, the only reason he'd been spared in Allwood's lair that day was because of Risa?

"If you truly believe that, then you'd do anything this 'animal' asks." A dark place grew in his heart. "Because this animal is dangerous and unpredictable."

The exit appeared. He swerved off the highway.

Allwood cried out when his mangled arm pressed against the door.

Although the professor had a charisma that drew people to him and a commanding presence, Demarco saw right through it to the person inside. A petty, shallow man who never cared about anyone but himself. The kind of man who would do almost anything to save his own ass.

If Allwood couldn't find a way to pass him through the security check point, Demarco would have to get creative.

———

Kellerman stared at the pod. Although he'd dreamed of becoming a time traveler, he never thought the day would arrive. Everything he'd worked for, every task the professor had assigned him, no matter how difficult, had been worth it.

Having a top secret security clearance meant he had to become good at lying or at least avoiding the truth, and the professor had only encouraged him in the deception game. They'd been a team. Kellerman had become his right-hand man and knew more than the high-ranking officers and politicians who funded the research.

But look how Allwood treated him after everything he'd sacrificed. Instead of bringing him closer in, the professor had begun pushing him away. Armas's arrival had been the first noticeable shift. The existence of the boy in this time increased Allwood's eagerness to complete the pods. It was the proof he'd needed that his wife had survived her trip to the distant past. The conversation shifted from the professor needing a knowledgeable companion to travel with him through time to the hope for a reunion with his wife and child. Kellerman became an after-thought.

He wouldn't take it anymore.

He wasn't some obedient dog who'd do anything Allwood asked.

All his decisions would now be about what was best for him. What *he* wanted. What *he* dreamed of.

The lieutenant spun around and navigated to a folder on the desktop. One that nobody noticed. A program he'd written months ago when he felt the professor slipping away and focusing more on his wife than on him.

He inserted the hidden code into the system and started the countdown. In ten minutes, after the machine had carried him to his new time and new life, all of the team's work would be erased. The formula they'd been working on for years would disappear. The bioelectric circuit design and the software he'd perfected to interface with them would no longer exist.

He smiled to himself when he'd finished.

Let the professor see how important he'd been to the work.

How much Allwood needed him.

After a few seconds of watching the timer count down, he rose, opened the plexiglass door, and closed it behind him.

The machine had a strange smell—damp but also intensely green, like a freshly mowed lawn. He climbed through the hatch. Beneath his feet the soft, organic surface clung to him. He touched the seat. The cool goo vibrated, which was unpleasant. But his travel should only last a few minutes, and then he'd be free of this time, free of the life he no longer wanted.

He thought fleetingly of his brother and sister and what they'd think. His family would mourn for a time, but the military would probably claim he'd been lost in some kind of accident. They'd receive his benefits and probably move on. And he? He would be living the life he should've had. He'd be in a place where his knowledge and insight would be worshipped.

After he sat down and strapped in, he pulled the organic restraint taut against his chest and clicked it into place.

The hatch hissed closed.

Kellerman took a deep breath, and his heart raced. Inky blackness enveloped him.

Allwood had never mentioned anything about the dark.

The machine began to spin, and as it did, bioluminescence lit up the interior. The minimal controls were visible, as were the walls that protected him from the time waves he'd pass through.

He gripped the restraint, closed his eyes, and waited.

CHAPTER 19

FROM INSIDE THE LAB, if someone happened to be present, the machine behind the plexiglass spun and spun and spun until it was a blur. A loud whooshing sound filled the small space that soon became deafening.

Then a computer screen lit up with a red warning: *Danger*.

The machine continued to spin. If someone looked closely, maybe it tilted slightly off its axis, maybe its green goo began to melt, and maybe the material that was supposed to withstand the rigors of time travel wasn't quite the right formula.

Maybe.

The whoosh turned into a whine.

The rounded sides of the machine pressed inward, creating an oblong shape. Then, instead of disappearing, the object imploded splattering green goo mixed with red onto the clear walls.

Silence filled the room.

Green and red chunks wetly dripped down the clear walls.

The computer's warning disappeared, Kellerman's countdown continued, and within minutes everything had been erased.

CHAPTER 20

LESS THAN A HALF-MILE from the highway exit, the road to Groom Lake turned to gravel. Demarco slowed the vehicle. With the sun low in the sky, strange shadows created dark patches that hid potholes and dips. Anyone traveling down this road would think it abandoned and turn around for the safety of the busy highway and the bright lights of Las Vegas in the distance. But Demarco and his passenger wouldn't be turning around. No, they would be following the road until it ended at their destination. No other option existed.

"Were you going to meet Kellerman at your lab?" The why of the lieutenant's mad dash from the pod landing site stood out as still unexplained in his mind. What prompted Kellerman to blow his cover? "Did he contact you while we were at the hospital? Tell you anything?" He glanced over at the man nursing his painful arm. "Where's your phone?"

"I lost it when you crashed into us back there." Allwood grimaced when the car bounced over a dip in the road. "Hope you didn't hurt your friends. That girl looked pretty banged up."

Demarco's mind returned to Charlie—the blood, the startled look on her face when he'd fled the scene with his captive. His vision fuzzed out. But it was for the best if she finally saw him for who he was: a man full of hate, a man obsessed with revenge. He had no room for anything else. This was who he was. His life had been distilled down to the actions he was about to take. After he achieved his goal, he didn't care what happened to him. He had nothing left in this time, nothing to hold him back from his plan.

"Where's Kellerman?" He turned the conversation back to Allwood's lackey and NCIS-A's mole. "Did he think you'd hide him? Keep him safe? Or was he going to be another subject for your experiments? Were you going to cut him open? Inject him with something? Alter his DNA for your own sick fun?"

"We're almost there." Allwood stared straight ahead.

Demarco noticed two faint lights in the distance. Not what he expected at a high security military facility. But perhaps the scaled down lighting helped with the hidden nature of the base and the secrets it held. Why draw attention? The badly maintained road, the minimal lighting—so far everything screamed: old, broken down, no longer used.

His headlights caught the white of a reflective sign with faded red lettering:

WARNING
Restricted Area
It is unlawful to enter this area without
permission of the Installation Commander
Sec. 21, Internal Security Act of 1950; 50 U.S.C. 797
While on this Installation all personnel and
the property under their control are subject
to search
Use of deadly force authorized

"What if I told you I have a working machine in my lab, a machine that would allow you to join your sister?"

The unexpected words hit the special agent like a concussive blast after an explosion. Demarco's grip tightened on the steering wheel. There was a chance to find Risa? "I don't believe you." But his mind raced at the suggestion. Reunited with his sister? He thought about what she must've gone through without him—the loneliness, the confusion, and the physical strain of such a massive time jump. Then there was Armas. She'd given up her child to one of these pods with the hope he'd find safety, or family, or Allwood. He wished he knew. Had she intended to join her son? Or had something happened to her?

"You should. It's all very real. I've been working for decades on the formula. When I found the Voynich manuscript on the internet, I knew it was Risa's work. I knew I could rebuild the machines even with a partial formula. The internet? Pretty amazing thing. When I figured out what it could do, even back in the late 1990s, something told me to search for answers, look for her. I knew Risa would find a way to communicate with me. But who knew she would speak from a place centuries earlier." The older man couldn't hide the scowl on his face.

"And Kellerman? What was his role in all of this, if you found Risa's work?"

"The formula was incomplete. I needed samples, and when my followers began to arrive—in the time I had selected before you interfered—I needed someone who could blend in and collect them for me without being recognized. Kellerman has been a great help to me in the last year. I have a machine waiting. That's why the senator was visiting. She wanted to see the culmination of twenty years of work."

A flare of adrenaline fired in Demarco's brain. "Why would you give me the chance, when you could use it and travel to any time you wanted?"

"I know you hate me," Allwood said and pushed his body back into his seat. "I know you blame me for everything that has happened to your family. There's no way you'll let me walk out of this alive." The professor made an odd noise in his throat. "If you leave me in this time and allow me to live, I'll give you the chance to be reunited with your sister."

An empty feeling hollowed out Demarco's stomach. "It's all your fault, so why wouldn't I blame you?"

"I'll give up everything, destroy my work. No one will ever hear from me again. I'll end it all tonight."

Demarco knew deep down Allwood was a liar and a charlatan. But the desire to rescue his sister and save her from a lifetime of isolation, such as he'd experienced, was strong. It tugged at him with a force he didn't think possible. Every moment he'd spent with Risa on the farm flashed through his mind. She'd been determined, intelligent, but also kind. A kindness that had led her to Allwood in the first place. She believed his words and joined in his passion. She'd made a mistake, and she had paid for it with the loss of everything she ever knew, even the loss of her child. The suffering she must had endured. He couldn't bear it. What if Allwood spoke the truth?

"Take me to the machine."

———

After another ten minutes of driving down the gravel road, they approached the guard shack standing outside rusted fencing. Although a spiral of barbed wire ran the length of it, the age of the base showed. Or was that intentional to keep prying eyes away?

Demarco turned off his headlights.

A young airman in BDUs motioned for him to roll down his window, another man in uniform hung back by the guard shack and gripped his rifle.

Demarco pressed on the electric window button. A warm, dusty wind blew inside.

"Badges?" The airman peeked in the RAV4. "Oh, professor, I didn't recognize the vehicle. How are you this evening, sir?"

The professor nodded and smiled a tight smile. "Fine, fine."

The airman gave Demarco a quizzical look.

"He's my security—from NCIS." Allwood nodded at Demarco who flashed his identification.

"Something up?" The airman signaled to his partner who headed for the gate and entered a code. The chain-link shuddered and then slowly rolled to the right on rusted wheels to open.

"Some sort of silly threat." The professor used his uninjured arm to shrug. "All I know is the base commander called me this afternoon, assigned this guy from Nellis, and now he has to follow me wherever I go. Irritating, but I can play along."

Demarco kept his face impassive. He wanted to press on the gas and fly through the open gate. Allwood's lab was somewhere behind this fence. He'd waited half a dozen years for this moment, and he wasn't about to let his impatience take over and destroy his chances. Besides, if the professor had told him the truth, there might be a way to rescue his sister. Maybe that was the only avenue for him anyway. What did he have left in this time? Nothing. He'd burned every bridge and ruined every relationship with his actions today. Even if he came out of this unscathed, he'd have to start all over in a new place with a different name. Could he handle that again? He'd barely kept his sanity when he'd done it the first time.

The airman stepped back and waved. "Come on through."

"Thanks," said Allwood. "I'll have to give you the tour sometime."

The young Air Force guard raised his eyebrows. "Really? That'd be cool."

Demarco crept through the gate.

———

At night, Area 51 gave off an eerie feel. The lighting was minimal, the signage almost non-existent, and row after row of identical warehouse buildings indicated a lot more secret research could exist here than Allwood's.

"Your sister was truly remarkable, you know."

The professor appeared more relaxed than he had the entire trip, which set Demarco on edge. "Where's your lab?" Everything looked the same, nothing stood out to him—wide, low greenish-brown buildings with white doors on the front and sides. Depending on Allwood to find what he needed made him uneasy.

"The code—in the Voynich manuscript and in our machines—was something she created." Allwood stared out the window and watched as they passed by building after building. "Did you know that?"

"No." It ticked him off that Allwood teased him with facts about his sister. It had been so long since he'd seen her climb into a pod and disappear, he could barely remember her features, much less the intelligence she displayed. His memories tied back to her collection of plants, her drawings in her sketchbook, her mischievous smile when she bested him in class. Less than two years younger, but so obviously smarter than him in many ways even at a young age.

"We left notes for each other at the stone bridge, and she attempted to teach me. She saw it as a way for our people to communicate secretively. I only had a minimal grasp before your thugs showed up, and we had to escape."

Demarco grunted.

The stone bridge had been a landmark between their village and the ruins of an earlier time. Their parents had forbidden them to go any further than the bridge. The ruins held untold dangers from their ancestors that could threaten their way of life. That information had been passed down from grandparents and great-grandparents and great-great-grandparents. The warning went so far back nobody knew who had started it or why. But they all obeyed...until Byron Allwood came along preaching his nonsense about transformation and becoming something more than human. Better than human.

"I loved her for her mind, her brilliance," the professor continued. "For things her family never noticed, never praised. She was beyond her time, beyond all of you—even me. I can see that now. When we were separated in time, and I found myself alone, without her, without our people—well, I'm sure you can understand how disorienting it was."

Demarco gritted his teeth. He remembered all right. He thought he was going to travel to a distant place on earth, and instead he made a decision that changed the course of his entire life. Forever. No going back. No fixing things. His parents wouldn't be born for hundreds of years. He had no idea if decisions he made in this time would affect their existence. His head hurt at the thought.

"I wished I'd been a better student. That would have made things so much easier." Allwood brushed dust off his clothes with his good hand. "Until your team found someone who could translate the manuscript, I had to rely only on my memory and the few bits of code she'd taught me." Allwood gently lifted the wrist of his broken arm and set it in a different position on his lap. He sucked air between his teeth. "Where did you find your translator? I'd hired several over the years, and they'd all failed. Told me translation was impossible. That dozens of people over hundreds of years hadn't been able to break it. Then, within weeks, your newest team member, the young lady in the accident I believe, managed to figure it out. I wonder how that was possible?"

Charlie.

Demarco imagined her earnest face when she'd listened to his story. The first time he'd shared it with anyone. Why did it have to be her? Why did she have to be the one? Anyone but her. The one person who could translate the text, who could uncover the whole scheme, and who'd revealed his sister's fate and her role in everything.

"You can stop here." Allwood pointed at an unlit building like all the other buildings, except this one had a familiar yellow-and-black motorcycle parked alongside it.

Kellerman.

"This is the building you want. The lab is inside." The older man straightened up in his seat. "Behind those doors is the way to reunite with your sister and put this all behind you."

Demarco parked, turned off the engine, and decided what he would do.

CHAPTER 21

CHARLIE NAVIGATED USING her cell phone. Surprisingly, it had been as easy as typing 'Area 51' into her mapping app to find a route to the military site. As the sky grew darker, though, identifying the landmarks they needed to take the right exit became harder. "I can't believe someone uploaded a picture of the entrance." She held up her phone so the commander could see a clear photo of a chain-link gate manned by guards. "I thought it was a highly classified, well-protected base."

Orr shrugged. "Everyone knows where the NSA is located, but you don't see random conspiracy theorists driving through the gates."

Charlie's mind flashed to I-95 and the familiar turn-off to her stepfather's work place. "True."

Orr turned on the headlights, and the reflective lane striping lit up. "You think Allwood would help Demarco get on the base if he knew what Demarco was thinking?"

"Good question." How would he make it through security without a badge or having his name on an access list?

Luckily for her, Commander Orr had connections through his father who'd worked at the site decades ago before his disappearance. When they'd decided on their destination, he'd made a couple of phone calls, and in less than an hour, they had everything they needed to enter the site. Some admiral or other had arranged it. Charlie had no idea Orr's family background and the clout their small office, NCIS-A, could wield when needed.

Orr gave her a quick glance. "Could Allwood want him to reach his lab?"

She smoothed her hair back from her face. "Are you suggesting the professor might be setting up a trap?" Her mouth went dry.

"Maybe."

A directional sign lit up under the glare of their headlights. "We turn off at the next exit." Her stomach quivered. They were only a few miles away, had no weapons, and would arrive completely out of their element. They'd be right in Allwood's backyard. It wasn't a good idea. In fact, it was a terrible idea.

"If you were trapped in a car with Demarco and knew he wanted to kill you, what would you do to save your own ass?" the commander asked.

Orr's speculation turned her mind in a different direction. If they didn't intercede, lives could be at stake. She thought of the woman in the hospital who had been murdered by a man she trusted. Allwood had convinced her to climb into a pod and travel through time. She had depended on him for everything, and he'd turned on her. If Allwood could do that to someone who'd trusted him completely, what could he do to someone he hated? Someone who'd chased him through time? Someone who would do anything to eradicate the man he blamed for everything bad in his life?

As they approached the exit, a decaying white mobile home a hundred yards from the highway appeared in their headlights. What poor misbegotten soul had decided to build a life for himself so far outside Las Vegas and miles from any civilization?

It dawned on her at that moment how far away they were from people and police and safety. Maybe it was one of the reasons Demarco wanted to end it here. Away from prying eyes. A score could be settled, and no one would be the wiser. Demarco was clever enough and angry enough he'd find a way to hide what he'd done. A secret base in the middle of the desert with incredibly high security? No one would interrupt him. No one would stop him. No one would get in his way.

Her armpits grew damp.

Charlie expanded her map in order to see more clearly what terrain lay beyond the exit to Area 51.

Orr turned off the highway.

"Do you think you can drive faster?" she asked.

"This road looks rough." Orr kicked on the brights.

The reality of what they were about to do settled heavily inside her. Her gaze bounced from one side of the road to the other—only sand and dirt and empty nothingness surrounded them on both sides. "I think we're running out of time."

Orr glanced over at her, gave a nod, and pressed on the gas. The old truck lurched forward and carried them further into the desert.

———

Demarco followed the injured Allwood to the back of the warehouse, where a dimly lit door awaited them. As they passed by the motorcycle, the special agent touched the engine with the back of his hand. Still warm. Kellerman had arrived not too long ago. Allwood didn't even give it a glance. He had no idea Kellerman had stolen it to put miles between himself and his former co-workers.

What had the young lieutenant discovered that had sent him on the run and exposed his subterfuge?

Demarco prepared himself for the possibility that Kellerman might be inside the lab waiting for his boss. A pre-arranged meeting? An opportunity to change their plans now that Kellerman's cover had been blown? Or was it something else? Information obtained from the dead woman in the hospital or something that had yet to be revealed to the NCIS-A team?

"Remember who has the upper hand here, Allwood." Demarco focused his attention on the wounded man who limped as he walked and held his arm close to his body. Did Allwood know this day would come? Had Allwood suspected he would follow him into the unknown, climb inside a pod, and join him in time traveling madness?

The older man paused, keeping his back to Demarco, and said, "I'm only interested in both of us getting what we want."

They approached the door. A keypad was affixed on the wall next to it. Allwood pressed a series of numbers, and the door beeped twice.

Demarco wished he still had his gun or his taser—both useful weapons. But he'd known a time when neither of those things existed, and he'd had to use other means to control his enemies. If Kellerman were waiting behind the door, he needed to be ready.

Allwood pulled on the knob. It opened. In the blink of an eye, Demarco slid an arm across Allwood's throat, pulled the man close, and whispered in his ear, "Nice and slow. We wouldn't want anyone to get hurt."

Allwood grunted and slowed his movements.

Demarco noticed lights were on inside, which told him Kellerman wouldn't be lying in wait. Too exposed. Too visible.

The professor's body tensed. "Are you going to let go now?" he croaked. "I'm offering you everything you ever wanted, and this is how you treat me?"

Demarco wanted to crush the man's throat, shut him up forever. "Not everything." He swallowed the bile that rose in his throat, released his hold on the man, and thrust him forward into the building. It would be so easy to snap his neck. He'd done it before to men stronger and more capable than Allwood. Or he could find a sharp object inside and stab him in the heart. And he'd do it without remorse, without guilt, without a single thought in his mind but vengeance.

They entered a small vestibule—plain, utilitarian, with no indications of what sort of work went on inside. A stairway to the left led up a flight of metal stairs, and several closed doors spanned the length of the white, unadorned wall in front of them.

To gain back some control, Demarco bit the inside of his cheek.

He craved to know more about the secrets inside this place. If he gave in to his baser instincts, he'd kill Allwood before he learned what had been hidden behind security codes and military protection. What vile experiments had he conducted?

Allwood headed for a door on the right. "This way."

"I want to see it all. Everything. I want you to walk me through every square inch of this space and show me what the military has been funding all these years. With this time's technology and the government's money, I can't even imagine how twisted your research has become."

"Twisted?" Allwood spat out. "Is that what you think? My life-saving therapies—"

"Life-saving? Is that what you call horrible disfigurement and manipulated DNA?" Demarco planted himself on the hard concrete floor. His muscles quivered. "A perfectly healthy human being reduced to a freak without knowing the long-term implications of your experiments? What did you promise the poor victims who came to you for help?"

"People came to me because no one else cared. I was the only one who attempted to improve their lives, make them something better. Your kind would leave them to suffer."

"Risa needed no improvement."

"I didn't do anything to anyone that I didn't try out on myself. Your sister saw what could be achieved and begged me to fix her. She knew she could be so much more with a few tweaks—smarter, stronger, better."

"A few tweaks? I saw what you did to her. You disfigured her."

"I made her more beautiful."

"She was perfect the way she was."

"She didn't see it that way," Allwood said. "And who are you to tell her what and who she should be? That was one of the reasons she ran away and came to me. I could see her potential. I could see what she could become. She trusted me completely and was involved in every step, every surgery, every genetic manipulation."

"Stop." Demarco gripped the back of Allwood's neck. "I can't listen to your lies anymore."

The older man shook off his hand. "If only she were here now and you could speak to her, she'd tell you the truth."

A muffled sound echoed down to the vestibule from the floor above.

"Someone's here," Allwood whispered.

Was the professor surprised or merely a good actor?

Allwood peered up the dark steps. "No one should be in the building this late. Unless—"

Demarco's assumptions about Kellerman and why he'd fled for the lab dispersed in his mind like falling snow into dry air. "Unless what?"

"Unless that fool betrayed me." The older man shuffled toward the stairs. "I told him it wasn't ready, but he was so eager. So stupidly eager."

"What wasn't ready?" It made no difference to Demarco if he saw the upstairs of Allwood's lab first or the downstairs. If something upstairs made the man grow concerned about what Kellerman may be up to, Demarco was perfectly fine following him and finding out more. Everything was going to end tonight. He would make sure nobody else would ever follow Allwood's path, rebuild his discoveries, or move ahead on any of it. Then he could climb inside one of those machines, take one last trip back in time, and destroy the Voynich manuscript before it could ever be discovered and translated. The work, the partial formula, every little scrap of the evil machine had to be destroyed. Demarco only trusted himself to make sure it would happen. He might be trapped in a more primitive time for the rest of his life, but at least he would be with his sister. He could find a way to make her trust him again, love him again. They could save each other from the loneliness and aguish that came with being a time traveler.

The professor took each step with care. When his injured left leg pushed up on a step, he hissed between his teeth. "Help me, you idiot. Kellerman is about to ruin everything."

Demarco brought his shoulder up under Allwood's good arm and helped him climb the stairs. When they reached the second floor, Allwood pointed to a dark hallway lit only by a few downward pointing lights.

The professor untangled himself from Demarco and hobbled down the hall. "The lab's down there. Hurry!"

Although his gut told him not to trust, Demarco's curiosity burned. If Kellerman wanted to access the room Allwood was leading him to, then it must contain something important. That traitor had shown his true colors back in Lake Havasu—his loyalty was only to himself. He'd known from Kellerman's first day at NCIS-A there was something off, but Orr had seemed thrilled to have someone with his tech skills on the team. Now it looked as if the commander had chosen poorly.

Allwood breathed heavily but seemed to have found a second wind. When he opened up his stride a little too much his wounded leg collapsed under him.

Demarco caught him before he went down. "Easy, old man, you don't want that leg wound to bleed worse than it already is." Besides, if the professor passed out, how would he access the room the man seemed so eager to reach? He again offered Allwood his shoulder in support.

With the help of Demarco, Allwood neared a door that looked like all the other doors in the warehouse. No markings on it. No indication of what went on behind it. Maybe as a way to control the secrecy?

"You need to help me with my badge." Allwood's broken arm was useless and the other was slung across Demarco's back and shoulders.

A white card reader, like the ones at the Washington Navy Yard, hung on the wall. "Where is it?" He patted the pockets of Allwood's suit jacket.

A strange whirring sound emanated from behind it.

"Goddammit, it's too late." Allwood snarled.

"Where's your badge?" Demarco snapped. If Kellerman was on the other side of that door, he wanted to know what he was up to. Who cared if it was 'too late'?

"My inside pocket."

Demarco felt inside the lining of the jacket.

"Hurry." The professor stomped his good foot. "We don't have much time."

"Got it." Demarco pulled out Allwood's badge and waved it in front of the card reader.

A metal ker-thunk sounded indicating the door was now open, followed by a muffled explosion.

They burst through the door.

Demarco's eyes landed first on the blood-and-goo streaked Plexiglass in one corner of the room. "What the hell?"

Allwood freed himself from Demarco's support and grabbed for a roller chair next to a bank of desktop computers. "The idiot. Why couldn't he wait?"

Demarco pointed at the mess behind the clear protective wall. "Is that Kellerman? Was that a pod?"

The professor nodded dumbly and lowered himself into the chair, staring at the screens. "He destroyed everything. All my work."

The special agent approached the enclosed area that had housed his former co-worker inside a pod. "Why did it blow up?" A chunk of goo slowly slid to the floor. Was that a body part partially coated in more green gunk? *Oh, Kellerman, what did you do?*

Allwood tapped furiously on a keyboard. "I don't think I can stop it. Do you want to see your sister again? Help me."

Demarco turned away from the sordid scene and focused his attention on the professor. "What do you mean?"

"All of my work. That stupid lieutenant of yours must've created a hidden instruction to destroy the formula I've been working on." Allwood typed while lines of code disappeared in front of their eyes. "The formula to build another machine. If we can't stop it, neither of us is going anywhere."

CHAPTER 22

AS DEMARCO APPROACHED THE COMPUTER, his stomach hardened. "Wait, you were going to put me in that machine, weren't you? The one that exploded and killed Kellerman?"

Allwood focused on the lines of codes in front of him as if Demarco didn't even exist. The older man was so intent on his precious research, he didn't even realize he'd exposed his sinister plan.

"You snake." Demarco's hands curved as if they were strangling the professor's neck. "I never should've trusted you."

"All of my work. Ruined." Allwood's hands shook as he navigated the screen with a wireless mouse. "Years of experiments, trials, formulas. That bastard." With an angry grunt, he picked up the keyboard and smashed it on the desk.

Demarco spun the chair around. "You were going to kill me."

The professor's eyes were fever bright, and he clung to his seat with his good hand. "And you weren't planning the same?" He raised an eyebrow.

A mirthless laugh escaped the special agent. "All these years, and you are the exactly same person. You haven't changed at all."

"Neither have you." The older man kicked at Demarco with his good leg and turned back around. "Let me save what I can." He reached down and pulled the cord from the wall to permanently shut off the computer and whatever program had been operating.

"My team will have to sort through this disaster in the morning. We'll find a way to rebuild."

Allwood thought he'd return to business as usual? After he'd murdered a woman, lured Kellerman to his untimely demise, and who knows what else? Even though Demarco wanted nothing more than to follow through on his dark thoughts and strangle the life out of his nemesis, the blinging of a phone caught his attention.

Kellerman's phone.

The young lieutenant had left it on the desk before he'd foolishly tried to escape in an experimental pod. Guess he thought he wouldn't need it in whatever time he'd chosen as his destination.

Maybe there would be a clue on it that would expose Allwood's sick plans. Could there be more in this massive warehouse than Genesis Machine pieces and parts? Was he still conducting human experiments and DNA manipulation?

He reached for it.

Allwood beat him to it. "Not so fast." In a flash he'd typed a six-digit code with one hand and unlocked the phone. He must've seen a look of surprise on Demarco's face. "You think I wouldn't know how to access his phone? Nobody works for me unless they are willing to share everything."

The screen displayed an email that Kellerman must've had open before he'd made his fateful decision to enter the pod.

As he read the email message, Allwood's face paled. His gaze slid to Demarco. "Would your translator's name be Charlene Cutter? The one who so cleverly deciphered the Voynich text?"

Demarco's mind froze. Why was this lunatic bringing up Charlie? What did Kellerman dig up about her? "Leave her out of this."

A slow smile spread across the older man's face. "Oh, you don't know then, do you?"

"Know what?" The gleam in Allwood's eyes was evil. The hair rose on the back of Demarco's neck. He grabbed at the phone. "What does it say?"

"Charlene and a brother." Allwood's face beamed. "I didn't know she'd given birth to twins."

"I don't understand." Demarco's adrenaline spiked. The truth had been right in front of him, and he'd ignored it. The unusual capabilities. The odd connection to the manuscript. He took a step backward. "No, it can't be."

"Yes," Allwood said. "Charlene Cutter is my daughter."

AS ORR SLOWED DOWN, the truck headlights played across the entrance to Area 51. It looked identical to the photo online: a chain link fence topped with razor wire, a simple guard shack, and a few external lights. With the sun completely set, night had swept across the desert, enveloping them in total blackness. The sight of bright lights and civilization—even if it was high-security civilization—brought an unexpected release of all tension in Charlie's body.

"Now we'll find out if my contacts did as promised," Commander Orr said as two uniformed airmen approached.

One of the men rested a hand on his sidearm and stayed a good fifteen feet away from the truck. The other tapped on the window glass.

Orr rolled it down.

"I'm sorry, sir, this is a secure site. We'll have to ask you to turn around."

Orr flashed his NCIS-A badge. "I was told you'd be expecting me."

The airmen's eyebrows shot up, he stepped back, and gave a quick salute. "Yes, Commander. I'm sorry, sir. We didn't expect you to arrive"—he eyeballed the junker the high-ranking officer drove—"in a truck."

"Stand down, airman."

The young man dropped his salute and gave a hand signal to his partner to back off. "It'll take us a minute to open the gate. Never seen it so busy this late in the day."

"Oh?" Orr tilted his head. "You've had other visitors tonight?"

The other airman opened the gate and waved at Orr and Charlie to move forward.

"One of our civilian scientists. But he does that sometimes—shows up at night. Whatever he's working on must be really important."

Orr nodded. "Sounds like it. I appreciate your help tonight, airman."

"Sir." The guard dipped his chin and stepped back from the truck.

Orr pushed on the gas and crept through the gate.

As they left the two guards behind, Charlie looked over her shoulder and watched the gate grow smaller. "You made that look so easy."

Orr shrugged. "It was."

"I thought for sure they'd notice my hands." She held them up to show the commander how much they shook.

"No worries, Petty Officer Cutter. I have this under control. All we have to do now is find the right building." He scanned the multiple rows of old military warehouses that lined the road.

"Should we have asked back there?" Charlie jerked a thumb.

"Ask where Allwood did his experiments? That might've made them suspicious of our motives."

"Maybe." She bit her lip. "But I'm worried it will take us forever to find them by ourselves, and I don't think we have a lot of time."

"I know what Demarco's vehicle looks like. He wouldn't expect anyone to follow him here, so I doubt he hid it from view."

Charlie's phone rang.

Orr's eyebrows furrowed. "Dr. Stern?"

Her stomach dropped. "It's my brother." *Chad.* He'd returned her call at the worst possible time. But she couldn't put off talking to him. His life could be in danger if she waited much longer to share the distressing news. "Could you pull over?"

"What?" He lifted his foot off the gas.

"I need to talk to my brother—privately." Her body flashed hot and cold. This might be her only opportunity to tell Chad the truth before everyone knew.

"Cutter—"

"Please, sir. I wouldn't ask unless it was important."

"We don't have time for this. I'm sure your brother can wait."

The phone rang again. The sound made her grit her teeth. "Sir."

"Hang up."

"What?"

Orr reached for her phone. "Hang up. You can call your brother when all of this is over."

Charlie leaned away and quickly answered it. Her breathing accelerated. "Chad, did you get my text?"

Even though her brother was thousands of miles away in Spain, his voice came through clearly, "I talked to Mom."

Her stomach bottomed out. He knew. "I'm sorry."

Orr grunted. She'd defied him, and he wasn't happy about it.

"What do you have to be sorry about? You didn't know anything either. We both were kept in the dark." He let out a sigh. "What I don't understand is, why would you tell Mom we were in danger? People take DNA tests all the time and find out family secrets. This doesn't change how I feel about Dad. Who cares?"

Charlie swallowed and gave a quick glance in Orr's direction. She had to warn him. "It's the truth. Believe me. I wouldn't say that if I didn't mean it."

"Spit it out, Charlie. I don't have time for your nonsense."

"When everyone finds out, both of our lives are going to change."

"Why? Who is this Byron Allwood guy?"

Orr braked the truck. He pointed across the road at a dark warehouse that looked like all the other dark warehouses they'd passed. "There's the car and the motorcycle Kellerman stole."

Dammit.

She didn't have enough time.

"He's a very dangerous man, Chad." She leaned forward and

rested her head in her hands. "I have to go. Watch your back." Charlie hung up the phone.

The commander parked next to the SUV. He turned off the engine and asked, "When everyone finds out what?"

Could she trust Orr with the truth? Or would he hand her over to the government to be poked and prodded? She'd only known him for a few weeks. Had they built any kind of rapport that might work in her favor?

She stared at the warehouse in front of them. Demarco and Allwood were inside. Terrible things could be happening, and only she and Orr could stop it. No one else. If she'd trusted the commander to have her back in this situation, couldn't she trust him with the truth, too?

"We need to find a way inside before it's too late." Charlie unbuckled her seatbelt.

The commander touched her on the arm. "What's going on, Cutter? What dangerous man are you talking about?" He scanned the dark building. "Is there something I need to know before I go in there?"

Charlie let out a measured breath of air. By herself, she was no match for the two men inside. They'd rip each other to pieces. Together, she and Orr could stop them—maybe. "Dr. Stern called me while we were at the hospital lab. She told me the DNA results had come in." Her heart pounded. To say the words aloud made her feel faint. "I was a match."

Orr's brow wrinkled. "A match for what?"

"Armas is my half-brother." She looked down at her hands in her lap. It was hard to believe she'd only received the information herself earlier that day. It felt like a lifetime.

"What?" The commander flinched. "How is that possible?"

With the truth out, she couldn't hold back the rest. "Armas is Bryon Allwood's son. The translations in the text, plus what Angel told me—well, it's the only possible conclusion. Years ago, Allwood arrived in a pod that landed in Corpus Christi. He somehow met my mother and then disappeared before my brother and I were born. My mother thought he had died. He's my father —the man who started this whole thing, who created these time machines, who murdered that poor woman in the hospital, and he seems bent on continuing his dangerous experiments no matter the cost. Now can you see why my brother might be in danger? Why I might be in danger? You think the government would let the two of us lead normal lives knowing we're connected to Allwood?"

Orr sat still and quiet.

"Sir?" His silence unnerved her.

"Is that why you could translate the text so easily?"

"I never knew my real father. I don't know that my abilities had anything to do with—"

Orr tipped his head backward. "Then how did you do it?" He ran a hand down his face. "How?"

"I don't know." She shook her head. "I've always had an ability with languages, codes, puzzles."

He held up a hand. "Stop. I don't have time for this." He worked his jaw. "What you just told me? I can't handle it. Not now." He pointed at the warehouse. "We've got to deal with this shit. The fact you are some time traveler's kid? I don't even know what to do with it. I'm barely keeping up here—the stuff about Demarco? Now this?" He gave a strangled cry. "I don't have a choice right now but to work with you. You understand?"

She nodded.

He pointed a finger in her face. "Don't fucking dare double cross me, Cutter. You got it? I need to know you have my back."

"And I need to know you have mine. That you aren't going to hand me and my brother over to some agency once this is over."

"You have my word." His back straightened. "I have more questions for you."

"I know."

"Just because I'm not asking them now, doesn't mean I don't want answers later. I barely can grasp the concept of time travel, much less the fact you are a half-sister to a boy who was born five hundred years ago."

"If it helps, I'm still trying to grasp it, too. Everything I thought I knew about myself, my parents, my life—"

"Understood." He stared out at the warehouse. "You ready?"

Charlie nodded.

They both exited the truck and approached the forbidding building.

Were they too late? Demarco had traveled through time to seek out his vengeance on the professor. It was an anger so deeply seated, Charlie feared what they might find inside.

DEMARCO REELED BACK after Allwood told him the content of the email on Kellerman's phone. "That isn't true." His mind went completely blank. "You're lying."

Smart, beautiful Charlie could never be this evil man's daughter.

Never.

Impossible.

Nausea filled his stomach.

"Oh?" The wounded and weakened older man seemed to grow stronger. He scanned Demarco's face. "So you care for this girl?" His thin lips curled up in a wicked smile. "Maybe even love her?"

"Shut up." Suddenly, the room was too small, the air too stale. "Show me the rest. Show me every goddamn thing in this place that you've been doing. I want to see all of it. Come on, get up!" He grabbed Allwood by his broken arm and yanked him out of the chair.

Allwood cried out in pain.

The sound made Demarco happy inside. He wanted more of it. Every dark thought he'd ever had about Byron Allwood filled his mind.

The older man bent over and hobbled toward the door. "I wonder what Charlene would think of you if she could see you now? Torturing her father and treating him worse than a dog."

The smirk had been wiped off his face and replaced with a grimace.

Pain made Allwood obey. Pain made him listen.

"You are not her father." Demarco dragged the man out of the room and pushed him toward the stairs. "Charlie is nothing like you and never will be."

"Charlie, yes, Charlie." Allwood grabbed the railing and slowly took a step down. "So she was able to translate the text, when no one else could. Seems as if my experiment, as you call it, worked as planned."

"Take me to your research," Demarco barked, ignoring the man's remarks. All of his focus needed to be on destroying everything. "Where do you keep your samples? There must be more in this place than one room. Show me or you'll have worse than a broken arm."

"Didn't you wonder how she did it? Why was it so easy for her?"

They reached the bottom of the stairs, and Allwood headed to the left.

"She's a very intelligent woman." Demarco kept his voice cool, but he wanted to scream.

My God, Charlie—his daughter? Why did it have to be him? Why?

"Ah, but she's more than that." The professor hugged his injured arm closer to his body. "The DNA manipulation. The attempts to build a better human—she is proof that it worked. Her intellect must far surpass the norm. Do you know how many centuries were spent trying to translate the Voynich manuscript? Everyone thought it impossible."

As they headed toward a set of double doors at the end of a short corridor, Demarco thought about when he'd first met Charlie—a pretty young woman in Navy summer whites accompanied by Stormy. They'd been about to hop on a plane for North Dakota. He'd thought her too new, too untested for the job, a poor choice for such an assignment. But she'd proven him wrong. Every time he thought she'd break under the pressure, she'd surpassed his expectations.

And now he knew why.

It was as if a cold ocean wave hit him.

Charlie was so accomplished and so capable and so ahead of everyone else because she wasn't a normal human being. She was altered. Had she known she was different? Was it something she could sense?

Nobody else had been able to translate the text, and then this slip of a girl, barely out of college, managed to figure it all out in a few weeks?

His mind jumped to the last time he saw her, crawling out of the overturned SUV, a hurt look on her face as he'd grabbed Allwood and ran. She'd trusted him, and he'd betrayed her for his own purposes. He was so focused on Allwood, he didn't even take a few moments to make sure she was all right. How easy it had been to do it, and he hated himself for it.

He shoved his captive forward, and a rush of delight flowed through him when the older man whimpered.

Charlie, you don't know what kind of man you fell for.

He'd learned to be callous and cruel. Once he'd made the time jump, he'd had nothing to care about, nothing to live for. All that had mattered was revenge. A seething hate had grown inside him over the years, and he'd tamped it down as best he could and pretended to the new world around him that he was exactly like them. But he knew he wasn't. He knew he'd done horrible things no one in this time would be able to understand.

But, Charlie, you could've changed all of that. If only...

"Charlie is very special," Demarco said quietly. "She's nothing like you."

Allwood reached the doors. These were not protected with a key code. "Once this is over, promise you'll let me go. Promise you'll let me live out my existence in peace."

"What made you think I'd promise you anything?"

The lights snapped on.

A huge space filled with rows and rows of 'rooms' crafted out of thick plastic sheeting appeared before them.

"What is this?" Demarco strode ahead of the limping professor and pulled back the sheeting of the first room he saw. Microscopes, petri dishes, and scientific equipment he didn't recognize covered the top of a stainless steel table on wheels. Small green mini pods sat inside glass boxes on another smaller table—one had partly disintegrated and another seemed to be changing color from green to gray. "Are you still perfecting the formula?"

Allwood sidled up next to him, huffing. Blood loss and pain seemed to be draining the energy from him. He would be so easy to kill, but Demarco had to know everything first. How many people worked in this massive warehouse? Who else had access to the data? He wanted no one to be able to recreate the vile machine that had taken him away from his family, that had separated him from his sister forever, that had brought him nothing but sorrow and loneliness. If he could spare others from such a fate, he would do it. No matter what it took. Since there was no way for him to travel back to Risa, everything would have to end here.

"These are some of our prototypes, yes. You have no idea how long it took me to reach this level of work." Allwood entered the space, his eyes aglow. "Risa had been the true architect of the material we needed. It had been her vision. I only understood it at a basic level. But I've learned so much since then." He picked up the case with the partially disintegrated orb. "The material needs to be flexible, yet strong, living yet capable of resisting forces that would destroy most organic life. Because it is alive, you know."

Demarco crossed to another room hidden behind plastic. "What about other work? Other experiments? This can't be the only thing you're working on here." When he peeled back the sheeting, he saw more pods, more equipment.

"That's everything. I needed another machine. That's all I wanted. These fools in the military were more than happy to give me everything I asked for to create one. I wrote all kinds of proposals for the government, hoping the next one would grab someone's attention. All I needed were a few assistants, some money. I knew they couldn't resist what I was selling—a machine that could travel through time."

"You told them you were from the future?"

"Of course not. That would've been ridiculous." Allwood set the pod on the table and followed Demarco. "But I had enough knowledge to sound as if I knew what I was talking about. You'd be surprised how easy it is to convince a senator or a general to throw a few million dollars your way—especially if you tell them you might sell your work to the highest bidder. When I was awarded my first contract, I left Corpus Christi and Charlie's mother. I didn't need to be saddled with that kind of responsibility."

The emotionless way he spoke of abandoning a woman pregnant with his children disgusted Demarco. Had she merely been a diversion until Allwood achieved what he wanted?

Demarco moved to the next room. It was better to focus on what was in front of him. He couldn't let his emotions get the best of him, or he'd act in haste. He needed to be methodical about what he would do. There was no room for mistakes. When he pushed past the plastic, he saw more green goo, more half-constructed pods. Could it be that Allwood was only interested in traveling to Risa? That all of this time and effort and money—and the death of Kellerman—had only ever been about reuniting with her? The answer seemed too simple.

"You aren't going to stop, are you?" Demarco gestured at the different attempts at creating the correct material. "This warehouse is full of prototypes. That's not the sign of a man who is done with his research."

"I swear to you, I am." Allwood crept toward him and lifted his good arm in the air. "I swear."

Before Demarco could act, the older man brought a heavy glass beaker down on his head.

CHAPTER 25

ORR AND CHARLIE circled the outside of the warehouse looking for signs of life and a way inside. The rusted metal siding covering it screamed for a new coat of paint. Guess the military spent its money on expensive experiments rather than building maintenance. The few visible windows were either covered up or too high to peek through.

The commander, who'd found an old flashlight under a blanket in the cab of the truck, played it across the structure. "I don't see any activity, nor do I see any sign labeling this place a laboratory."

Charlie approached a door on the side of the building and tried opening it. "They have to be in there. Why would Kellerman and Demarco park outside the same warehouse? This has to be Allwood's lab." She made her way around back. "Besides, if you were doing classified research, would you really put a sign up advertising the fact?"

"Point taken," Orr said. As she headed toward the back of the building, he lit up her path. "Be careful. There's a lot of boxes and junk piled around here. I'm surprised the Base Commander doesn't crack down on it. If I were in charge—"

The back of the warehouse was even darker. None of the street lighting reached that far. She stumbled over a rock, nearly losing her balance. But there was another door back here.

"Hey, look, a keypad." This had to be the entry point. The side door didn't have such a lock. She smoothed her fingers over the keys. "We enter through here."

A ripple of fear ran through her. The quietness made her think the worst had already happened. What could they be walking into?

Orr flicked on his flashlight and lit up the keypad. "We don't know the code, and we don't have time to make guesses."

"Give me a minute. We might get lucky." Charlie went into code breaking mode. What number sequence would Allwood use? Maybe she could figure it out. She tried the year of his arrival: 1996. A red light lit up next to the numbered keys.

Nothing.

As she entered different codes, Orr tried the door, then ran his hands along the door jam, as if he could find a secret weakness to exploit. After a few minutes with no result, he grunted. Then he stepped back and examined the whole side of the warehouse.

Charlie was oblivious. She rooted around in her mind, running through the code possibilities. What about the letters on the keypad? Maybe Allwood used a word code instead of a number code.

"Waste of time, Petty Officer." Orr's voice sounded far away.

She waved him off and continued trying codes: numbers, letters, number and letter combos.

Wait, what about the obvious? RISA.

Suddenly, she heard the roar of an engine. The old truck drove up alongside the building, made a big U-turn, and positioned itself behind her. The solid front of the truck faced the wall of the warehouse.

What was he doing?

She turned, and the blast of light from the headlights nearly blinded her. She held up her arm in front of her eyes.

He leaned his head out the window. She could barely make out his silhouette. "Move!" He waved a hand.

The engine revved.

God, he was going to ram it.

Her heart seized. She scrambled away from the keypad, the door, and the building.

No way to sneak up on Allwood and Demarco now.

Once Charlie moved out of the path, the commander let off the brake. The truck barreled toward the rusty warehouse. Repurposed Vietnam War era warehouses might seem indestructible, but both of them were about to find out if that was true.

As the front end of the truck crashed into the door, the wall caved in around it. A godawful screeching coupled with a loud boom echoed into the desert surrounding the base.

CHAPTER 26

BYRON ALLWOOD SMASHED the glass beaker across Demarco's brow.

The bastard.

Pain exploded behind his eyes. Warm, wet blood ran like a stream down his face. Head wounds always were a mess of blood. He touched his forehead.

Shit.

A tiny tremor of fear swept through him.

Allwood had tricked him into believing he was weak and losing strength by the minute. Somehow the old beast was tougher than he'd thought. Maybe a result of his DNA experiments?

Before the special agent could act, the professor followed up his surprise attack with a slash to Demarco's neck using a sliver of broken glass.

Heat seared across his throat. He clutched at the new wound and backed up a few steps into a wall of plastic sheeting.

The older man limped forward, his face a mask of fury. "You destroyed everything in my old life. I'm not going to let you do it again." He gripped the broken glass so hard, blood dripped from his good hand. "You are too stupid to understand, too pathetic to see what could be. We'll end up right back where we started if nobody tries to change things, tries to make humans better than the animals they are now." He slashed the air.

Demarco pressed up against the sheeting, feeling behind him for an escape route or something he could use as a weapon. Blood dripped steadily into his right eye, blinding him. He wiped at his head wound with the back of his arm. "How would we know what to change in this time, Allwood?" The man believed he could alter the future? What madness was this? "We don't even know when the *Zhadang* happened or if it even happened. Everything we learned as children was built off of long ago memories. We don't know if it's true."

Allwood's eyes snapped in the dim lighting. "We could see the ruin all around us. The shells of buildings and technology that surpassed what I have in this very warehouse. What could I achieve with the better brain I've created, the stronger body, and with Risa by my side—" He let out a strangled cry and lunged at Demarco.

This time, the older man didn't catch him off guard. Demarco bent his head down, let out an animalistic growl, and rushed at Allwood, butting him in the gut. Adrenaline surged through him so, at first, he didn't feel the second slice of the glass across his scalp.

The two tumbled to the ground together. Allwood let out an agonizing yelp when he landed on his broken arm.

Demarco grabbed hold of Allwood's wrist and banged his hand on the concrete floor, forcing the piece of glass out of his grasp. Then he pressed a knee into the professor's chest using his full weight. He didn't care if Allwood suffocated.

The professor spat in his face. "Not every community did as well as yours. Some of us starved. Some of us watched our friends die, our brothers and sisters, our parents. And nobody cared. Nobody came to make sure we had enough to eat, enough wood to heat our homes. By spring, we were left to raise ourselves...the children who'd made it. Buried our dead who'd been left in the barn all winter, chewed by rats and God know what other creatures." He gasped for air. "Do you know what a body looks like after its been nibbled on for months? What parts do you think a rat likes best? The soft parts—the eyes, the lips, the face. You think I should've left well enough alone? Look around you." With his bloody hand he gestured at the lab. "The technology we have. The ease of living. All the things our families should have had. But no, some stupid idiotic fools hundreds of years before we were born ruined it all. Destroyed everything. With no thought or care about those of us who came after. I'm not going to let that happen again."

"Shut up." Demarco leaned into his face. "I don't want to hear your excuses. Are you trying to make me feel sorry for you? You aren't the only one who suffered loss, who saw horrible things, who walks around every day with memories he tries to forget, tries to put behind him, tries to pretend never happened."

But the man's words did affect him. They dredged up hard winters, summers with too much rain and devastated crops, serious illness and horrible deaths. Things people living in the twenty-first century couldn't even fathom.

"Yet you hate that I wanted to find a way to change that misery? People joined the Genesis Project because they were begging for a better life—begging *me*."

Demarco stared at the older man and blinked. He released a small amount of pressure on Allwood's chest.

Everything he'd thought about Allwood's followers changed in that instant. They were people who'd wanted something better, something more. He'd lumped them into one pile: the enemy. Because they were different than he was. Because they hoped for an escape from the difficult lives they'd led in the aftermath of a long-ago war. As he thought about the wonders around him: electric lights, automatic heating and cooling, even the clothing on his back—the way he'd grown up had been a struggle every day.

Could he blame people for wanting to make a change? Could he blame them for trusting the wrong person?

An explosion of sound broke them apart—a screeching, deafening roar. The walls around them shuddered, and Demarco thought the ceiling high above would collapse on top of them, bury them, and end everything.

He closed his eyes and waited.

———

Charlie's breath caught in her throat. She scanned the devastation left behind in the truck's wake. The wall around the door had bent and then caved as if a boulder had smashed into it. Hard to believe an old pickup could do so much damage. As she stepped through the ruins, twisted metal, pink insulation, and live electric wiring blocked her path.

"Be careful." The commander pushed open the truck's driver's side door, which was blocked by the mangled door frame, and squeezed his body through the opening. "Let me grab the flashlight."

The wiring sparked. She sidestepped it.

A set of stairs led up to a second floor, but debris littered the bottom few steps making passage difficult. Charlie picked her way through it. Spying a broken two-by-four that had once framed the door, she grabbed it. At least she had some kind of weapon. Nothing in Boot Camp had prepped her for this. She knew about gas masks, water tightness, even how to fight a fire on board a ship —but what if she had to engage in hand-to-hand combat? Her legs trembled beneath her.

The commander appeared with the flashlight in one hand and a crowbar in the other. "Come on, we only have a few minutes to take advantage."

"Advantage?"

"I'll bet they weren't expecting a truck to drive through the wall."

Charlie nodded. The upstairs appeared dark, but down the hall a faint glow under a set of double doors caught her attention. "This way, sir!"

They burst through the doors into a massive space full of plastic sheeting creating dozens of individual enclosed spaces.

Where was Angel? Kellerman? Allwood?

The massive impact had knocked over some of the temporary walls, exposing lab equipment, computers, and greenish blobs of all shapes and sizes encased in glass. Some of them had fallen and broken open, a familiar green ooze spilling onto the concrete floors.

Movement caught her eye. Two men grappled on the floor.

Angel, blood dripping from a head wound, had his hands around Allwood's throat. The older man's face was turning blue.

She rushed the men and raised her weapon. "Stop it, Angel! Let him go!"

Angel stiffened, looked up, and gave her a hardened glare, a look she'd never seen in his eyes before.

He knew.

He knew she was Allwood's child.

Angel's words resounded in her head: *Any child of Allwood's would be an abomination.*

Although she tightened her grip on the wood, she took a step back. A splinter pressed into her palm.

"Demarco," Orr said, "it's over. Don't make this worse on yourself."

Allwood took advantage of the distraction and the loosened grip around his throat and scrambled away, putting distance between him and his captor.

Angel sat back on his heels and let his arms fall to his sides. "Kellerman's dead."

A wave of shock ripped through her. "My God." She lowered her makeshift weapon. "Did you—?" Her gaze locked with Angel's. She couldn't say the words. Had he lost control? Was Kellerman his first victim and Allwood his next?"

His brow wrinkled. "No, of course not. Do you really think I would? That I'd be capable of—?" He looked down at his hands that had been at Allwood's throat only moments earlier. Color rose in his cheeks. "You don't understand: he attacked me."

"Professor," the commander asked, "are you all right? Do you need medical assistance?"

Allwood had scooted away from Angel until his back had hit a cabinet. "Keep him away from me." He touched his throat. The odd position of one arm indicated a serious break.

"Kellerman died in a pod that lunatic built." Angel pointed at the older man. "He's trying to rebuild the machines. God knows what he planned on doing with them. We have to destroy this place and everything in it."

Charlie looked more closely at the equipment around her, the mini-orbs of green, some still encased in their protective glass, others spilled on the floor.

She picked up an unbroken glass container with a perfect round blob inside it. "Are there more full-size pods?"

Orr, Angel, and Charlie turned to look at Allwood.

Distant sirens sounded.

"They'll be here soon," Allwood said in strained voice. He struggled to his feet. "Who do you think they'll protect?" A cold smile spread across his pale face.

"Why, you son of bitch," Angel growled and stepped forward.

Orr grabbed him by the arm. "We've made enough of a mess as it is." The lights flickered as if to emphasize his statement. He scanned the length of the massive space. "There's a lot of money in this room. The last thing we want to do it piss off the wrong people."

"Sir," Charlie positioned herself between her estranged father and her teammates, "we are the only ones who understand the implications of this kind of research. Think about what might happen if the military could create workable pods."

"But you know what will happen, don't you, Charlie?" Allwood turned his odd eyes on her. "Base security will show up, arrest the three of you, and my work will continue. The commander knows he's in over his head. If you help me complete the formula, I'll say you're my assistant and that these two were the instigators. We could work together—father and daughter."

Orr shifted his focus to Charlie.

"Shut up!" Demarco hissed between clenched teeth. "Leave her out of this." He struggled to pull out of the commander's firm grasp, but his injuries had weakened him.

If Angel hadn't figured out her parentage yet, he knew everything now. She swallowed her fear. "I don't want any part of this. I don't care who you are."

The sirens grew louder.

"They're almost here. Last chance, Charlie. You could continue your work on the translations. Didn't it feel right using that magnificent mind for something so impossible? A challenge where no one else had succeeded? I understand that desire."

"You don't know anything about me. You abandoned my mother and left her to raise me and my brother alone." The chunk of wood rested heavily in her hands. She'd never been a violent person, but Allwood was pushing her to her limits. "You don't care about me. You don't care about my mind. You only care about your obsessive need to be better than human, to be smarter than everyone else."

A laugh sputtered from his thin lips. "I understand you well enough to know you want to use your intelligence. You crave finding a puzzle worth solving, a mystery worth uncovering. Real work. Real achievement. Real discovery. I made you that way, Charlie. I created you, whether or like it or not."

"Stop it. You didn't make me." But deep inside she had doubts. Deep inside she worried about what ran through her bloodstream. Was she normal? Was she a freak? Is that why she felt as if she never fit in? Too smart, too fast, too everything. The only one who'd understood had been her brother. He hadn't struggled with the differences as much as she.

"You bastard," Angel spat out. "Let me throttle him." He managed to break free of Orr's grip and lunged at the professor.

"Demarco, stop!" Orr commanded and raised the crowbar he held.

The special agent tackled Allwood, and they landed in a heap.

The faint smell of smoke hovered in the air.

The electrical wiring that sparked earlier must have set off a blaze.

"Shit. A fire will rip through this place," Orr said. "We don't have much time."

The two injured men grappled on the floor.

"Angel, please!" Charlie held the two-by-four in her hands. She didn't want to hurt anyone, but if she had to, she would. "We have to go."

Orr dropped the crowbar, grabbed Allwood by his good arm, and hauled him up and away from Demarco. "This ends now. The fire will be our cover."

The smoke grew thicker.

"What about Allwood?" The special agent, disheveled and

bloody, spat on the floor. "He murdered someone. We can't let him get away with it—and we can't let the experiments here continue."

"Agreed." Orr's gaze flicked from Demarco to Allwood. "Security will be here any minute. What do you suggest we do?"

The lights flickered out and plunged the warehouse into darkness.

CHAPTER 27

A FEW DIM emergency lights kicked on.

Orr snapped on his flashlight and bounced the thin beam of light off the plastic sheeting around them.

"I think we take him with us," Charlie said, "and hope the fire destroys everything. Without Allwood or Kellerman, that should slow down their research."

"Slow it down?" Angel's nostrils flared. "No, it has to end." With a grunt, he swept his arm across a stainless steel table covered in organic samples and knocked them all to the floor. Shards of glass and goo flew in all directions. Then he ripped through the next plastic partition like a bull through a matador's cape and dumped over another table. "I won't have them hurting anyone else." He shoved a chair out of his way and proceeded to the next space.

"He's lost his mind," said the professor as Orr made sure he stayed put.

Charlie chased after him. "Angel, wait!"

"Kellerman died in one of those machines. He'll convince someone else it's safe, toss them in a pod, watch them die. How many times is he allowed to do that before someone stops him? What about the possibility of using the pods? What would the military change if they got the chance? That sort of power is too dangerous."

"What happened to Kellerman was horrible." Charlie shivered at the image that popped into her mind. He didn't deserve that. "But if we're caught here, we'll end up in prison. What we've seen tonight must be protected behind a slew of special access requirements. They'll never let us out or we might reveal their secrets."

Angel's eyebrows came together. "At least Kellerman managed to erase any trace of their work from the computer systems."

"What?"

"Kellerman might be a traitor, but he managed to set off some sort of automated self-destruct. Allwood tried to stop it, but I don't think he succeeded. They should be operating on an intranet like we do back at the office, right?"

Charlie nodded. Even though Angel hated tech, he'd learned a few things at least. "So no data storage outside of this building." She scanned the dimly lit space around them. "The only bits of formula they have left are the samples in this room?"

"Right." Angel breathed heavily and wiped at the blood still dripping down his forehead.

"Hey, I have an idea." Orr played his flashlight across the wall next to another exit door blocked with some high shelves covered in cardboard boxes.

"What is it?" Charlie eyed Angel. Would he be able to contain his rage and wait until they could make a coherent plan? "Security will be here any minute." She coughed.

The smoke grew thicker.

The commander had forced the professor to walk to the wall he'd lit up. "It's a deluge system. Not very common, but makes sense in a space this size."

"Deluge system?" Charlie asked.

"The sprinklers above us. Instead of a fire sprinkler being set off individually due to heat, a deluge system releases water all at once from every sprinkler simultaneously." He tapped a fire alarm next to a complex system of pipes. "Only have to pull this."

"But that will put out the fire," Angel said. "We want this place to burn."

"With this kind of system, there's no way the place will burn down. Eventually, the conditions in the building will set it off automatically," Orr pointed out. "But the problem isn't the building, it's the organic materials they're trying to recreate."

"Yes." Angel's body straightened.

"The organic materials dissolve in water." Charlie picked up on the commander's thinking. They'd seen it several times already—a pod landed in the water and then liquefied into nothing within minutes. "I think you have something there, sir."

"Without the computer data, plus making sure we dissolve all the samples—it would make it impossible for research to go forward. Especially with Allwood gone."

"Gone?" The professor jerked his head. "Where am I going?"

"You're coming with us to Nellis," explained Orr. "We have an extra seat for you on the flight back to DC."

"You can't do that to me." The older man attempted to wrench free of Orr's grasp. "I'll call the senator. She'll put a stop to this."

"Who said you get a phone call?" Angel gave a wicked smile barely visible in the low light.

The sirens grew even closer.

"Sir, we have to work fast before it's too late." Charlie lifted her head to look across the rows of temporary walls. Could they finish in time?

"I'll take care of this one first," Orr lifted slightly on the professors twisted arm. "You two start smashing and dumping."

Angel and Charlie looked at each other. He gave her a wavering smile. For now they trusted each other. But after it was all over? What would he do to the daughter of his enemy?

A chill ran through her.

———

Angel and Charlie each selected a row of cells to tackle and methodically smashed beakers and containers in each one. Any green goo had to be exposed. Mini refrigerators were overturned and contents spilled onto the concrete floor.

Charlie used her chunk of wood to sweep across counters and tables. Using brute force, Angel overturned everything in sight.

The floor was awash with broken glass and clumps of the experimental pod material.

The smoke in the space grew thicker. The sprinklers would go off any moment.

Orr quickly secured Allwood with an extension cord and muzzled him with some duct tape, then grabbed a large garbage can at the end of one of the rows. "Put any slides in here. A can full of water should ruin them."

Charlie scooped up two trays of glass slides sitting next to a microscope and discarded them into the container. Angel passed her with a stack of trays to do the same.

Orr dragged the can to the middle of the space and joined them in tearing the place apart.

The sirens intensified.

"Faster," the commander said. "We don't have much time."

The three of them scrambled.

Angel threw more trays of slides into the can. "Done."

The build-up of smoke finally set off the deluge system. No need to pull the alarm. Every sprinkler head in the massive warehouse turned on simultaneously. Sheets of water poured into the space.

Charlie jumped when the cold water hit her skin and dropped the two-by-four. She still had several trays full of samples to expose. "Angel, help me."

The special agent rushed to her aid and burst through the sheeting behind her to reach the last of the organic samples and mini-pods.

Through the high windows, red flashing lights bounced off the ceiling.

"They're here." Orr trotted toward their captive. "We have to leave. Now."

"Give me a second." Angel kicked over the last refrigerator, and the remaining samples spilled out. Water from the sprinklers melted the experimental substance into a greenish watery mess, which drained into a grate near the center of the space.

"It's working." Charlie swept an arm across her brow to clear her vision and watch as the organic materials turned into liquid.

"This way!" Orr held Allwood by the cord that entrapped him. He headed in the direction of an emergency exit on the side of the building.

Charlie and Angel stared at one another. The force of the water rained down on them.

"Are you coming with us?" she asked. Would he want to be part of their team, or would he balk at associating with Allwood's daughter?

His face was unreadable. Her mind flicked back to his attitude in Devils Lake—although he'd been part of NCIS-A, he'd been operating alone and with his own agenda. No wonder he'd kept to himself and had a standoffish demeanor. Now she and Orr had showed up at the lab and had ruined his plans.

"Let's go." Angel grabbed her by the elbow and helped her across the slick concrete floors toward the exit through which Orr had already disappeared.

His touch on her arm was comforting. She wanted to believe he'd changed and that he understood her connection to Allwood was not her fault. But maybe this sudden decision to work with her and Orr was merely about his own escape, his own survival.

They burst through the exit doors.

Charlie shivered in the cool desert air, her wet clothes clammy against her skin.

The emergency vehicles had pulled around back where the smoke and flames had probably been most visible. They only had mere moments to act before they'd be discovered.

"Your keys," the commander held out a hand. "Give them to me."

Angel lifted his chin. "If I can be in charge of Allwood."

Orr scanned the professor. His shoulders were rounded, his head hung low. "Fine. He shouldn't be much trouble now."

Angel handed Orr the keys to the stolen SUV, and the commander shoved the professor in his direction.

They crept around to the front of the warehouse. A murmur of voices drifted toward them from the crash site at the back. More help might show up any minute.

Orr pressed a button and unlocked the vehicle. Angel shoved

Allwood into the back seat, quietly shut the door, and then opened the hatchback.

Charlie's brow wrinkled.

The commander was more interested in leaving the scene without being noticed, rather than paying attention to Angel.

The special agent closed the hatchback and handed Charlie a plaid picnic blanket. "You look cold. Maybe this will help."

She accepted the blanket without a word. Angel climbed into the back with the professor. As she took the front passenger seat, she wrapped the musty-smelling fabric around her shoulders. Maybe he didn't hate her after all?

Orr started the car, backed out slowly, and drove away from the warehouse without any headlights. As they neared the base entrance, the commander turned them on, but also made a phone call. "We'll be ready for wheels up in three hours," he said to someone on the other end.

The guard who'd let them onto base must've recognized the SUV as Allwood's because he opened the gate before they even arrived.

As the gate shut behind them, Orr, Demarco, Charlie, and Allwood sped for the highway.

AS THEIR PLANE took off from Nellis Air Force Base, Charlie stared at the seat Kellerman had occupied when they'd arrived. Although she knew he was dead, she had trouble processing it. She'd spent many long hours working with him, talking to him, getting to know him. It would be difficult knowing his family would never hear the true story of his death. How horrible.

Commander Orr approached her holding two steaming Styrofoam cups. "You look as if you could use a warm drink."

She accepted the coffee, and the picnic blanket slipped off one shoulder. "Thank you."

Orr shifted his gaze to the back of the plane where the special agent, his wounds now bandaged, sat next to the restrained professor. "I'm not sure I can trust him with Allwood, but what choice do I have? It's a long flight back to Andrews. We need an eye on that guy until we decide what to do with him."

"What are we going to do? With his lab destroyed, he's the only one with any information about how to create more machines. People are going to start looking for him."

"I know." He sipped his coffee. "But until we read the reporting on the fire at the lab, we have to keep our heads down."

"The guards know we were there. Won't someone start asking questions?"

"Let me worry about that, Cutter." Orr's friendly, relaxed

demeanor shifted into serious commanding officer mode. "I don't know about you, but it's been a long and confusing day."

Her gut clenched. In the lab, she'd spilled the truth about her background. Now both Angel and Orr knew everything. What would happen to her?

"Don't worry, Petty Officer." It was as if the commander read her mind. "Your secret is safe with me. You and your brother will have nothing to worry about."

"But the DNA—"

"I'll take care of it," he said.

"I don't understand how that's possible."

"Dr. Stern has a very good relationship with the head of the lab at NSA. They're used to providing classified results to a host of federal customers." He tapped a finger on the side of his cup. "Besides, they don't really know why we were processing these samples. At this point, we can ask for them to be destroyed."

"True." If the DNA results went no further than the NCIS-A office, shouldn't that be the end of it? "But Demarco—"

She looked over her shoulder. Angel's penetrating gaze met hers. She shivered and turned around.

"I'll speak to him."

Did the commander understand the pure hatred Angel felt, not only for Allwood, but for all of his followers? Even his own sister? She didn't trust him. He could decide to turn on her at any moment to rid himself and the world of an 'abomination.' What about Chad? Would he ever be safe from Angel's wrath?

"I don't know if that will be enough." Orr was seriously underestimating the depths of Angel's feelings. She'd seen them first-hand. The fire in his eye when he spoke of members of the Genesis Project altering their DNA still shook her to her core.

"Drink your coffee, get some sleep, and we can all talk about this tomorrow at the office." Orr patted her arm.

When he moved to rise from his seat, she grabbed his sleeve. "Don't leave me alone."

His brow wrinkled. "Today really shook you up, huh?"

"Why don't you look at me differently after finding out I'm Allwood's daughter?"

"Why should that matter to me?" He angled his body to face her. "It did shock me to hear it, and it took a little bit of brain power to understand how that was possible, but the minute I began believing in time traveling pods, it wasn't too hard to come around to it." He shrugged. "If your connection to Allwood is what helped you translate the manuscript, I'm glad you're here working for the good guys."

She nodded. "I don't want anyone on the team to look at me differently or treat me differently. Nothing has changed. I'm still Charlene Cutter."

"That's exactly who I still need on this team. You're an excellent asset to the group. I'd be crazy to let you go."

"Thank you, sir." A sudden lightness filled her. "I don't want to work anywhere else."

Orr flashed a smile. "Good."

DEMARCO WATCHED as Orr and Charlie chatted. Inside he was a writhing mass of conflicting emotions. After today, where did he belong? He'd reached his years-long goal: finding the man who'd stolen his sister and destroyed his life. Now what?

The knowledge to build the machines no longer existed except in the pages of a manuscript only Charlie seemed able to translate and the mind of the man seated next to him. Demarco was stuck. A man between lives, between times. A stranger here, yet not a stranger. He'd never return home, and he'd never travel to his sister. He wiped the grit from his eyes. Any trust he'd built with the team had been irrevocably destroyed by his actions. What would happen to him once they landed?

"I'm thirsty," Allwood said.

The older man didn't look good—broken, bleeding, weak. It was as if the battle they'd fought in the warehouse had used up the last of his energy.

"I suppose I could give you some water." Demarco tested the plastic restraints the commander had used once they'd made it to the plane. They seemed solid enough. Besides, where could the man go? They were flying tens of thousands of feet in the air.

He rose from his seat and worked his way forward to grab a bottle of water. As he neared the row where Charlie sat, he felt her eyes on him. It pained him to think about her connection to

Allwood. How could such a terrible man produce such an exceptional daughter? Everything he'd told her about how he viewed the followers of the Genesis Project and his feelings toward Armas came to the surface. He fisted his hands. She must hate him.

He grabbed two bottles and headed toward the back of the plane, keeping his gaze unfocused. His work with A Group was probably over. He'd never have to see her again after today. That might make things easier. He could forget. He could go back to the life he'd lived before she came, before he'd managed to lie his way into a job. The lonely, distant life of a man without a past or a future.

When he reached Allwood, he held out the bottle. "Here."

The professor sat slumped in his seat.

Demarco frowned. "Wake up." He prodded the man's good arm with the cold water bottle.

Nothing.

Was he breathing?

"Shit." He grabbed a wrist and felt for a pulse. "Sir, I think we have a medical emergency here."

The thought of losing the one person besides himself who cared about and remembered Risa, hit him hard. Even though Allwood was a murderer, a mad scientist, and a charismatic liar who harmed people and ruined lives, it perturbed him to think he'd no longer exist. Maybe he wanted justice, maybe he wanted vengeance, or maybe something else entirely. But watching Allwood slip away didn't seem fair.

He dragged the man to the floor and began chest compressions.

The professor's eyes were partially open. Demarco shivered at the emptiness in them.

Orr appeared at his side. He didn't know if Charlie was there, too, but what did it matter?

"What did you do?" the commander asked.

"Nothing. I swear to you." He continued to press against the thin man's chest. "He asked for some water, and then when I came back—"

Charlie knelt next to Allwood and picked up a limp wrist. "He doesn't have a pulse."

As Demarco looked down at the man he'd hated, his vision blurred and a heaviness settled in him. "No." Who would he talk to about Risa? Who would understand what it felt like to be transported to a time with nothing and no one familiar?

"He's dead, Angel." Charlie touched his shoulder. "It's too late."

"No." He slowed his rhythmic movements, knowing what she said was true, but not wanting it to be real. "He can't die." He needed this man. He needed someone to hate, someone to blame. Someone who understood.

"It's over."

His shoulders slumped.

"There's nothing else we can do," the commander said.

Demarco grabbed his unopened bottle, grunted, and hurled it at the bulkhead. It exploded in a shower of water.

———

The last few hours of the trip had gone by in silence. Charlie had assumed Angel would be pleased with Allwood's death. But his violent reaction when he threw the water bottle had surprised her. After that, Angel seemed distracted and isolated himself in the last row of seats. The commander had put himself in charge of the body, wrapping it in a tarp that he'd found stowed in one of the cargo nets and dragging it out of the aisle to lay next to the body bag of his follower. Charlie had returned to her precious manuscript translations because it was easier to lose herself in the mysterious symbols rather than assess her feelings about what had happened.

Maybe she was numb to it. Maybe too much had happened too quickly, and now she was in shock. It was hard to know. Byron Allwood was her father, and both he and Kellerman were dead. That was more than enough to jolt the system.

That fact hit her hard: the man she'd always thought of as her father was not.

She reassessed her relationship with Harrison Cutter—the man who had given her her name. He'd taken on a woman pregnant with another man's children, which gave Charlie an entirely different perspective on him. The clashes she'd had with him over the years seemed clearer to her now—the two of them were different, and he knew it. He knew there was no DNA connecting him to her or to Chad. Anything a parent might be proud of would be seen through that lens. Someone else's child. Someone else's blood. Someone else's joy. Not his.

No wonder her mother had been so defensive of her father's actions over the years. "But he loves you, Charlie," she would always say. "He only wants what's best for you." At the time it had come across as so typical 'dad,' to be overprotective and controlling to the point of irritation. But maybe he had been so protective because he knew the truth. And that truth would've been so damaging and hurtful once it was revealed—their real father had left them, hadn't wanted them, had actually hid himself away for more than twenty years to avoid his responsibilities. Her real father had been a selfish man who didn't care anything about the woman he'd hurt and left pregnant and alone.

What might have been if Byron Allwood would've lived? Her mind was empty of thought. She couldn't think of any situation where she'd insert Allwood into her life. In fact, every scenario she came up with, Harrison Cutter's face filled in. Because he'd been there her whole life. Yes, he drove her crazy. Yes, he could be overbearing and tough. Yes, he expected too much from her. But that was probably because he knew she had the talent to achieve more than she'd dreamed for herself.

What did it matter if the dead man in the plane had given her half her DNA? It meant nothing to her, really. She was Charlie Cutter, and she worked for NCIS-A. None of her achievements were Allwood's. Everything she'd accomplished, she'd done on her own with the support of Harrison Cutter.

Allwood was gone, his work destroyed, and he would never hurt anyone again—especially not her or her brother. No one beyond her team and her family would ever know the truth about her connection to Allwood. The commander had made clear it changed nothing about how he viewed her or her skills.

She focused on the iPad. The Voynich manuscript symbols leapt off the page at her. She'd found her true calling with her team. How satisfying it had been to feel supported, listened to, and respected, to know that her knowledge, skills, and interests were of value and had purpose.

The plane landed with a thud. They were home.

What would the next assignment be for A Group? Their main directive to pursue any evidence of alien life on earth had been turned upside down when they'd uncovered a time traveling secret that had lain hidden for centuries. Her body tingled at the achievement. But she needed something more. Something equally challenging, equally intriguing. Her mind craved the stimulation.

The commander strolled up to her seat. "So, Petty Officer Cutter, are you looking forward to being back in the office?" The awkward silence that had hung over the last few hours disappeared.

"Actually, I was thinking about Armas." Her half-brother needed her more than ever. "I'd like to visit him, if that's possible."

"We'll have to ask Dr. Stern. He's still very touch-and-go as I understand."

Charlie nodded. She wanted to stay positive about his recovery. He'd been through so much in his short life. "Then it will be good if I stay busy. I hope you have some new work for me." She said it in more of a teasing tone than anything. They'd have weeks of reports to catch up on regarding what happened in Lake Havasu, and it was still to be discussed if they'd report on what really happened in the warehouse.

"I might have something new up my sleeve," the commander answered mysteriously. "But I'd like to wait for Chief to make it back. The hospital left a message, and he's going to be released later today."

The plane taxied to a stop.

What did Commander Orr have in mind?

———

The small team stood together on the tarmac at Andrews Air Force Base. It was right before dawn, but the rising sun was hidden behind a morass of gray clouds. Only a muted glow told them it was sunrise.

"Dr. Stern is going to meet me here with a transport for the bodies. She'll do some tests and then we'll dispose of them," Orr said. "Word out of Area 51 this morning is that there was a lab accident that caused two deaths. Not sure if they'll bother digging to find out its only Kellerman's remains in the warehouse. Demarco, you said the body was quite damaged."

Angel nodded.

Orr acknowledged his affirmation with a sigh. "There's also a bit of frantic chatter in the intel community about a highly classified project having to be shuttered for the time being."

"Still hard to believe we were able to leave the scene without incident." Charlie thought about how easy it was to drive off into the desert while emergency services worked to stop what was left of the fire. "Are you sure they won't come looking for us?"

Even though Charlie had thought Angel had slept most of the flight home, the dark circles under his eyes told a different story. Would Orr be recommending him for disciplinary measures?

"My base access was tied to another Area 51 office, and the Commanding Officer at NSA Washington approved my request." Orr stood with legs apart and arms crossed. "If they want to take it up with Captain Schultz, they are more than welcome."

"So the truth remains safe behind TOP SECRET YARDARM privileged access only?" Charlie asked.

"Correct. The three of us will combine the details of last night into a report for cleared personnel only, which is quite a small circle," Orr said. "I'll give you two a few days to type something up, then I'll handle the final report."

"Will I still have access to the office?" Angel frowned.

Orr had to know what he was asking: was he in any trouble?

"Of course. You are a necessary part of our team. Especially now that we're down a man. Until we can find a replacement for Kellerman, I'm relying on everyone more than ever."

Angel nodded.

Charlie's stomach twisted. She had a small hope that Angel would be shuttled to a different office after his behavior, so she wouldn't have to see him again. It would be so much easier than having to worry about watching her back. What if Angel turned on her?

Orr changed the subject, "On that note, can you give Petty Officer Cutter a ride back to her room?"

She broke out in a cold sweat.

"Of course, sir." Angel wouldn't look at her.

Charlie opened her mouth to argue, then stopped. What good would it do?

"We'll have a team meeting tomorrow in the office," Orr said. "0730 sharp."

"Yes, sir," she said. Would Orr share everything with the team? Even the most secret of truths?

When the commander headed back up the ramp into the plane, the two of them stared at each other for a few moments. Orr wouldn't send her off with Angel if he thought she would be in danger, would he?

"I'm parked in this direction." Angel pointed using his hand as a directional arrow.

As she followed behind him, her mind was a whirlwind of questions, worries, fears. "Why?" It was the one question that stuck in her mind. "Why did you do it, Angel?"

"I had to." He kept walking with his gaze focused straight in front of him. "Allwood was the only thing that kept me going in this time for many years. Without that motivation, I wouldn't have survived, Charlie."

He spoke her name with a gentleness that surprised her.

She mulled over his answer and willed her heart to slow down.

They reached his Landcruiser, and he unlocked the passenger's side first, opening the door for her. Her stomach fluttered. Why was he being so kind? He hated her father and by extension should hate her.

When he joined her inside the vehicle, he didn't start the engine right away.

Charlie took the opportunity to press him. "Why didn't you explain your fears to Commander Orr? Why did you feel the need to strike out on your own, steal someone's car, take Allwood hostage—"

"And abandon you." Angel gripped the steering wheel. "I'm sorry I left you after the accident, Charlie. I wasn't in my right mind. I had to stop him. Orr would've made me follow the rules, call the authorities, agree to whatever BS the military would do to cover up what they'd been working on. I couldn't let that happen. I couldn't let Allwood get away with it. He was evil, Charlie."

The tiny hairs lifted on the back of her neck. "Which means you think I'm evil, too."

"What?" His posture became rigid.

"I'm his daughter. You must hate me." Her hands shook. She clasped them in her lap so he wouldn't notice.

"Before I met you, I never would've thought this world held anything I'd value. I thought I'd lost everything that mattered. But you proved me wrong, Charlie. There was something in this world that I cherish more than anything else." He turned in her direction, and his eyes searched hers. "Why did you think—?"

Using all the courage she could muster, she met his dark gaze. "I'm tainted, I'm an abomination." But a tiny little piece of her wanted to believe him.

"I was wrong." Tentatively, he touched her arm. "Everything I said was wrong. I understand that now."

"How can I believe you?" She thought back to the moment she'd seen past his rigid exterior and saw the hurt man behind it. Had that ever been real? Who was Angel Demarco? "Am I supposed to forget what you told me?"

"The information we uncovered yesterday exposed Allwood's true feelings toward his followers. My God, he even killed one of them. Those poor people were charmed by that charlatan. He experimented on them as a means of further refining his techniques before he tried the genetic manipulation on himself. It was always about how his followers could benefit him. Even my sister —he used her for her knowledge of plants and organic chemistry to build the time traveling machines. He never intended to take these people with him. I think he merely used them to disappear—one time traveling pod stands out. But a whole host of them landing at once? It was a good cover for someone who never wanted to be found again. It was wrong of me to blame his victims for what he did to them. You were one of them. But what's even worse is you had no choice in the matter." He cupped her cheek in his hand.

Her eyes filled with tears. "And my brother? And Armas? What about them?"

"All I know, is that I can't imagine life without you. I love you, Charlie."

Her pulse raced as he leaned in.

"And if loving you means I have to let go of some of my beliefs and acknowledge some of my wrongheaded thinking, then that's what I have to do." He brushed a strand of hair from her eyes. "I can't go back to the life I had before. I need you."

CHAPTER 30

TWENTY-FOUR HOURS LATER, Charlie, Angel, Stormy, Dr. Stern, and Chief Ricard sat around the conference table in their office, while Commander Orr stood behind the podium. A strange current ran through the room with the notable absence of Kellerman. As each one entered and sat in their usual seats—Kellerman's spot remained empty. Yes, he'd been part of their team, but once Orr explained to everyone what happened on their trip out West and how he'd died, the odd sensation dissipated some. They hadn't really known Kellerman as well as they'd thought.

"I gathered us here this morning to discuss my plans for NCIS-A going forward. I will need each of your expertise to bring this plan to fruition. I presented my idea to the Commanding Officer for NSA Washington, and he signed off on it late yesterday. He was briefed on our mission, and is in full support of this next phase."

"Next phase?" Charlie asked.

Those seated around the table gave each other confused looks.

"Stormy, can you turn off the lights, please?"

The lights dimmed, and the commander projected a slide on the screen. "As we learned on the flight to Nellis, Chief and Kellerman were able to identify dozens of radar signals over the last twenty-five years or so that indicate a pod landing." A world map appeared with a number of different colored dots sprinkled across it. "The yellow dots you see are recent radar signatures captured in the last five years. The red, blue, and green dots are all from older time periods as you can see here." He used a laser pointer to draw attention to a key in the bottom right-hand corner that lined up the different colored dots with different years, going all the way back to 1996—Allwood's arrival.

He clicked to the next slide. "The first part of our initiative will be tracking down these pod landings. We will start from the most recent and work our way backward. The goal will be to find out if there are any survivors. Just like Byron Allwood, Armas, and the woman in the hospital at Lake Havasu, not all pod landings result in the traveler's death. Stormy and Chief will team up on this task. Chief has been studying these signatures for a while now, so he is the most familiar with the locations and the possibility for survival. Petty Officer Storm has a knack for data tracking and, let's face it, she has a kind face. I think witnesses will trust her more easily than some of the rest of us."

Charlie smiled to herself, thinking about the first day she met Angel and what she thought of him.

"What's the second part of our initiative?" Angel asked.

He'd shared with Charlie his nervousness about the meeting. He didn't believe yet that the commander had fully forgiven him for some of his actions in Nevada. In fact, he still expected to lose his clearance and his job, and maybe even face charges.

"I'm glad you asked, Demarco. This second part wouldn't work without you." Orr clicked to another slide that read: *Greeting Committee.*

"What does that mean?" Charlie asked.

"We are expecting more arrivals. We aren't sure how many pods were created—I'm hoping we can use the data in Byron Allwood's phone, recovered by Petty Officer Cutter, to find out more—but because we had three pods land in the last month, more could arrive any day. We need to welcome these people, provide for them, explain where they are and what has happened. Rather than our original mission of hunting down aliens, we are searching for humans who have been lost to time. This will be a humanitarian mission. I'd like Petty Officer Cutter and Special Agent Demarco to head the committee."

"Why did you say the second initiative wouldn't work without Demarco?" Chief asked.

Everyone turned their attention to Angel.

"I don't mean to put you on the spot, Demarco," Orr said, "but the fact is we need your help on this one. I think you should let the rest of the team know why."

Angel blanched.

Charlie hadn't been expecting that. Angel's secret could wreak havoc with the small amount of trust that remained between the team after Kellerman's betrayal.

Orr gave a quick nod. "It's okay, Demarco. They need to know. It will help them understand."

Chief Ricard focused a penetrating gaze at Demarco. He'd already learned the truth about the special agent in Lake Havasu and had been standoffish ever since he'd entered the conference room. Demarco had, after all, flipped the car that had caused him major injuries. Charlie wasn't sure how the chief truly felt about Angel after finding that out.

"What is it?" asked Stormy. "Why is everyone so quiet?"

Dr. Stern appeared thoughtful.

"It's okay." Charlie laid a hand on Angel's thigh. If he wanted to leave his past behind and accept this new life in a new time, he needed to know when to trust and share his connection to all of this.

Angel looked down at the table and rubbed his hands together. "I don't think I can be a part of this, sir."

The special agent avoided eye contact with everyone in the conference room. "I think it's a mistake for me to continue here. I appreciate the offer, Commander, but I don't think it would work out." He stood, slipped his lanyard and badge over his head, and set it on the table.

Dr. Stern frowned and reached a hand toward him as if she wanted to stop him.

Charlie's brow wrinkled. "Wait, Angel. We can take it slow." She looked to Orr. "Can't we, sir?"

Angel set his jaw. "Please don't, Charlie." He headed for the door. "I'll clean out my desk and go."

As he exited, Charlie scooted back in her chair and shot a glare at her superior. "You're asking too much of him."

Orr raised an eyebrow. "I gave him a pass on everything. I kept the authorities off his back. He owes this office an explanation, and it starts with the truth."

Chief Ricard's lips pressed flat.

Dr. Stern scanned the middle-aged enlisted man who sat across from her. "Don't even think it, Chief."

He held up his hands, palms out. "I didn't say a thing."

"You were thinking it," the doctor said. "You think you're so perfect?"

His mouth gaped open, then closed.

"What's going on?" Stormy asked. "I feel as if I need the Cliff-Notes." She looked to Dr. Stern.

"Isn't anyone going to stop him?" Charlie looked around the room at what remained of their team. "He might've made some mistakes, but he saved all of us. He stopped a madman from following through on his insane plans."

"Go after him, Charlie," said Dr. Stern.

She nodded and disappeared out the door.

CHAPTER 31

CHARLIE ROUNDED the end of the cubicles and headed straight for Angel's desk. "What do you think you're doing?"

He leaned over a banker's box he had already filled with his jacket and the few sparse personal belongings he'd allowed himself in the office: a single small African violet, a postcard of the Lincoln Memorial, and a visitor's guide to Washington D.C. "I'm cleaning out my desk. What does it look like I'm doing?"

"Everyone wants you to stay on the team."

"I'm not interested."

"Why? Is it because Orr wants you to tell everyone where you came from? Who you are?"

He straightened, leaned against his desk, and rubbed the back of his neck. "That's some of it. Look, I'm packed. I'm going. You can follow me if you want, but I'm not going to change my mind." He picked up his box and headed for the door.

Charlie followed. "What else is there to be afraid of? Everyone back in the conference room is ready to continue forward on our new mission, and once you explain your past, they'll understand why you did what you did. They'll forgive you."

They exited into the hall, which was quiet and empty of foot traffic.

He smirked and shook his head. "Right. They'll forgive me. Even Chief?"

She checked the hall in both directions. "They believe in time travelers now," she whispered. "That would've been the biggest hurdle to overcome."

A pair of men in fatigues walked purposefully toward them.

Charlie and Angel split apart to let them pass.

They both watched the men until they turned a corner and disappeared.

"It's not only the team I'm thinking about." Angel headed toward the elevator in the opposite direction. "I'm more than a time traveler, Charlie. There are things I've done. Things I'm not proud of."

"Haven't we all?" Why was he so scared to own up to his past? This was his 'get out of jail free' moment, and he was squandering it by worrying about how he'd be perceived. Who cared what any of them would think?

He stopped mid-stride. "You don't get it. It's not about telling the team about who I am, it's about things I've done. Things that would terrify you. You'd barely be able to look at me if you knew. Imagine if one of Allwood's followers steps out of a pod and sees me. What if they know who I am? Remember. Orr doesn't understand that, and you barely understand that." He pressed hard on the elevator call button.

"We'll greet them as a team. Show them things can be different in this time. We don't have to be enemies. This is your opportunity."

"And if they don't believe me?" He passed by her to enter the empty elevator.

She followed.

"They will learn to believe, Angel." She touched him on the arm. "I promise. I know you're a good man inside."

His eyes searched her face. "I'm only good when I'm with you."

The elevator doors closed, leaving them alone in the quiet. Only a few floors, and they'd reach their destination.

She met his gaze. "Then don't leave me. Because you are the one that helped me find my true calling, the reason I was born. I'm part of the future but also part of the past." A fluttery feeling intensified in her chest. "We can bridge the divide together."

CHAPTER 32

Six months later....

ANGEL DROVE his Landcruiser down a familiar road in Colchester, Virginia toward the Occoquan River. It was barely past dawn in late February, and a thin veneer of snow lay across everything. The Mid-Atlantic was headed for spring, so this would likely be one of the last snows of the season.

"Looks a lot different in the winter, doesn't it?" Charlie stared out the windshield and wished she'd dressed a little warmer, but she and Angel had been in bed at her new apartment when the alert came through—another pod landing at very familiar coordinates. No time to second-guess her outfit. A local landing was a godsend. She should be glad they didn't have to hop on a plane and fly to Portugal.

"Are you sure these are the right coordinates?" Angel asked.

"Yes." She showed him the yellow dot on her cell phone from the map Commander Orr had texted her. "You've asked me that three times already."

"It doesn't make any sense."

"Why? Chief showed us the map of all the landings they've tracked from the radar data. About sixty percent of them seem to be clustered around the Maryland-DC-Virginia area for some unknown reason. It makes sense we'd have another landing here."

Angel slowed down as Bell Avenue narrowed, and the woods closed in on them. It would open up soon to reveal the large mansion at the end of the road. The spot where they'd recovered Armas.

Charlie's heart twinged.

Armas.

Her half-brother.

It had taken weeks for him to come out of his drug-induced coma, but ultimately the anti-toxin treatment had worked. He still suffered from some muscle weakness, but Stormy made sure he consistently met with his physical therapist. After he'd been released from the hospital, Stormy had decided she and her husband would become his foster parents—there could be no official adoption, as he had no record of birth and no parents to sign away their rights. A special department that was assisting with their 'Welcome Committee' duties at the Social Security office, helped create documentation that would pass scrutiny once Armas became an adult.

Although Charlie felt a deep attachment to the boy, Stormy had the necessary family structure and support such a child would need to grow up and mature. Stormy's children had bonded with Italian-speaking Armas and had even begun to learn simple Italian phrases using a language learning app. Charlie's life and schedule would've been too erratic to take on such responsibilities, but she and Angel visited him whenever they could. The most shocking thing had been seeing Angel leap into the role of uncle full throttle. His love for his nephew grew each time they visited the Storm house. As time had passed, Armas had begun turning into a regular American boy—so little of his previous life existed in him except for an occasional Italian word or phrase. He was young and adaptable and happy—despite the horrors of his illness and the loss of his mother.

Angel parked the vehicle. "The radar tracking indicated the pod should be landing any minute. Any suggestions for recovery?"

They both stared out at the dark green river, knowing the water temperature was probably a lot colder than the last time Charlie swam out to rescue a time traveler.

"I can do it." Thank God the team had invested in some cold water gear—neoprene suits, dive masks, and even snorkels. She was the stronger swimmer of the two, but it would take time to don the suit and prep for a rescue, if necessary.

As they contemplated their next steps, they both witnessed a massive fireball burst through the low-hanging clouds and streak across the sky.

"Shit!" Angel scrambled outside without even putting on his coat.

The pod landed ten yards from shore in a massive explosion of water.

"I'll suit up," Charlie said, heading for the back of the Landcruiser. She grabbed a suit, stripped down to her underwear, and prepped for a swim.

Angel had scooped up a stack of blankets and was halfway to the brand new dock that had been built since their last trip here.

Although at first he'd been hesitant in his role as official 'greeter' to the couple of arrivals they'd met in the few months since their new mission began, the experience had proven quite positive. The startled look on people's faces as they exited the disintegrating pods was quickly replaced by fear when Charlie and Angel approached with towels, dry clothes, a bottle of water, and some food. He would launch into his short introduction about who he was, what time they were in, and how their team was there to help.

Orr had described it to Charlie and Angel like a witness protection program. "We are going to help travelers who are lost create a new identity, find a place to live, find a job, and make sure to connect them with other travelers."

She zipped up her suit and charged down the rugged slope to the beach. The pod door had already opened, and a figure was attempting to navigate her next steps with cold water lapping at the edge of the doorway.

"Wait!" Angel yelled at the person who emerged. "Let us help you."

The figure's head snapped up, as if suddenly aware she wasn't alone.

"Quick, I think I might've spooked her."

Charlie joined him at the end of the dock. "I'm on it." She dove into the water with a life vest and swam quickly to the sinking pod. The suit protected her well from the cold water, but when the freezing water hit her face, it reminded her of the risk she was taking. With powerful strokes, she reached the pod in no time. Her unusual strength and endurance, likely created in her DNA by Allwood, didn't bother her anymore. Instead, she relished the thought of being able to help people who'd been damaged by the same man with the skillset he'd created in her. A full circle of sorts.

A middle-aged woman wearing a roughly-made dress stood in the open doorway, her bare feet exposed to the cold water rushing into the pod. *"Dov'è sono? Chi sei?"* She had long brown hair threaded with gray and milky blue eyes full of fear. "Who are you?" As she clung to the edge of the doorway, the soft organic material broke off in her hand. She gasped.

"You don't have much time before it disintegrates." Charlie treaded water and handed her the orange life vest. "Put this on, and then I can help you to shore. My colleague is waiting for us."

The woman shifted her gaze to the dock where Angel stood with his hands in his pockets and his hair lifting in the breeze.

"We can reunite you with other travelers, if you'd like." Anything to coax the worried-looking woman out of the sinking pod. "Please, take the vest."

Her pale eyes snapped to life. "Others?"

"Yes."

The woman snatched the life vest and slipped it on. Charlie talked her through snapping the plastic buckles and tightening the straps. As the new arrival pulled the second strap tight, the pod heaved to one side causing her to fall into the water. She screamed.

Charlie swam for her, knowing the shock of the cold water must be terrible. The faster she could maneuver the woman to shore, the better. Angel had blankets waiting, then they could load her into the Landcruiser and blast the heat before they launched into their welcome message and the steps that would happen from there.

She grabbed hold of the inflated bladder that held the woman's head above water and managed to swim them both to the dock in record time. When they reached it, Angel lent a hand to help them both up the metal stairs at one end.

As the woman came out of the water, Angel gave an incredulous stare. "Risa?"

Charlie's brow wrinkled.

The woman scanned him from head to foot. "How can this be?" she asked in a shaky voice. "How can you be here? Am I dreaming?"

"Dearest sister!" Angel gathered her in his arms, unbothered by the cold water that dripped off of her, and hugged her hard.

"How is it possible?" Her whole body shook.

Charlie unfolded one of the wool army blankets Angel had brought from his vehicle and rested it across Risa's shoulders. "We need to move her into the Landcruiser. It's freezing out here."

Charlie had never seen Angel shed a single tear until now. After everything he'd been through, after the realization he may never see his sister again, after knowing he'd never be able to return to his time or see his family and loved ones—he'd never cried when he explained everything to her. But as he held his younger sister close, he bawled. Years of repressed emotions poured out of him—every fear, every sense of loss, every moment of loneliness he'd suffered.

When a few minutes had passed, and both brother and sister managed to gather themselves, Charlie asked, "Would you like to see Armas?"

Risa's eyes teared up for a second time. "He's here?" Before she could collapse to the wooden boards beneath her feet, Angel held her up. "My God, he made it?"

He gripped his sister tightly. "Yes." His eyes shone. "You named him after Dad?"

Risa met her brother's gaze and nodded.

"Will he even recognize me?" She touched her wet hair that

had turned mostly gray. "He was so small back then. So very very small."

"A boy will always remember his mother," Charlie said. "Come, let's take you somewhere warm and talk about your future with your son."

"My future." Risa pulled the blanket close around her body and smiled.

As Angel led his sister toward the road, Charlie held back. The sight of the two long-lost siblings walking together after having been separated by hundreds of years of time made her forget everything else. Who would have thought when she first joined NCIS-A all those months ago that she would end up in the most rewarding job a person could have—saving those lost in time and making a place for them? How many more travelers would they encounter in the coming years? Angel couldn't remember the number of pods he'd seen that day when he'd climbed inside one himself.

"Are you coming, Charlie?" Angel looked back at her. She'd never seen his face so relaxed, his body so loose. The weight of worry and guilt had been lifted.

She straightened her posture, and, in an unhurried fashion, walked to the end of the dock to join them. "Yes, I'm coming."

Behind her the last of the pod sank under the waves. Any evidence of Risa's arrival disappeared.

Onto the next rescue.

The End

Join K.J. Gillenwater's newsletter and receive a free science fiction short story

IF YOU LIKED THIS BOOK...
TRY READING 'AUTOMATED'

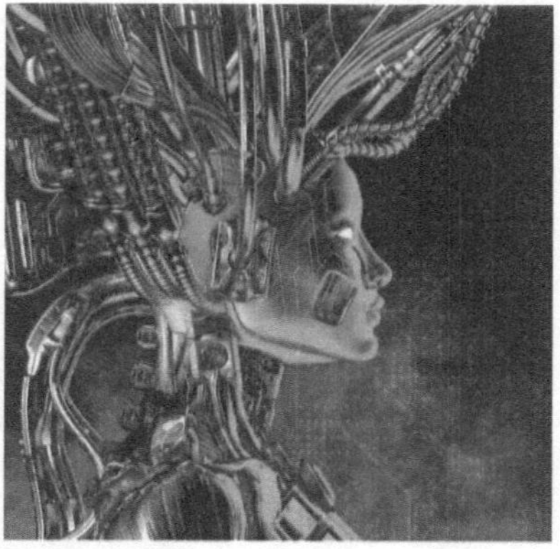

AUTOMATED: Available only in the U.S. Kindle Vella store!

When Eli visits Chicago in 2043, he is shocked to find his dead wife reborn as a robot. Replica humans are illegal to manufacture, so who would create such a thing and why? As he delves deeper into the mystery surrounding his wife's past, her secrets begin come to light. Who was she? The discoveries he makes will shatter his world and bring him face to face with an enemy he never knew he had.

Start reading now!
First three episodes are always free.

K. J. Gillenwater worked as a Russian linguist in the U.S. Navy, spending time at the National Security Agency doing secret things. After six years of service, she ended up as a technical writer in the software industry. She has lived all over the U.S. and currently resides in Wyoming with her family where she writes government proposals and squeezes in fiction writing when she can. Visit K.J.'s website for more information about her books and what's coming next. www.kjgillenwater.com.

- The Genesis Machine Trilogy: Inception, Decryption, and Revelation
- Revenge Honeymoon
- Illegal
- Aurora's Gold
- The Ninth Curse
- The Little Black Box
- Acapulco Nights
- Blood Moon

Short Stories & Short Story Collections:

- Skyfall
- Nemesis
- The Man in 14C
- Charlie and the Zombie Factory